KIDNAPPED IN GAZA

DAVID AIKMAN

13-digit ISBN 978-1-4675-2661-6
10-digit ISBM 1-4675-2661-4

Readers interested in free excerpts from Kidnapped in Gaza
and David Aikman's other books are invited to visit the website
www.kidnappedingaza.com

Dedicated with gratitude to Jean Max, bureau manager in the Time Jerusalem bureau when I served there, and to all my wonderful co-workers in the bureau.

ACKNOWLEDGMENTS

Many people made this book possible, starting with the correspondents, reporters, and staff of Time Magazine when I was working in the bureau.

I would also like to thank Chuck Cobb for his excellent suggestions on Arab and Palestinian matters and Robert Berger for his careful attention to important details in the manuscript.

Great thanks to Barbara Casey, my agent, for her diligent work in seeing this project through and for my publisher, Ron Chepesiuk, for seeing the possibilities.

I

THWAT! THWAT!

The calm of the early evening in the Judean Hills was shattered, propelling me out of the rattan chair I was sitting in to see what had crashed into the living room wall above my head. I had just commented to my host about how lovely the Judean Hills could look at this time of the day, when the sun casts a warm golden glow into the valley. But my attempt to break the ice with someone I badly wanted to interview had now been suddenly and brutally interrupted.

Before I could react, the upper part of the window, partially opened to allow a cooling breeze to flow through the compact living room, cascaded to the floor with a deafening clatter. Shards of glass flew in all directions.

"Richard Ireton! Get down on the floor! Quickly!" my host barked like a drill sergeant as he leapt from the other rattan chair in the living room. "They're shooting at us!"

I had only an instant to ponder the redundancy of Dr. Amnon Rubinstein's words before diving to the floor where I tried, absurdly, to somehow make my tall, lanky frame blend in with the cool gray tiling of the two-story home in Efrat, about a half-hour drive south of Jerusalem. Unlike most of the Israeli communities in the West Bank – which vocal critics called "settlements" – Efrat's residents were mostly Israeli professionals, with a high concentration of lawyers and physicians. Dr. Amnon Rubinstein, of course, was a physician.

Thwat! Another round hit the wall in almost exactly the same place as the first. It narrowly missed an Arab tapestry that had caught my attention when I entered the room just a few minutes earlier.

"Well, at least he's consistent," said Amnon drily, raising his head a few inches above the floor and looking at the shattered window. I was too shocked to reply. Instead, I tried to quiet my loud, rapid breathing. A cold sweat had formed above my upper lip and my heart was beating furiously.

We both lay there for a few more seconds, waiting to see if another round would come crashing into the house. We could hear excited voices outside, and the sound of running. After a few seconds firing broke out again, but this time it came from close by: someone in the settlement was shooting back.

Amnon leapt to his feet and ran out of the room up the stairs, probably to see if he could spot the sniper from a window upstairs. I stayed on the floor. To my great annoyance, I was trembling now in addition to breathing heavily.

Outside there was more shouting, followed by the sound of children's voices, frightened and urgent. A woman shouted back at them in a high-pitched voice. I'd arrived in Israel just six months earlier from being bureau chief for *Epoch* Magazine in Hong Kong and my Hebrew was rudimentary at best, but they were apparently asking her what they should do. I could only guess at her reply.

Just a minute or two later, Amnon came loping down the stairs, two at a time, and almost leapt back into the room. He stood fully upright now, almost my height but lanky for an Israeli, with his hands on his hips. Amazingly, he was grinning as he spoke, and his voice was clear and high. "It's okay, he's gone now."

"How do you know?" I asked. The question was pure reflex. Reporters never take anybody's word for anything.

"Because I built a concealed observation window in the roof upstairs," Amnon replied, apparently not taking offense that I had questioned him. In fact, he sounded rather proud as he explained, "I can scan the whole of the valley opposite from it and not be observed. I spotted the fellow – actually there were two of them – and saw them scrambling down the hillside. They just got picked up by a passing car."

"Who do you think they were?" I lapsed automatically into my journalist mode now, hitting the second of the 5-W's-and-an-H formula for good reporting: Who, What, Where, When, How and Why.

"That's a good question. Probably not Hamas. They're on their best behavior right now," Amnon said, referring to the largest and most influential Palestinian militant movement. The Hamas charter called for the destruction of Israel. After it won the Palestinian Authority's general elections in January 2006, it had taken over Gaza violently and brutally two and a half years later, even throwing some PA officials from Fatah to their deaths from rooftops. But Hamas had cut back almost completely on suicide bombings in Israel and had been cajoled by some Arab governments into entering negotiations with the Israeli state. The ferocious Israel army assault into Gaza in December 2008 had reduced Hamas's ability to launch operations against Israeli targets in Israel and the West Bank. Hamas was now deliberately discouraging any "freelance" violence against Israelis.

"I'd say some fairly extreme group, perhaps the Al Aqsa Martyrs Brigade," Amnon continued knowledgably, speculating about the militia group linked to Fatah, the Palestinian nationalist movement founded by Yassir Arafat. "Fatah has been trying to make a comeback recently and wants to be seen in the forefront of action. Or perhaps some splinter group from Islamic Jihad, who knows? Anyway, they don't like us and they want to let us know they don't."

"Could they be Hezbollah's people?" I asked, wondering about the Lebanese pro-Iranian Muslim group that had dominated the politics of Lebanon and was also openly committed to the destruction of Israel.

"I've no idea. I don't think Hezbollah has much of a foothold in the Territories," Amnon said, using the term Israelis all use to refer to what is more commonly known as the West Bank. "Do you know something about that?"

"No, but it seems logical enough. Ever since the 2006 war in Lebanon, you have to assume that Iran has been trying hard to get its hands around the Palestinian fighters here in the territories. Iran almost certainly ordered up that Lebanese action a few months ago. Hezbollah is a Shiite group, but Iran, which is also Shiite, has supported Hamas. I'd imagine they'd be quite happy if Hezbollah could open some franchises in Gaza and the West Bank," I said, not because I thought Amnon needed any explanation of the complexities of political struggle in the Middle East power but because I was thinking out loud about this region and its politics that was still new to me.

"Yes, you're probably right. Look," Amnon said, changing the topic, "if you're not too shaken, let's continue the conversation in a place where there's no danger at all of getting hit, my fully furnished basement."

"I didn't think any of these houses in Efrat had basements," I said.

"Most don't," Amnon agreed. "But since I work at Hadassah I guess some people think my safety is important." He was being modest. Dr. Amnon Rubinstein was Israel's best trauma surgeon and worked at the world-renowned Hadassah University Medical Center. "When I bought this house I discovered that there was a special fund to pay for shelters for Hadassah physicians to ensure they stayed as safe as possible." Amnon chuckled. "I suppose physicians who are dead aren't very useful," he added, laughing at his own joke.

I got to my feet, brushed off a few shards of glass that were still sticking to my clothes, and followed my host downstairs to a carpeted, book-lined room which was comfortably, not to say sumptuously, furnished. A leather arm chair was set perpendicular to a matching three-seat sofa. On the walls between the bookcases were masks and spears from Africa. Atop a table next to the wall was a tableau featuring a stuffed mongoose in mortal combat with a stuffed cobra, the sort of thing sold in kitschy tourist shops in Thailand. Amnon noticed my interest in it.

"I picked that up when I was at a medical conference in Phuket," he said. "As you know, the mongoose always wins when it's pitted against the cobra. Sometimes I feel we and the Palestinians are locked in a cobra-mongoose fight. The question is, which are we, the mammal or the reptile?"

"That's an unsettling idea," I said, collapsing into the sofa. "Couldn't it be a different sort of fight, say two kangaroos tussling over their women and turf, but neither of them wanting to finish the other off?"

"Well, I think it could have been if the Palestinians thought of the struggle that way. I think they've acted as though it's all a zero-sum game; either them or us," Amnon said. I knew what he was referring to. Israeli and Palestinian delegations had started secret talks in Oslo in 1993 that resulted in a grand public peace-making ceremony on the White House South Lawn in September 1993. "Oslo," as everyone called it, was hailed as a major step in the peace process, but there were plenty of people who objected to it. Israel's Prime Minister Rabin had himself been assassinated in 1995 by an Israeli extreme nationalist for having conceded to the Palestinians what the assassin considered the irrevocable land of Israel. The "Oslo" agreement was supposed to end in a final settlement by 1999 and the Israelis, in theory, would by then have withdrawn from most of the towns and communities they had established in the territories. Presumably, Efrat would have been one of the vacated Israeli communities.

But the "peace process" that seemed to be so promising after the "Oslo Accords" had then foundered. Ariel Sharon, the Israeli Prime Minister in 2005, had ordered a pull-out of all Israeli citizens in settlements near Gaza, but that didn't seem to improve Israeli-Palestinian relations. In fact, the opposite happened. Hamas crowed that the Israeli withdrawal had occurred because of successful "resistance" to Israel. Hamas meant, of course, suicide bomb attacks on Israeli civilians. Hamas – or its allies in Gaza – had then launched from the vacated Israeli settlements, among other locations, an unrelenting rocket fire from Gaza upon towns in Israel proper. That, in turn, had prompted the Israeli assault upon Gaza at the end of 2008.

Amnon's words about a "zero-sum-game" sobered me. Then, taking up from where our conversation had been interrupted by the sniping, he said, "Listen, can I get you a cold drink? I think it's too early for anything stronger than that."

"Yes, thanks, whatever you have. Juice would be fine."

While Amnon ran back upstairs to fetch the drinks, I stood up and surveyed the books on the shelf. It had always been fascinating to me how much you can learn about people from the books they are willing to display in their homes. I skipped over the several Hebrew titles, which I couldn't read, and scanned the English spines. It was a mixture of fiction and non-fiction: *The Hunt for Red October* by Tom Clancy and *The Testament* by John Grisham, but also *The Clash of Civilizations* by Samuel Huntington, *Six Crises* by Richard Nixon, an English translation of Plato's *Republic*, *The New Atlantis* by Francis Bacon. Amnon was obviously broadly read. Curious about the Nixon volume, I flipped through it. A handwritten note on the inside cover caught my eye: "For Dr. Amnon Rubinstein of Hadassah, with many thanks for fixing up old Harry a few weeks ago." It was signed by hand, "Richard Nixon."

Just then, Amnon came back downstairs with two glasses, loping as usual. Noticing the Nixon book in my hand, he laughed.

"Wondering how I got hold of that, no doubt?" he said. "Harry Wasserman was a Jewish supporter of Nixon who had an emergency appendectomy during a visit to Israel about fifteen years ago. I was the surgeon on duty at Hadassah at the time and performed the operation. I never met Nixon before he died, but he sent me the book when Wasserman got back to the US."

"Nixon was a very keen supporter of Israel," I noted.

"He was," said Amnon. "Though he made his share of crude anti-Semitic comments."

"True," I said. "But wasn't it Nixon who saved Israel's hide during the 1973 Yom Kippur War?" I asked.

"You bet," said Amnon. "Without those massive US re-supply airlifts either the Syrians or the Egyptians might have overrun us."

There was a pause in the conversation. I felt that Amnon was sizing me up, as though he wasn't really sure why I'd asked to visit him. We had been introduced to each other by an Israeli journalist for *Ha'aretz*, the politically liberal Hebrew daily, who knew that I wanted to meet an Israeli physician whose medical ethics and natural compassion had not been tainted by the squalor of the daily Israeli-Palestinian confrontation. Did such a person exist? Jewish medicine had assumed an exalted place in my mind, not only because Jewish physicians had been famous for their skills since the Middle Ages and had been courted by Christian and Muslim rulers alike, or because more than fifty Jews had received the Nobel Prize for medicine. Was there something about Judaism itself that fostered special compassion in the field of medicine, I wondered? I thought a physician at Israel's leading university hospital, Hadassah University Hospital-Ein Kerem on the outskirts of Jerusalem, might have the answer. After all, the hospital had been nominated in 2005 for a Nobel Peace Prize to recognize its equality in treating patients, its ethnic and religious diversity and its bridge-building efforts.

When I learned that Dr. Rubinstein lived in Efrat, in the heart of the Gush Etzion block of settlements that the Israelis established in the West Bank after 1967, I pressed for an invitation to meet him in his home in that troubled area.

Most Israelis do not view the settlements in Gush Etzion, which means Etzion Bloc, the way they view many of the more isolated communities in the West Bank: as outposts in Palestinian territory inhabited by religious Jews, often Americans, who seek to make a statement by populating Palestinian areas with a Jewish presence. For many years, these "religious" settlements had been something of a liability for Israel's army, the Israeli Defense Forces or IDF, because Israeli troops always had to be based nearby to protect the communities against the constant threat of attack.

But most Israelis viewed Gush Etzion as a "consensus" settlement, meaning they felt it was a legitimate extension of Israeli territory. After all, the Gush Etzion Jewish pioneering communities had been in their current location in the 1930's, long before Israel's war of independence. Gush Etzion consisted of about eighteen communities comprising some forty thousand people. I had learned a lot about it that afternoon in Kefar Etzion, or Etzion Village, the site of the original Jewish settlement that dated back to the 1920's and 1930's and had been wiped out during the 1948 Israeli war of independence. An eccentric local Israeli veteran who seemed to be minding the museum part time had told me that one hundred twenty-eight of its several hundred defenders were shot down in cold blood after they had surrendered to the Arabs. The whole Etzion area, identified as it was with Jerusalem's struggle to survive during the 1948 war, seemed to be a "consensus" block. Even most Israelis on the far left of the political spectrum, I was told, would be unwilling to part with it in any "land-for-peace" swap with the Palestinians.

But I wanted to visit Efrat for more than its historic significance. I wanted to see what it was like living in a community which had been distinctly dangerous to reach by road during the Second Intifadeh of 2000-2004. Palestinian gunmen had fired on cars on the road to and from Jerusalem, and had sometimes tried to kidnap the residents. Why would anyone live in such a dangerous place when he could reside safely in Jerusalem or even within "Green Line" Israel; that is, the Israel of borders recognized internationally after the 1949-1950 armistice talks that concluded the War of Independence?

"You said on the phone that you wanted to talk to an Israeli physician who had lots of experience treating both Israelis and Arabs," Amnon said, taking the initiative in the uneasy silence that had briefly enveloped us after we had settled into his cozy basement retreat. "Is that right?"

"Yes," I said. "Medicine in Israel seems to have been one of the few areas where Jews and Arabs work together, and get treated together. I'm curious why."

Amnon sighed and then laughed. "Let me tell you," he said. "Ever since I trained as a physician in Tel Aviv it's been the same. We treat whoever comes in, whether he's Jew or Arab, whether he's insured or uninsured, whether he can pay or not, whether he's an IDF soldier or someone who tried to kill an IDF soldier. I think it's part of the Jewish genes, it's in our DNA," he said reflectively, then added, "And don't forget, when Hadassah was started in 1912 by contributions from American Jewish women, there weren't any Israelis, there were just Palestinians, some of them Arab, some of them Jewish. Hadassah's charter made it absolutely clear we were to treat anyone who needed medical attention who lived in this area. Now, of course, that understanding isn't shared by everyone who lives here. In 1947, as the fighting between Jews and Arabs began to get really heated, a convoy of nurses and physicians from Hadassah Hospital on Mount Scopus in Jerusalem was viciously attacked by Arab irregulars and several physicians and nurses died. But that hasn't prevented us from continuing with the tradition. We treat anyone who comes in the front door, or more often, who is carried in the front door."

"Even terrorists?"

"Even terrorists. One of the most remarkable fellows I patched up had been shot in the stomach in the shoot-out that followed the take-over by Fatah gunmen of the Church of the Nativity in Bethlehem in 2002. He was wounded during the first days of the fighting but wasn't allowed to leave the church for four days. By then, he was dying from all kinds of horrible infections. When they finally let him out and he was brought to Hadassah, we had to clean several kilos of maggots out of his stomach. It took months and several operations to get him better," he paused, remembering. "And the trouble we had to go through to get permission to do all these operations! We had to send one of our social workers – at considerable risk, I might say – to his family's village on the West Bank and locate his mother. His mother couldn't read, so an uncle had to read to her the document she needed to sign so that we could go ahead with the operation."

"Did the fellow show any appreciation for all the trouble you were going to, to keep him alive?"

"Yes he did. He became a model patient, taking trays of food around to other patients, helping sweep the floors, do odd jobs."

"Did it stop him from being a terrorist?"

"I couldn't say. We lost track of him. But Shabak – you know, the abbreviation for our internal intelligence services – let him go back to his family, reckoning it was unlikely he'd do any fighting again. Oh, and you remember that tapestry on the living room wall upstairs, the one that caught your attention on the way in?"

"You mean the one the first bullet barely missed?" I had been struck by the quilted tapestry, a stylized map of Bethlehem made of cotton but richly embroidered with silk thread.

"Yes. The mother of the terrorist I treated sewed that herself for me. She was so grateful that we saved his life."

"Have you treated Israelis wounded by suicide bombings?" I asked.

"Of course, all the time, though not so many recently, thank God. We've been more successful than previously at foiling the attacks."

Amnon looked intently at his glass, as if scrutinizing carefully the particles of fruit in the punch he was drinking. I watched him silently, then asked, "Can I ask why you decided to live here, which, as we've just experienced, isn't exactly the safest place for an Israeli to live?"

"Two reasons. First, a family one," Amnon gestured to a group of framed photographs on a low table in a corner of the room that I had not noticed before.

"My mother and her first husband both came from Poland and both were religious," he said, handing me a faded wedding portrait of an unsmiling girl who looked barely out of her teens and a boy not much older, looking incredibly serious. "They owed their lives to a Polish gentile family who sheltered them during the war from both the Nazis and anti-Semitic Poles. When they moved to Palestine in 1946, they settled in Kefar Etzion, believing they were redeeming the land of Israel by living in its heartland. My mother, then pregnant with my elder sister, was among the last of the women and children living here to be evacuated in January 1948, with the help of Brits," he recalled, referring to the time when Gush Etzion was completely surrounded by Arab forces but the British government still technically ruled Palestine. My mother's first husband was killed here after the whole block fell to Arab Legion forces in May 1948. He and more than a hundred others were all shot, by the way, after they had formally surrendered to the Arab Legion. After independence was won, my mother moved to the Tel Aviv area and remarried. I was the first son from her second marriage. She was living on a kibbutz at the time and she never stopped reminding my half-brother and me as we were growing up that if she had been able to choose, she would be living in Judea in Etzion. I didn't think about it very much until I started working at Hadassah-Ein Kerem and needed a place to live. Efrat had already been developed for some twenty years and it was only about twenty to thirty minutes from Jerusalem. My wife Leora and I visited the community, saw that there were nice houses and apartments available, met some of the people and found that they were quite normal, and decided that we'd like to live here. We don't regret it, in spite of the – what shall I call it – occasional excitement.

"Oh and there's another, more practical reason why we're here. We simply didn't like living in Jerusalem itself. Too claustrophobic."

Just then Rubinstein's wife, Leora, appeared in the doorway. A tall woman in her 40s with a striking, aquiline face, she had piercingly dark deep-set eyes. Her hair was cut fashionably short and she was not wearing a headscarf, as most of the wives of Efrat did, being religious Jews. She wore a simple, sleeveless red cotton sundress that left her shoulders bare but descended to slightly above the knee. She wasn't classically beautiful, but she was strikingly attractive and carried herself with a quiet dignity that I had seen displayed by only one other woman, my Filipina girlfriend, Trish.

Just thinking about Trish momentarily stopped me in my train of thought. It had been months now since we last saw each other in person. After my adventurous escape from the coup attempt in southern China, I had remained in Hong Kong only a few more weeks before moving to Jerusalem.

I rose as Leora came into the basement and introduced herself before Rubinstein could. "Yes, Rick, Amnon told me you would be visiting us today," she said, confidently. "I see you have a soft drink. Do you need anything else?"

"Nothing, thank you," I said, "but I do have a question. Where were you during the shooting just now?"

"Having coffee at a neighbor's house," Leora said matter-of-factly. With a half-shrug, she added, "She made sure the children weren't in the line of fire and we went on drinking our coffee."

"As simple as that?"

"As simple as that. We live in a dangerous part of the world, Rick. You can't let a bunch of half-educated fanatics disrupt your life."

"Excuse me, but how do you know the shooters were a bunch of 'half-educated fanatics?' They might have been graduate students from Birzeit University," I countered, referring to Palestine's first institute of higher education.

"Yes, they might have been, but they would still have been 'half-educated' and 'fanatic.' Only a fanatic thinks you can build a better life by arbitrarily killing people you don't even know and who are not trying to kill you. And only a person whose education has not gone above waist-level is dumb enough to think that you will drive people from their homes by taking clumsy pot-shots from a nearby hillside."

Amnon was watching his wife with a slight sideways glance, as though uncertain whether she'd say something that he might have to explain further. But he didn't contradict her.

I was a little annoyed by what she had just said. I had Palestinian friends and none of them was dumb or fanatic. "I certainly don't want to contradict you," I said cautiously, "but have you met any of them?"

"You mean Palestinians?"

"Yes."

"Of course. We have a clinic in the town that is open for minor medical needs. We treat the local Arab villagers. For more serious situations they go to Hadassah, and Amnon can patch them up. I work at the clinic."

"Are you a nurse?" I asked, but instantly regretted it as I saw a quick anger flash across her face. It was the same look I'd seen in Trish when I had also inadvertently insulted her on our first date.

"No, I am a physician. I did my residency at Johns Hopkins in Baltimore and I specialize in pediatric cases." She looked straight at me as she said this, and suddenly I felt very small indeed.

Leora continued, "I understand, however, why you might think I was a nurse. After all, I am a woman, I don't dress frumpily as you might expect female physicians to dress, and I assume you thought that Amnon, the famous Hadassah trauma surgeon, would have a little wifey who'd once been a starry-eyed assistant at one of his major operations." This was said without rancor or bitterness.

"I'm so sorry," I mumbled in humiliation, "you must think I'm a walking parrot of sexist stereotypes. I do apologize."

Now Amnon came to the rescue. "My dear Rick," he said, "I can assure you that Israeli men, in spite of having women all over the armed forces, can sometimes be so chauvinist that they make American males all look like hyper-sensitive wimps. I'm sure that Leora was flattered that she struck you as young enough to be a nurse fresh out of her training. Weren't you, Leora?" he said, turning to his wife with a grin that bordered on a smirk.

She laughed with a great roar, and my tension subsided. I took it as a good moment to make my departure. I wasn't sure there wouldn't be more shooting, and I didn't want to drive back to Jerusalem on a dangerous piece of road after dark. More importantly, the shooting that had just happened in Efrat might be part of a pattern of renewed violence across the West Bank.

I needed to get back to Jerusalem to find out. I thanked the Rubinsteins, made excuses about deadlines, and quickly made my way up the stairs. My last view of the Rubinsteins was of Amnon on the front porch of his home, his arm around Leora. They seemed to be sharing a good laugh; I suspected it was at my expense – no doubt something about the naiveté of newcomers to Israel.

I was still feeling slightly flushed from the embarrassment of my clumsy remark to Leora as I drove back to the main road leading to Jerusalem, the Hebron Road. In my few brief months in Israel, I'd already driven in the "Territories," or *slakhim*, as the Israelis call the West Bank, often enough to know well the road to Ramallah, to the north of Jerusalem, and its tediously slow checkpoint for Palestinian cars heading into Jerusalem. But Efrat was on the other side of Jerusalem, and Palestinians were far less frequently encountered on this road. Even so, I knew there would be checkpoints manned by Israeli border police. At least I wouldn't have to drive alongside what I regarded as a real eyesore: the "fence," which in parts of the road north of Jerusalem was an actual wall. The Israelis had built it to protect traffic from Palestinian snipers and to make it harder for suicide bombers to penetrate Israel proper from the West Bank.

The visit with the Drs. Rubinstein was my first to a private home in an Israeli settlement and the first time I had met Israelis who were regular middle-class professionals who had chosen to live there. Until now, I had assumed, as most Israelis assumed, that most of the people who chose to make their homes in the settlements were religious Jews determined to live out their vision of "redeeming" the land that God had first called the patriarch Abraham to settle in more than three millennia earlier. It was a surprise to find that ordinary, relatively secular Israelis might want to live in the Territories too.

Reflecting on this and the shooting as I drove from Efrat, I realized that I was more shaken by the incident than I had allowed myself to admit. Amnon had said that he'd seen the shooters climbing quickly into a car that pulled up on a dirt road near where they had been shooting from. Then the car had driven away fast. That ought to have brought some sense of closure to the whole incident. But it didn't. The shots that came through the window could have killed me if I'd been standing up. They were brutal reminders of how fragile life was here. It was only four decades after the Six-Day War that had brought the Etzion Bloc back under Jewish control and nearly six decades since Israel had come into existence amid a storm of fighting between Arabs and Jews. I wondered if the violence would ever come to an end.

I drove back to Jerusalem more slowly than usual. I needed time to digest it all, to make sense of the mayhem I had just experienced. The road meandered between the folds of the hills, with the sun reddening in the west and descending low over them. The shadows were lengthening. I passed two Arab boys ambling in the opposite direction of the traffic on a donkey beside the road. They looked up as I passed and smiled, which cheered me momentarily. *Well*, I thought, *not everyone here hates everyone else.*

Then, as the road curved into a bend between two steep embankments, I heard two rifle-shots. *Oh no, not again. I've just been through all that.*

I wasn't driving fast but I braked hard anyway, and then slowed the car down to walking speed, continuing to follow the curve of the road. I saw no cars ahead of me in either direction – *That's a bit strange at this time of day* – and when I looked in the rearview mirror I could see no vehicles behind me either.

Before I could digest this fact, three more shots cracked out in succession followed by a burst of automatic rifle fire. I wondered whether to stop driving or continue forward until I could see what was happening? Prudence, of course, said to stop, but this was a developing story and I was trained to follow developing stories. And if I didn't, there'd be more than just some hollow laughter the next time I met up with my fellow reporters for a drink at the American Colony Hotel bar. I would face guffaws and some awkward questions. "You came across shooting on the road to Etzion," I imagined them saying, "and you didn't bother to check out what was going on? What kind of hack are you?" The British reporters could be especially savage in this vein, and the last thing I wanted was a reputation as either a lazy or a timid American reporter. So I kept driving, albeit at a slow crawl.

I'd barely rounded the curve when I saw the jeep. It was a standard Israeli military jeep, similar to what the Americans had used in World War II. But it had standard Israeli fittings, desert camouflage with a metal grill over the windshield to protect the glass and the jeep's occupants from rocks and even grenades. It was parked at a sharp angle on the right side of the road, suggesting that it had come to a sudden halt. As I watched, two soldiers leapt out and took cover behind the armored steel front doors. One was talking into his radio; the other was scanning the nearby hillside with his binoculars in wide sweeping arcs. He was in a half-crouch as he panned: it seemed he hadn't located the source of the firing, and didn't want to present himself as a target as he searched.

I stopped about one hundred yards behind the jeep, snatched a small pair of binoculars from the glove compartment and got out. Not wanting to become a sniper's target as well, I followed the soldiers' example and crouched behind the Subaru. I focused the binoculars first on the soldiers and then tried scanning the same hillside the one soldier was looking at. Almost immediately, I saw three men – presumably Arabs, because one was wearing a *keffiyeh*, the traditional Arab headdress – crouched behind two rocks on the hillside. Two of them were armed with AK-47 assault rifles and they popped up to fire off a burst at the soldiers. It occurred to me that they might have been responsible for the earlier shots I had heard. Their shooting didn't seem to be very accurate.

Just then, the Israeli soldier with the binoculars gave a shout – he'd spotted the snipers too. His comrade picked his Galil, the standard-issue Israeli infantry combat rifle, and I could see that it had a telescopic sight attached. I couldn't hear what they were saying, but from the gestures it was plain that the one with the binoculars was indicating where the snipers were. In one swift motion, the Galil-equipped soldier rose from behind the jeep door, pivoted his rifle to a resting position on the open door, and fired two shots at the hillside. I swung my small binoculars back to the hillside.

It was either a very well-timed or a very lucky shot. The soldier's bullet caught one of the Arabs in the chest just as he popped up to unleash his own wild burst of AK fire at the Israelis. It was the one wearing the *keffiyeh*, the signature Arab headdress made famous by Yassir Arafat. He crumpled immediately in a single slow but unbroken fall to the ground. The other two Arabs quickly pulled the body behind the rocks and hid. They probably hadn't expected such a real firefight. Meanwhile, the Israeli soldier with the Galil made a rash move. He stood up from his crouch, perhaps looking for another clear target on the hillside. But just then one of the Arabs sprung up and fired off another burst from his AK-47, hitting the Israeli shooter. He fell to the ground with a cry, clutching his shoulder.

The other soldier moved quickly to drag him out of the line of fire, propping him up behind the jeep's armored door. I expected the two unwounded Arabs might press home the attack quickly, taking advantage of the new numerical advantage of two-to-one, but instead they half-dragged, half-carried their comrade, who looked quite dead to me, up the slope and disappeared. His red *keffiyeh* fell off as they were dragging him up the hillside, but one of the other Arabs quickly picked it up. They apparently had decided to make good their escape before Israeli reinforcements arrived, as they surely soon would.

Deep quiet now fell over the scene, broken only by the trill of crickets in the Judean Hills and the groaning of the wounded Israeli. For the second time in less than an hour I was face-to-face with the brutal, and to me, incomprehensible, violence that seemed to haunt the ancient hills and valleys of the Holy Land like a permanent morning mist. Once again, my pulse was racing. A sweat had broken out again on my upper lip and the adrenaline rush made my whole body feel like a tightly wound coil.

Before I could think through what to do next, two more jeeps roared up and stopped near the jeep with the wounded soldier. A half dozen Israeli soldiers leapt out. Some took up firing positions protecting the group from anymore hillside attacks. Meanwhile an Apache attack helicopter clattered overhead, evidently trying to locate the fleeing Arab shooters.

I couldn't decide whether to stay lying on the ground until the Israelis noticed me, or get up and introduce myself to the newly arrived reinforcements? Each response had its problems. To continue to crouch by my car barely one hundred yards away from where an Israeli soldier lay bleeding, perhaps seriously wounded, might provoke the military reinforcements to direct their fire against me before asking any questions. On the other hand, to walk up to the entire group unannounced might also provoke them to shoot at me.

I decided to walk slowly towards them with my hands in the air. That way, if they thought I had been one of the shooters, at least they would know that I was surrendering.

I had not walked more than ten yards before one of the newly arrived soldiers saw me and started to shout angrily at me in Hebrew. Since I had no idea what he was saying, I decided the best thing was to just stand still with my hands still raised. Two other soldiers approached slowly, their rifles trained on me. It was the first time I'd ever been so close to a gun trained on me. It wasn't pleasant.

"I'm an American reporter!" I shouted. "Media! Press!" The two soldiers looked at each other and lowered their rifles. An officer now walked up and demanded in English, "What are you doing here? Did you see what happened?"

"Yes, I saw it all. I was driving back to Jerusalem from Efrat when I saw the military jeep in front of me stop and apparently take fire from the hills," I said in a rush – relieved that someone spoke English and feeling a sudden need to unload what I'd just seen. "I stopped my car and stayed by it until the shooting from the hillside stopped and you arrived."

I was ready to tell him in more detail about what had happened but the officer interrupted. "Let me see your press card," he said authoratively, though he didn't look more than his mid-twenties to me.

Slowly and carefully I reached into my jacket and took out my Israeli government press pass, the standard issue with a mug shot for all foreign and Israeli reporters accredited to cover news within Israel. The officer took it without comment, scrutinizing it carefully. Without looking up he said, "Do you have any other ID, a passport?"

I did. I'd taken to carrying my passport with me everywhere since hearing of a Dutch reporter who'd been detained by a previously unknown Palestinian group while covering as story in Ramallah, the West Bank town just north of Jerusalem that contained the West Bank headquarters of the Palestinian Authority. If the man had been able to prove that he was Dutch, he would have been released immediately instead of being kept by some unshaven thugs in a new unfurnished apartment for twenty-four hours.

The officer took my passport without looking up and leafed slowly through the pages. Then he turned and yelled back to the soldier communicating by radio with headquarters. I heard my name and passport number being read out. Turning back to me, he said, "Stay here." That seemed an extraneous comment to me. With Galil rifles and Uzi automatics hanging from practically every uniformed Israeli in sight, I wasn't about to go strolling off.

The radio erupted with loud static, and a voice in Hebrew seemed to be confirming that he had heard my name and passport number correctly. Then one of the few Hebrew words I do understand came through the radio: "*Rega* (wait)."

"You know," the officer took up the conversation again, "my father has been a reader of *Epoch* Magazine since he came here from New Jersey thirty years ago. He often complains that it's biased against Israel, but I don't find it so much against us." He cracked a slight smile as he said this.

Good, I thought. *This may not take too long.*

The radio emitted more squawks and static and conversation. The officer listened and then smiled more broadly. "Okay, they know who you are at the *Kirya*," he said, referring to the big Israeli Defense Forces compound in Tel Aviv that is the nerve center of the entire Israeli military machine and keeps track of all foreign reporters in-country. "But before we let you go, you need to tell me what you saw here."

I told him. When I started to describe the Arab shooter going down, the officer interrupted.

"You saw him fall? Are you sure of that?"

"Yes, and I saw his body being carried off by the two others. I don't know whether he was dead or not, but he went down quite abruptly."

"'Abruptly'? What do you mean?"

"Like the life had gone out of him. I've seen people being shot dead by police on TV, and it looked like that."

"On TV? Where do you see that?" the officer asked incredulously.

"In the States. They sometimes show live police car chases and shoot-outs on local TV. There are even TV channels that show little else."

"No way. We'd have an uproar here if that sort of thing were shown on TV. We see far too much death in real life as it is."

He paused. I thought better than to respond to his comment. There wasn't a single Israeli family that had not lost relatives or loved ones, or did not know someone who had, in the suicide-bombing climax of the 2002-2004 Palestinian Intifadeh against Israeli rule.

"Okay, so what happened after the guy went down?" he asked.

"His two comrades pulled him out of the line of fire."

"And then they went away?"

"No, then one of them fired a burst at the two soldiers in the jeep and hit the one who had shot the Arab. Only then did they leave."

"You are very observant," said the officer carefully.

"It's my job. I'm a reporter," I said simply.

"All right. Thank you for telling me what you saw. You can go now. But don't be surprised if someone follows up with more questions when you get back to your office. Are you in Tel Aviv or Jerusalem?"

"Jerusalem. It's the TV people who generally live in Tel Aviv."

"Okay. Be careful now as you drive back." It was a redundant warning. All I wanted was to get back to Jerusalem and veg out with a stiff drink in my hands.

I walked back to my Subaru, started the engine, and drove away from the scene slowly. Only when I had turned a bend in the road and was out of sight of the soldiers did I resume normal driving speed. I'd stopped shaking and perspiring, but now suddenly I felt very tired. By the time I arrived in Jerusalem on the Bethlehem road, the sun had gone down completely. But amid the darkness, the sky in the West was still suffused with a pale, pinkish glow.

II

AS I HAD TOLD the Israeli officer, I lived in Jerusalem. My one-bedroom apartment was on the second floor of a large, stately old house in the German Colony, just off Emek Refaim Street. I considered myself extremely lucky to have found it within days of moving to Israel from Hong Kong six months earlier. I could have gotten more rooms for the same price in an Arab-owned apartment north of Jerusalem. Many of my foreign correspondent colleagues had done this. But all of them had rather conspicuously fastened their sympathies to the Palestinians. I didn't want to get type-cast the same way. I'd seen too many good reporters get sucked into this or that political movement and lose their professional skills.

It was easy finding a really nice niche in a pleasant neighborhood because prices had sky-rocketed in recent years. The German Colony, as its name suggested, was an elegant, upscale section of Jerusalem originally populated by German gentiles in the second half of the nineteenth century. Since the 1980's and 1990's it had become gentrified, with stylish restaurants and shops. At the height of the 2002-2006 Intifadeh one of the restaurants had been attacked by a suicide bomber.

As with all the buildings in Jerusalem, this one was faced with the magnificent, golden-hued Jerusalem stone that gives the city the name "Jerusalem of Gold." I'd gotten into the habit of driving to the Mount of Olives, just east of Jerusalem, shortly before sunrise after *Epoch* Magazine had been put to bed in the wee hours of Saturday morning to sit and gaze at the sun climbing from beyond the Jordan River behind me and peeling away the shadows of the buildings and walls of the Old City. I savored those rare moments of peace and quiet, usually so lacking in a reporter's life and even more so in this conflict-ridden part of the world. At that hour of the morning the daily cacophony of East Jerusalem — donkey carts, trucks, drivers honking their horns — hadn't yet made itself heard. As a reporter, one aspect of the job I never enjoyed was the noise that reporters always made when they were assembled together, and this happened a lot in Jerusalem. The early dawn hours on the Mount of Olives was a tonic to my spirit.

I loved the fray of reporting, the adrenaline rush, the competitive spirit, the need for quick reactions to instincts. But from childhood I'd also relished being alone, if possible in the midst of natural beauty. I used to worry my mother a little in my high school years in the college town of Grand Rapids by peeling off from normal afternoon activities onto the shore of Grand River and just spending hours watching the activity on the river. I'm not sure why I derived such peace from being by myself, because I was pretty outgoing socially and generally scored in the extrovert part of the Myers-Briggs test. People seemed to notice too my unusual juxtaposition of personality traits: the delight in being by myself, and the gusto of being with stimulating people.

As I switched on the lights to the empty apartment, I had a momentary spasm of delight, once again, that I was now living in Jerusalem and covering one of the perennially most compelling front-page stories of our times. When I was growing up in Grand Rapids, Michigan, I had certainly dreamed of more ambitious things than following in my father's footsteps and becoming an electrician. But I had never imagined that within just a few years of graduating from journalism school at Northwestern University and graduate school at Berkeley I would be on the staff of *Epoch* Magazine, leading weekly news magazine in America and the world. Nor that just a few years after that, I'd be making headlines myself by playing a key role in stopping a military takeover of the Chinese Communist government by rogue elements of the Chinese army who had fallen under the influence of a weird meditation cult that practiced Qigong.

The China and Hong Kong experience had taught me, the hard way, that it is sometimes not so easy as a reporter to separate yourself from the action on which you are reporting. And what about the personal factors, the friendships and romances which seemed inextricably bound up with the "objective" factual developments that you are supposed to be covering?

Well, there would be plenty of time in the future to try to put all that into perspective. Meanwhile, here I was in Jerusalem being dragged unwillingly into one part of the violence that always seemed to be happening somewhere in what was often called, quaintly, "the Holy Land." My little nook in the German Colony was as good a place as anywhere to take stock of things and plan my next move. I'd found the apartment by following up an ad in the *Jerusalem Post*, which led me to Esther, my landlady.

She was decidedly quirky. A meticulously dressed Polish Jew who had stayed behind in Poland for a few years after World War II before coming to Israel, she was a widow and evidently well off, for she traveled quite frequently to various European destinations. I'd thought her a little fussy when I went to see the apartment for the first time. She had rattled off a long list of what she didn't want me to have in the apartment: she didn't want me bringing in a billiard table – *why on earth would I want to bring in a billiard table, and if I did, what could be so dangerous about one?* – she'd rather I didn't have drinking parties, would I not paint the walls of the apartment, and if I brought lady friends to stay the night, please no more than one at a time? When I heard this last injunction I couldn't help bursting out laughing. *Did she think I was such a Lothario that I'd be setting up two-fers in the apartment?*

But she was serious. "First, if you have two women they are always noisy," she said, as though she'd seen this sort of thing countless times. "Second, there's a security situation. Two women sometimes gang up on a single man and rob him." *W-e-l-l, I guess that's possible*, but I didn't let on to Esther about my skepticism. From my numerous experiences of renting in new cities, both as a graduate student and a reporter, I'd learned that if a landlord's rules were not inherently unacceptable, there was little to be gained by questioning them. Doing so only risked rejection as a renter.

Ironically though, I realized just a few weeks after moving in that the issue of two women staying overnight might not be academic after all. I badly wanted my girlfriend Trish to come over from the Philippines, but I knew as plainly as the midday sunshine in Jericho that she wouldn't be coming alone. When Trish had first visited me in Hong Kong, I'd almost sabotaged the relationship before it could get started by inviting her to stay in my apartment. In this day and age, an invitation like that would normally raise few eyebrows, and certainly no previous girlfriend had ever objected. But Trish was different. She was both unconventional and independent-minded, in addition to being spectacularly beautiful. More alarmingly, she had come under the influence of a zealous African-American lady missionary who believed firmly in old-fashioned morality. Trish made it unambiguously clear that she would not sleep with me – or with anyone – outside of marriage.

In discussing a possible trip to Jerusalem, Trish had also emphasized that Clarissa, the missionary, was coming along too. Clarissa was a Pentecostal from Richmond, Virginia who had come to the eccentric conclusion that God wanted her to go to Hong Kong to tell the Chinese about Jesus. I'd met her at a reception not long after her arrival in Hong Kong, and in a quixotic surge of what I thought might pass for charity, took her for tea at the swanky Mandarin Hotel, whereupon the good-hearted lady had all but adopted me. I had no one but myself to blame for the influence she now exercised over Trish, for I was the one who had thrown them together in the first place. Clarissa had bailed me out on short notice when I was rushing across the border into China to cover a story, having completely forgotten that Trish was due to arrive that morning. Clarissa had met Trish at the airport, mothered her around Hong Kong and, it seemed, had converted her in short order from a sophisticated, exceptionally attractive, professional woman to a pious, God-fearing saint who wanted to please God more than her boyfriend. More than once it had struck me how ironic it was that I, a direct descendant of Oliver Cromwell's son-in-law and right-hand-man, was much less a Puritan than a house-trained pagan, eager for every scrap of approval from his long-legged inamorata, but quite unable to have my desired way with her. I had come to discover, however, that I loved Trish enough to be willing to put up with her demands that she remain chaste before marriage.

When *Epoch* decided to send me to Jerusalem, Trish was dismayed that I would be even farther away, but Clarissa was thrilled. Like so many evangelical Christians I'd met, she was fascinated with Israel, the land she believed God in the Bible had promised to the Jews, his chosen people. She seemed to think Israelis were a breed of Biblical supermen transported through time into the third millennium. I thought this was both ludicrous and naïve. As a reporter, I had quickly become acquainted with the good, the bad, and the ugly among Israeli citizens and knew they were no better or worse than anyone else. But Clarissa insisted on holding to her cherished views, formed through a dozen books she'd read describing Israel's seemingly miraculous beginnings in the War of Independence of 1948, and Christian prophetic books predicting this or that great event before the Last Days. She seemed to love the Jews, though it occurred to me that she didn't have much to go on since, other than some co-workers in her government career in Washington, she actually didn't know that many Jews personally.

Fortunately, Clarissa still had a good sense of humor despite her religiosity. She had guffawed over the phone when I had told her a joke a rabbi told me about how his view of the Messiah's identity differed from the Christian's. The rabbi said that when Jesus finally arrived in Jerusalem, he was going to ask him, "Excuse me, Sir, is this your first visit to our city?"

Clarissa and Trish had started talking about visiting Israel almost as soon as I arrived. But it had taken months for them to coordinate their schedules and make the arrangements. It was assumed from the outset that they would be coming as a package; if I wanted to see Trish at all in Jerusalem, Clarissa was going to be part of that package. They had finally decided that they would first join an organized tour to see the sights around Galilee, Masada, and the Dead Sea, finishing up with the group in Jerusalem for four days. Once the rest of the group had left, Trish and Clarissa would come stay at my apartment. Esther would have to cope with that as best she could.

It was pretty annoying having a chaperone hanging around Trish, but I was so eager to see her that I was willing to put up with it. And our almost daily emails and frequent phone calls were good, but they made me only long for more of her. I'd actually come to enjoy at several different levels our e-mail exchanges. As a journalist, I was impressed both by Trish's writing style, which showed itself elegantly in e-mails, and her quick mind and varied interests. She would go into fascinating literary digressions about everything under the sun since her mind was crammed with literary material. She was also, in her current job as public relations officer in a major hotel chain, having a wide variety of social experiences: a meeting with Philippine partisan veterans of World War II, a visiting young female opera soprano from Norway, a lecture on the more venomous aquatic life in the waters off the Philippines.

Trish had honed the skills of writing and expressing herself in conversation when her family, ever itinerant because of her father's professional training as a surgeon, a job that took him to the US and many other countries, would assemble the four sisters and conduct spontaneous reading seminars. All four sisters were good-looking, but they added to looks formidable minds and a well-stocked memory of everything they had ever read. At these informal family salons, the girls were encouraged to give free rein to their ideas and imagination, but Luis de los Santos, a surgeon as well as a well-rounded Filipino intellectual, would challenge them to defend their ideas in front of sisters who were routinely competitive and even aggressive with each other.

All this cerebral activity during Trish's upbringing had caused me some surprise in the first few months of our romance. Sometimes she'd unintentionally embarrassed me in conversation with friends by being far better informed about literature and ideas than I was. Now I wondered how Trish could be bothered with the rather ordinary-sounding job in public relations. Granted, the hotel chain was an international one and the guests came from far and wide. But I'd have imagined her more readily in a distinguished academic career. "Tricia de los Santos, PhD." It sounded rather grand. I'd asked Trish herself about this before I left Asia to come to Israel. She made it clear she had no taste for the academic life. "First of all," she said, -- somewhat petulantly, I thought – "academic bureaucracies are snake-pits of infighting, petty squabbling over turf, and idiotic regulations about the way you list the graduate courses you took thirty years ago. Second, academic salaries are pittances, miserable pittances. You'd need to have a relative who won the Publishers' Clearing House sweepstakes to function comfortably there."

By "function comfortably" I knew what Trish meant. It meant having a nice apartment in an upscale part of town, going out to dinner and drinks rather often, and making sure her personal wardrobe was really, really chic. Trish wasn't extravagant, but she was certainly expensive in her tastes, and she seemed to regard it as a natural right that she would have a job with a sufficient salary to afford them. All this amused me. I had never met anyone like her, and I knew I would never meet anyone else like her. But she was hard to catch, much less land.

Walking through the apartment, I went into the kitchen and poured myself a glass of sabra. I decided I needed something soothing before turning on the evening news. Most locals scorned the Israeli after-dinner chocolate and orange liqueur – it was for tourists, they said. But I had warm memories of my introduction to sabra: by an Italian professor in Guangzhou, China, Guiseppe Petrolucci, a charming and brilliant Italian academic who was researching Chinese history's rich tapestry of peasant rebellions. Petrolucci had earned a special place in my heart because he was the one who had arranged my getaway from a gang of Chinese ultranationalist thugs when I'd become embroiled in the coup attempt in China.

My sabra in hand, I collapsed onto the worn sofa and switched on the TV to watch the day's Israeli newscast. Even though my Hebrew was rudimentary, I could understand from the context and the images what the stories were about. Sure enough, both the Efrat shooting and the ambush of the IDF jeep were leading items. The story on the jeep was short, which I thought was a good thing because I didn't want any reference to get out that I, a Jerusalem-based reporter, had been there. But the shooting at Dr. Rubinstein's house in Efrat got quite a bit more air time. Amnon Rubinstein was newsworthy not only because he was Hadassah-Ein Kerem's head of surgery but also because he was a conspicuously secular and prominent Jew living in a West Bank settlement of mostly religiously observant Jews. A reporter was interviewing both Amnon and his wife Leora in their home, by the shattered window, but since I couldn't understand what they were saying, I switched to CNN International.

A reporter was on a Paris street describing an anti-Jewish march by mostly Islamic, Arab demonstrators shouting slogans such as "Death to the Jews!" They had also roughed up a few bystanders on the street, one of whom started to run away and had been pursued by the demonstrators but had apparently escaped. CNN then aired footage of a similar though bloodier incident a few weeks earlier in Paris and showed a curly-haired young man who looked to be in his late teens being carried off on a stretcher.

"It's not clear why that young man was set upon, or today's near-victim," the correspondent in Paris said, gesturing toward the scene behind him, "but one thing is certain: he was in the wrong place at the wrong time."

Turning to the Paris gendarmes who were clearing the scene, the reporter now asked, "Do you know if the people who were attacked were Jewish?" I thought the question was not only unprofessional, but actually outrageous. Was the reporter implying that, if the victims *were* Jewish, the attack would have somehow been justified? The police officers didn't reply, but someone in the crowd shouted, "Tell the world, Paris is getting to be a dangerous place for the Jews." The camera swung to the crowd, but it was impossible to see who had spoken. The reporter resorted to an old standby: the man-in-the-street interview.

"Do you feel safe in this part of Paris?" he asked a middle-aged man. I wanted to roll my eyes at his crass question.

"Well, would you feel safe," the man replied, "if a bunch of thugs entered your neighborhood, shouted murderous slogans, and then beat up someone at random?"

"Do you plan to stay in France?"

"Not if they can't keep the streets safe."

The reporter turned back and looked into the camera to resume his stand-up: "As you can tell, Parisians are nervous and angry after this incident. Whether the government can convince people that they are going to crack down on these demonstrations, which so often lead to violence, is an open question. If they don't, there are elections in the autumn when ordinary French people will have a chance to express their own views on the matter. From Paris, this is Brian Watford for CNN."

The next item was a domestic American news item, so I turned down the sound. I was stunned by what I had just seen. I'd worked in Brussels for *Epoch* Magazine before being sent to Hong Kong, and I'd never come across any anti-Semitism there. Of course, Belgium wasn't France and didn't have the demographics of France where fully ten percent of the population is Muslim, almost all of them Arabs from North Africa. The country was host to the largest Jewish community in Europe, around six hundred thousand. But an attack in broad daylight on French Jews?

Parts of Europe were beginning to look like *Kristallnacht*, the night in 1938 when rampaging mobs of Nazi storm troopers and ordinary German citizens caught up in the Nazi frenzy smashed thousands of windows of Jewish synagogues and businesses. The name referred to the millions of shards of glass on the streets of German cities glittering in the light of headlights and torches carried by the mobs. That night, November 8-9, 1938, came to symbolize the beginning of the end for the Jews of Germany and Europe under the Nazis. Was *Kristallnacht* now coming to Europe — coming moreover by stealth as the Continent became progressively swamped by immigrant blocs of increasingly radical Muslims? It was a frightening thought.

I checked my e-mail to see if Trish had responded to my morning e-mail to her. She hadn't. Tired, still shaken by the two shootings, and a little grumpy, I decided to call it a day.

I slept well, and was about to get into the shower when the phone rang. Wrapping a towel around myself, I went back into the bedroom to pick up the phone. This was one aspect of the journalist's life that I hated: you could never ignore the phone because it might bring news of some breaking story. I mentally kicked myself – not for the first time – for failing to get caller ID on my home phone.

"Rick?" The caller's voice was distinctively British.

"Yeah. Who's this?"

"Patrick Cavenagh here. I guess you saw the TV item last night on that shooting on the road to Jerusalem?"

My antennae immediately went up. My name had not been mentioned on the TV report, so why was Cavenagh calling me? I was rather ambivalent about Cavenagh, a long-time Jerusalem-based correspondent for *The News Report*, a left-of-center British daily. The man was extremely funny, especially after a few drinks, in describing his reporting experiences, and he had been generally friendly towards me. On the other hand, he was unmistakably biased in his reporting on Israel and he had scant respect for American politicians, especially Republican ones. He lived with his Palestinian-American girlfriend in a northern suburb of Jerusalem that was predominantly Arab. He seldom missed an opportunity to depict Israeli actions against Palestinian terrorists as an ongoing part of what he always described as Israeli oppression of the Palestinian people.

"Yeah, I saw that piece too," I said cautiously. "What's on your mind?"

"Well, I recall your saying the other day that you were going to drive to Efrat over the weekend and talk to some of the settlers there. I wondered if you had done so yesterday and whether you saw anything happen on the way back."

He was definitely clever. Over drinks with several people in the American Colony Hotel bar two weeks ago, I had made a passing reference to my plan to visit Efrat, and Cavenagh, with his razor-sharp, Oxford-trained mind, had snatched the information out of a general conversation and stored it carefully in his mind. But what to say to him? Should I admit that I saw the shooting at the jeep and risk becoming part of the story – never a good thing for a reporter to do – or should I just lie about it all, or at least try to play dumb? If I denied any knowledge of the shooting, Cavenagh might discover through sources in the IDF that a foreign reporter had been on the scene and learn that it was me. I'd then lose all my credibility with the foreign correspondents in Israel.

"As a matter of fact, I did see some of what happened," I said, wondering where Cavenagh was going with this. "As you guessed, I was in Efrat yesterday visiting someone and was on my way back to Jerusalem when I heard shots on the road just ahead of me. I stopped the car in case someone tried to shoot at me as well."

"So you were quite close to the jeep with the two Israeli soldiers?"

"About a hundred yards from it. Hey, if you don't mind my asking, where is all this going?" As a reporter, I was used to *asking* the questions, not answering them.

"You're right, I should explain myself before asking questions of a fellow-hack. Well, I've got Palestinian sources who say the true version of what happened yesterday is a lot different from what the IDF put out."

"What do they say happened?" I shot back. I was back in my accustomed role of being the one asking the questions.

"Sorry, Rick, I can't say at this point. I'm still following it up. But your version is that the two Israel soldiers stayed by their jeep the whole time you were there?"

"My version?" I really disliked Cavenagh's tone and what he was suggesting. "Is what I say I saw just a 'version' of events in your book, perhaps comparable to what some little old lady in Bournemouth said she saw on the Beeb last week?" I'd counterpunched deliberately with the reference to the Beeb, journalists' slang for the BBC which is notorious for being critical of Israel, sometimes quite ferociously.

"Well, I know you prefer watching Fox," Cavenagh replied. In journalistic terms this was a real insult. I had no objection to Fox TV, though I generally disagreed with its conservative coverage, but the British reporters detested it because they thought it reflected rah-rah Americanism. I'd met many Fox reporters and they were thoroughly professional and serious about their reporting. Why was Cavenagh getting so personal?

"Look, Patrick, I'm telling you what I saw because that's what you asked me to do. Are you accusing me of lying?" I decided to be blunt.

"I'm not saying you'd want to lie, Rick," Cavenagh smoothly responded. "But you know as well as I do that the Israeli military spokesman's office often peddles a version of events that bears scant relationship to the truth."

"Well, are you saying that the TV story last night wasn't what happened?"

"I have good reason to believe it was not."

"Well, you're saying then that I'm a liar."

"No, I'm saying that the IDF may have wanted you to believe that what you thought you saw was the truth, when it wasn't."

"How is that possible?" I was really exasperated. "I heard the shooting, I stopped the car, I saw the Arab sniper get shot by the Israeli soldier and then get hit himself. Within about two minutes reinforcements arrived. Neither of the soldiers had moved at all."

"Well, the Palestinians must have moved. I'm perfectly certain that they didn't hang around to sign autographs for the IDF."

"Yes, of course they beat it fast. But I couldn't see them after they had dragged their wounded or dead fellow-shooter out of the line of sight of the Israelis."

"That's precisely the point. You couldn't have seen everything that happened." There was a pause now at the end of the line. I wasn't sure whether Cavenagh was having doubts about what he'd been told by his Palestinian sources, or still believed them and was figuring out how to prove that I had gotten the story wrong. Now Cavenagh changed tack.

"Did the Israeli reinforcements who came on the scene talk to you about what you saw?"

"Yes they did. They asked me to tell them what I had seen." For crying out loud, I was darned if I was going to tell Cavenagh every detail of my encounter with the Israeli soldiers on the road from Efrat. The conversation was really irritating me now. Who was this British reporter to subject me to something resembling a cross-examination in order to back up his own "version" of the events that had taken place?

"And you did?"

"Of course. One of their guys had been hit and seemed to be bleeding pretty badly. I had no reason to conceal from them what I had seen. An officer wanted to see my press credentials and I showed them my Israeli Government Press ID and my passport as well. He looked at them both carefully and then told me to go."

"Did he say he'd be in touch with you later?"

"No." I wasn't going to volunteer that he said someone else might be in touch with me.

"But nobody from the spokesman's office has followed up yet?"

"Absolutely not. Look, I'm sorry, but I'm finding your questioning downright aggressive. I certainly don't mind giving you a fill on something that I saw happen, and which is no longer exclusive, but you seem to have a conspiracy theory about the IDF."

"With good reason. On almost every major incident of abuse of Palestinians they've been lying all along. Now I'm close to proving it."

"In the case of the ambush of the jeep?"

"No, in their follow-up pursuing the Palestinian shooters."

"What happened?"

"I'm sorry, I can't give you the details yet. But it won't be long before this is a helluva story."

"And you're going to break the story?"

"Well, I'm going to be the first with all the gory details."

"Well, good luck to you, then. Listen, Patrick, I'm sorry, but I can't chat any more. I've got things to do this morning."

'Yes, you probably have," Cavenagh with a sort of lazy drawl that bordered on disdain.

What did that mean? There was something about Cavenagh's entire tone that grated on me. Cavenagh was letting me know that he thought he'd uncovered a major scandal of Israeli abuse of Palestinians. He was going to go with this story no matter what I said I had seen on the road. It left a sour taste in my mouth. But Cavenagh wasn't finished.

"Just fyi," he concluded, "I think the Beeb's got a line on this story too. It'll be on in the next bulletin of the world service. I'm sure your little old lady in Bournemouth will be watching. Thanks for your fill. Bye." He hung up before I had a chance to come up with an equally scathing rejoinder.

It was still a few minutes before the top of the hour, so I turned on the TV again and switched to BBC World. It was the business report, and an Indian entrepreneur was recounting his success in selling computer systems in the Gulf. I was still sour, and the man seemed irritatingly cheerful as he told his story.

"Oh, go and sell some chapattis," I muttered to the TV set, but regretted it immediately: I was stereotyping the businessman, not to mention sounding downright racist. Sobered, I decided I had just enough time to dash into the bathroom for the shower that had been interrupted by Cavenagh's call.

I was just buttoning my shirt when the doorbell rang. *Who the heck?* I opened the front-door to find my landlady Esther standing on the landing, smiling broadly. "Hello, Rick, I hear you had some excitement on the way back from Efrat yesterday?"

Startled, I couldn't help exclaiming, "For crying out loud, the whole of Jerusalem seems to know where I was yesterday afternoon! How on earth did you find out?"

Esther was nonplussed by my outburst and said placatingly, "Don't be silly. Israel is such a small country that everybody knows everybody else's business. I've got a nephew in the army and he was in the unit that came upon the ambush on the Etzion-Jerusalem road after it had ended. His officer said there had been an American reporter on the scene and his name was Ireland or something. When he told me that, I knew it had to be you."

"Listen, Esther, come on in. I've been told that the BBC has got a report on the incident and the next newscast is about to start. I'll get you a cup of coffee."

I thought better of letting Esther know what kind of story it would be. I didn't want to pass on to her the hints of Israeli brutality against the Palestinians that Cavenagh claimed had taken place in the hills above the shooting.

Esther had been a widow quite a few years, but though she was in her 50's she had kept herself in good trim. She practiced yoga every day and took regular Pilates classes. Her face was almost perfectly round, something I had never seen before. She had long legs and wore tight-fitting pants that flattered her. This morning, she was in a very tight pair of jeans and a short fitted bright red top that showed off her slim figure. She'd dropped by the apartment once or twice before for no obvious reason, causing me to wonder if she was flirting with me. It was flattering, of course, but awkward. I certainly didn't want to start anything with a landlady nearly twenty years older than me while I was pursuing Trish and trying to hold on to her affections when she was thousands of miles away in the Philippines. On the other hand, I didn't want to anger Esther by rejecting her flirting – if that is what it was – outright. "Hell hath no fury like…" kept passing through my head.

I had just managed to make some coffee in the French press Trish had given me when I left Hong Kong before the BBC World News started. I sat down on the sofa next to Esther to watch. There were items on North Korea, on the approaching American presidential election, and on a squabble between Germany and Russia over natural gas supplies. But the fourth item was obviously what Cavenagh had been referring to:

"In the Israeli-occupied West Bank yesterday," the anchor was intoning, "there are reports of three Palestinian prisoners being killed in cold blood by Israeli soldiers after being captured by an Israeli patrol. Our correspondent Christopher Blakely reports:

'When Palestinian gunmen fired from the hillside on an Israeli jeep yesterday, along the road that goes from Jerusalem to the West Bank settlement of Efrat, an Israeli reinforcement detachment gave chase to the three snipers and captured them. A Palestinian eye-witness says he saw one of the Israeli soldiers aim his rifle point-blank at the Palestinians, who had surrendered and had their hands in the air, and fire three shots. He said the men died immediately.'"

Esther had grown very tense on the sofa next to me and glanced at me a couple times. I pretended not to notice.

The reporter went on, "I talked late last night with Khalil al-Jaffar, a school teacher from a nearby Arab village." The camera then panned in on the face of a very agitated young man who said, "The soldier, he shoot three times and the Palestinians, they fall down dead. This an atrocity, this murder."

The camera returned to the reporter who wrapped up his report: "The Israeli Defense Ministry is usually prepared for these allegations, but when I called a few minutes ago, they said they had no information about the incident. They said they were standing by their previous report of the ambush on the Jerusalem-Etzion Road. But with the American Secretary of State due here for discussions of US-Israeli relations and the peace process in a few days, this incident is sure to aggravate the atmosphere of the talks with her and the already tense state of Israeli-Palestinian relations."

I glanced sideways at Esther. She looked furious. Before the reporter had even finished speaking, she had rounded on me: "Is that what you wanted me to see, Rick, another lie about our soldiers in the Territories? It makes me sick how you foreign reporters invent these stories to embarrass Israel."

Now it was my turn to be placating. "Esther, I'm really sorry. I had no idea what was going to be in that report other than that it was going to be about what I saw myself. A British reporter called me only a few minutes ago and said I should watch the BBC news."

"Yes, I am not surprised that's what he suggested. The British hate us. They've never forgiven us for driving them out of Palestine."

"Oh come on, Esther," I found myself in the surprising role of defending Patrick Cavenagh and the Beeb, "none of today's reporters were even alive when the British were running Palestine." I stopped, not wanting to say that there wasn't any bias against Israel at all among many British and other European reporters. Frankly there was. But I liked many of these reporters. I thought that they were, in general, pretty professional, and I didn't like all reporters to be lumped together into the category of anti-anything.

"You're right, Rick, there must be some other explanation for why they just hate us. They *hate* us. Perhaps it's because this generation of Jews won't go meekly into the gas chambers."

I was shocked. I'd had a few conversations with Esther, but they'd been cordial and she'd shown no animosity. Now she was getting really bitter. I didn't know how to move her off the topic which was causing her such anger. Thinking quickly, I said, "Well, there's one thing the English *goyim* are always raving about, and that's how good-looking Israeli women are." I'd used the Hebrew word for gentiles – *goyim* – hoping that the light-hearted touch might deflect her anger a little. I paused. She cracked a slight smile.

"Okay," she said in a lower-pitched voice, obviously a lot more relaxed. "I admit that my blood boils when I see how the foreign journalists report about us. Of course, you're different, Rick."

"Different? How so?"

"Well, I've always thought you tried to be fair to us. You do stories that are on a hundred different subjects. Two weeks ago you were doing a windsurfing contest in Nahariya, and last month you were out wine-tasting on the Golan. This weekend you took the trouble to drive to Efrat to find out what made a secular Jew want to live there. You don't just focus week after week on how the Goliath state of Israel is finding more and more ways to oppress the Palestinians."

I was embarrassed. I didn't want any of my colleagues to think of me as pro-Israel, but I did happen to think that there was more to covering Israel than the endless headlines about Palestinian demonstrations. I responded carefully.

"Look, Esther, I'm sure you think all foreign journalists in this country spend all of their time thinking up ways to bash Israel. I'll admit that quite a few of them have a pretty jaundiced attitude. But I'd say most of us don't have an agenda. We're hacks. We know what news is, and we follow it. Unfortunately, most of the news that's made in this country is about Israeli-Palestinian stuff. Like it or not, that's what we call 'the story', and like it or not, most of us are going to spend most of the time covering it." I was on familiar ground here. Over the years I'd had to give a similar defense countless times in response to the common complaint that the media only reports "bad news."

"Actually, I like Israelis," I continued. "I have found this to be an amazingly interesting and talented country, and I think it deserves better coverage than endless shootings and other violence. But my liking for the people here won't stop me from reporting things you probably don't want me to report."

She fell silent. I had made a reasonable case for my profession. I hadn't convinced her to like the Beeb, much less to feel any sympathy for Patrick Cavenagh, but for the time being, until some new reporting provocation stirred up her outrage, I'd drained some of the venom from her animus. I decided that now would be a good time to make my case for Trish and Clarissa coming to stay.

"Esther, can I talk to you about something related to my renting this apartment? Something that has nothing to do with the news."

"Try me, Rick."

"Well, I know you said that you didn't like drinking parties or two women staying overnight but I wondered if you'd let two women friends from Hong Kong and the Philippines – only one of them is a girlfriend – spend a few nights here next month?"

"Only one of them is a girlfriend. Who's the other?" She was clearly intrigued, and any lingering annoyance over the previous topic of conversation vanished.

"She's old enough to be my great-aunt, and sometimes I think of her as that. She's a missionary who lives in Hong Kong."

"A missionary!" Esther was aghast. "I don't want any missionaries here," she said in a tone that would brook no argument.

I immediately realized I had used a word that had ugly connotations to most Israelis, even to secular ones. A "missionary" in the Israeli context was someone – usually an American Christian – who tried to persuade Jews in Israel to stop being Jews and to become Christians. To an Israeli, the word not only conjured up the thought – ugly to most Jews – of "converting" Jews into Christians, but also harked back to the societies, particularly those in Eastern Europe, that had for hundreds of years persecuted Jews for *not* being Christian.

"No, no, Esther," I hastily replied. "I don't mean what you are thinking of at all. She's a missionary to the Chinese, lives in Hong Kong, and she loves Israel and the Jews. She wants them to go on being exactly what they are. Actually, she's African-American."

"She's black? How interesting. Why does she want to convert the Chinese?" Now Esther was intrigued again.

"Well, you know what these Fundamentalists are sometimes like." As soon as I said this, I felt a stab of conscience. It was a crude stereotyping of a woman I admired and respected, even if I didn't agree with her view of things. I tried to recover, "I mean, Christians who belong to evangelical churches always believe they've got to tell other people why they are the way they are."

"You mean, give their testimony?"

"Why, yes, that's what they call it," I said with some surprise. "How do you know that expression?"

Esther looked at me rather pityingly. "Rick," she said, "I wasn't born yesterday. Even in Israel we have programs on TV about the Fundamentalist churches in America."

I realized I was close to striking gold.

"Well," I said, "she's from one of those churches, and when I was in Hong Kong I was nice to her once not long after she arrived, and she did me a good turn or two as well. Trish is Filipina. She's my girlfriend – at least, I think she is – and Clarissa sort of took her under her wing when I had to go out of town suddenly and Trish was visiting me."

"So is Trish a Fundamentalist too?" Esther asked.

"Well, not exactly. But she sort of looks on Clarissa as a favorite aunt."

"So you won't be sleeping with Trish when the pair of them arrive?"

Her blunt question startled me, but I was also secretly rather amused. Israelis could be utterly lacking in any diplomatic niceties.

"Well, no, to be honest. Even if Trish were here alone, she wouldn't let me."

"Then you'd better get another girlfriend. Every man needs his outlet."

This made me laugh out loud, and this time Esther joined in. I knew she was just teasing. She watched me intently for a few seconds, then sighed.

"Well, I can see now. You're in love with her. You'll have to marry her."

I felt my face turn red. This made me really uncomfortable. Esther saw that and had mercy on me.

"Of course Trish and Clarissa can stay, Rick. Promise me though that you'll introduce me to them both."

"I will, Esther, I will."

III

JOURNALISM IN AMERICA has undergone major, sometimes wrenching upheavals since the 1990s, but to my relief one thing that had not come unglued was the network of bureau managers that keep the *Epoch* foreign bureau system humming along. In Hong Kong, I'd had Lucinda, a paragon of discretion, diligence, intelligence and humor. She'd saved me from embarrassment more times than I cared to remember, reminding me of a forgotten story deadline or of the impending visit of some *Epoch* corporate bigwig.

Epoch seemed to have innumerable Lucindas around the world. They were usually women of a certain age, some single, some divorced, some happily married. What they all had in common was an unusual loyalty to the magazine that was demonstrated time and again through amazing feats of efficiency and last-minute resourcefulness.

Lucinda's counterpart in Jerusalem was Margaret Rosewood, an *oleh* – an immigrant to Israel – from Birmingham, England. Margaret was happily married to an art dealer who'd made the transition from Britain to Israel fifteen years earlier. He had been married at the time but had gotten divorced. When he met Margaret, he discovered both intelligent companionship and a formidably well-organized mind and manner. Like Lucinda, Margaret was impeccably discreet. Unlike Hong Kong, the problem the bureau manager faced in Jerusalem was not corporate apparatchiks painting the town red; there was no "town" in Jerusalem to paint. Hardcore carousers in Israel inevitably gravitated to Tel Aviv where the atmosphere was less religious and the many excellent restaurants and nightspots were happy to entertain any visitor who could pay his bill.

No, the challenge for the Jerusalem bureau manager was entirely confined to the bureau itself. Bureau chiefs came and went, but the local reporters always stayed around. Some of them had been writing for *Epoch* for decades and had strong ideas about what next week's story should be and, for that matter, who should report it. The Friday morning story conferences could be acrimonious affairs as the local reporters vied with each other for priority in reporting. I found it all rather amusing, but Margaret didn't. That's because it usually fell to her to bandage up the wounded pride of the reporter I had passed over. Often, she served as an appeals court for the squabbling reporters behind the bureau chief's back. I was more than grateful for the way she shielded me from such small-minded strife, and I trusted her judgment in these affairs implicitly. Like Lucinda, she'd lived through several bureau chiefs and knew how to ensure that each one looked good within the *Epoch*'s bureau chief system. It was not entirely altruistic; Margaret's salary was tied to her work performance. She was one of the highest-paid *Epoch* bureau managers and was determined to keep it that way.

The bureau was located on King George V Street not far from the always crowded Hamesh Bir department store. The bureau was a lot less glamorous than Hong Kong's, and I had been annoyed from the first day I stepped into the bureau that some predecessor of mine had chosen the third-floor office space with scant regard either for its size or surroundings. The rooms were small and drafty in winter, and the building didn't have an elevator. About the only thing going for the bureau space was its convenient location: right next to the entrance of Ben Yehuda Street, a traffic-free pedestrian street, and a few hundred yards from the government press center in the Beit Agron building

I parked my car in an underground lot on King George V Street and walked the few blocks back to the bureau. On this early spring day, the mood of people on the street was relaxed. Although suicide bombings were not quite a thing of the past, Jerusalem had not had one in several months. The street was filled with the usual cadre of IDF soldiers, both men and women with their rifles slung casually over their shoulders, as well as on-duty border guards with their green berets, and the occasional knots of *haredim* ultra-orthodox Hasidic Jews in their quasi-uniform of black frock coat and broad-brimmed fur hats. Passing a convenience store, I momentarily considered buying an ice cream, but then decided against such an indulgence so early in the day. I did stop at a newsstand to buy a copy of our rival magazine, *Newshour*. The cover made me chuckle: cats and the American obsession with them. Two recent bestsellers about cats had topped the *New York Times* book list, and *Epoch* had run a cover on the topic several months earlier. "Well, we beat them on that one," I muttered to myself with satisfaction as I leafed through the magazine.

I had resumed walking when what I saw in the international news section of *Newshour* stopped me dead in my tracks. Our competition had not only scooped us, *Newshour* had gotten a twin-exclusive: an interview with one of the senior Hamas figures and a parallel interview out of the Beirut bureau with Hasan Nasrallah, the leader of Hezbollah.

"Oh boy," I worried aloud, "what'll they be thinking in New York?" In *Epoch* jargon, "New York" referred to the editorial bosses back at headquarters: Christopher Reddaway, the managing editor, and the foreign desk chief and my boss Burton Lasch.

"Good morning, Rick," Margaret greeted me cheerily as I entered the bureau. She was always the first to arrive, shortly before 9 each morning, and she went through the night's bureau email before anyone else started work. Jerusalem, like Hong Kong, was not an early-morning place, at least for journalists, and for that I was grateful.

"Anything interesting?" I asked. This was my standard routine each morning with Margaret.

"Well, there's an email for you from someone in China. Says his name is 'Yayo Fanmee' or something. He seems to know you. He plans to come to Israel in the next few weeks."

For the second time in as many minutes, I stopped in my tracks. "Yao Fanmei," I said, half to myself and half in response to Margaret. "So he's coming after all?"

"Do you know him?" Margaret asked innocently.

"Know him? I saved his life by getting him out of Guangzhou in the middle of that anti-government military coup in China last year. I last saw him in the Philippines, which is where we both ended up on someone else's yacht."

"You mean he was working with that CIA guy you also helped get out of China?"

"No, I met Yao completely independently of Chuck McHale, but we both ended up on the same smuggler's speedboat to Hong Kong and on the same yacht to the Philippines. Poor Yao must have heaved up every meal he'd eaten in the previous three months on that trip."

"Well, what do you think he's doing coming here?" Margaret followed up intelligently. "China has diplomatic relations with Israel but it's been courting all the Arab nasties it can find, from Sudan to Hezbollah. Is this just a social visit, a sort of get-together for the sake of old times, or something else?" Margaret was as sharp as any of the bureau's reporters.

"Beats me. Knowing Yao, the Chinese government wouldn't be sending him unless they wanted to find something out that they don't know through their embassy in Tel Aviv or from their own spooks in the area."

"Well, you're probably the only person in Jerusalem that Yao knows so I'd assume he wants to find out something from you."

"That's probably right. The question is, what?"

Margaret ignored my rhetorical question. She was moving briskly through her morning briefing, which included whatever she felt was worth noting from the Hebrew-language dailies. This was another one of the many ways Margaret was invaluable to me. Although I'm better than the typical American in picking up new languages, I just hadn't had the time to learn much more than the basics of spoken Hebrew.

"There's an interesting and lengthy story in the Davar weekend edition about a young French Jew who was beaten within an inch of his life by Arab demonstators in Paris who were shouting, 'Death to the Jews!'"

"When did that happen? Was it over the weekend?"

"Oh no. It was more than a month ago. The guy was walking home from the Sorbonne when he was set upon by Arab residents of Paris apparently looking specifically for someone Jewish to beat up."

"What happened to him?"

"Well, the police managed to rescue him before he was killed. He was hospitalized and started making almost immediate plans to emigrate from France to Israel."

"Interesting story. There was an item on TV last night about another anti-Jewish demonostration by Arabs in Paris. Not a nice place to be right now. What else?"

"There's a piece in *Ha'aretz* – that's Israel's most authoritative left-of-center daily – quoting *The News Report* online edition saying that IDF soldiers yesterday murdered captured Palestinian gunmen in cold blood not far from the road to Efrat. Weren't you going to Efrat yesterday, Rick, to talk with that surgeon from Hadassah?"

"Yep, I went, I saw, and I reported," I replied. It was a lame attempt to conjure up Julius Caesar's famous words after conquering the Gauls: "*Veni, Vidi, Vici* (I came, I saw, I conquered)."

"Oh, it was a Caesarian operation, was it?" Margaret quipped, her medical pun swiftly deflating my classical pretensions. I decided the best escape from more humiliation was to stick to the subject at hand.

"I saw that ambush of the Israeli jeep with my own eyes, and I also saw the back-up squad arrive. One of the gunmen on the hillside had clearly been shot – I don't know whether he was alive or not – and the other two dragged him out of sight. As far as I know, the other two escaped. So Patrick went with the information he had, did he?"

"I don't know what information he went with," her voice rising in the tones of the distinct "Brummy" dialect of Birmingham, England Margaret had explained, soon after I arrived in Jerusalem, that many Americans couldn't understand her speech because it was heavily regional from Birmingham. The shortened term for the dialect was "brummy." She went on, "But the Ha'aretz story has him quoting Palestinian sources – wait, let me see who it says spoke to him … um, here, it says, 'a school teacher, who observed Israeli soldiers shooting down two Palestinian gunmen who had already surrendered and were prisoners.'"

"Do you believe that?"

"No, of course not," Margaret answered without hesitation. "I don't believe it precisely because if it happened it would immediately become public knowledge. Even if a Palestinian school teacher hadn't been there, someone in the squad would have turned the shooter in. Who knows, there might have been a reservist in the unit who was a law professor —"

"I believe it!"

The voice was that of a young man speaking heavily Israeli-accented English. It was Rafi Eitan, a Tel Aviv University graduate student in international relations who was interning with us for a few months. Rafi was from a well-to-do North Tel Aviv family of totally Ashkenazi provenance — none of his Jewish ancestors in Europe had been born closer to the equator than Mainz, Germany. In less than two weeks after arriving in the bureau he had established himself as politically the most left-leaning of anyone in the bureau. The only person in the bureau who was, even by Israeli standards, close to the nationalist right was Ira Blumenthal, an older reporter who'd worked many years for the *Boston Globe* before immigrating to Israel. Ira almost always voted for the conservative political party Likud, and was proud of it. Professionally, he was a first-rate journalist who focused mainly on political reporting, and it was hard to discern from his *Epoch* reports where his personal sympathies lay.

The rest of the bureau was centrist to liberal. Before Rafi came, the most outspokenly liberal-leftist staffer was photographer Benjamin

Lifshutz who'd migrated to Israel from a "displaced person's camp" in central Europe just after World War II and had photographed every major event in Israel's history since the 1948 War of Independence. Benjamin was an old Laborite and had probably never voted for any political party other than Labor and its successor, Meretz. In fact, when he first came to Israel, he'd lived for several years on a kibbutz, one of the early agrarian pioneering communities to which an entire generation of socialist-inclined Central European immigrants had gone. Because of their tradition, they had long been hothouses for left-wing politics in Israel. He thoroughly disliked the nationalist right, and had been quite dismayed when Menachem Begin came to power as leader of the Likud and prime minister in 1977. But Lifshutz had also been around long enough to have witnessed firsthand the brutality of Israel's wars, most of which were defensive battles for survival against attacks instigated by its Arab neighbors. And from photographing various diplomatic events that followed the 1993 Declaration of Principles agreement between Israel and the PLO, he'd met almost every major Palestinian figure. Lifshutz knew the West Bank and Gaza almost as well as any Palestinian, and he didn't believe every allegation of Israeli brutality.

But Benjamin Lifshutz was out on assignment this morning, so Rafi, who had just walked into the bureau, had a clear run with his ideas.

"I believe it," he repeated, "because we've been an occupation force since the beginning and occupation forces inevitably commit atrocities. Only last month a captain was court-martialed for ordering his troops to beat up some Palestinian teenagers they'd caught throwing rocks at our jeeps. It's got to be true."

I find this kind of dogmatism particularly irritating, and demanded of Rafi, "How do you know? Were you there? That's a ridiculous assertion to make if you weren't an eyewitness, and frankly, it's just bad journalism. Just because the IDF has been brutal in the past, even sometimes committed atrocities—if it ever has—that's no reason for accepting at face value allegations like this on the say-so of a Palestinian school teacher — if indeed he ever said that to Patrick Cavenagh."

"You don't think Patrick's making it up, do you?" Margaret's right eyebrow shot up quizzically. "I know he doesn't like Israelis, but I've never thought his reporting was actually dishonest."

I paused. "Well, I'm not saying that Patrick made anything up. I just think he might not have exercised his usual professional skepticism, that's all."

Rafi looked about to comment, then seemed to change his mind. I wondered if he recalled the tongue-lashing I'd given him his second week in the bureau when he'd impudently suggested that I had not visited enough Arab countries. "I'll keep that comment in mind as soon as you become *Epoch's* next foreign editor," I'd said sarcastically.

"There's only one way to begin to get to the bottom of this story," I now said to Margaret. "That's to get Karim onto it. Is he around?"

"Yes, but he's probably not going to be much use. He only got back from the States yesterday. It will take him a few days to get up to speed."

"Well, he'll just have to do it faster than that. We've got to get onto this story fast. We don't want another Mohammed al-Dura story poisoning the entire atmosphere for reporters here. One more tale like that and the government press office will have us all wearing bull's-eyes on our backs with the words 'foreign correspondents' underneath."

Mohammed al-Dura was the name of a Palestinian boy who was allegedly killed by Israeli military cross-fire. His supposed final moments of life were caught on film by a French TV crew and the clip was broadcast worldwide in 2002. The authenticity of the footage was questioned from the beginning, but it took several months before the true circumstances of the videotape were laid bare. The French TV film crew had been coaching Palestinian children to appear on camera throwing rocks at Israeli jeeps. No one ever confirmed that Mohammed al-Dura's body had even shown up in a Palestinian mortuary, and careful investigation of the firing positions of Israeli soldiers at the time Mohammed al-Dura supposedly died showed that the soldiers could not possibly have been responsible for his death. The French TV producer who had put the piece together was fired. But by then it was too late. Mohammed al-Dura had become yet another mythical figure in the David versus Goliath struggle of innocent and peaceful Palestinian civilians quietly resisting the implacable Israeli occupation forces.

"Yes, we certainly don't need another Mohammed al-Dura incident," Margaret said with a sigh. "I'll call Karim up and tell him to get to the bureau right away."

"No, don't do that. Tell him I'll meet him at the Adelphia restaurant in East Jerusalem. Normally, I'd go to the American Colony. But it's always crawling with British hacks and I don't want it to get out yet that I'm looking into Patrick's allegations. And the Adelphia will be easier for Karim than summoning him here to the bureau. That way maybe he won't resent me for not letting him get over jetlag."

"Right, I'll make a reservation at the Adelphia," Margaret said as she headed for her desk. "Oh, and before I forget, there's a small package for you." She turned and grinned at me: "It's from the Philippines." Within a just few short weeks of my arrival, Margaret had managed to pry enough information out of me to know about Trish.

I retreated to my dreary corner office. It had only one window, set so high on the wall that it was impossible to see anything out of it. None of the bureau offices, including the bureau chief's, had had a new coat of paint in at least a decade. The small rug in front of my desk was littered with cigarette burns, the legacy of a bureau chief three generations back who'd annoyed everyone with his chain-smoking and against whose habit no one had had the temerity to protest. A wooden cupboard in the corner was covered in dust. Piled on top of it was a stack of week-old *Jerusalem Posts* and inside were two liquor bottles — half a Gordon's gin, and a nearly full Johnny Walker Black Label — and, as a sort of protest against this elite liquor collection, two bottles of Maccabee beer, Israel's most famous domestic brand. Of course, they were not chilled, and of course there was no tonic water to accompany the gin. The days of leisurely "pours," *Epoch*'s word for a round of drinks in an editor's or bureau chief's office at the end of the week, seemed to have petered out, whether the victim of new, faster-paced, Internet-driven journalism, or a general lowering of the conviviality at *Epoch*, I didn't know.

I sat down and tore open the padded envelope bearing Trish's neat handwriting. Inside was a thin box and something loosely wrapped in white tissue paper. Unwrapping it quickly, I laughed out loud when I saw what it was: a silver business-card case inscribed with the words "The Scribe's Particulars." How typical of her: slightly eccentric and very witty. I held the silver case in both hands for a long moment before putting it aside on my desk. I was tempted to send her an immediate email of thanks, but decided to do that later when I was not so pressed.

I skimmed the *Jerusalem Post* quickly just to be sure I was up on the latest events in and around Israel of the previous twenty-four hours. Then I turned my attention to emails. Glancing at the subject headings from various levels of *Epoch*'s editorial system, I decided they could all wait. What I really wanted was to see if Trish had written again.

We'd been corresponding via email, and though it was a regular exchange, I was always disappointed on the days when she didn't write. I suspected Trish was a little hesitant to appear too forthcoming. She'd first said she loved me that day when we'd met in a lovely Manila garden after my escape from China with CIA operative Chuck McHale and Yao Fanmei. That had also been the first time we had kissed. It embarrassed me now to find myself dwelling like a 10th grader on the memory of that first encounter with her soft lips. We'd kissed a few times since then – too few as far as I was concerned, but I accepted that. I had come to realize that I could either accept Trish on her terms or lose her, but that hadn't always been the case. The relationship had ended almost before it began when Trish came to visit me in Hong Kong and I'd suggested that she stay in my apartment. To my astonishment, she had made it clear there was going to be absolutely no sex with me – or anyone else – before marriage. More than once, I'd wondered if it was worth it to be single, chaste, and at the same time in love with someone who held to such old-fashioned moral standards and who lived thousands of miles away. It wasn't as though there was nothing available closer to home. Israeli women were no more promiscuous than those of any other nationality, but when they liked a guy they were unrestrained in expressing it. Trish seemed to have caught a strong dose of Christianity from her missionary friend in Hong Kong, Clarissa, and she was not, apparently, going to be shaken out of it. As an agnostic, I was just grateful that she had made no demands that I convert or something horrible.

I glanced quickly down the list of senders' names in my Inbox and immediately spotted her moniker: trishdeloss. It wasn't just the stunning good looks that all five of the de los Santos daughters shared.

In conversation, Trish could be both funny and witty, sometimes punning so quickly that I had a hard time keeping up. But she had a tart tongue too, and liked putting in his place anyone who started sounding pretentious. I had spent quite a lot of time in the Philippines after the China adventure, and getting to know Trish. I once had felt obliged to apologize in Manila Hong Kong to an American businessman a day after Trish had thoroughly thrown him for a loop at a dinner party with the American political officer at the Embassy. The man made the mistake of claiming to be a connoisseur of English literature, a statement that was like a declaration of war for Trish. No one, but no one, she thought, knew as much about the subject as she did.

The businessman went prattling on about how much he enjoyed reading Chaucer, and how, as a long-time bachelor, he found it difficult to meet women who shared his passion. Trish had immediately jumped into the conversation with the crack: "It seems that what you need is a good 'povre widwe.'" Only the political officer, who had been an academic before joining the Foreign Service, caught the joke, and burst out into a hacking, sputtering laugh. The businessman looked stricken, not understanding Trish's literary allusion. She rescued him with a laugh and an explanation: "'Povre widwe,' means 'poor widow,' and she's the heroine in the opening line of Chaucer's *Pardoner's Tale*. If she were poor enough she'd laugh at all your literary allusions."

The first secretary thought this was just about the funniest thing he had ever heard, and his hacking laugh crescendoed through the room. "For goodness sake, I like that!" he exclaimed. "Trish, you should go into business as a literary wit-trimmer, someone who trims wits to make them illuminate conversation better." This time, everyone around the table laughed, even the businessman.

"My dear Rick," the email from her began, "I've had a really bad day so forgive me if I cry on your shoulder a little. Andros – you know, my new boss, that fiery-tempered Greek — said my presentation for the Viscayas Development Group was totally lacking in substance and ordered me to start from scratch. This is the first time any boss has ever suggested that my work was sub-par, and I had actually worked particularly long and hard on that presentation to show him what I am capable of. I feel sort of crushed." It was a longer email than usual and went into great detail of her previous workday and the challenges of adjusting to this new and apparently hard-to-please boss. I was delighted by her greeting – "My dear" – which she had never used before, and the "cry on your shoulder" request. I would be delighted for Trish to cry on my shoulder or, for that matter, any other part of me. But there was no mention of the silver business card-holder. Perhaps she'd sent it several days earlier.

I was sinking into a mild reverie about her when the phone rang, jolting me back to reality. I snatched it up and answered automatically, "Ireton."

An unmistakably Chinese-accented voice said in English, "Is that Mr. Ireton?"

I recognized the idiosyncratic and slightly ponderous style of Yao Fanmei speaking English. I responded in Mandarin, "*Wo jiu shi* (Yes, it's me)."

"I'm coming to Jerusalem on the 20th of next month," Yao persisted in English, "Will you be there then? Did you get my email?"

"Yes, Fanmei. How good to hear your voice. It's been too long. You're coming to Israel? What brings you here? I thought they'd converted you to academic life in Beijing." I heard measured, polite laughter from the other end of the line.

"*Dui-le, wo xianzai shi yanjiuyuan* (That's right, I'm now a researcher)," Yao replied, reverting now to Chinese, "*buguo wo mei wang wode lao pengyou men de shiye* (but I've not forgotten the profession of my old friends)."

So Yao *was* coming to China on government business, almost certainly to gather information that the Chinese government didn't think it was getting from its conventional sources. By "old friends" he must have been alluding to his former colleagues in the Public Security Bureau where he had held a significant job in Guangzhou before getting caught up in fast-moving turmoil when a powerful element of the Guangzhou Military Region initiated a coup attempt against the central government. If they had succeeded, there would almost certainly have been a war between China and the United States over Taiwan, the breakaway island province. Yao had managed to alert contacts in Beijing to what was afoot and I had engineered his escape from Guangzhou just in the nick of time as the coup got under way.

"Fanmei, I will be delighted to see you and show you around this town, indeed this country, as much as time permits," I replied in English, my Mandarin abilities faltering. "But I need you to send me by email the details of your flight arrival. I'll come pick you up. Do you need a place to stay?"

"No, thank you. The people who are sending me are keeping America's economy afloat. They can afford to pay for my hotel." And he laughed in that polite, measured way, again. I didn't understand his reference at first, but then realized that Yao was alluding to China's purchase of U.S. Treasury Bonds that kept the American economy solvent after years of huge trade deficits.

"Yes, your government is certainly paying our tab," I replied.

"'Tab?' what is the meaning of 'tab'?" Yao asked.

"Tab means a bill, a check in a restaurant. I was agreeing with your comment that China's profits from foreign trade are what pay for America's profligacy" – then corrected myself, realizing "profligacy" wouldn't be a word Yao would know – "I mean, America's extravagant ways."

Inwardly, I was relieved. I was delighted to accommodate Clarissa and Trish, especially now that Esther had approved the arrangement, but I really didn't want a mid-level Chinese government bureaucrat staying with me and one, moreover, who was probably connected with, if not on the payroll of, the Chinese foreign intelligence.

"Well, can we make a hotel reservation for you?" I asked, following up politely.

"No, thanks, the embassy will do that."

"Right, then I'll look forward to seeing you on the 20th of next month. Send me your details by e-mail."

"Yes, I will do that. Thank you, Rick, and see you soon. Goodbye."

"Rick, it's Karim on line two," I heard Margaret say loudly through the office door.

"Thanks, Margaret." Now I had to change gears rapidly. Yao was polite, even formal, and I was always confident I knew where I stood with Chinese, even with Chinese officials. They were seldom emotional with you and if they didn't like you or what you were saying, they didn't let on, at least not right away.

It was different in the Arab world and I had not quite known how to proceed at first. Arabs too were very polite, often exquisitely so. In fact, compared with the often brusque Israelis, Arabs were generally more openly hospitable and gracious, the Bedouin tradition of hospitality towards all strangers seemingly embedded in their genes. On the other hand, I had found it necessary to be especially careful in conversation. A single ill-phrased comment or a carelessly selected adjective could elicit an outburst of indignation and emotion. Undoing the damage could sometimes be very difficult, I'd found. For example, shortly after arriving in Israel, I'd gone to Ramallah, the first major West Bank Palestinian city north of Jerusalem, to meet a Palestinian lawyer whose assessment of the political mood of Palestinians was, according to Karim, generally quite sound.

"How often do you come into Jerusalem?" I had asked. It was the sort of question that was standard at the start of an interview, and I was totally unprepared for the emotional outburst it unleashed.

"How often?" the Palestinian lawyer barked back. "Because I don't have Jerusalem residency or any close relatives in the city, it takes me at least four hours just to get through the Israeli checkpoints! Do you think I can even consider coming 'often' to Jerusalem under such circumstances?"

"I'm sorry," I hurriedly replied, trying to mollify the man, "I had no idea that it was so difficult for you."

"It is difficult for all of us," the doctor replied. "Look, we are under occupation. How can you move anywhere 'often' if you are under occupation?"

The encounter had made me aware of the paramount need to maintain journalistic objectivity. Our instructors at Northwestern's Medill School of Journalism had drummed this into us while acknowledging, of course, that absolute objectivity is humanly unattainable. Nonetheless, we were taught that there was always more than one side to a story and our job was to present as true and accurate a picture as possible.

In this case, my natural sympathies lay with Israel's innocent civilians who for several years had been mindlessly murdered by suicide bombers. That made me predisposed to accepting the Israeli arguments for the need to construct the security fence which the Palestinians called "the Wall." It ran down the Green Line that marked the legally recognized international boundary of Israel in its pre-1967 borders and the West Bank, which until 1967 had been ruled by Jordan. But now I was also hearing from Palestinians that the fence completely disrupted their lives.

For some, it meant that they were forced to go through a ponderous security checkpoint just to visit a relative a few hundred yards from their home.

After that interview, I closely studied the pathway taken by the fence and understood that, in places, it actually gobbled up land that technically was part of the West Bank. The Israelis insisted that the fence was in no way intended to be a permanent boundary marker between Israel and what might become a Palestinian state, but few Palestinians were convinced.

"Karim, thanks for calling me. How was Boston?"

"Oh, very good. My daughter is now a senior at Boston College and graduates this May. She wants to go on to law school."

"Well, I've heard you describe Fatima as a good arguer," I said. "Now you've got proof of it. Where's she been accepted?"

There was a brief pause, as though Karim was embarrassed to answer the question. "Well, she's been accepted by Harvard, Stanford, and Duke, but she didn't get into Yale, which she wanted to badly."

"Heavensakes, Karim, the three places you just mentioned are not exactly Podunk State University."

"Yes, but Fatima wants to change the world, and Yale has the best international human rights program."

"Indeed it does. Still, you must be very proud of her. Congratulations."

"Thanks, and yes, I am proud of her. But that's not why you called, is it, Rick?"

"You're right, Karim. I can't tell you anything over the phone, but there was a report on both the BBC and in the British *News Report* that something really bad happened on the West Bank yesterday. I want to talk to you about it."

"I know what you're referring to," said Karim. "I've already started looking into it. Margaret said that you wanted to meet for lunch at the Adelphia. Would one o'clock be okay? I think the checkpoints are quite busy this morning."

"One o'clock's fine, Karim. See you there." We hung up.

Karim Nasr was the Jerusalem bureau's Palestinian reporter. Everyone in Israel's foreign press corps thought he was simply the best. In his late 40s, he was older than the average Palestinian journalist working for a Western news organization. More importantly, he had the advantage of having lived in the United States and being a U.S. passport-holder. He'd become a naturalized U.S. citizen while teaching at Whitman College in Walla Walla, Washington after getting his doctorate at the University of Portland where he'd specialized in modern Middle East history. With his facility in written Arabic and his familiarity with the situation on the ground in Palestinian areas, he would have been an asset to any university or any news organization.

Perhaps more significantly, Karim was respected equally by Westerners, Palestinians, and even Israelis for a quality not related to his academic background or his personal experience, and, frankly, not assumed to be present in many Palestinians: He was, quite simply, totally honest.

THE ADELPHIA RESTAURANT was generally regarded as the best non-hotel restaurant in East Jerusalem. Of course, the American Colony Hotel down the Nablus Road offered more refined dishes and a pleasanter atmosphere, but I had chosen the Adelphia for a more serious reason. The American Colony Hotel was constantly humming with diplomats on short-term assignments to Jerusalem, foreign correspondents either based in Israel or passing through, and Israeli officials on the murky fringes of Israeli-Arab negotiations. I was sure to run into someone I knew or who knew me, and the one thing I absolutely didn't want right now was to have any hint of my controversy with Patrick Cavenagh bruited about by the foreign press corps. Even though meeting with Karim was an entirely normal thing for the *Epoch* bureau chief to do, just the briefest of social encounters could bring questions. I could imagine Cavenagh's buddy, Steven Palling of the *Morning Express,* running into us and saying, "Ah, Karim, so nice to see you. Checking up on that murder by the IDF in the West Bank yesterday?" I just couldn't risk where that sort of encounter or a follow-up to the question, either.

Karim had been *Epoch*'s Palestinian stringer – that is, a non-staff reporter who is paid a retainer to ensure that *Epoch* has first dibs on any news he uncovers – for some twelve years. He was born in Ramallah, the West Bank city just six miles north of Jerusalem that served as the headquarters of the Palestinian Authority, or at least the Fatah part of it, as opposed to Hamas, which was located in Gaza. But since the armed takeover of Gaza by Hamas in June 2007, Ramallah has been the only place where Palestinian officials who were reasonably moderate and modern could be found. Ramallah even had a large population of Palestinian Christians, though their numbers had dwindled dramatically over the decades due to emigration to the United States, Australia, and elsewhere. On the other hand, there were a large number of American-born Palestinians living in Ramallah, which contributed to something approaching the trendy, shopping mall youth culture visible from Los Angeles to London.

The Islamists who had founded and now controlled Hamas hadn't succeeded in extending their takeover of Palestinian government to Ramallah, though they dearly wanted to. They'd been pushing hard to gain power in the West Bank, and their influence was felt in society in a vaguely menacing way. From time to time, they would harass young women they considered immodestly dressed or they would menace the young men who hung around those women. Fewer women went out on the streets now without the *hijab*, the obligatory headscarf for all Muslim women. Karim's wife Leila thoroughly resented this, and persisted in appearing in public without the head covering, her long deep chestnut hair swinging freely past her shoulders. Karim often scolded her about this, worried that a passing squad of Islamic radical youths might decide to pick on her and beat her up — or worse. Although they both were born into Muslim families, they were for all practical purposes agnostic.

Karim's education had been broad and varied. He'd attended the Anglican School in Jerusalem, an international school that was a favorite among Jerusalem's expatriates but which also admitted a handful of Arab and even Israeli students. That was where he had acquired his excellent English. After graduating from Bir Zeit University with a bachelor's degree in politics, Karim had pursued graduate studies at the University of Oregon in Eugene, then spent five years there working on a master's degree and then a doctorate in political science. That was followed by his five-year teaching stint at Whitman College in Walla Walla, Washington. During that time, Karim and his wife both became

US citizens, which meant they could have remained in the United States permanently. But after Leila completed her own master's degree and was aiming for a doctorate in English literature, Karim decided to haul the entire family back to Ramallah. Neither of their two American-born children, Bassam and Fatima, could read or write Arabic at more than elementary level and they had become increasingly reluctant to speak Arabic at all, catching that common affliction of immigrant children to America: hostility to their cultural and linguistic origins. If Karim and Leila didn't get them back to the West Bank and immerse them in Palestinian Arab life soon, their children would lose their Arab heritage forever. Karim, who was proud of being both Arab and Palestinian, didn't want that to happen. So Bassam and Fatima, aged twelve and eight respectively, were uprooted from their comfortable suburban American life and, whining constantly, dragged back to Ramallah. That had been a decade ago. Karim had taken up a position teaching politics at Bir Zeit before becoming the *Epoch* stringer. It paid enough to eke out his modest salary as a stringer, though *Epoch*, in appreciation of his unique skills and expertise, had steadily bumped up his salary to the point where it was higher than that of some of the Israelis working in the bureau.

"Great to see you, Karim," I said as I joined him at a table in the corner of the restaurant. Karim was unusual among the Arabs I had met not just in being prompt for appointments, but early. Sometimes this annoyed me. Though I was usually punctual myself, I often tried like most journalists to squeeze more into a time-slot than there was actually time for. It meant that sometimes I was seriously late for an appointment. I was, to be sure, always embarrassed when this happened. Although I wasn't late today, Karim was still there before me.

We chatted about personal news for a while: Karim's time in Boston and my few days at an *Epoch* bureau chiefs' meeting in London.

"Is Lasch still in charge?" Karim asked.

"Was he ever not?" I countered.

"No, but I know that he and Reddaway have been sniping at each other for years."

Karim's observation annoyed me a bit. It happened to be true, and everybody at the magazine knew from week to week who was up and who was down in the great rivalry between the foreign editor and the managing editor. But, his experience and journalistic savvy notwithstanding, Karim simply *wasn't* an *Epoch* correspondent. He wasn't a total outsider obviously, but he wasn't a member of the club, either — not a staff correspondent or a staff writer, let alone an editor or regular correspondent. But I knew I couldn't afford to pull rank with Karim. I really couldn't afford to irritate him right now.

"Yes, and you and I know that's a product of a natural antipathy; reporters always think editors don't know how to ask questions and editors always think reporters don't know how to write."

"They're probably both right," cracked Karim. I laughed, which seemed to please Karim. Despite his absolutely fluent, colloquial English, Karim had something of a complex about not being Anglo-Saxon and thus not always being attuned to all the niceties of Anglo-Saxon tribal culture and humor. He enjoyed it when he said something that amused an American.

"I think you know why I wanted to talk to you, Karim," I said. But before I could continue, a waiter approached with two huge menus. One thing was indisputable about the Adelphia: the service was excellent. I paused – in East Jerusalem restaurants, it was prudent to be careful about talking in front of the waiters — and we both studied the menus quickly before ordering St. Peter's fish which is found only in the Sea of Galilee, or Lake Tiberias as the Israelis call it. When the waiter had taken our order and was out of earshot, I continued: "Have you heard anything about what happened yesterday on the Hebron road between Jerusalem and Gush Etzion?"

"But weren't you there yourself?" Karim countered. "I heard that you went to Efrat over the weekend. You must have seen something."

"I did. In fact, I saw the ambush moments after it started. I saw one

Palestinian shot and severely wounded, perhaps killed, and I saw the Palestinians shoot one of the Israeli soldiers. Then the reinforcements arrived and I left. What about this allegation, then? Are you at all convinced that, after the ambush got under way, the Israeli soldiers climbed the hillside, captured the two gunmen and their wounded accomplice, and then shot them all at point-blank range?"

Karim drank from the glass of water in front of him first, then carefully looked around the restaurant. Then, lowering his glance to the table, he replied in a voice so low that I had to strain to hear him.

"I know what the BBC reported," he said carefully. "I also know that both Patrick Cavenagh and the BBC man interviewed a school teacher from a village near Gush Etzion who said he saw Israeli soldiers shoot the three Palestinians in cold blood." He paused. I studied his face intently.

"Well, did it happen?" I blurted out when Karim didn't continue.

"I don't believe it did, but I need more time to investigate."

"Why don't you believe it?"

"Because I don't think the Israeli army would be that stupid."

"They've done stupid things before."

"Yes, but cold-blooded murder? You can't keep that many secrets in Israel. The army here is composed of kids drafted from all sectors of society. If it had happened, you can be sure that someone on the Israeli side would have heard of it by now. You've got groups of reserve officers who refuse even to serve in the West Bank and Gaza. The soldiers in yesterday's business weren't part of an elite Israeli unit — a brotherhood of combat veterans who have all sworn a blood-loyalty oath not to betray each other."

"Well, what about the Palestinian school teacher? Isn't he credible?" I asked. Playing the devil's advocate is an essential part of journalistic digging.

"Of course he's credible. The question is, was he telling the truth? The whole thing doesn't ring true to me. After all, he's just one witness. Of course, as a Palestinian, I'm supposed to say that I believe him. But as you know, Rick, we Palestinians don't always tell the truth even when we're morally in the right. What is it that you like to quote Henry Kissinger as supposedly having said?" He made a clumsy attempt to mimic my fairly good imitation of Henry Kissinger's German accent: "Just because I'm paranoid doesn't mean zat somvun isn't following me."

He added, "Just because the Palestinians suffer under Israeli occupation doesn't mean that everything they say about the Israelis is always true. Sometimes it's a lie. But I think that, as a reporter, one should simply tell no lies."

I was struck deeply to hear Karim say this. I knew him to be a meticulous, honest reporter who could be relied upon not to be swayed by exaggeration on the part of his sources. But this was the first time I had heard Karim articulate so clearly a journalistic principle rooted in a Western understanding of truth. That understanding held truth to be a value above any political, philosophical, or religious cause, no matter how heroic that cause might be. In journalism school, my instructors had hammered into us that good reporters reported the news without bias. Of course, in reality, complete objectivity is impossible, but journalism in America more than in any other country held the ideal of objective truthful reporting as about the highest professional value one could seek. I'd heard plenty of Americans – usually political conservatives – write off the entire journalistic profession because a few reporters were seriously biased. I wondered how Karim had stumbled onto this principle. Probably not through Islam, I thought, because while that religion sets great store by justice, it has a much less elevated view of truth-telling.

"I think," Karim was now saying, "that the school teacher probably came under pressure to say what he said."

"What sort of pressure?"

"Any sort. Anything from denying him promotion to a threat to deny his children access to good schools, to direct physical threat. You know, I'll tell you something: That ambush on the road to Gush Etzion was a failure. The gunmen lost one man while on the Israeli side only one soldier was wounded."

"Do you know which group sent them?"

"No. It could have been Islamic Jihad, or Hamas, some Fatah faction, or even Hezbollah. They are beginning to be very active, you know."

"If it was a failure, why would they want to accuse the Israelis of an atrocity?"

"Because they were embarrassed. Somebody lost face. You can't let the screw-up – the botched ambush – be the last word on the business, so you create a new incident to distract people. Perhaps you can push that hard enough so it becomes international. Now you've got a new incident that might get people all riled up. They did this with the Mohammed al-Dura affair and it worked, so they just might try it again."

"Do you mean that once it was clear the ambush hadn't worked, someone decided to make this into an Israeli atrocity and found a convenient Palestinian school teacher to arm-twist into making a false statement?"

"Exactly. Of course, I can't be totally sure just yet, but it certainly seems to be likely."

"Well, don't they have to produce the bodies of these men who were allegedly murdered by Israeli soldiers? I thought Palestinian funerals were almost always opportunities to demonstrate the iniquity of the occupation."

Karim winced, but all he said was, "Yes, our funerals can be very emotional." He continued, "No, it would be very easy for three alleged 'mothers' of the slain men to come forward and say that the families had insisted on immediate burial for their sons. The school teacher could claim that the bodies were all taken away immediately and buried. Of course, the Israelis might eventually prove that the three so-called mothers didn't even have sons, or that one of the young men was killed in a traffic accident, or that another was not even dead but actually alive and well and working as a bouncer in Las Vegas. But by that time, the propaganda damage would have been done and the media would have moved on to other stories. People's attention-spans are very short, you know."

"How do you think we should cover the story, then, Karim?"

"You know, it would be very dangerous for me to work on this too much. If even Fatah knew that I was uncovering evidence that an alleged atrocity against Palestinians never even took place, my life wouldn't be worth very much – or Leila's. I cannot be seen looking into this at all. But I can do one thing that won't put me at too much risk. I can obtain the names of the alleged murder victims, get some background on them, and give that information to you. You'll have to handle the rest of it, I'm afraid."

"Well, that's a start."

The waiter now showed up with our first course, a basket of warm pita bread and *houmous* and *techina,* a Middle Eastern dish of creamed chickpeas and sesame paste that I always enjoyed. The conversation shifted back to personal news, this time to the upcoming visit by Trish and Clarissa. I'd revealed much more about my relationship with Trish to Karim than to any of the Israelis in the *Epoch* bureau. Perhaps it was because I felt just a little safer with Karim since he, as a Palestinian and an Arab, was something of an outsider, as was I.

"So, she's coming in a few weeks?" Karim asked with a smile as he cut into his St. Peter's fish. "And this missionary friend, Clarissa, is coming with her?"

"Yes."

"Won't that be a little awkward?"

"Yes, of course, but without Clarissa there'll be no Trish," I said with a sort of wry smile.

"You mean Trish won't see you unless Clarissa's there? That's how good Palestinian Muslim families do their courting. Perhaps you should become a Muslim, Rick." Karim laughed at his own joke.

"No, I am not chaperoned every time I'm with Trish," I said. "It's just that Trish wouldn't feel she was being honest with Clarissa if she came all this way from the Philippines to see me without Clarissa coming along."

"Does this Clarissa have some sort of hold on Trish or something?"

"No, but Trish seems to have gotten her Christianity from Clarissa and she is careful not to do anything without checking with Clarissa."

"But I thought she was born Roman Catholic?" Karim responded.

"Well, she was, but you know how these Protestants talk about being 'born again'? I guess that's what's happened to her."

"I see. So there's no sex, then?" Like a good reporter, Karim didn't pussyfoot around with his questions.

I was equally straight in my answer. "Not before marriage, apparently."

"Are you going to marry her?"

"I don't know. We'll have to see how things develop."

Through the ice cream that followed, we were both silent, lost in our private thoughts. I could only guess at what was on Karim's mind – perhaps his struggle with being a loyal Palestinian under the combined pressures of the Israeli occupation and the poor moral choices of some of his Palestinian compatriots. I was contemplating more low-brow questions: was it really worth it to live a monk's life in order to secure Trish's ultimate affections, and would Trish, virtuous, beautiful and brilliant as she was, be the most compatible choice for a wife after all? For that matter, did I even want to get married?

Karim was the one to break the silence as the coffee was served.

"You know, Rick, I sometimes wonder whether it's worth my being here at all. I could have stayed in America, gotten an assistant professor's job after Eugene. Leila would have been happy teaching English literature somewhere or other. I came back because I wanted my children to receive the most formative part of their education with other Palestinians, speaking and reading Arabic, and seeing if there might be some place in our society for them to be useful. But sometimes I wonder if I made the right decision."

"I think you did, Karim," I replied without a moment's hesitation, though I was not sure why I was so emphatic about it. "Heaven knows, there are so many lies coming out of this part of the world that people who are interested in truth are really rare. I think you made the right decision."

"I hope so, Rick. I hope so." On that note, we ended the meal, paid the bill, and headed towards the door.

We were on the point of parting just outside the restaurant when there came into view the last person I wanted to see me having lunch with Karim: Patrick Cavenagh. He was approaching the restaurant on foot from the direction of Salah ed-Din Street, East Jerusalem's main road. Deep in conversation with a Palestinian I didn't recognize, he didn't notice us at first. But he looked around as they approached the door of the Adelphia and locked eyes with me. He smiled, and I braced myself for a sarcastic comment. But it didn't come.

Instead, he stopped abruptly in front of me and Karim and said, almost formally, "Good afternoon. I see you two have been at work already on yesterday's events. This is Abdul Husseini, the new director of the Palestinian Human Rights Center. Abdul, this is Rick Ireton, bureau chief for *Epoch* Magazine, and Karim Nasr, his Palestinian stringer."

Husseini's eyes narrowed; he seemed to be sizing us up. Looking pointedly at Karim, he asked, "So you tell the American reporter what he should know about us Palestinians?"

I thought he sounded menacing, but Karim didn't flinch. "I tell him what I see and hear," Karim replied pleasantly. "He makes his own decisions about what he should know."

Husseini countered quickly with a question in Arabic that I didn't understand, and Karim responded with an equally rapid reply. They were behaving like stray mutts sniffing at each other in a park.

"Oh, by the way, Rick," Cavenagh cut in, "The European Union Human Rights Commission is already reviewing reports of yesterday's murder with a view to making a possible official complaint to the UN Security Council. Timing ought to be great," he added smugly, "because the Secretary of State is due here in a few days." He flung this at me as he and Husseini turned and strode through the Adelphia door. Obviously, he was not interested in my reply. Cavanaugh's parting words were, in effect, the sarcastic put-down I had anticipated at the beginning of the encounter.

Taking leave of Karim, I said, "Let me know as soon as you get any information about the supposedly murdered men. I have a feeling this thing is going to move very fast."

"Yes, I think it will," said Karim. We shook hands and parted.

I decided to start back to the *Epoch* bureau on foot since getting a cab anywhere near the Old City can be difficult. The walk would also give me some time to think.

It seemed to me that I had three options with this story: a) let it unravel as Cavenagh wanted it to and watch the world discover yet another "atrocity" committed by Israeli troops against the occupied Palestinians; b) offer a sort of sniffling dissent by coming forward as an eyewitness to at least the first part of the incident, namely the ambush; or c) push hard to get to the bottom of what happened, including, if necessary, exposing the Palestinian school teacher, Khalil al-Jaffar, as a liar. The third course would involve some danger, if not for me, possibly for Karim, if it became known that he was my primary source for exposing a journalistic fraud. And of course, if I succeeded in proving fraud, I would incur the undying enmity of Patrick Cavenagh and quite a large contingent of the foreign press corps sympathetic to the Palestinian cause.

I realized I needed input from my boss Burton Lasch, the foreign editor who had sent me to Jerusalem, and before that, to Hong Kong. It was because of Lasch's concern about a college friend who had disappeared in China that I been dragged into my previous major journalistic adventure. I reckoned Lasch now owed me one. With the time difference, Lasch was probably having breakfast or getting ready to go to the office, but I knew it was all right to call. After all, Lasch had a habit of calling his reporters at the oddest hour of day or night – basically whenever the fancy struck him and with the unlikely assertion that he hadn't a clue what time it was in some far-flung bureau. But Lasch also made it clear that he was just as willing to take reciprocal calls from his reporters anywhere in the world if anyone was in trouble or facing some professional dilemma.

I stepped into a doorway just opposite the Old City of Jerusalem and punched in Lasch's cell phone number. I looked around carefully to see if anyone was paying any attention to me. Good, I was alone.

Lasch anwered his cell phone on the first ring. "Lasch," said the familiar laconic voice with its Boston accent.

"Burt, Rick Ireton here." I decided not to bother with any chit-chat, but jumped right into the reason for my call. "I'm calling from Jerusalem, of course, and I've got a situation I need your advice on.

"I was eyewitness yesterday to an ambush of an Israeli jeep on a road outside Jerusalem – in the West Bank. A Palestinian sniper was killed – at least, I saw him shot – and an Israeli soldier wounded. Reinforcements arrived very quickly and the other two Palestinians apparently took off. But the BBC is now reporting that Israeli soldiers captured the three Palestinians after the ambush and then shot them in cold blood."

"What does Karim think happened?" Lasch brusquely broke in.

"He doesn't believe the Israelis would be that stupid. The Beeb quoted a Palestinian school teacher who claimed to be an eyewitness to the murder. I've asked Karim to check into the ID's of the alleged murder victims. But a fellow-reporter, a Brit, seems determined to turn this into another Mohammed al-Dura incident."

"A *what* incident?"

Lasch had clearly forgotten the name, though he certainly knew about the controversy. I reminded him now: "He was the small Palestinian boy who was filmed a few years back supposedly dying in his father's arms under Israeli gunfire. You remember, of course, that the case was later exposed as totally fabricated by a French film crew. But proof of that came too late to influence the international scandal that developed in the wake of the incident."

"Who's the British reporter you just referred to?"

"Patrick Cavenagh, of *The News Report*."

"That spells trouble," Lasch observed drily.

"Why?"

"Because Cavenagh was behind that attempt to prove that British soldiers had been torturing captured Taliban prisoners in Afghanistan. The effort fizzled because there were too many witnesses refuting the allegations. But before it was exposed as a false accusation, questions were asked in the House of Commons and much of the press scurried around trying to get corroboration. The strange thing was that there undoubtedly had been violations, but not in the incident Cavenagh focused on. He seems to be a perennial muckraker. Sometimes he's been right – and good for him – but I think his judgment isn't that good."

"Well, how do you suggest I go about this, Burt? I'm not eager to be seen as defending the Israeli government against the wicked foreign media and – "

"Yeah," said Lasch, interrupting again, "it's not fun playing the role of foreign-reporter-goody-two-shoes."

"But I just can't sit around doing nothing when I think there's a deliberate attempt to fabricate news. That just goes against every journalistic principle I've been taught. What do you think?"

"You're a good reporter, Richard. You don't need me to tell you that you have to look into this. But don't let the fact that you were an eyewitness color your judgment. Be prepared for the possibility that the Palestinians *were* murdered. But as long as you approach the controversy with a genuinely open mind, you'll do fine."

Phew. I felt an almost instant release of tension in my gut. My instinct had been to investigate the ambush story aggressively. Now that I knew Lasch was behind me, I felt more confident about following it.

"Thanks, Burt, that's very helpful. I'll be in touch if there are developments you need to know about."

"Right, and take care. There are some bad guys out there."

"I know. I think I just met one."

"Who?"

"Abdul Husseini, the new head of the Palestinian Human Rights Center. I'd never heard of him before today, but I was with Karim and he asked Karim, quite cynically, what kind of information he provided *Epoch*. Karim cleverly replied that he told me only what he saw and heard, and that I was the judge of whether that information was useful or not."

"Good for Karim. He's worth a lot to *Epoch*."

"I agree. Well, I'd better get cracking on this story, so I'll sign off here. Bye, Burt."

"Bye. And be careful."

As I hung up, I recalled ruefully that Lasch had said the exact same thing last year when he sent me from Hong Kong to locate his lost friend in Guangzhou. That "adventure" culminated in a hair-raising escape from Guangzhou's organized crime bosses that landed me in Manila. Hearing the same words again from Lasch brought little comfort.

I decided to get back to the bureau as quickly as possible, so this time I flagged down a taxi. I knew what my next step should be. I called Esther for the contact number of her nephew in the IDF who had been in the back-up squad after the ambush. She agreed to my request only after I promised that her nephew, Yossi, would not be mentioned in anything I wrote.

Margaret greeted me with my phone messages as soon as I got back to the bureau: "Karim called and says he has the information you wanted, someone from the Palestinian Human Rights Center wants to talk to you, and the IDF spokesman's office wants you to talk by phone with the Defense Minister. What have you done, Rick, to merit all this attention?" she asked with a good-humored smile.

"Nothing that you don't already know about. Well, that's not quite true. I bumped into the new head of Palestinian Human Rights when I was coming out of the Adelphia Restaurant with Karim. He was there with Patrick Cavenagh. I'm surprised he's already following up on me.

Margaret, first things first. Get me Karim on the line."

"Right."

I had barely gotten behind my desk when the phone rang. It was Karim.

"Rick, I've got their names," he said. "Are you ready to take them down?"

Karim then carefully spelled out the Arabic names for me.

"What do you know about them?" I asked.

"I was told that all three were students at the An-Najah University in Nablus, so I immediately called up the university pretending to be calling from an American grad school to get references for one of the students. I took a chance that the university wouldn't have caller ID and that whoever answered couldn't know where I was calling from and also wouldn't recognize that my accent wasn't native-born American. I gave the name of one of the students and said I was calling to confirm that he had studied at the university. Rick, the registrar's office said they had no record of such a student. I politely said thank you and hung up. I've now asked my bother's son Ahmed to call again in an hour's time and pose as a reporter from *El Quds* newspaper requesting official reactions from the university on the murder of their students. I'll let you know what my nephew find's out."

"Did you get any info on the other two?"

"I couldn't ask the registrar about all three students or they might have been suspicious. But Leila has a cousin at An-Najah and she told me that she's never heard of the other two, though she obviously doesn't know all the students. Just as importantly, she also said there's been no gossip on campus about An-Najah students being murdered by the IDF."

"Good work, Karim. You got onto that real fast." We hung up and I called Margaret to get Palestinian Human Rights on the line.

"Thank you for calling, Mr. Ireton," the voice on the other end of the line said. "I'm Ahmed Husseini. I understand from Mr. Cavenagh that you saw what happened during part of yesterday's incident on the Jerusalem-Gush Etzion road. Is that correct?" I felt a stab of irritation. How many other people had Cavenaugh blabbed to about where I had been over the weekend?

"That's correct, Mr. Husseini," I replied tersely. *Why was he being so irritatingly formal?* "What can I do for you?" I added, making no attempt to mask the condescension that had crept into my voice.

"As you know, the BBC has reported the atrocity that took place after the incident. I wanted to know what you are reporting about it."

The insolence. It's none of al-Husseini's business what I or Epoch *Magazine want to report about anything. He can just wait to read the story in the magazine like anyone else.*

"Mr. al-Husseini, I'm sure you know that we don't discuss stories we are working on before they appear in the magazine. I'd be very happy to ensure that a copy of the magazine is sent to you in the mail, if you are interested. Of course, as you know, it won't be printed until the weekend, so it'll be a few days, I'm afraid."

It was a crisp put-down. I could almost feel al-Husseini's rising anger through the phone line.

"Mr. Ireton, I am sure you realize that this incident could turn into a major international incident, likely to be mentioned in both the Security Council and the General Assembly."

"Which incident?" I asked, even though I knew exactly what al-Husseini was talking about. I was employing a standard interviewing technique: an open-ended question. It was a way to get al-Husseini to reveal his views and possibly to slip out with new information that I didn't have.

"Yesterday's atrocity," al-Husseini exploded. *Boy, it doesn't take much to get this guy hot under the collar.* "I think you know exactly what I mean. It's going to be important that people know that you weren't at the scene of the ambush when the murders took place."

"Mr. al-Husseini, I can assure you that *Epoch* makes every effort to gather all the facts for the news stories that we report. Whatever the details of this incident are, this will be no exception."

There was a pause at the other end of the line. Presumably, al-

Husseini was trying to decide whether or not to continue his aggressive line of questioning. And maybe he realized that he couldn't bully me, because now he not only backed off a little but tried to sweet-talk me. "Mr. Ireton, you have a reputation of being a very thorough reporter," he said. I thought he was laying it on a bit thick. "The Palestinian people would be disappointed if, on this occasion, you failed to draw the right conclusions about what took place." *Was that a threat?* I wasn't sure, but now I was sure that I really didn't like this guy.

"Mr. al-Husseini, I thank you for your concern that reporters be thorough and accurate. I share it. Do you have any other questions?" I asked.

Al-Husseini grunted in the negative, brusquely said goodbye, and hung up.

I now asked Margaret to call back the Israeli Defense Minister, Yoram Ben-David. Ben-David was an Ashkenazi Jew whose parents had immigrated to Palestine before World War II and who had served for eight years as a career military officer. He was widely respected in the often dog-eat-dog world of Israeli politics. For one thing, ethnically he was something of a throwback to the days when the Labor Party dominated Israeli politics and Ashkenazi Jews of European origin populated Israeli politics to the exclusion of just about everyone else. His cabinet colleagues represented the newer breed of Israeli politician: more Sephardic, more religious, more populist in outlook than the traditional Labor Party residents of upscale districts in North Tel Aviv. I had never met him, but I had heard others in the press corps speak well of him.

"Rick Ireton?" the rather loud voice on the line asked.

"Yes, Mr. Minister."

"I'll be very direct with you. Did you see any of our soldiers behaving towards Palestinians in inhuman ways yesterday?"

"No, sir, I didn't. But I need to be very clear that what I saw was only the first few minutes of what took place."

"I expect you know what the Palestinians are alleging?"

"Yes, sir, I saw the BBC report."

"But you didn't see anything like that yourself?"

"No, sir, I didn't."

"Good. As you probably realize, people who are not friendly to the Government of Israel are going to try to turn this into an international scandal."

I had to be careful now. I couldn't appear to be a reporter who was willing to let the Israeli defense minister think I was prepared to back up in public the official position of the Israeli government. My phone was certainly tapped by the Israeli Shin Beth, the internal security services, and more than likely it was also tapped by some Palestinian security agency – I knew that at one time thirteen such agencies were in operation.

"Mr. Minister, I'm well aware of the implications of this story if it's confirmed. That is why I am investigating it with great care."

"Good. That is all I wanted to know. Thank you. If you need to know anything, please give me a call." *Was he serious?* Israeli cabinet ministers did sometimes give their private or mobile phone numbers to some trusted Israeli reporters, but almost never to a foreign reporter. So I pounced on the opening.

"That's very kind of you, Mr. Minister. May I have a number where I can reach you easily?" I wasn't about to let the conversation end without getting a direct phone number for him.

"Certainly. I'll give it to you, but only on the condition that you don't share it with anyone. If just one other reporter calls me up on this number, I'll cut off any further contact with you. Is that understood?"

"Yes, Mr. Minister."

Ben-David then gave me the number.

That was a coup. I wondered how long it would be before I would need to use it. I smiled inwardly. *Well, that was one good side-benefit from the weekend's events.*

Moving fast now, I got up from my desk and went out to see Margaret. "Do you still have that spare mobile phone we got for Reddaway when he was here two months ago?" I asked.

"Yes, but I don't know if the battery is properly charged or not."

"Don't worry, I only need it for ten or fifteen minutes. I don't think it's associated with anyone in this bureau, is that right?"

"No, it's not." An amused smile of understanding came over her face. She looked at me quizzically, but said nothing.

I walked out of the office, turned right onto King George V Street, and then up the first right turn, Schatz Street. Once I was certain that no one was within earshot, I called up Esther's nephew.

"Yossi?" I said. "This is Rick Ireton. I think your Aunt Esther has mentioned me to you. She gave me your number because your unit arrived at the ambush on the Jerusalem-Etzion road yesterday just a few minutes after I got there. Can you talk?"

"I can talk, but my English is not good," Yossi replied slowly. His accent was almost a caricature of an Israeli sabra speaking English. "I have a sister in Jerusalem. She speaks good English. Can we meet with her there?"

"Of course. That would be much better than speaking on the phone. When can we meet?"

"I can see you this evening, but it will have to be late. After 10 o'clock. Where do you suggest?"

I had to think quickly. Once again, it was important to avoid being seen by the wrong people, if possible. I'd not succeeded in doing that at lunchtime, but it might be easier in the evening.

"The Crowne Plaza Hotel," I suggested, "in the rooftop bar."

"Ten o'clock, then. My sister's name is Reina. She is very beautiful."

Wow, I thought. *What next?*

V

I SPENT MUCH OF the remainder of Monday afternoon in the bureau looking over accounts. It was a part of the bureau chief's job that I absolutely detested. I have no head for figures and the bureaucratic aspect of it all always drives me up a wall.

Which expense goes in which budget category? The criteria seemed almost theological. If a luncheon meeting took place with a source, it was "Bureau Entertainment," but if it was with anyone connected – even remotely – with *Epoch*, it fell in the "Bureau Functions" category. But what happened if Burton Lasch was in town, and he brought along a guest who also was a source? If the bean-counters in New York saw the name "Lasch," they'd demand that the meal be categorized as "Bureau Functions." But if Burton's friend showed up at exactly the same restaurant at exactly the same time the following week and repeated the exact same story word for word that he'd told us the previous week, it would now have to be "Bureau Entertainment."

Then there were the annoying expenses the bureau had incurred for Reddaway's wife. She'd arrived on a later flight than her husband, stayed the first night at a different hotel, and had no money to pay the bill. So Karim had put it on his own American Express card. He'd been immediately reimbursed by the Jerusalem Bureau, but now the bureau had to get the money back from New York. How the bean-counters dealt with Reddaway and his wife was not my concern, but the hassle of following up on expenses that had fallen through the bureaucratic cracks infuriated me. Fortunately, Margaret was a model of efficiency in assembling the various pieces of paper on which the expense reports were based, and all I had to do was keep track of them, sign for them, and write the requisite memoranda covering my backside in inter-office communications. But the whole process always put me in an irritated frame of mind.

And in the midst of it all, an email from Trish arrived telling me that she and Clarissa had changed their scheduled visit and the itinerary. So then I had to phone up all the hotels booked on the non-group part of the itinerary. Trish could be infuriating with her last-minute changes of plans. Most of the time, I thought it was a charming quirk of her personality, but just occasionally it really annoyed me. Now I had to go back to the hotels whose reservations' staff I had cajoled for the original reservation and plead with them to change the date without jacking up the price. I secretly thought that, with her profession being hotel public relations, she could have handled all this herself. But she coyly kept insisting that since it was my part of the world I would know far better than she did where she and Clarissa ought to stay. It was particularly irksome because Israel's spring tourist season was well under way and hotel rooms in many locations were hard to come by. It made me wonder if Trish sometimes took for granted my devotion to her. She was actually surprisingly unspoiled in spite of her peremptory way of ordering people around when she was in her I'm-in-charge mode. Of course, she certainly liked expensive clothes and the perquisites of a successful professional career, but when she said that she could drop all that if there were a cause she really believed in, I don't think she was making it up. She was genuinely appreciative of my efforts to please her most of the time, but having grown up in an affluent family, which in the Philippines meant having people at her beck and call, she had acquired a habit of sending people scurrying this way and that, and that included me sometimes.

None of that, however, detracted from my enjoyment of her emails. This morning she had quoted from Ben Johnson's play, *The Alchemist*, to describe perfectly in two lines the appearance of a guest at her hotel:

"And your complexion, of the Roman wash,

Shot full of black, and melancholic worms

Like powder-corns, shot at th' artillery yard."

It had quickly become clear at our very first dinner together in Hong Kong that Trish's knowledge of English literature didn't just exceed mine by a factor of three or four, but exceeded that of most college professors. At times since then, I'd been reduced to scrambling for dictionaries of quotations or relying on Google searches to understand Trish's high-brow literary allusions. But I didn't mind; in fact, I was flattered that Trish shared her literary passions with me in her emails.

The pleasure of Trish's e-mail was but a brief escape from the long hours of bureau tedium. After dealing with the accounts, I'd had to listen to a forty-five-minute whine by Ira Blumenthal, the American-born long-time bureau reporter about a political story on the Knesset, Israel's parliament, that he claimed should have been assigned to him because he was the one who had first suggested it several months before. When the idea was resurrected at a bureau meeting last week, Ira had been out of town visiting a relative in the Galilee and Ari had grabbed the story. Now he and Ira were squabbling over it like kids fighting in the schoolyard at recess. It amazed me how petty people could be when they felt that the professional turf they played on was about to be encroached on.

Finally, around 5 p.m., as the others drifted out of the bureau, I was left relatively undisturbed. Margaret always left the office precisely at 5.30, returning to a pleasant house in Rehavia, an upscale district of Jerusalem that had grown up in the 1920s. Her husband's job had afforded them an elegant, Ottoman-style house that they had decorated with exquisite taste. I always enjoyed their dinner parties, not only because of Margaret's excellent culinary skills and the invariably interesting guests, but because she and Solomon had decorated and furnished their home with both warmth and style.

I was going through the newspapers and magazines that accumulate on my desk at the beginning of each week when my phone rang. It was still a few minutes before 5.30 and Margaret's voice came through the open door, "Karim's on line one."

"Rick, I've got some interesting information for you. Can you talk?"

"Yes, Karim, but call me back on the cell phone that Reddaway used last month when he was here. Do you still have the number?"

"I think so. Hold on a moment while I look. Yes, I have that number. Okay, I'll call you right back."

When the cell phone that Reddaway had used rang, Karim started without preamble. "My nephew called An Najah College about an hour after I made the first call. Boy, the story there had changed completely in one hour. Their line now is that the whole college is grieving the martyrdom of the three students. Classes are being canceled and there's going to be a week of official mourning. Instead of what they had told me – that they had never heard of the students, or at least never heard of one of them – the college is now saying that they have bios for each of the victims and that their former professors are available for interviews. Someone picked up fast on the need to invent legends – isn't that what the spy people call it? This is all going to make the Mohammed al-Dura incident a tea party."

"A tea party? Where did you pick up a British expression like that?" I asked, amused.

"I don't know. Probably from a British graduate student at Eugene," Karim replied distractedly.

"Okay," I said, focusing back on the topic at hand, "what do we do with all this information?"

"Nothing. We can't, at least not without revealing that I've started looking into whether this story is a fraud."

"Have you followed up on Khalil al-Jaffar, the school teacher who claimed to have witnessed the murders?"

"He's completely gone to ground. People I talked to said he was in hiding because of fears that the Israelis might try to make him change his story. They say he'll only come out of hiding if the UN investigates the incident."

"Well, okay, I can understand that, at least from their point of view. But if he's a school teacher, we should be able to find out more about him. He must have attended a teachers' training college somewhere, and there aren't many of those in the West Bank. It's possible that he got his qualifications in Gaza, but I don't think it's likely. Listen, Karim, I know it's a pain, but can you discreetly contact teachers' colleges and try to find out where this fellow studied? We may get to him through a classmate or someone else who knew him in college."

"Right. I'll call you again if I find anything. Which number should I use, your regular mobile or this one?"

"This one. For all I know this may be bugged as well, but it may take the buggers more time to track it than to keep up with my regular mobile or the office phone."

"I've never heard you use a British profanity before, Rick," Karim said with a laugh.

"What profanity?" I asked distractedly.

"Buggers. You should look it up. The British meaning of the word is not pretty."

"Okay, I get you now," I said. He was getting me back for giving him a hard time earlier in the conversation about his Briticisms. "Keep up the good work, Karim."

"Right, bye."

Margaret had left by the time I hung up the phone, and the bureau was empty except for Ari. I wondered if he was working late because of an attack of conscience after our heated exchange in the morning. He was methodically going through back issues of the bureau's Hebrew-language newspapers now, both to ensure that everything was in order and to see if there was any important story the bureau had missed. Before I headed out myself, I made a point of stopping to say a few kind words to Ari so that he would know that there were no lingering hard feelings.

On the street outside it was that magical time of day when Jerusalem seemed to catch its breath and bask in its own natural beauty. The limestone facing of the buildings – the "Jerusalem stone" as it was called – was transformed by the setting sun into a wondrous luminosity. In one of the few beneficent consequences of the often unhappy 1922-1948 British rule of Palestine, the British authorities had required that all new buildings in Jerusalem be faced with the beige-gray stone that over the years had come to be the trademark color of David's City. Israeli authorities had been happy to continue the practice after the War of Independence ended in 1949. The result was that all of Jerusalem's buildings – from the walls of the Old City to the churches on Mount Zion, from the new modern architecture of the Haddassah hospital complex on Mount Scopus to the YMCA or that Jerusalem landmark, the King David Hotel – now reflected the old British regulation. I loved the limpid sunset hour when the city stretched itself out languidly in its beauty. I loved also the wild flowers that grew copiously in the nooks and crannies of pathways and the edges of parking lots, the great bushes of wild lavender, the clumps of hawthorne and rosemary. I'd often snatch at the lavender as I walked by, rub it between my fingers, and enjoy the enchanting aroma.

Where to eat? I didn't want to go back to my apartment in the German Colony and then come back into town again to meet Yossi. I certainly didn't want to go to the American Colony, let alone the Adelphia Restaurant because of the possibility of more encounters with Cavenagh or other colleagues in Jerusalem's foreign press corps. I retrieved my car from the underground parking garage on King George V Street and, on a whim, drove over to the Renaissance Hotel on Herzl Boulevard. I'd been there a few times before and enjoyed sitting in the large lobby lounge watching the Orthodox Jewish families who stayed there on their extended visits to Jerusalem, often over Jewish holidays. When the Shabbat rolled around and the hotel essentially shut down, with the check-in counter screened off from the rest of the lobby lest the Orthodox Jews be troubled by the sight of fellow Jews working on the Sabbath, their children would run wild throughout the hotel, giggling and screaming as they played. Their parents didn't seem to make any attempt to control them at all. It also amused me to watch the Christian tour groups who sometimes stayed in the hotel, altogether indifferent to the rhythms of the Jewish Sabbath in Jerusalem but not to the rambunctious energy of the Orthodox children there. Half of them probably had read Focus on the Family founder James Dobson's stern prescriptions on how to deal with obnoxiously noisy children.

The road to the Renaissance Hotel passed just below Israel's parliament, the Knesset, and just above the Israel Museum where the Dead Sea Scrolls are on display. Along the way, the wonderful aroma of Mediterranean pines in Sacher Park wafted across the road. The best place to enjoy the rich scent of those pines was atop Mount Scopus. The clusters of ancient trees that could still be found there had a restorative effect on me and they were another of my favorite haunts when I needed solitude.

After parking the Subaru in the parking lot out front, I walked towards the hotel lobby. As usual, security guards at the door were inspecting everyone's packages, briefcases and handbags, but they waved me through airily when they saw I was empty-handed.

Inside, I looked around carefully to make sure there was no one I knew before settling into a large leather chair in the lobby lounge. The lobby lounge had a snack and drinks service, but it was milk kosher, which meant that a cheeseburger was out of the question. I ordered a smoked salmon sandwich instead, and settled down to read the paperback translation of French writer Honore de Balzac's novel, *Pere Goriot*, I'd brought along. Trish had written enthusiastically about it some days earlier and I was content to read for a few hours before my rendezvous with Yossi and his apparently beautiful sister, Rayna. In spite of my affection for Trish, I couldn't help feeling a certain glee at the prospect of meeting this Rayna woman. Israeli women can be stunningly attractive, and I wondered just how "beautiful" she was.

At 9.45 p.m. I paid my bill, got back into the Subaru and drove the few hundred yards up the hill to the Crowne Plaza. The hotel commanded a magnificent view of all of Jerusalem. Built in 1973 in the western part of the city not far from the Binyanei Hauma Theater. The hotel was the focus of a lot of controversy because of its location atop the highest point in West Jerusalem where it protruded into the Jerusalem skyline like the classroom joker relentlessly raising his hand. Originally part of the Hilton International chain, it was now a Holiday Inn Crowne Plaza.

I walked slowly, almost carefully, into the nearly empty hotel lobby. Presumably the Christian tour groups from America that regularly stayed there had already turned in for the night in anticipation of an arduous early morning trek to the Red Sea or Masada. Two male clerks behind the check-in desk were chatting idly. I looked around the lobby again but didn't see anyone who might be either Yossi or his beauteous sister, so I got into the elevator and went up to the top floor. On exiting it, I was startled by the ambient light of Jerusalem all around, framed perfectly in the rooftop bar's windows and brighter than the light in the bar itself. Trying to appear inconspicuous, I started to walk fully into the bar, but was stopped dead in my tracks and could only just stare dumbfounded for a moment. A young man sat half-facing the back of the bar, sipping a drink through a straw, but it was the woman sitting on the barstool next to him that stunned me. She was so drop-dead gorgeous that I couldn't even begin to describe what was so striking about her. She was quite tall – I guessed her to be nearly as tall as me at six feet, one and a half inches – and so thin she looked as if she would have to be a professional model. If it were possible, her face was even more striking than her figure. I'd seen plenty of beautiful faces – in Asia as well as in Israel – and yet was puzzled why this particular woman's face was so captivating. Then it hit me: it was absolutely perfectly proportioned – the nose, the eyes, the cheeks, the forehead, the lips, the chin, all setting each other off, without fuss or false emphasis. Her hair was light brown, almost blond, and very wavy – the rest of her might have been natural, but the hair had obviously been crafted in a salon. From where I was standing a few feet away, I could hear her laughing, a boisterous, broad, uninhibited laugh which invited others to join in.

Of course, she had to be Yossi's sister. I walked briskly forward towards the young man and the woman. Extending my hand to Yossi, I pointedly ignored the radiant beauty on my left and said, "Hello. I think you must be Yossi. I am Rick Ireton."

Yossi smiled broadly. "Esther, my aunt, she says a lot of things about you," Yossi said, still smiling, the sounds of sabra English rolling out pleasantly. While he was speaking, I was conscious that the heavenly apparition at my side was observing me coolly and carefully.

"This is my sister, Rayna. Now, I said she was beautiful, didn't I?" The comment broke the ice and I laughed as I turned to face her. As we shook hands—her hand was incredibly soft but her grip was surprisingly firm—I was astonished anew. I had met beautiful women before, and Trish was dazzling, but not even Trish had mesmerized me the way Rayna was now doing. I was going to really have to work hard to focus on Yossi's story to keep from drooling during the interview like a long-celibate convict, particularly since Rayna would be translating for Yossi.

Yossi himself seemed to be very young. I guessed only eighteen or nineteen. His face was as handsomely proportioned as his sister's, and his light, curly hair, which evidently hadn't been combed for several days, gave him a slightly rakish look. He was not in uniform and he was wearing the ubiquitous garb of young Israeli men: a tee-shirt – black in this case, with the English words "Tell No Secrets" on it – and jeans. He was palpably good-natured, and his quiet, cheerful voice set off that of his sister in a charming way.

As for his sister, she exuded a femininity that was almost intoxicating. I don't think I have ever been so beguiled by the sheer physical beauty of a woman who was as close to me as Rayna now was. First there had been her figure, then her face. Now, as her deep brown eyes searched my face – *What was she looking for?* – my own eyes roamed. Her breasts were not especially large, but her waist was more petite than most women outside of Asia and her hips were perfectly proportioned to the upper half of body. She was exquisitely shaped. I had never seen anyone so perfectly proportioned.

I suggested that we move away from the bar to a table in the corner. A middle-aged couple, totally engrossed in each other, were the only other people in the bar. It probably would not be difficult to keep our conversation out of earshot of anyone else. I silently thanked some unseen creator for arranging this meeting so late in the day. Any earlier and it would have been difficult to get Yossi and Rayna out of ogling range of anyone who happened to also be at the bar.

When the waiter came over to take our order, Rayna said without hesitation, "Grapefruit juice," while Yossi asked for a Maccabee beer, a favorite local brew in Israel. Realizing I needed to remain stone-cold sober, I ordered an orange juice. This seemed to amuse Rayna, who asked, "You don't want a Scotch? I thought foreign correspondents always drink Scotch?"

"Perhaps so," I said, matching her smile, "but this foreign correspondent likes to be clear-headed when he's conducting an interview." *What I mean is, sitting next to you I'm intoxicated enough as it is without a drop of Scotch or any other inebriant. How am I going to keep my mind on the interview?*

Mercifully, my thoughts were soon diverted by Yossi's story as it came out in carefully constructed English paragraphs interpreted by Rayna.

"You know, I saw you yesterday on the Jerusalem-Efrat road," Rayna translated for Yossi. "You were being spoken to by our officer, a lieutenant. I found out your name, or something like your name, from one of the other soldiers in our unit, as well as the name of your magazine.

"After we had called an ambulance for Itzhak – he was the one who was wounded – we were told to climb the hillside and see if the snipers were still hiding there. We searched for about an hour and found nothing—nothing, that is, except a large pool of blood behind one of the bushes. Probably, that was the position he was firing from and where he was hit. We were also looking for any weapons they might have abandoned when they took off. But we found no weapons either. The snipers had completely disappeared, taking with them the man who was shot."

"How many soldiers were involved in the search?" I interrupted.

When Rayna interpreted the question into Hebrew, Yossi started shaking his head. For the next few minutes, the two were engaged in what seemed to be a good-natured disagreement in Hebrew. Finally, Rayna turned back to me with a look that was both apologetic and embarrassed. "I'm sorry," she said, "Yossi is not willing to discuss numbers because that is a military secret."

"I understand," I said quickly, "and I certainly don't want to give the impression that I am trying to pry any military secrets out of him. I don't need an exact figure, but it would help to know whether it was a hundred or fifty or fewer?"

Yossi answered immediately when Rayna translated my question. "Much less than fifty," he said, "not even thirty."

"After your unit arrived to reinforce the ambushed jeep, and after the ambulance came, did any other Israeli soldiers arrive?"

"No, no one else came. When we finished searching, we drove back to our bases in Israel."

"Do you know what the BBC reported?—that the three Palestinians were captured after the ambush along the Jerusalem-Hebron road and were shot in cold blood?" I asked, suddenly feeling very fatigued and wanting the interview to end.

"That is an absolute lie!" Yossi almost shouted in Hebrew, drawing the stares of the couple at the bar as well as the bartender and waiter. Rayna translated this, looking almost as angry as her brother.

Then she spoke for both of them. "You know, in Israel we have freedom of the press and foreign reporters are allowed to travel freely almost anywhere in the country. Somehow, though, they overlook the parts of Israel that are extremely successful and concentrate only on the things we are struggling over. What we are literally paying with our lives to achieve is how to survive as a healthy society while constantly being attacked by people who want to destroy us, even kill us all. I know that because of our security needs we have sometimes behaved very badly towards the Palestinians. That is wrong, and our press itself often points out when we have done bad things. But why do foreign reporters here spend so much time looking for crimes against the Palestinians to write about and almost no time at all reporting what the Palestinians are doing – and during the *Intifadeh* doing on a daily basis – against us? Tell me Rick – can I call you Rick? – what do you think about this constant stream of foreign criticism of Israel? It's not so bad in America, but in Europe it's awful. European reporters seem to hate us as soon as they arrive."

This was a conversation I had found myself in a dozen or more times if at all. I thoroughly disliked it, not only because I thought a critical attitude towards the government – any government—was quite natural, even healthy, for a reporter, but also because I disliked having to defend journalists, whether that be specific individuals or the entire foreign press corps, against charges of bias. It was coming, moreover, too soon after a similar conversation with Esther. Wearily, I turned to Rayna and Yossi and said, "Rayna, I know that many Israelis think the same thing and I'm sure you have your reasons for it. I'll try to answer that – I'm sure inadequately – in a moment. But can I just ask a few more questions of Yossi?"

Rayna translated this for her brother and he nodded.

"Let me get this straight. You came with the reinforcements, stopped on the road until the ambulance had come and picked up the wounded Israeli soldier? Then a group of fewer than thirty soldiers climbed the hillside searching for the snipers or any abandoned weapons. All that you found in that time was a pool of blood under a bush? Have I got that right?"

"Yes," said Yossi, without waiting for Rayna to interpret.

"Then – and this is for both of you – how would you suggest disproving the assertion that three Palestinians had been murdered on the Jerusalem-Gush Etzion road?"

Yossi replied instantly, speaking rapidly, but pausing to allow Rayna to translate.

"There is only one eyewitness who said he saw it happen. We certainly didn't see him. Find him and question him. Ask him how many Israeli soldiers he saw. Ask him what happened to the bodies. Ask him exactly where it happened. Go there and see if there is any blood on the ground. Produce the bodies. Find out if he has any terrorist connections –"

"And how would I do that?" I interrupted.

Yossi spoke rapidly to Rayna, looking at his watch at the same time.

Rayna spoke again. "Rick, Yossi has to get back to his base before midnight, so he needs to leave right now. I have some suggestions about following this up, if you don't mind staying after he's gone."

Don't mind staying! You're probably the most beautiful woman I've ever seen in my life and you're asking me if I would I mind staying?

Yossi got up quickly, shook my hand, kissed his sister on both cheeks, then turned back to me. "Good luck," he said in English. "You need lots of luck in Israel." He walked swiftly toward the elevator.

"How is he going to get back to his base?" I asked.

"He has a friend with a car in the same unit. Yossi will call him and they'll meet up near here."

In the presence of this absolutely stunning woman, now willing to devote her attention to me, I felt a mixture of exhilaration and panic. I chided myself inwardly. *Grow up, Ireton! She's just a woman like any other, and she just happens to be unusually good-looking. Focus on the story!* But try as I might, I could not disentangle myself from a growing obsession with Rayna. It was utterly foolish; I had spent barely half an hour in her company, but I was already allowing my thoughts to range into some pretty heavy fantasies about her.

"Let's order another drink," she said. I liked the "let's." *That means "let us." That means she thinks of us as doing things together.* Feeling like I was dreaming, I beckoned to the waiter and turned to Rayna.

"Another grapefruit juice?" I asked.

"Well, now that my brother's not here, I'll order something stronger."

"Your brother controls what you drink?" I asked in amazement.

"He doesn't control it, but he doesn't like me to drink any hard liquor. I think he thinks it's unladylike." As she said this, she laughed quite charmingly, her mouth broadening into a wide smile. A long ago memory flashed through my mind: my mother saying that a big smile was always a good sign on any woman, "broad and generous," she had said.

"Vodka and orange juice," Rayna said without hesitation when the waiter came.

But I was in a quandary. I knew I needed to keep my wits about me, but the idea of unwinding with a stiff drink with this lovely woman was more than tempting. What happened next was something I couldn't have dreamed up myself even in my most overheated romantic imagination. I ordered an Amaretto. It was smooth and pleasant and not so strong that it might lull me into any foolishness. "Let's sit over there," she said, pointing with her slender hand to the black leather bar sofa against the wall. "We can talk more easily and more comfortably." As I sat down, she placed her left hand lightly on my right arm as if to make sure I wouldn't move too far away.

What's happening to me? I've never felt almost overpowered like this by a female before, not even by Trish. Trying to steady my wits, I struggled for the first time to focus on what Rayna was wearing: a dark green cotton dress, simply cut, and not even revealing any cleavage, but showing off vividly the extraordinarily curvy lines of her figure. She had a deep-green ring on her left hand – probably Eilat stone – and, now that I was paying close attention, I saw that she also wore a necklace of matching color. But what struck me most powerfully now was not what she was wearing, or even her exquisite figure. It was the totally natural feminine flow of all her movements. Some women, inexplicably to me, seemed to possess this natural grace. Trish, for instance, was compact and graceful in her movements. But Rayna seemed to have a natural way of doing everything in a way that exuded femininity – picking up a glass, sitting down, rising from her seat to kiss her brother. I couldn't explain even to myself what it was exactly, but I certainly recognized it.

"How long have you been in Israel, Rick?" Rayna asked once we were seated side by side.

"About six months," I said. "I'm sorry my Hebrew is completely rudimentary."

"Oh, you do speak some Hebrew, then?" she said, her eyebrows arching up charmingly.

"*Ani medaber i kitsat ivrit, aval lo tov meod* (I speak a little Hebrew, but not very well)," I replied.

She laughed loudly, but not mockingly.

"Most foreigners can't even say that after more than a year," she said flatteringly.

"And where did you learn your amazing English?" I said, endeavoring to match her volley of compliments.

"In England. I lived there for six months and attended an English-language school in Brighton. By the way, I learned that Englishmen are not cold and reserved but quite romantic. Only they are clumsy about the way they express it."

I was astounded. Why was she telling me about the romantic characteristics of Englishmen? *For that matter, why is she sitting close enough for me to feel the warmth of her body through her dress?* For the first time that evening, faint, very faint alarm bells began to go off in my mind. *All this is far too quick. What is she up to? She obviously knows what a hypnotic effect she has on men. Why has she targeted me?*

I wasn't sure how to respond to Rayna's remark about romantic Englishmen. Was she leading me on for some great seduction scene? And if so, why? Now a sort of hack's instinct to discover motives was kicking into action in my mind. I decided to play along, at least for the time being.

"Clumsy?" I said. "How so?"

"Well, they send you flowers, like men of any other nationality, but instead of waiting to see if the girl will call to say thanks or follow-up, they want to – what's that expression? – 'gild the lily' with immediate phone calls and visits. They don't allow enough time for sentiments to crystallize. A woman loves to be pursued, even pampered, but she needs space and time to decide how she's going to respond."

"I take it you handled this clumsiness with the requisite skill?"

"Oh, I like you!" she exclaimed. "My experience with Americans is that they are straightforward and direct, but not as witty as the British."

More alarm bells. She seemed to want to make it clear to me that she was an experienced woman, that she'd been around and learned all sorts of things about the behavior of men of different nationalities. Though she didn't realize it, Rayna was diluting the effect of her natural beauty and charm by what she was revealing about herself.

But I was still intoxicated. She wore a light scent that I recognized as Christian Dior. Part of my mind wanted to bask in the aura of her beauty and femininity forever. Part of it was saying, "*Be careful, be careful.*"

Curiosity about her kept me asking questions.

"Well, you've given me your judgments about British men and American men. Do you prepare yourself for battle, as it were, before you meet with different men?"

She laughed again, a wonderfully infectious, uninhibited laugh.

"Well, Mr. Ireton," – and she sounded teasingly serious as she said this – "you might like to know that when Yossi told me Esther wanted me to act as translator for him in a meeting with you, I took the trouble to do a Google search on you. I'm impressed. You're quite famous, you know."

"Famous? I suppose you came across information about all those activities in Hong Kong last year?"

"Yes, but not only that. I see that when you were in high school, you were chosen as the 'student in the class most likely to succeed.'"

"How on earth did you find that out?" I asked in amazement. "It certainly isn't on any website I know about."

"Well, you obviously don't know as much about your classmates as they know about you," she said teasingly, once again touching my right arm lightly with her left. Once again, I felt as if I'd received an electric jolt.

"How so?"

"You know you can find out where your former high school classmates are by accessing certain websites. Well, it's true that you have to pay for some of them, but, I thought, what the heck, let's find out as much about this American reporter as I can. I got onto the website for looking up old classmates, discovered who your high school class president was and who was voted 'student most likely to succeed.' It was you!"

No one had ever paid as much attention to my background as this woman had, this incredibly beautiful young woman who was sitting next to me. Once again, in the penumbra of her allure and charm, I felt myself at risk of tumbling down a slippery ice slope. What was alarming was that I did not want to stop myself from falling farther.

Suddenly, my mobile phone rang, a sharp, jarring buzz that I had deliberately chosen to ensure that I wouldn't miss calls in noisy places. *Saved by the bell!*

"I'm sorry," I said to Rayna as I reached into my jacket pocket.

"Ireton," I said, as crisply as I could.

"Richard," said a voice I would recognize even amid the cacophony of a rock concert, "I'm so sorry to call you at this late hour. It's probably late in the evening in Jerusalem now, isn't it? It's Clarissa. I need to talk to you about my travel plans with Trish."

Clarissa. My missionary nemesis. The woman who had persuaded Trish not to stay in my apartment when she was visiting me in Hong Kong. Arrrgh! I wanted to shout over the phone, but didn't.

"Clarissa, I'm tied up right now. Can I call you back later?"

"Oh yes, of course, Rick. It's the early morning here in Hong Kong now. I'm up and I'll be available all morning."

"Thanks so much. Goodbye."

Rayna looked perplexed. "Clarissa? Is she your girlfriend?" she asked, rather intrusively, I thought.

"No. She's a missionary I used to know in Hong Kong."

As I said this, I felt a twinge of conscience. "Used to know" was a lie. She was still a friend and she was coming to Jerusalem quite soon and would be staying with me.

"Well, I don't want to keep you from talking to your old Hong Kong friends," Rayna said, teasing. "And I need to be going soon anyway. But there's one thing… you said you'd talk about why foreign reporters are so hostile to Israel."

I sighed deeply. I'd only been in Israel six months, but I was already tired of this question. I certainly understood the Israeli anguish behind this question, but the reporting situation in Israel was far more complex than non-journalists realized.

"Okay," I said, taking a deep breath. "It's true that some foreign reporters are really hostile – unsympathetic even – to the existence of Israel. But for the rest, it's not a question of their being especially hostile to Israel, it's that they are instinctively sympathetic to the underdog. As most reporters see it, Israel holds all the keys and the Palestinians are virtually prisoners in their own land."

"Wait a moment!" she interrupted, waving her hand impatiently. "You are saying it is '*their* land'?"

Her voice rising in anger, she continued. "Don't you know that the Balfour Declaration of 1917, which announced that Britain favored a homeland in Palestine for the Jewish people, never defined what 'Palestine' was? What you reporters call 'the West Bank' was part of the Palestine referred to in the Balfour Declaration. After Israel declared independence in 1948, it was invaded by the Jordanians, held by them, and then annexed by the Kingdom of Jordan without so much as a nod to what the Palestinians wanted. If the Palestinians thought the West Bank was 'their land' between 1948 and 1967, why didn't they tell that to the Jordanians?"

"Hold on Rayna," I said, annoyed that the conversation had gone in this direction. "I'm not making any declarations about who has the stronger legal claim to the land of Palestine mentioned in the Balfour Declaration. We both know that's an incredibly complex issue. What I am saying is simply that the Palestinians feel so hemmed in by Israeli roadblocks and restrictions on their movement throughout the territories that they feel they are prisoners in their own homeland. I'm not making any judgments on the issue of land ownership; I'm just trying to explain the attitudes of some foreign reporters. Israel, with its tanks and helicopters and fighter jets, seems to be the Goliath in this struggle. And the Palestinians, who admittedly now have a few guns and can let off bombs but who basically can just throw rocks, are seen as the David. You wanted to know why some foreign reporters are so critical of Israel. I'm saying it's because they see the Palestinians as the underdog."

Now it was Rayna's turn to sigh deeply. "My gosh, it's hard," she said. "If a nation gets strong enough to defend itself effectively, simply because it can stand up to attacks from outside, it becomes a Goliath. Maybe we Israelis should start learning the Philistine language." She almost spat out this remark.

"I'm sorry," I said, not wanting her to grow morose, clam up, or heaven forbid, want nothing more to do with me. "I'm certainly not saying that I share that perspective. I'm just saying that, to understand the seeming hostility of some foreign reporters, you have to understand the attitude behind it."

There was a long silence. Rayna stared straight ahead as the waiter put our drinks on the table, then sipped her vodka and orange juice slowly and carefully.

"You haven't asked me what I do," she said with a smile that broke the tension as she leaned forward from the wall to look fully at me.

"Well, there really hasn't been a chance for me to ask, and we've been talking about things you wanted to talk about," I said, again unsure where she was leading the conversation. "Okay, what do you do?"

"I'm in the army, like Yossi."

"In the army!" I was incredulous. "Then why aren't you in uniform and how come you don't have to be back at some base or other like Yossi?"

"I do have to get back to Tel Aviv, though it's not really a base. I have a lot of freedom to come and go."

I was puzzled. As far as I knew, the only place where anyone in the army reported for work in Tel Aviv was *Hakirya*, the huge defense ministry complex in the middle of the city. I didn't want to appear to pry, though she *had* asked me to inquire about her professional life. I took a stab at one possibility.

"Let me guess now: you are in intelligence. That would explain your excellent English." I paused, momentarily stumped how to continue the conversation. Then I had a brainwave. "If you are in intelligence," I asked, "why on earth would you be allowed to speak with a foreign reporter?"

Rayna looked back at me with an absolutely enchanting smile. "I haven't admitted that I'm in intelligence," she said. "As for talking to foreigners, no one in the army is supposed to do that without permission. Perhaps I was authorized to."

I caught the implication instantly. "And would that be by someone very, very high in the defense establishment?"

"Yes," she said simply. "Look, it's getting quite late and I have to get back to Tel Aviv. If you need anything else you can call me on my cell phone. If you do, don't give your real name. Just say that you are 'Michael'."

"Why not say my real name?"

"Don't ask. Just say 'Michael'."

"Okay, I understand the parameters of this thing. But let me ask one other hypothetical question. Are you authorized by someone very high up to answer questions that I would otherwise ask him?"

She smiled again. Oh, it was heaven when she smiled.

"Yes," she said.

"Well, then I am going to take you up on something you said while translating for Yossi. You said you had some suggestions for how to check up on the Palestinian school teacher."

"Okay, I'll do that. First, you check into all the teacher training institutions on the West Bank and in Gaza. See where he studied."

"I've got someone doing that."

"Good," she said approvingly, and she smiled again. I felt like my second-grade teacher had just patted me on the head. "Next, you get the yearbooks for the past three years of An-Najah University. See if there's any mention of the 'alleged' students who've been murdered."

"And how would I do that without broadcasting to every Palestinian nasty within a hundred miles that I'm trying to expose their martyrdom story?"

"Tel Aviv University has a section of its library devoted to Palestinian institutes of higher learning. I think they would have copies of the yearbooks."

"How do you know that?"

Rayna laughed with that boisterous laugh that invited everyone within earshot to join in.

"Don't ask, Rick, please don't ask."

"Okay, what next?"

"Check the archives of the Terrorism Information Center outside Tel Aviv. See if there are any Al-Jaffars there."

"Can I call you to get confirmation of what I dig up?"

She paused before answering, as though this possibility had not occurred to her. "Yes," she said slowly, then added quickly, "but I won't give you specific information. I'll only confirm or deny what you might have found."

"Got it." This was actually more than I had hoped for, and I was thoroughly satisfied with such an arrangement.

Before I could ask anything else, Rayna had arisen from her seat, extended her hand for another very firm handshake – *such a contrast with the softness of her skin!* – and walked out of the bar towards the elevator.

She didn't look back, leaving me sitting alone at the table, stunned. The waiter came to the table with the tab for our drinks, and looked surprised that I was alone. He seemed on the point of asking a question but then, apparently thinking better of it, just put the check on the table and went off again.

Clarissa. I needed to call her back. Oh, what awful timing that woman had!

I dialed her Hong Kong number and heard it ring three times.

"Clarissa, sorry I couldn't speak just now. I was in a business meeting."

Another stab of conscience. The meeting with Yossi had been about business, but the conversation with Rayna had not really been just business.

"I wanted to confirm all the details of our arrival, Rick. We'll be coming to stay with you on the 19th, after we've done all our touring. Will that still be okay? Or would you like us to stay in some guesthouse or hotel?"

"No, the 19th is fine, Clarissa. You'll be most welcome. Anything else you need to know?"

"What clothes should I bring?"

Urrgh! I hate it when women aske me that! What do I know about women's clothes?

"Well, I don't honestly know. I will tell you that the temperature can be in the 80s during the day and down in the 50s at night. Less extreme in Galilee and the Mediterranean coast, more extreme down by the Dead Sea."

"I won't be staying there, just visiting."

"Well, that's the climate. I hope that helps you decide what to pack."

"Yes, that helps a great deal." A pause. "Rick, is everything all right? You sound a little preoccupied."

Preoccupied? Rayna has my head spinning!

"Well, I can't tell you secrets, Clarissa" – *why am I saying this?* – "but I've certainly got some challenges on my hands."

"Yes, I can tell." *Did she sense anything about another woman, about Rayna?* "Well, I'll be praying for you, Rick."

My heart sank. That was the last thing I wanted to hear right now.

"Thanks, Clarissa. See you at the end of next week."

I hung up, left enough shekels on the table for the drinks and a tip, and headed out. *What on earth next?*

VI

FOR THE NEXT two days, I must have seemed obsessed with the story of that alleged atrocity in the Judean Hills. The *Epoch* Bureau had learned not to bother me when I was on the scent of a story; I could be irritable and snappish if someone tried to distract me, especially with what seemed to me some trivial matter. Margaret was good at announcing an early-warning system to the bureau so that even the most obtuse reporters – Rafi being one of them – would learn to steer a wide berth of me.

The story of the alleged atrocity was now front-page news in all the international press. It was being called "The Al-Jaffar story" because of the school teacher who had first made the allegations about the murders. But it didn't seem to be going anywhere. From the Palestinian side there were unlikely to be any more developments until Al-Jaffar surfaced somewhere. He'd gone to ground after making his first allegations to Patrick Cavenagh of *News Report* and Christopher Blakely of the *BBC*. I doubted that, as some colleagues thought was the case, Al-Jaffar was frightened that the Israeli security services might be trying to reach him, dissuade him from repeating his story, and even silence him. If anything like that happened, Patrick Cavenagh would make sure it was on the front page and above the fold; the Israeli government would end up looking even more brutal and clumsy than it already did after the initial allegations by the school teacher.

But in the morning I allowed myself to be briefly distracted from the Al-Jaffar affair by attending a reception hosted by the Ministry of Absorption.

There had been quite a large recent intake of immigrants into Israel from several countries, and many newly-arrived *olim* were going to be there. Israeli and foreign journalists had also been invited. The absorption authorities evidently wanted the new *olim* to benefit from the wide net of contacts made available to them. Perhaps they also hoped that the reporters might learn a thing or two about Israel's absorption policies.

I had not wanted to attend the reception, but had been badgered into it by Ira Blumenthal who said that foreign correspondents needed to meet the Jews who were continuing to come to Israel and to learn about what had prompted many of them to do so. "Well, you old Bostonian," I had ribbed Ira before heading off to the reception, "I suppose you know a thing or two about being a newcomer."

Ira had not understood at first what I had meant. It was not until I was already out the door that Margaret had explained to him that Bostonians, of all Americans, had been familiar with the sting of rejection as immigrants. "Weren't there signs on the windows of boarding houses, 'No Irish'?" she asked. Ira grunted in a way that could have been in agreement with the idea, or dismissive of it. His own family had immigrated to the US in the 20th century from western Ukraine.

In the lobby of the Ministry of Immigrant Absorption, close to the center of Jerusalem, there had been some effort to convert the rather gloomy ministerial reception area into something that, at a pinch, might have been described as welcoming. Silver plastic balloons, filled with helium, were anchored to tables on which a spread of light snacks had been placed. One table had an ice-filled bowl containing cans of soda. The whole lobby was noisy with the new *olim* and the reporters, and I recognized a handful of foreign correspondent colleagues. Scooping up a can of soda from the ice-filled bowl, I picked my way through the crowd towards another table at which an official was accepting job resumes. I couldn't help comparing the place I now was to the entrance hall of a large funeral parlor.

The hair that regularly flopped across my brow was being especially annoying this morning, and I kept sweeping it away with my unencumbered hand. I almost tripped as I approached a knot of new immigrants among which a rather pretty blond in a summery dress was slowly and rather loudly telling a story to another new *oleh* – at least, that is what I took him to be – who seemed quite mute. It occurred to me that he might not know what she was saying, because she was speaking English. I decided to take a chance that he spoke French. "Good morning," I said, extending my hand. "Perhaps you don't speak English. *Parlez-vous Francais? Etes-vous recemment arrive en Israel?*"

The young man smiled in evident gratitude that someone had rescued him from a monolingual purgatory. Perhaps he did know a few words of my language, but he certainly didn't feel very comfortable using it. "*Alors, je parle anglais comme une vache espagnole* (Well, I speak English like a Spanish cow)," he said. "*Pourquoi vous parlez francais tellement bien* (How come you speak such good French)?"

"*J'ai vecu deux ans en Belgique* (I lived in Belgium for two years)." The pretty blond girl looked quite blank, so I quickly realized I'd have to move back and forth between English and French to keep the pair communicating. She soon introduced herself as Svetlana, from Novgorod in Russia. The tongue-tied young man said he was Jean-Louis, and had been in Israel only a few days. In a somewhat avuncular manner, I attempted to play matchmaker. "Svetlana," I went on, "Jean-Louis needs a little encouragement both at making friends and at speaking English. Could you help out?" I then translated into French for Jean-Louis what I had just said. "Svetlana was just telling me where she was from," I continued in French. "It's the town of Novgorod, a little south of Saint Petersbourg, if you can picture that."

"Yes, I have read about Novgorod," Jean-Louis said hesitantly, his English heavily shrouded in his French accent. "It is, how do you say, a very interesting city. The Mongols never came there."

Svetlana brightened sharply on hearing this.

"You know that?" she asked. "Most people don't."

"Yes, and I think there have been some Jews living there for a long, long time."

"Well, not so many now," she said, her face becoming serious. "The nationalists have been creating unpleasantness for quite a few years. Are there any problems for Jews in France?"

"Are you kidding?" said Jean-Louis. "In Paris a few weeks ago I was attacked in broad daylight by a bunch of Arabs from the suburbs outside the city. I was lucky to get away with my life."

"You were physically attacked?" Svetlana asked, her eyes growing wider.

"They were shouting things like 'Death to the Jews!' and horrible stuff like that. They knocked me off my feet and would have probably beaten me to death if the flics hadn't showed up in time."

"How awful!" Svetlana said. "No one I know was actually attacked in Russia, but there were sometimes horrible roadside signs reading, 'Death to the Jews.' You certainly felt uneasy on buses. Gangs would sometimes get on and extort money from the passengers. If they found out you were Jewish, they'd throw you off, or even beat you up. A friend of mine tried to intervene when a Georgian was being beaten on a bus and he found himself being attacked and pushed off the bus. And those ugly signs; I heard of one family who stopped their car and tried to remove the sign. It turned out to be booby-trapped."

Jean-Louis looked baffled.

"Booby-zapped? What is that?"

I translated for the Frenchman. Svetlana, it turned out, worked for a Russian-language TV channel and was well plugged into the video community. Jean-Louis quickly made it clear that his working skills included training as a videographer. As the two of them conversed more and more animatedly, I smiled benevolently at them, made my apologies, and decided to make a quick departure. Before leaving the building, however, I recognized a Norwegian reporter at the door as I made my way out. "You know, I really like this scene," Arne said. "You've got all these disconnected strangers finding each other for the first time. It's most touching."

"I thought the same," I said, turning around to catch a final glimpse of Jean-Louis lighting up like a candle in front of Svetlana. "But I've done my Good Samaritan act of the day and I think I will get back to the regular news." Arne laughed without asking what I had meant by "Good Samaritan." I went back to my car parked a few blocks from the ministry and returned to the bureau.

There I learned that the tip about locating the yearbooks of An-Najah had paid off. I made another trip to Tel Aviv and found them in the Tel Aviv University library. I couldn't find the names of any of the alleged students in the yearbook, and I took the trouble to photocopy the pages of the relevant yearbooks. On the same trip, I visited the Terrorism Information Center outside Tel Aviv. A female soldier who didn't look older than 16 – but she had to be at least 18 to be in the Israeli army – accompanied me as I looked over some of the gruesome exhibits: the explosive vest of a woman potential suicide bomber who had been arrested at an Israeli roadblock, photographs of the aftermath of some of the successful bombings of Israeli buses, home-made daggers that had been confiscated from Palestinian prisoners in Israeli jails. "This one was used to attack a deputy warden who nearly died after the attack," explained my guide, who looked so young and innocent I found it incongruous that she was guiding journalists and members of the public through an exhibit of terrorist activities; I thought she'd fit in better as the dorm resident of a private girls' school.

But it was in the Center's archives that I found what I was looking for. There was a comprehensive list of every Palestinian ever apprehended by the Israeli military on any charge, whether the relatively innocuous stone-throwing to the much more serious charge of being a member of a terrorist cell. I was astonished that I was allowed access to the archives, for I assumed that they were classified as secret. But as soon as I had arrived in the unimpressive and rather cramped compound of the Center and identified myself, it was obvious that the red carpet was being rolled out. "We've been expecting you," said the impossibly youthful soldier who introduced herself as Corporal Regev. The name immediately triggered a memory in me. "Isn't that the name of one of the two soldiers kidnapped by Hezbollah in 2006?" She grimaced painfully. "He was my cousin," she said.

"I'm so sorry."

"Thank you. Now, what is that you want to see?"

"The archives of arrested Palestinians over the past few years."

"You know, we never usually open these archives up to foreigners. But someone very high up in the government told us to make an exception for you."

Rayna must have gone all the way up to Defense Minister Messinger to obtain that. For heaven's sake, where is this leading?

"Thank you."

At first, I was completely stumped. The archives were all in Hebrew. But Messinger-Rayna-Regev had anticipated this. Corporal Regev accompanied me into the backroom where everything was available on computer terminals and she translated for me, reading the initial Hebrew references and then telling me how to scroll down to get the information I was looking for.

I discovered that Al-Jaffar had been arrested twice by the Israeli military, once when a teenager for throwing rocks at an Israeli jeep, once because he had been the organizer of a road blockage by Palestinian youth. "No known terrorist connections," the description of him said. Puzzled and frustrated, I pushed back the thick waves of hair that fell over my forehead whenever I was trying to read something closely. A thought struck me.

"Do you have anything on Abdul Husseini?" I asked. I felt a little awkward as I posed the question. I wasn't sure whether it was ethical to acquire intelligence information about someone who was, to all intents and purposes, an ordinary Palestinian source.

"I thought you were never going to ask," said Corporal Regev with a smile.

"Why?"

She looked embarrassed when she answered. "Well, let's just say that he's someone we thought you might have come across in Jerusalem recently."

Good night. Is the Shabak keeping such close tabs on me as to know everyone with whom I'd spoken in the past seventy-two hours? Now it was I who was feeling uncomfortable. Burton Lasch had always warned me: "Be careful how friendly you get with intelligence sources. Almost certainly if you think you're using them, they'll be using you. That's why I have an absolute veto on any of our correspondents actually working with any such service." *Am I now being used by the Israelis?*

Corporal Regev turned off the computer screen and asked me to wait while she brought to me a file that was kept in a back room. She seemed also to have sensed intuitively the dilemma I was experiencing in obtaining access to all these documents.

"You understand, of course, that we are showing you these things on the understanding that you will never mention where you got the information. You can absolutely never mention your source as being the Terrorist Information Center. Actually, it's as much to protect you as to protect us. If some Palestinian groups knew that you had seen this material, they would probably never trust you."

I knew this, and it worried me.

"Here is the file on Husseini," she continued. "Actually some of the material is now open-source. If you do a Lexis-Nexis search of Husseini you will find his name, and these details came up in an *International Herald Tribune* story three months ago. Of course, don't say that you heard this from us." She laughed as she said this. *Duh,* I thought. *Why didn't I think of Lexis-Nexis for all of these guys?*

Husseini's background was fascinating. He was related to the famous – or notorious, depending on your point of view – Haji Amin al-Husseini who had been Grand Mufti of Jerusalem in British Mandate Palestine before World War II, had actively encouraged Palestinians to riot against both the British and the Jewish *yishuv,* or settlement in Palestine, and ominously had not only raised a division of Balkan Muslims for the Werhmacht in World War II, but had encouraged Hitler in his plans for the Final Solution, the Holocaust that led to the deaths of six million Jews. I wondered momentarily if Patrick Cavenagh knew this much about Haji Amin, or if he knew of Abdul Hussein's family connections with the former Grand Mufti. Abdul Husseini had grown up in the camps in Jordan, and had been active in PLO activities there. He had, however, become something of a religious Muslim in his teenage years and was thought to have joined the Muslim Brotherhood, an international Muslim association founded by an Egyptian, Hassan al-Banna, in 1928. Though the Muslim Brotherhood claimed currently to be non-violent, its ideology had been the foundation of an entire generation of Muslim terrorists and organizations. In Gaza, Hamas had been formed as the Palestinian wing of the Muslim Brotherhood.

"Husseini's Muslim Brotherhood associations are in Jordan," the report read, "but Husseini is believed to have close connections with senior Hamas figures in Gaza. He may even have some sort of official status, though secret, within Hamas. It has been speculated that, should Hamas come to power in the Territories in Judea and Samaria, Husseini would play a key governing role." I wrote all this down in a notebook and then handed back the folder to Corporal Regev. She was smiling.

It was time to go. I was still feeling a little uncomfortable over my privileged access to Israeli intelligence data, and I did not want to risk the possibility that someone else from the foreign press corps might spot me at the Center. While the archives themselves were not open to the general public, the museum itself was open to anyone who wanted to visit.

I thanked Corporal Regev for her help and expressed condolence for her kidnapped cousin whose remains had eventually been returned to Israel in a swap of live Hezbollah prisoners for the remains of dead Israelis. But I was not finished with reporting in Tel Aviv.

I dialed the number that Rayna had written out on the piece of paper in the Crowne Plaza. It rang twice before being picked up.

"This is Michael," I said. "Can you talk?"

"Not right now. I'm in a meeting. Are you free in a couple of hours?"

"Yes. Where?"

"The Herzliya marina. There are several outdoor restaurants there. We can eat and talk."

Eat and talk. Where is this going?

"Where shall we meet?"

"Just go and stand looking at the largest yacht in the marina. I'll find you."

It felt really good that I was going to see Rayna so soon again. I experienced a sort of "buzz" at the idea. At the same time, I sensed a third voice in my mind cautioning me to be careful. It was a voice I knew from experience was part of an instinctive warning system that had kept me out of trouble in several reporting situations. It was obvious Rayna had been sicced onto me for purposes that were entirely in the interests of the Israeli government, and not necessarily those of honest journalism at all. If I fell heavily for Rayna, as was probably her intention and that of her superiors, right up to Defense Minister Messinger, there would certainly be a price to pay. Israeli friends often used to say, cynically, about your close connections with some political or military source, "Why are they letting you get so close? It is not because of your beautiful blue eyes."

I arrived at the marina several minutes before the appointed time, parked my car in the visitors' lot – which required payment – and wandered around as the Mediterranean sun sank lower in the west. Just as I loved Jerusalem, so I loved the Mediterranean coast of Israel – there wasn't any part of the Mediterranean that I didn't love – and I relished the smell of the salt air and the sound of the waves. The marina itself opened up to the ocean only by a series of protected seawalls, and sailboats and motor yachts flowed in and out of the calm waters. Looking around at the young couples strolling along hand-in-hand and at the vacation atmosphere of the place, I thought I might just as well be at any marina in the entire Mediterranean. What did these carefree young people know of a developing human rights scandal that was bearing down on their country like a runaway freight-train?

I sauntered among the sumptuously-fitted yachts that were a testimony to Israel's booming economy and the high-tech millionaires who had done so well out of it. Many of these were recent Russian immigrants. In fact, as I strolled over to what I thought looked like the largest yacht in the marina, I caught snatches of Russian spoken here and there by confident-looking and well-dressed young men, invariably talking into mobile phones as fast-moving entrepreneurs always seem to do. Many of these were accompanied by drop-dead gorgeous blondes with long legs. I couldn't help wondering how many of these were actual Israelis and how many were part of the sexual trafficking that had become for many years a major Israeli social problem. I'd read of women in Russia and the Ukraine being promised "waitressing opportunities" in Israel and elsewhere by smooth-talking agents who spoke of riches and huge opportunities in return for a large down-payment to an "agent." There was no "waitressing," of course, only rape and cruelty at the hands of a pimp who took away their passports and forced them into prostitution to pay back the original down-payment.

I was so lost in thought about this that I failed to notice at first the slight Dior scent that wafted my way as Rayna approached me from behind. "*This* is not the largest yacht in the marina," she said with a charming laugh. "I had to search you out as a bloodhound sniffs out an escaped convict."

"I'm sorry," I countered weakly. "I was distracted by the human sights in this marina."

She laughed again. Then she took my hand. "Come on, I know a very nice Italian restaurant closer to the sea than most of the other restaurants here. Do you like Italian?" she asked, as she led me off.

Like Italian? I'd eat a week's sauerkraut if I could eat it next to you.

But "of course," was all I could muster. I felt like a lamb being led to the slaughter.

The restaurant was small, was on the second story of a building, not around the wooden deck of the marina, as most of the others were. It was obviously known by regular devotees, for the customers all seemed to be better-dressed than the average visitor to the marina. All the tables looked to be full, but as Rayna approached the maitre d', still pulling me by the hand behind her, she spoke a few words to him and was shown to an unoccupied corner table with a wonderful view of the Mediterranean over the marina's seawall.

"This is really nice," said Rayna, who finally released my hand. "It's one of my favorite places outside of Tel Aviv proper." Evidently, she was not a stranger to pleasant eateries. I wondered who paid her bills.

In the flattering light of a setting afternoon sun, Rayna looked even more ravishing, if that were possible, than she had appeared when I first met her. In contrast with the dark green dress, fully appropriate for a bar that she had worn that night, she was now dressed in a pastel blue dress that fell to slightly above her knees. This dress had more cleavage, and I marveled again at how perfectly formed and proportioned she was.

She wore eye makeup that complimented her dress and for the first time I realized how huge her eyes were. They were brown, the most commonly occurring eye-color for Israelis, and they drew in the attention of everyone who looked at her face. In the daylight, however, I noted that I had probably underestimated her age the night before. She was definitely above her mid-twenties and probably into her early thirties. That would account for the confident, knowing attitude she had towards men. It was certainly not cynicism, but I thought it might become cynicism if she remained single for another three or four years.

I realized again this evening that one of Rayna's most attractive characteristics was that when you talked to her, she was never the slightest bit distracted by things going on around you or her. She seemed to focus intently on everyone she was talking to as if she were homing in on them. It was very flattering to be with someone who appeared to have such an intense interest in you with such laser-like focus. But because she was so dazzlingly attractive, it was also a little intimidating. I suspected that she was not patient towards people she spoke to who were not themselves fully engaged in the conversation.

"Well, how was the Terrorism Information Center?" she asked over a glass of Pinot Grigio that we had both ordered.

"They were extremely friendly and helpful."

"Good. We wanted that to happen."

We? Whom does she mean? The Head of Israeli Military Intelligence, the Defense Minister, Rayna and her indeterminate military friends? Or perhaps all of them. I decided to probe.

"I realize someone in *Hakirya* wanted this visit to be a success. Did it go as high as the minister?"

She laughed again. "Goodness, you are inquisitive. You don't think I can give you an answer to that, do you?"

"I don't know, but you'll have to admit I would be incurious if I didn't ask."

"Incurious. What an interesting word. I hadn't expected you to be rather literary."

"I don't think I am. I just think incurious is a nicer word than half-witted."

"Well, obviously I can't say who said what or when. But did you get everything you needed?"

"As far as any of the Palestinians were concerned, yes. And thank you, whoever the powerful friends were who agreed to let me into the archives. But I have two other questions. First, why do you think whichever Palestinian group set up the sniper attack on the Jerusalem-Efrat road went to such lengths to accuse the IDF of an atrocity? Sniper attacks on that road have been frequent enough in the past. Some of them have been intercepted. Others have not been. What was so important about this one that, when it failed, all this hullabaloo about an atrocity came up? Second, the Terrorism Information Center had nothing on Khalil al-Jaffar that tied him to any of the usual suspect groups. So why was he trotted out to make the allegations?"

"Answer to question one and question two: we don't know. We were hoping you could find out as a reporter."

"You know perfectly well that I am not allowed to share any information with any intelligence organization. That is a fireable offense at *Epoch*." I was surprised at the vehemence with which I said this. Perhaps I was more conflicted than I realized at the favor I had received from the Israeli authorities.

Rayna pushed her chair back from the table a little to observe me from farther away than was possible where we were sitting, which was not next to each other, but on perpendicular sides of the small table. The gesture surprised me a little. I wasn't sure what she was up to.

"Don't think we haven't thought very carefully about the dynamics of your relationship with us," she said coolly. "I could probably cite *Epoch's* written regulations on the subject. Let me see now, 'Correspondents are also prohibited from making their services available to any intelligence-gathering organization, including those of the US.' Am I right?" And before I could reply, she added. "We are not asking you to share anything with us. Just do your job. 'Tell no secrets' is the sort of thing government employees should constantly observe. That was what Yossi's tee-shirt said, if you remember. 'Tell no lies' ought to apply to journalists. Unfortunately, in Israel and almost everywhere else, it doesn't always work that way, in either case.

"Don't worry," she continued before I had a chance to say anything. "We are not going to do anything to compromise your relationship with *Epoch*, or for that matter with any of your colleagues. I think you know which of your colleagues I mean."

Rayna's apparently intimate knowledge of *Epoch's* restrictions on intelligence contacts stunned me. What else did she know? Perhaps she knew about Trish. Perhaps she'd read my emails to Trish and hers to me.

Once again, Rayna seemed to read my thoughts. "Don't worry," she said with a half smile, "*I* haven't read any of your personal emails, much less listened to any of your phone calls. Frankly, I haven't got time to pay attention to that, even if I had access to it. And I don't have access to everything. And something else you shouldn't worry about. We are not interested in learning anything from you before *Epoch* Magazine appears on the newsstands."

"Well, you had some good suggestions last night about what would be worthwhile looking into. What are you suggesting at this point?"

As soon as the words were out of my mouth, I regretted them. By even asking for reporting suggestions from Rayna I was crossing an invisible line that separated journalism from something else altogether.

"Sorry, I take back that question," I said quickly before Rayna had a chance to reply. "That was not very professional. Forgive me."

Rayna seemed strangely touched by this. She reached over and momentarily placed her hand on mine. Once again, a shiver went through me. Boy, she was hot.

"Rick, I'll not presume to advise you where to go and what to do on a story. I did help out last night and today because I was prodded to give you a sense of direction. But where you go from now on is up to you."

"But you said you would know wherever I went."

She chuckled and sighed. "Yes, I suppose we will be able to find out."

We had by now gotten through the main course, she with angel hair pasta and I with an especially good veal piccata. We'd ordered a full bottle of *Pino Grigio,* and by the time the entrée was over and it was time to choose desert, it had loosened the tongues of both of us. I learned that Rayna came from a distinguished Israeli military family that had first seen action in her grandfather's generation in the War of Independence. Rayna had wheedled out of me the existence of Trish and her place in my life. The admission to Rayna of Trish's existence actually smoothed over an indefinable tension between us, at least a tension on my side. Rayna was frank about the problems of being a woman officer in the Israeli army – she turned out to be a captain – because of the continuing macho tradition among Israeli male officers. "I expect you get hit on quite often," I said, as the *Pino Grigio* had its effect.

"Often? Are you kidding? Like several times a day."

I burst out laughing at this admission. "Now there's a military secret you've just disclosed to a foreigner," he said.

"Oh no," she shot back. "Everyone in Israel knows this. It's just as well the Palestinians haven't got their hands around this problem. But I expect with time, they will."

Just then the manager of the restaurant came over to the table. It was obvious that he and Rayna knew each other rather well, but I knew better than to be inquisitive about this. He was carrying an elegant leather attaché case.

"Forgive me, please," he said in English with a strong Italian accent. "My brother is a craftsman in fine leather and he asked me to show some of his crafts to my customers in case they are interested in purchasing them. May I show you some leather items?"

I looked at Rayna and she gestured that I was free to look at the collection if I wanted to. We had just gone through an excellent Zabayon desert. That, Rayna's proximity to me, and the *Pino Grigio*, made me feel decidedly mellow.

"Go ahead," I told the manager.

The selection that was in the briefcase was exceptionally well crafted. There were belts, wallets, and leather key-chain cases. I decided to buy a belt and a wallet, reaching into my own wallet to pay in shekels. Rayna looked at both of my purchases, expressed admiration, and then asked the manager, "Can your brother inscribe Mr. Ireton's initials on both of these items? That would not only be very elegant but a security measure against his losing them."

"With pleasure," said the manager, "but he will have to leave them with me. If he provides an address I'll have them sent on as soon as they are complete. We can probably get them back to you in twenty-four hours or so."

"Sounds fine to me," I said, and I gave my card to the manager.

I paid the bill with a credit card and walked slowly out of the restaurant with Rayna. She slipped her arm into mine as we walked down the stairs of the restaurant to the marina deck level. Once again, a shiver went through me. That ancient, cautionary voice was still audible in my mind, but I decided I didn't want its advice any more. Things were just too delicious right now.

"Can I take you back to Tel Aviv?" I asked.

"Isn't that out of your way? If you drove back towards Tel Aviv by the most direct route, you'd pick up the Ayalon freeway to Jerusalem. I'm at the other end of town."

"Well, I'm in no great hurry tonight. Besides, I certainly owe you one or two."

"No, Rick, you don't owe me anything. But I'll accept your offer."

We drove back, mostly in silence, to where she lived, which was indeed quite close to Hakirya, on Herzl Street. I decided to be gallant and got out of the driver's side of the car to open the door for her, which seemed to surprise her.

"Well," she said as she elegantly extended her legs from the Subaru, "I am being treated well today. Not just a fine Italian dinner but impeccable – may I say European? – manners."

I was about to extend my hand to shake hers with, but before I could do it, she had leaned towards me and given him a gentle kiss on the cheek. Then, as I stood there, amazed, she uttered a quick "Bye" and disappeared into the front door of the apartment building.

I stroked my face carefully where she had kissed it. Then, with an impatient Israeli driver honking the horn behind me, I got back into the car. I turned on the radio in the Subaru and listened in near-bliss to a superb performance of Beethoven's Fifth Symphony as I drove back to Jerusalem. The Subaru, groaning just slightly, accelerated past trucks and buses as the freeway from Tel Aviv climbed into the Judean Hills leading to the entrance of Israel's historic capital. In the dark, I knew that scattered along the sides of the road as it climbed through the steep valley were the carcasses of ancient armored cars from the War of Independence. They had been left there, carefully repainted over the years to protect against the ravages of rust, as reminders of the cost that had been paid to keep open the road to Jerusalem during the siege of the city by the Jordanian Legion in 1947-1948. The night now hid them but oddly, when returning to Jerusalem at night from some function in Tel Aviv, I always thought about them.

"You got a call last night from Trish." It was Margaret talking, with a grin and twinkle in her eye. I had come into the bureau in mid-morning and I was unprepared for the cascade of information that poured over me from all sides. "She and her friend Clarissa have put forward their visit to Israel by a week. Something about a mix-up with the travel agency. They'll be coming in two days."

"Two days? That means they will want to stay at my apartment the following week, after they've done all their out-of-town touring. And that coincides almost exactly with the anticipated arrive of Yao. The best-laid plans ... Terrific."

"You mean your Chinese friend?"

"Yes."

"But he won't be staying with you, will he?"

"No, but I'm sure he'll expect to be waited upon by me while he's here. It's not a question of selfishness at all. It's just that he has no idea how busy reporters are, and in China if some semi-bigwig shows up in a new town, he fully expects all the local grandees to pay court."

"Well, don't worry. I'd be happy to handle Trish and Clarissa while you explain to Chinese intelligence all the ins and outs of the Israeli-Palestinian issue."

I laughed at this, and then added, "But why did Trish call the bureau? She has my mobile number."

"Have you forgotten? You've been using Reddaway's phone since Monday. Trish said she tried you on your own mobile and got no answer. She seemed a bit worried by that, but I assured her that you were running around on an important story. Well, that didn't seem to set her at ease. '*How* important?' she wanted to know. I suggested she look at the latest issue of the *International Herald Tribune*. That seemed to satisfy her.

"By the way, how was yesterday?" Margaret seemed to sense that I had had an interesting evening.

"Amazing. They really pulled out all the stops. I've certainly got some leads. But I'm stuck with this Al-Jaffar fellow. Nobody seems to have anything on him or know anything about him."

"Well, I think that may be about to change. Karim asked if you'd be in this morning and I said I thought you would be. He's on his way to see you. Oh, and this came to you from Tel Aviv by special courier. You certainly seem to have rung some bells there."

She handed me a small, padded package. I couldn't imagine what it was, so borrowed the scissors on Margaret's desk and cut it open. She watched me carefully. Inside were two compact, neat cardboard boxes. I opened them with extreme curiosity. In one was the wallet I had selected and paid for at the Italian restaurant in Herzliya barely twelve hours earlier, now neatly engraved with my initials on the inside. In the other box was the belt. My face must have conveyed an expression of mixed astonishment and delight.

"My goodness, why on earth did they rush this? I ordered the engraving of my initials just last night, at the time I bought it in a restaurant. How on earth did they turn it around so fast?"

"Well, someone must have told them," Margaret helpfully offered. "Perhaps you were having dinner with someone who told the belt-maker later what your initials were. By the way, who did you have dinner with last night – if that's not too personal a question?"

"With the army officer who translated my interview with Yossi the night before last."

"A he or a she?" Margaret followed up. She was grinning from ear to ear and her short, salt-and-pepper hair was bobbing as she suppressed a giggle.

I sighed. "A she. A very remarkable she."

"I see," said Margaret, adopting an expression of mock gravity. "Well, I see our Defense Ministry can sometimes do its homework quite well."

I didn't know whether to comment on this or not. I thought better of it and retreated into my own office.

Examining the inside of the box more carefully, I saw Rayna's business card. Scrawled on the back were the words, "Thanks so much for a lovely dinner. Now, please wear the belt right away, just to please me."

I found himself trying to untangle in my mind a kaleidoscope of different emotions: a macho sense of conquest, excitement that such a gorgeous female had taken considerable trouble to get a piece of leather engraved overnight and sent to me for arrival first thing in the morning, a hack's innate suspicion that if something seemed too good to be true, it probably was, and slight guilt that I was, in effect, receiving a gift – well, not exactly a gift because I had paid for it myself, but an item that her connections had made very special for me – from a woman who was not my actual girlfriend. All of that was combined with an immense feeling of having been flattered to the skies.

The belt was actually exceptionally well-crafted, made of thick ox-leather and with minute, precise stitching in the seams. It was, in fact, just a tad thicker than I was normally comfortable with, but it fitted easily enough through the loops on my pants. I decided to put it on right away. Looking at myself in a small mirror tacked onto the inside of the cupboard behind my desk, I admired the result.

The phone rang. "Karim's here," said Margaret.

I made sure I had a notebook and pen on me before going out into the reception area. There I found Margaret and Karim deep in conversation about the fortunes of the Boston Red Sox. It had been a disappointing season, whose only highlight had been that the Red Sox defeated the New York Mets at an away game early in the season. "I tell you, that Velasquez fellow is a great pitcher. It's just that they haven't used him properly all season." Margaret, being a Brit, had acquired all her baseball knowledge – it certainly didn't qualify as expertise – from her husband Solomon and from Ira Blumenthal's generally grouchy Monday post-mortems on the previous day's game.

"Well," I said on exiting my office, "I see that our two primary sports commentators are getting into it."

Karim lauged uproariously. "I tell you, I only know anything about this team because of what Fatima has told me," he said. He shook my hand and immediately suggested that we go for a walk. I knew that when Karim had a walk in mind it was because he had information so confidential that he worried that someone bugging the bureau might catch it.

We walked up St. George's Street towards the Plaza Hotel and Independence Park, which we then entered. I scanned the area carefully in case we were being shadowed or – unlikely, but not impossible – some unfriendly person was trying to eavesdrop on our conversation from a distance using an electronically enhanced listening device. I'd often seen such things advertised in mail-order catalogues in the US, and I always wondered whether they worked. But I didn't want someone to try the thing out on me. I had also become conscious that Shabak, the Israeli domestic intelligence service, itself might be tailing me; hadn't Rayna suggested as much?

"Okay, Karim," I said when I was sure that we were not being listened in on, "what do you have?"

"Three things that may interest you. First, Al-Jaffar's name doesn't come up among past graduates at any teacher training institute in the West Bank or Gaza. It's possible that he was trained in Egypt but we can't be sure. At the school where he is said to have worked, no one answers the phone and there is no website for it."

"Which village was he from?" I interrupted.

"From al-Jiffri. It's quite near the spot where the sniping took place."

"Okay, what are the other two?

"Palestinian El Quds has taken over as the agency handling all the enquiries into the shooting. An-Najah refers everyone who calls back to them. Your newfound friend Mr. Husseini is the go-to person on this." Karim smiled sardonically.

"Well, Patrick seems to have an edge there already."

"What about the BBC guy who did that TV report?"

"Christopher Blakely?"

"Yes. Do you know him? Maybe he's more approachable than Cavenagh."

"You know, that may be true. He was out of town at the time the Beeb ran his story. I think he went to Cyprus immediately after the weekend. If he's only just returned, Cavenagh may not have had time to warn him against telling me who his source for the story was. I'll call him up as soon as we're through. So what's the third item?"

"You won't like this at all. Al-Jaffar's gone to ground in Gaza. Hamas has taken him under its wing, saying that he wouldn't be safe in the West Bank because the Israelis could get to him more easily."

"Well, will Hamas let him talk to reporters while he's there?"

"They may. But you know what Gaza's like now. It's an extremely dangerous place. Not only is it very uptight because of the recent Israeli incursion, but hardly any reporters go down there because of the threat of kidnapping. Hamas is also awaiting the arrival of a delegation representing the UN Security Council to investigate the allegations of murder. And, of course, the Secretary of State will probably be there in a few days."

"When will that be?"

"Both visits are scheduled to take place next week."

"So the only chance of getting to Al-Jaffar before his story becomes cast in concrete as a UN document is to get to Gaza before next Wednesday?"

"Right."

"And is there any way to make contact with Al-Jaffar in Gaza without going through Husseini?"

"There may be. But it will be very risky. If Husseini heard that you were trying an end-run around him, he could get quite nasty. What I suggest is – "

My mobile phone – the one I had borrowed just a few days ago – rang with a jarring, samba-like tune. "Excuse me, Karim," I said, flipping it open.

"I'm sorry to interrupt your meeting with Karim, but I think this is important. I'm sure you are going to be thrilled to hear this news, but your Chinese friend is at Ben Gurion." It was Margaret in her best don't-interrupt-the-boss tone.

"That's impossible. He's not due in Israel until next week."

"He knows that, and he's very apologetic. He says the ticket was for an earlier departure date than the travel people told him. Even the Chinese Embassy was confused and so they didn't send anyone out to meet him. You're it, I'm afraid."

"Rats. It couldn't have happened at a worse time. Well, thanks for letting me know, Margaret."

I hung up and frowned. "Karim, my friend, would you mind driving with me to Ben-Gurion? I've got to pick up a Chinese official who's visiting Israel for the first time."

"What sort of official?"

"Well, he's actually a friend of mine. To be quite frank, I helped get him out of China last year when he was in a very perilous spot."

"Of course I'll come with you, Rick. But what about Gaza?"

"Well, it's a risk to go there, but I'm taking the chance that Al-Jaffar's handlers will figure that access to Al-Jaffar by Western reporters will serve their cause better than scaring them away by the threat of kidnapping."

Karim looked very serious. "You know, some news organizations based in Jerusalem won't allow their reporters to go into Gaza. What does Lasch say?"

"Lasch doesn't know anything about my plans to go into Gaza. But I can predict what he would say, if I asked him. 'I trust your judgment, Rick. Just know that *Epoch* never expects any of its correspondents to take any risks to life and limb for the sake of a story.'"

"Let's go then," Karim said. "I assume we'll take the Subaru."

"Yes."

VII

WHEN KARIM AND I arrived at Ben-Gurion Airport, we passed the checkpoint at the perimeter gate with relative ease. I was worried that the checkpoint guards might give Karim a hard time, aware that he was a Palestinian in spite of his American passport. But the border police manning the checkpoint merely asked me as the driver, almost as if it were an afterthought, to pop the trunk. They glanced inside it and waved me on.

We both spotted Yao at the same time, almost immediately after entering the arrivals' hall. Crowds of well-wishers were milling around waiting for passengers from incoming flights and glancing at a TV screen which showed the faces of passengers clearing customs before they arrived at the meeting point. But Yao was literally sitting on a suitcase almost in the middle of the hall looking distinctly dejected. I was within a few feet of him before Yao realized that someone had come to meet him in this strange country, someone, moreover, whom he knew and regarded as a friend. He brightened immediately.

"Well, hello, I uh, how wonderful to see you," he said, the long vowels of Mandarin infecting his English. "Wonderful" came out as *one-der-fool*.

"Fanmei, welcome to Israel. I knew you'd eventually get here when your parting shot in the Philippines was 'Next year in Jerusalem.' I want you to meet Karim Nasr. He's the Arab affairs reporter for *Epoch*. Karim, this is Mr. Yao of the Beijing Institute for International Affairs. He's an old friend."

Karim extended his hand to Yao and seemed surprised at how firm the handshake was. He'd met Chinese students and scholars before, of course, both at the University of Oregon and at Whitman College. But he'd never met any Chinese officials. He was as curious as I was to know what had prompted the Chinese official to come to Israel, or, more to the point, why the Chinese government had sent him there.

I wanted to know immediately if Yao had a hotel reservation, and if so, where. Yao showed me a print out on which was written "Beersheba Hotel, 214 Hayarkon Street, Tel Aviv." I had never heard of it, which bothered him. I had a brief vision of struggling up three flights of stairs with Yao's luggage and a grumpy female Central European Jewish concierge following close behind muttering about inscrutable Orientals.

"The *Beersheba* Hotel?" I asked. Later, Karim told me he thought that I had asked this question rather impertinently.

"My institute in Beijing has sent scholars to Israel before, and they told me they had used this hotel. I understand it's not luxurious, like the Hilton, and it's not on the beach, but it's clean, has an elevator, and is rather quiet."

Satisfied that Yao had not been assigned to some fleapit abode in the middle of what had once been Tel Aviv's red light district, I scooped up Yao's modest suitcase and the three of us returned to where I had parked my car in the public short-term parking lot. On the way into town we exchanged small talk. Yao asked politely about Trish. Karim seemed surprised at how much he seemed to know about her.

I assumed that Yao would be tired after his long flight from Beijing and that he probably would not be in the mood for a meal. We settled for a coffee and conversation in the Beersheba Hotel coffee shop.

"My friend, I'm delighted you've finally made it here. I'm curious, though, what your research project is." If I could have done so, I would have put "research" in inverted commas as I spoke. But I didn't want to be rude.

"Well, my main interest is Gaza and Hamas. I certainly plan to go down to Gaza and talk to officials there, and the embassy has made arrangements for that. But I am interested to discover how much support Hamas has on the West Bank."

I glanced at Karim as Yao said this and noticed that the Palestinian was smiling slightly. "I think that Karim here may be able to help you on that subject," I said levelly.

Karim said, "As you probably know, Hamas does not have much support on the West Bank, but it is growing. I can tell you that Fatah is worried about it. Frankly, so am I and my family."

"Is that so?" Yao asked. "Why are you concerned about Hamas?"

"Because I don't want to live in an Islamist state," Karim said. "Would you? Would you like to see your wife harassed on the street by young men with beards because she's not wearing a *hijab*, or your children indoctrinated into believing that the highest merit for a Muslim is to be a martyr and to die while killing lots of Jews? You need to know that for a Palestinian the choice today is either continued Israeli occupation or the rule of the imams. What a choice!"

The tone of Karim's question and comments was angry and sardonic. I'd seen glimpses of this in Karim before, but seldom so forcefully expressed.

"Would you be willing to introduce me to some of your friends on the West Bank? Could I also meet some of the Hamas people on the West Bank, if that is possible? I have some connections with Hamas officials in Gaza. Rick, is it okay if I ask Karim for this assistance?"

"Of course, Fanmei. If Karim can arrange what you need, he will. If it's impossible, he'll tell you directly."

Yao's almost cadaverously thin face, the result of having been born at the height of the great starvation during China's Great Leap Forward of 1958-1961, twitched slightly at this. He turned full-face towards Karim. "If I am not asking a rude question," he said, "how are you as a Palestinian able to come and go freely into and out of Israel? I thought there were tight restrictions on the movements of Palestinians all over the West Bank, with scores of roadblocks."

"There are tight restrictions. But I have an American passport so I can go through the checkpoints – usually, but by no means always – with little trouble. For other Palestinians, it's a nightmare. My own brother, who is a doctor at a hospital in Ramallah, needs seven or eight hours to visit our ailing mother in Hebron."

I was amazed. Karim had never told me this before, and as the Palestinian recounted the detail to Yao, his voice almost quavered with indignation. I felt somewhat awkward; humanly speaking, Karim had every right to be indignant about his frustration with the living conditions of Palestinians in the territories, but the revelation of this little fact about his own brother opened up new areas of potential awkwardness with me and with the Israelis in the *Epoch* bureau. They were, as I've said, of course, somewhat left-of-center in their Israeli domestic political views – except for Ira Blumenthal – and they had often sympathized with Karim's various tales of problems of life under what Karim and all Palestinians called Israeli occupation. But hitherto, Karim had never mentioned any difficulty faced by a really close relative.

Of course, the way the Israelis controlled the West Bank was much more complicated than straightforward occupation. Ever since the Oslo Accords peace process that started in 1993 Israeli authorities had gradually handed over to the Palestinian authorities all local authority in Palestinian municipalities. In fact, Israeli individuals very seldom ventured into the heart of West Bank cities; they might be turned upon by Palestinians at any moment and the Palestinian Authority police could not be relied upon to protect them. The way Israel controlled the West Bank, however, was through a complex system of road-blocks dotted throughout the area along its network of roads. The purpose of these was explained by the Israeli government as security; Israel wanted to prevent the passage of known terrorists or arms from one area of the West Bank to the other, let alone across the "Green Line" into Israel proper.

The "security barrier," in many places an ugly concrete wall reminiscent of the Berlin Wall, ran along much of the boundary between Israel and the West Bank, not to mention through parts of Jerusalem. Israelis believed – with some justification – that it had succeeded in reducing terrorism drastically. Palestinians resented it even more than the roadblocks because it seemed to them to be a land-grab.

In places, the Palestinians had been successful in Israeli courts in forcing the Israeli military to restructure the route of the fence to keep it from slicing off parts of Palestinian-owned land. But most of them felt that the combination of the roadblocks and the encroachments of the fence was progressively reducing the land that would eventually become available to them for a state. As for Israeli residents in the settlements, they could spend much of their time driving back and forth along roads built by the Israeli military and scarcely ever see a Palestinian Arab at all. I wondered how much Yao knew of the minutiae of Israeli-Palestinian relations. I was intrigued not only by the questions Yao was asking, but the replies that Karim was giving.

I decided to cut the meeting short, not only because Yao's eyes, puffed and bloodshot through fatigue, were beginning to blink, but because I didn't want to impose on Karim too much. Assured that the Chinese embassy would come for him in the morning, Karim and I said goodbye and left the hotel.

There was something of an awkward silence between Karim and me as I drove the Subaru onto the access ramp for the Ayalon freeway back to Jerusalem. Finally, I broke it. "I am so sorry about your brother's problems," I said. "Is there anything you think I could do to help?"

Karim looked sideways at me for a few moments before replying. "What can you do, Rick? You don't control the Israeli military, you can't be seen being too partisan towards us, and you have no way – at least I don't think so – of taking my brother's case to the Supreme Court."

I bit my lip. I couldn't tell Karim that the Israeli Defense Minister had called me up personally and given me his private mobile phone number. I couldn't reveal anything about Rayna. But a plan was forming in my mind.

"You're right, of course, Karim. I absolutely do not give orders to the IDF or have access to the justices of the Israeli Supreme Court. But I will put my thinking cap on about it."

I realized as soon as I had said this that it sounded feeble. No amount of "thinking caps" would enable his brother to move noiselessly through Israeli military checkpoints. We talked on the way about my plans to try and find Al-Jaffar in Gaza before the UN team got to him. Karim once again warned me that it would be very dangerous for me to travel to Gaza. "Well, I think you are right, Karim," I finally said with a sigh. "But it sticks in my craw that this Israeli atrocity story is making the rounds without being carefully investigated by reporters."

"Mine too. Have you seen Blakely yet?"

"No, I nearly forgot about him. I'll call him up now and see if I can meet him after I have dropped you off. I suppose you want to go to the bureau?"

"If it isn't out of your way."

"Of course not." I handed Karim the phone as the road left the Valley of Sharon, swept past the ruined Jordanian fortress at Latrun and began to climb up into the Judean Hills. Once again, it was dark. Karim had to squint to locate Blakely's phone number. Once the number started ringing on the other end, Karim handed the mobile back to me.

"Blakely," the mellow British voice said at the other end.

"Chris, it's Rick Ireton here from *Epoch*. Actually, I'm on the way back from Tel Aviv. Any chance I might drop in on you in the next forty-five minutes?"

"Good Lord, Rick, I've literally walked in the door from Cyprus. Can't it wait until tomorrow?"

"I'm sorry, Chris, but it really can't. In fact, I can't even tell you by phone what it's about. But I promise it won't be boring."

There was a chuckle at the other end of the line. Christopher Blakely, half a generation older than most of the Jerusalem-based foreign correspondents, and indeed almost the age of Karim, was famous for complaining that so much of the news he had to cover was "boring." The word was pronounced with an especially disdainful lengthening of the b-o-r part of the word, making it sound a little like *baw-ring*. For all of his cynicism and his pose as an absent-minded, rather detached reporter, he was thoroughly professional. He shared something of the almost constantly critical attitude towards Israel of his other British colleagues, but he lacked the apparent animosity of Cavenagh. He was also something of a *bon vivant*, enjoying copious amounts of good food and good wine. On the subject of wines, he was far from hostile to Israel, boasting that he had "discovered" an obscure label of a Burgundy-type red grape from a vineyard on the Golan Heights, that part of Syrian territory originally captured by Israel during the Six-Day War of 1967.

But calling Blakely out of the blue was a gamble. If the BBC man talked to Cavenagh before I reached him, the game would be up; Blakely would be as forthcoming as Mount Rushmore.

We were almost up the last stretch of the Judean Hills and had just passed the turn-off for the village of Motza Illit. On impulse I turned to Karim sitting beside me and asked, "If you found out that this Al-Jaffar fellow was lying about the al-Jiffri atrocity story, what would you do about it in my place, Karim?"

"I'd tell the truth."

"I thought you'd say that. It's an honor to work with you." I felt strangely emotional as I said this. I found myself blinking back tears. The Palestinian merely stared straight ahead, stoically.

I dropped Karim off at the *Epoch* bureau where he had left his own car and drove over to the tall apartments called the Wolfson Buildings overlooking the Valley of the Cross and the Knesset building. The ancient monastery that gave the long stretch of low-lying land between the hills of Rehavia and the Knesset its name was an old Greek Orthodox monastery that claimed to have been built on the site of the copse of trees from which the wood for the Cross of Christ had been made. At night, the ancient walls of the compound were floodlit, as was the entire Knesset Building, a 1966-vintage structure whose design had been as passionately argued over by its architects and Israeli domestic critics as any topic ever considered by the Israeli political establishment. Some critics argued that the building didn't look sufficiently "Israeli," its surrounding decorative and structural cluster of columns allegedly borrowing from "classical" or even "international" styles. I had never bothered with these internecine squabbles among Israeli architectural esthetes; I thought the building handsome enough and a good venue for the often noisy parliamentary squabbling that constituted Israeli domestic politics.

The Wolfson Towers had gone up in the 1970's and offered a handsome view both of the Knesset and the Valley of the Cross. Their location for a journalist was excellent; close to the Knesset and Jerusalem's cluster of government offices, HaKirya, and yet only a short drive from the Israeli government press center in Beit Agron and Jerusalem's finer restaurants (and for that matter, the *Epoch* Bureau on King George Street). Perhaps even more useful for someone like Blakely, a bachelor (he'd been long-since divorced from a Laura Ashley-clad scion of a distinguished family from the English county of Yorkshire), the apartments in Wolfson, in addition to having excellent views, were well appointed for convenient urban living. Blakely needed only a *metapellet* (daily help) to take care of his basic cleaning requirements. Otherwise, he barely needed to raise a finger to operate on a daily basis.

I parked in the visitors' lot and made my way up to Blakely's seventh-floor apartment. As the elevator stopped and I turned right to 7C, I sighed with relief. Blakely was in one of his heavy music moods, playing Mahler's Fourth Symphony loudly enough for me, who was somewhat familiar with Mahler, to have recognized it instantly through the apartment's front door. I pressed the bell and waited quite a while before the door opened. "Come in, dear Rick, come in," Blakely said, a glass of red wine in hand. "Now don't you think this is just the most divine music ever written? It's the *Ruhevoll* fourth movement. Listening to this, you wouldn't know what a tormented life Mahler led in Vienna, a Jew in the anti-Semitic capital of Europe, a Jew, moreover, who'd become a Christian; thus a double adversary: to the Austrians for his Jewishness, to the Jews for his Christianity."

While this monologue was being delivered, Blakely was filling a new glass with the red wine he himself had been consuming and was making his way, a tad unsteadily, across the room to where I was now sitting on the modern leather sofa. Blakely was overweight to the point almost of corpulence. That alone made moving around confined spaces a potentially hazardous endeavor for him, even without the mellowing influence of the red wine. He had a large, straight nose and thinning blond hair, curiously smooth cheeks, as though he hardly needed to shave, small, closely placed eyes that twinkled when, as now, his sense of being a simultaneous *bon vivant* and *aficionado* of fine symphonic music was approaching a paroxysm of pleasure. I took it all in with genuine pleasure. I liked Blakely, and I thought that the feeling was mutual.

"So, what's on your mind?" he asked distractedly, as the gorgeous music of Mahler spilled into the room from his expensive audio system.

"Al-Jaffar, to be precise," I said. "I saw your fine piece on the Beeb the other morning and was impressed by how quickly you had latched onto that story. Since I had been in the neighborhood of the ... the event, I was curious how you heard about it and got to Al-Jaffar himself."

"You were close to the incident?" Blakely asked, suddenly brought down to earth from the esthetic eerie where he had seemed to be perched for the last several minutes. "Where were you when all this happened?"

"Returning to Jerusalem on the Jerusalem-Efrat road. I stopped my car about one hundred yards behind two Israeli soldiers in a jeep who seemed to be pinned down by snipers on the hillside."

"Two Israeli soldiers! I thought there were at least twenty."

"There were when the reinforcements arrived, but initially there were just two."

"What did you see happen?"

I realized this could be a trap, so I took a sip of the wine that Blakely had offered and leaned back on the sofa. Thank God, it seemed certain that Blakely had not been in touch with Cavenagh since his arrival in Jerusalem. Still, I didn't want to be in the position of telling the

Englishman what I had experienced until the BBC reporter made it clear he would be forthcoming on his side of the picture.

I leaned forward again as the sensuous strings of Mahler filled the background. "Chris, we've been in on a few of the same stories, and I think we've always treated each other fairly. If I tell you exactly what I saw and heard, will you be as forthcoming about Al-Jaffar?"

"Well, you know I've got to protect Patrick Cavenagh. He and I shared the same source. I don't want to let him down."

I thought quickly. "You won't. I'm not competing with Patrick and I give you my word no one else will hear of your source. Listen, we're both working hacks. It's not in my interest to rip you or anyone else off. I think this town has plenty of interesting sources."

Blakely seemed to be weighing this up. "Could I call Patrick?" he asked. My heart sank like lead. If that happened, my entire game was up. *Think quickly again.*

"Well, this is not between Patrick and me and I've given Patrick the same fill that I'm prepared to give you. I'd prefer to keep this *entre nous*, or as the Israelis like to say 'under four eyes.' I don't know where they got that from."

"I think from German, as it happens. The Germans say '*Unter vier Augen*,' which is exactly the same thing, meaning between two people. Okay, I'm with you. So you tell your story first."

I recounted the whole tale, from my initial stopping in the Subaru one hundred yards behind the soldiers, to the apparent killing of one of the snipers on the hill and the wounding of one of the Israelis, to the arrival of reinforcements. I did not, of course, reveal that I had later received a personal phone call from the Defense Minister.

"That's all?" Blakely asked.

"That's all that I saw." *Wait a minute. Should I mention my debriefing of Yossi? If I do, I run the risk that Blakely will ask how an ordinary Israeli soldier knew enough English to speak with an American reporter.* I decided to hold that part of the story in reserve. I might need it later when cross-checking the details of Blakely's account.

"Now, what's with the Al-Jaffar fellow?"

Blakely didn't reply immediately, as though weighing in his mind what he had heard from me against the account that he had heard – and reported – from Al-Jaffar.

"Patrick and I were having a drink in the American Colony on Sunday evening. We were about to go in for dinner – incidentally, have you tried that sea bass they've started serving recently? Olive oil, bay leaves, and balsamic vinegar. It's delicious – sorry, I couldn't resist that reference. Anyway, we were about to go in for dinner when Patrick got a call from this Husseini fellow – have you met him? He runs something called the Palestine El Quds Center – who said he had a major breaking story. Would we like to be the first to break it? Well, I'm a sucker for scoops I must admit, especially if they come flopping into your boat when you're not even fishing. We looked at each other and said, 'What the heck!' – that's my Americanese breaking through – and he chuckled at his own humor, 'let's see what he has to say.'

"Husseini said he wanted us to meet someone who had a very important story we should know about. Could we come after dinner to his office in East Jerusalem?

"Well, it was actually within walking distance of the American Colony up the Nablus Road, and we were there inside ten minutes after the meal. Husseini introduced us to this fellow called Al-Jaffar who said he was a school teacher in the village of al-Jiffri in the West Bank. He'd been going for a walk in the early evening, he said, when he heard shots being fired not far away. He'd walked towards the noise to investigate, and on coming over a rise in the ground, he said he saw a group of Israeli soldiers surrounding three men lying on the ground. One of them was wearing a *keffiyeh*, so he assumed they were Palestinians. He seemed to be bleeding heavily, or perhaps he had bled to death already. Anyway, this Al-Jaffar fellow says he saw an Israeli officer stand over each of the men on the ground and point a pistol at the backs of their heads."

"Did he see him fire the pistol?"

"Al-Jaffar was vague about that. I had the impression that he'd turned and run before the Israelis spotted him. Husseini told us that Al-Jaffar had told him when he narrated the story later to him that he'd watched the Israeli officer shooting the Palestinians on the ground execution-style."

"But what do you think Al-Jaffar thought he really saw."

Blakely took a deep drink of his wine before replying. Then he seemed to screw up his narrow-set eyes and look at me quizzically.

"Are you suggesting that Al-Jaffar was lying to us, old boy?"

"I'm not suggesting anything, Chris. I'm just doing what they told us to do in J-School."

"Oh, of course. I forgot that they give degrees for studying journalism in America." There was a bite of condescension to the comment. But I ignored the remark. It was too important to keep Blakely on track. I laughed as good-naturedly as I could. "Yep, we colonials are a bit slow and need to be trained how to report," I said.

Blakely laughed back, apparently satisfied for the time being that I had no ulterior motives in my line of questioning.

"What I'm curious about, Chris," I resumed, "is how much of what you heard from Al-Jaffar is what he actually saw, and how much was what Husseini explained to him later he had really seen."
"You don't trust Husseini, do you?"

"Chris, it's not a question of trust. I've only met Husseini once. I have no experience of him to assess one way or another the reliability of his word. What's important in this story – and I'm sure you agree – is to decode what is reliably Al-Jaffar's account of what he was an eyewitness to and what Husseini later interpreted for him as what had actually happened."

"Yes, I see your point. Actually, I hadn't thought of that when we met with Husseini and Al-Jaffar on Sunday evening. I couldn't believe – and I'm extremely reluctant to accept now – that Husseini was inventing the atrocity story wholesale."

To cover up my own instinctive dislike of Husseini, I took another draft of the wine and asked Blakely, "What is this? It's awfully good."

"Actually it's South African. I know they've always had wonderful white wines – which we couldn't drink at all during the apartheid era because of the trade embargo on the country – but this Cape Cabernet Sauvignon is wonderfully mellow. But back to Husseini. Are you suggesting that he fed Al-Jaffar a story of what Husseini would like him to have seen and reported?"

"Oh Chris, you know as well as I do that people in this part of the world half the time don't know what they're looking at. The only thing I'm curious about is what Al-Jaffar told you he saw."

"You're like a ferret on this, aren't you?"

"Well, if what you heard from Al-Jaffar and Husseini the other night pans out, it's the biggest thing since Mohammed al-Dura."

Blakely grimaced. "Yes, French TV took a caning on that one."

"As they should have. But this is different. No one could remotely claim that you or Patrick constructed a completely fictitious scenario and then reported that as fact. Forgive me for inserting my interpretation, but since we don't seem to have any audio or visual corroboration, it may be Al-Jaffar and Husseini's word against anyone else's."

"Well, not just theirs. Patrick and I ran the story."

Turning towards Blakely, I for the first time saw signs of worry in his expression.

"I'm sorry," I resumed the questioning, "I've gotten a little distracted. Must be the Cape wine. Sorry to be such a nudnik, but did you hear from Al-Jaffar's own mouth that the Israelis – or one Israeli officer – executed three Palestinians lying on the ground."

There was a long pause.

"No. Husseini said that Al-Jaffar had phoned him and told him what he had just seen. He didn't say, 'The following are Al-Jaffar's exact words.'"

"Did Al-Jaffar go back to the bodies after the Israelis had left?"

"No. He said he was too scared of what might happen to him and so he phoned Husseini first thing."

I was a sufficiently experienced reporter to have developed an intuitive sense of when to back off on a certain line of questioning. Failure to do so at the right moment might provoke an interviewee into defensiveness and complete refusal to co-operate further. I sensed such a moment had come right now with Blakely. In fact, with the pause in the conversation, the Englishman thought he might actually be off the hook.

"Incidentally, wasn't Trish supposed to be coming to Israel around this time?"

I laughed loudly. "She was, and she is," I said. "God knows how I'll find time to do anything with her. The news in the place never leaves you in peace. And speaking of that news that we've been talking about, I've just got one more question. How on earth did Al-Jaffar, an obscure West Bank school teacher, have any connection with Husseini?"

"That's a very good question, and we asked Al-Jaffar that with Husseini there. Al-Jaffar said that he had recently been part of a Palestinian school teachers' group that met in Ramallah with education officials of the Palestinian Authority and Palestinian civic organizations. He'd met Husseini who'd given him his card. Al-Jaffar may have thought Husseini had connections to help him in his career. He didn't say that, but I surmised it."

I got up from the sofa and walked over to the balcony which looked out on the Knesset and the Valley of the Cross. Just below us across Ben Zvi Street was Sacher Park, which was usually thronged with Israelis picnicking or just relaxing. It was now completely empty. There were few cars moving back and forth, and Jerusalem was quiet except for an occasional ambulance siren racing in the distance. The sound of an ambulance siren was one that I, and Israeli Jerusalemites in general, dreaded hearing. Too often it meant that a Hamas suicide bomber had just blown himself up on a Jerusalem bus or at the entrance to a restaurant.

Behind me, Mahler was still playing and Blakely was helping himself to the last of the Cape red.

"Chris," I said, wandering back into the apartment, "a few things still puzzle me about this story. One is that no one has ever produced the bodies. Supposedly they were buried as soon as possible after the murders took place. That raises the question why the funerals were not public and indeed a major media event. If there's one thing the Palestinians like, it's an emotion-grabbing funeral of martyrs. Do you think this UN team is going to turn up anything stronger than what you and Patrick have already reported?"

That fleeting look of anxiety reappeared again on Blakely's face. "Well, I hope so, Rick. But I still have one question for you, if you don't mind. You say that you got back into your car and drove back to Jerusalem after the reinforcements arrived. How many soldiers were there in that group?"

"I'd say no more than fifteen to twenty and an officer, the one who wanted to see my ID."

"So you can't be sure that yet another group of soldiers didn't also arrive later and that therefore the group of soldiers who went up the hillside in search of the snipers was actually quite large."

"No, I'm satisfied that there were fewer than thirty in the search."

"How can you be so sure?"

"Because I talked later with one of the soldiers who was in the group that climbed the hillside." *That did it. I let Yossi out of the bag.*

"You did? How on earth did you get to him? It's almost impossible to get ordinary Israeli soldiers to talk about anything to us foreign hacks."

"Because my Israeli landlady had a nephew in the back-up unit that arrived on the scene and she persuaded him to talk to me."

Please, don't ask me about how we conversed.

"How many soldiers did he say went up the hill after the snipers?"

"Fewer than thirty."

"I suppose he had nothing to say about any executions."

"According to him, they didn't even find any bodies. They saw plenty of blood, but that was it."

"Phew! Could Husseini have sold us a bill of goods?"

"I don't know, Chris. All I know is that Al-Jaffar is no longer in the

West Bank or Jerusalem."

"Where is he?"

"He's apparently gone to ground in Gaza. Hamas is looking after him."

This time Blakely whistled loudly.

"Well, I'd better let Patrick know that. He's more up on this story than I am."

I felt another bolt of adrenaline in my stomach. I absolutely didn't want Cavenagh to know I'd gotten out of Blakely the information that Cavenagh had been unwilling to tell me.

"Well, that's fine, Chris, but sorry I can't stay for that conversation. I've got to make preparations for another short trip."

"Where to, if you don't mind my asking?"

"To Gaza."

VIII

I WAS EXHAUSTED after all the running around of the day before and slept later than I usually did: until nearly nine o'clock in the morning. It was already Friday; where had the week gone? So many different impressions had crowded in upon me in the past few days that my brain felt like one of those overloaded donkey carts I'd often seen Palestinians leading along roads in the West Bank and Gaza. I wanted to get to the bottom of the al-Jiffri massacre story. I had also found Rayna absolutely tantalizing, a sudden inruption in my cosmology of women. But now Yao had arrived, and would doubtless be calling me within a day or two to propose that we meet. Yao was extremely efficient with his information gathering and I knew that when we met again I'd be almost cross-examined on a host of topics that happened to interest him at that moment.

Then there was the nagging difficulty Karim had mentioned about his brother. I couldn't ignore that. Karim was just too decent to be left in the lurch with a brother unable even to visit their common mother without totally unreasonable delays. And now I had to think through a trip to Gaza.

I'd dreaded this. Cavenagh had been in and out of Gaza twice in the previous four months, but Blakely had avoided it like the plague ever since a BBC colleague had been held there for several weeks by kidnappers. I knew my boss, foreign editor Burton Lasch, would never ask me to go. I also knew that managing editor Reddaway would have seen Tom Corbett's piece on Hezbollah chief Nasrallah in *Newshour*. I could imagine the following conversation at one of *Epoch*'s Magazine editor's story conferences early in the week.

"Well, Burton, I see that *Newshour* has gotten to Nasrallah this week. Great story. Have we got anything in the works to match that?" Reddaway might have said with barely concealed malice.

"I think Ireton's working right now on that al-Jiffri massacre story. I don't doubt he'll come up with something very interesting," I imagined Lasch responding, to which Reddaway would probably retort, "Interesting? That's a good idea. We certainly don't want our correspondents to report things that are boring." That latter remark, I imagined, would be dripping with sarcasm. How the two men, Reddaway and Lash, could even work in the same building was a mystery to me. The rivalry they had engaged in for the three years that Reddaway had been ME (Managing Editor) was folklore not just within the corridors of *Epoch*, but throughout midtown Manhattan where the heavyweights of American news organizations were located. But I knew that Lasch was one very tough and experienced journalist. I didn't doubt that the eternal ping-pong match between them was as much a source of entertainment to the Boston-born Lasch as it was a source of annoyance to Reddaway, whose educational and cultural background was considered by some people to be "effete." His literary attainments were considerable – he'd written three well-reviewed biographies of James Joyce, Honore de Balzac, and Aldous Huxley – but he had arrived at the ME job at *Epoch* not by coming up through the ranks of writers and editors, but by being moved laterally from another magazine owned by the *Epoch Group*. That was *Urban Lifestyle*, not even a weekly, but a monthly that combined articles on trendy Manhattan restaurants with interviews and gossip about the Upper Midtown Manhattan social world. I had little respect for it and I remembered that many eyebrows had been raised in the corridors of the Epoch building when Reddaway had been given it.

Reddaway was curiously ambivalent about gumshoe reporting,

though some of the *Urban Lifestyle* reporters themselves needed to be virtual garbage-can sifters to keep up with the demand of the magazine for gossip. Reddaway had enough experience to know that painstaking, background reporting was essential for major news breakthroughs, but the details of it always bored him. Where Lasch almost always trumped Reddaway was, in fact, in the quality of reporting that his correspondents gave him. He was fiercely protective of the foreign desk component of *Epoch*, and his correspondents reciprocated that protection by being among the most competitive reporters in the business.

The phone – Reddaway's phone – which I often thought was the curse of my whole life suddenly snapped me into alertness by ringing by my bedside in my apartment in the German Colony. I'd been awake a few minutes, trying to plan in my mind how I would handle the various demands of the day.

It was Clarissa. "Rick, we've landed in Tel Aviv and we're about to head up to Galilee in a bus. This is so exciting – I've waited all my lifetime to come to Israel! I can't believe I'm here. It's so wonderful!" she burbled on. I tended to roll my eyes when I was at the receiving end of this gushing enthusiasm from evangelical Christians visiting Israel. But I liked Clarissa, even admired her in a strange way, and of course, where Clarissa was, Trish was not far behind.

Come to think of it, I felt rather miffed that it had been Clarissa who called me first, not Trish.

As if reading my thoughts through the phone, Clarissa was now saying, "Now I know you don't want to hear from a crabby old missionary like me" – and she laughed uproariously at her own joke – "and that the person you really want to talk to is a certain Filipina lady. Well, she's right here beside me. Here she is."

"Hi Rick." The low pitch of her voice always caught me by surprise. "We're a bit bushed from all the flying, but we're sure glad to be here."

"Hi, princess," I replied, genuinely thrilled now that Trish was in the same country. "How're you feeling?"

"Oh aching from the flight, and in need of a shower and all that stuff, but in good spirits. When do we see you?"

"Well, I think that's up to your schedule. When do you come up to Jerusalem?"

"Next Monday. We'll be in Galilee for the next few days."

"Trish, do you have a mobile phone that you can use here?"

"Of course, Rick. I can use my hotel mobile in any country in the world."

"It's the same number as the one I've used from here?"

"Of course. So we can keep in touch while the out-of-Jerusalem part of the tour is happening. Will you be in Jerusalem when we arrive next week?"

"Yes, but I'm heading out of town for a couple of days and won't be back until the weekend is almost gone."

"Where?"

"To Gaza."

"To Gaza! Isn't that incredibly dangerous? Don't they kidnap journalists there, even kill them sometimes?"

"Well, some bad things have happened. But I think in this case the bad guys will realize that it's an advantage to have me come there and let me return unharmed."

"How can you be so sure?"

"Well, to be honest, you can't be absolutely sure of anything in this part of the world. But the story I am working on is something they ought to want to have reported."

"Trish, Trish, we've got to board the bus now." It was Clarissa's voice shouting in the background.

"Very quickly, can I share the Gaza travel with Clarissa?"

"Of course, princess. I'll probably need her prayers."

"And mine. Bye, handsome."

"Handsome." She'd never called me this before and my head spun a little because of it.

"Bye. And enjoy."

The presence of Trish in Israel both excited me and made me uncomfortable. I couldn't develop any kind of friendship with Rayna while Trish was around. On the other hand, the presence of Trish made me conscious of the fact that I didn't really have the right to develop *anything* with Rayna. Rayna was confusing to me. She was a definite asset in my news-gathering, but she also presented something new and unexpected in my life: a female interest that absolutely rivaled Trish, but at the same time promised plenty of danger.

Thinking of Rayna reminded me of Yoram Messinger who was clearly behind Rayna. I decided I'd call the defense minister now, before getting to the bureau.

I punched in the number, and it rang exactly once.

"Messinger," responded a curt, low-pitched voice.

"Mr. Minister, it's Richard Ireton of *Epoch*. I'm calling you on this line only because it's a matter of some importance and I am heading out of town quite soon."

"Go ahead, Rick."

So far, so good. At least he wasn't barking back on the phone that he was too busy to talk.

"Mr. Minister, we have a Palestinian stringer working for *Epoch* called Karim Nasr. He's a good reporter and I've always found him to play the news straight. He's got a brother— "

"I know about Nasr," Messinger interrupted brusquely. "He's a reasonable man."

Know about Nasr? Does the Defense Minister of Israel have taps on the phones of every Palestinian working for a foreign news organization?

I decided not to pursue this line but to get straight to the point. "Well," I went on, "Karim's got a sick mother who lives in Hebron and a brother who's a physician in Ramallah. Karim says his brother needs seven hours to get through all the checkpoints to visit his mother. Do you by any chance have a "fast-track" procedure for certain Palestinians?"

"We do, and I'll get it fixed today. Have Karim come to the IDF spokesman's office in Jerusalem tomorrow morning and we'll give the pass to him to give to his brother. Anything else?"

I was bewildered. I couldn't imagine a defense minister responding to such a personal request so quickly.

"No, sir."

"How's the Al-Jiffri story going?"

This was awkward. It was one thing to be the messenger of bureaucratic benevolence to the brother of a fellow-journalist, but quite another to share reporting details with a senior member of a foreign government.

"I'm working on it, sir."

"I expect you'll be going to Gaza at some point."

How does he know that? For that matter, how should I respond to that statement – it wasn't really a question – by Messinger?

"Why Gaza?" I asked feebly, once again regretting the foolishness of the response as soon as it was out of my mouth.

There was a brief, cynical laugh at the other end of the line. "Well, you know," said the defense minister, "that we follow these things as closely as you people do, perhaps more closely sometimes."

"Yes, sir. And yes, I will be going to Gaza."

"I thought so. Good luck. You will need it. Now I have to go. Goodbye."

"Goodbye, sir."

Well, one good deed for the day: Karim's brother could now get to Hebron a lot faster than before. He'd still have to go through the checkpoints, but with the Israeli Defense Ministry special pass, each stop might take only a few minutes now. Karim himself didn't need a pass because of his American passport, but his brother would certainly benefit from it.

But what was the "good luck" all about? I found this faintly disconcerting. I decided to call Karim and give him the good news.

"Rick, how did you do that?" Karim asked over the phone in amazement when I called him.

"Don't ask. I happened to come across a useful phone number a few days ago, and I used it. Let's leave it at that."

"Well, whatever you did, a thousand thanks. I'll give the pass to Ibrahim tomorrow. It'll be in time for him to go to Hebron this weekend."

"Fine, Karim, but just remember that the IDF spokesman's office closes up tight in Jerusalem at noon on Friday in time for everyone to get home by Shabbat. I'd hate for you to have to let it slide until Sunday. Now, can I meet with you to discuss my Gaza trip?"

"Can we do that in a couple of hours or more? I've got to take Leila to a doctor's appointment."

"Fine. Let's meet in the bureau at 1.00 pm. I'll bring a sandwich for you."

"No, don't do that. Leila makes the best sandwiches between Tel Aviv and Amman. I'll bring one she made."

"Suit yourself. Bye."

But it wasn't fine. I knew that it could take two and a half hours from Jerusalem to any destination in Gaza by the time you had cleared all the Israeli checkpoints at the Erez crossing point, an ominously fortified pedestrian walkway between Israel proper and Gaza. Once at the border, I'd have to leave the Subaru on the Israeli side, make the crossing on foot, and pick up a car in Gaza on the other side. With a lot of luck, Karim could arrange something. Without luck, it would be a Gaza taxi. I'd done this a couple of times since arriving in Jerusalem, and I always found it creepy. UN and other internationally recognized vehicles were allowed to pass through the checkpoint into Gaza by the Israelis, but with private cars it was hit and miss. They might let you through, or they might stop you for a long interview with you. I thought it was simply easier to take the pedestrian route.

I showered and got dressed, was hastily fixing some scrambled eggs when my cell phone rang. It was Rayna. I thought quickly.

"Thanks so much for getting that belt engraved so quickly – overnight, in fact."

"Did you like it? I really want you to wear it. Perhaps it will be good luck for you."

"Good luck? Is it from a sacred cow or something? And by the way, I am wearing it."

Rayna roared with laughter at the other end of the line at this.

"Oh, you can be very witty sometimes. No, not a sacred cow. But who knows, a cow that, had it gone on living, might have followed you around affectionately."

Where is she going with all this? I thought. *This is a little strange at 10.00 a.m. on a Thursday morning.*

"Don't worry, Rayna, it's very elegant and I'm only too happy to wear it."

"I've followed bits and pieces on the Al-Jiffri story, and I thought that sooner or later you'd be traveling to Gaza. I think you should be very careful there. Your friend Mr. Husseini showed up in Gaza last night."

"My friend? Hardly. How do you know that?"

"Don't ask." *Now the shoe is on someone else's foot.* "What I mean is, Mr. Husseini is more complicated than you think. Let me just leave it at that. Anyway, take good care of yourself. Gaza can be a turbulent place."

"Turbulent? I think the right word is insane."

"You're right. Anyway, I look forward to dinner when you are next in Tel Aviv. Good luck, Rick."

She hung up. It was beginning to unsettle me deeply. First the Israeli Defense Minister and then Rayna had specifically cautioned me about how dangerous Gaza was. I didn't know whether Messinger had relayed to Rayna the details of his conversation with me – probably not – but Rayna presumably drank from the same information source as her boss.

Just a little irritable now, because I hated to receive warnings without any specific details to back them up, I grouchily and noisily loped downstairs to the Subaru parked on the street. I passed Esther coming up the stairs and greeted her as cheerfully as I could. I saw that she stopped to watch me head down the last flights.

Infuriatingly, the traffic was much heavier than usual. The journey by car, which normally took no more than fifteen minutes – on a good day, ten minutes – lasted exactly half an hour this time. There seemed to be more tourist buses than usual. I wondered if a large visiting Jewish group from the US might be in town. I also noticed a higher security presence than usual, always the sign that important visitors were in Israel and that, probably, they were going to be addressed at some convention or other by the Israeli Prime Minister.

At the bureau Margaret, sensitive as ever to her boss's moods, avoided chatter that might have grated on me. Matter-of-factly, she went over the Hebrew newspaper news and then added the bureau news of the day. Ira was going to be in the Knesset today doing that political story. Rafi, she thought I'd be interested to know, had been following a story from *Ha'aretz* about the funding of the Palestine El Quds Center. "It seems some Tel Aviv bank has been getting huge checks for them from somewhere in the Gulf," she explained.

"Rafi's working on that? I thought he presumed every Palestinian organization was working to inaugurate Nirvana in the Middle East and every IDF soldier was potentially a mass murderer, at least *was* already a mass murderer only it hadn't been proved yet." Margaret thought this very funny, as did Benjamin Lifshutz who was heading out of the bureau to photograph the Prime Minister speaking somewhere.

"Who's the group clogging the streets of Jerusalem?" I asked him just as he was halfway out the door.

"Oh, it's the New York and Los Angeles grandees of the Israel Bonds. The Prime Minister missed them on his US itinerary this year, so the mountain came to Mohammed."

"Are there that many grandees?" I asked. Lifshutz grinned.

"How many grains of sand make up Mohammed's mountain?" he quipped. Everyone laughed. Lifshutz left the bureau and I went to my office.

There were memos from *Epoch* in New York to digest and quite a lot of mail that I hadn't previously attended to. I'd missed last month's payment date for the Mastercard I generally used and they'd charged me a late fee of twenty-nine dollars. That was irritating.

I made quicker progress responding to bills and mail than I'd anticipated, and my sour mood gradually began to lift. Trish had called again from a rest stop on her way to the hotel in Tiberias, the first stop on their Galilee tour, and that had cheered me up. But something she said gave me pause.

"Rick," she said, "I've been thinking and praying about this Gaza trip of yours. Can it be postponed? I feel a real heaviness about it."

Another of Macbeth's witches? I was beginning to get really irritated by the number of people who seemed to be worried about my imminent visit to Gaza. I restrained my temper when responding to Trish.

"Have you told Clarissa yet?"

"Of course. She's been doing nothing but pray ever since I informed her. We've hardly had ten words of conversation on the bus."

"Well, does she think I'll be all right?" It was a rash question, but I had become emboldened by so many of the Job's comforters who'd wanted to warn me.

"Yes, she does. But she says you may encounter serious difficulties there."

"Goodness, everyone I've talked to this morning seems spooked by my plans to visit Gaza. You'd almost think I'm the only one who hasn't noticed the stain on my shirt."

"Rick, don't make fun of Clarissa. She really hears from God."

I was tempted to roll my eyes at this. It was God-talk that frustrated me because it was so far outside my own experience. I'd come to trust Clarissa's sincerity and experience as what she called a "prayer-warrior." But in spite of my several-month romance with Trish and the many references in her emails to spiritual experiences, I wasn't comfortable around people who talked in language that suggested they'd been instructed in it by the Almighty himself.

"I don't doubt, Trish. But please bear in mind that I'm an unreconstructed agnostic for whom this God-talk isn't always easy to take. I respect your faith and I respect Clarissa's. Indeed, I've seen it at work. But I'm not in the same place that you are, and I'm certainly not where Clarissa is."

There was a long silence at the other end of the line. Then, ever so faintly, I thought I heard the sound of Trish sobbing. It stung me to the quick. I'd fluffed my lines again and it mortified me. Trish was just too precious to treat lightly.

"Trish, I'm so sorry. I've hurt you with these hobnail boots of my skepticism. Just make allowances for me as a hard-boiled hack, trying to make sense of an extremely complicated and at many times very inhospitable world. Believe me, when going to a place like Gaza now that it's controlled by Hamas, I am not above asking for your prayers of protection. And Clarissa's. Especially Clarissa's. She seems to have some hotline to heaven."

Now Trish laughed through her tears. "She does, I know. But I think you ought to know too that I'm more than just someone who prays for you. I really care for your safety. I really care for *you*. I love you."

"I know you do, Trish, just as you know I love you."

"When are you setting off?"

"For Gaza?"

"Yes."

"This afternoon, as soon as I can get from Karim all the details I need."

"Well, go with God. Our prayers will be constant behind you."

"Thanks, Trish. Enjoy Galilee. I love you and…God bless you."

I'd never said that to anyone before. It sounded strange, but also rather comforting.

I hung up a bare minute before the buzzer on my desk phone rang again.

"Rick, Karim's here."

"Thanks, Margaret. Send him in."

Karim almost bounded into the room with a grin from ear-to-ear on his face. I guessed why it was there.

"Rick, I picked up the checkpoint pass for Ibrahim at the IDF spokesman's office this morning. Thank you so much. When I called my mother about it she asked me to express her very warmest gratitude to you. Ibrahim is absolutely thrilled."

"Well, I hope it works the way it's supposed to. I'd like to hear from you how Ibrahim gets along the next time he goes to Hebron."

I decided to risk the coffee shop of the Plaza for some coffee. I badly wanted a *latte*, partly because I had been late getting up and suspected that, physically speaking, I still wasn't firing on all cylinders. Karim ordered an ice-coffee. I sipped my latte greedily.

"I've made arrangements for you to be picked up on the other side of the Erez crossing into Gaza by a driver I usually call on during trips to Gaza," Karim began right away.

"The man you should call when you are in the city of Gaza is Hasan Madani. He's an aide to the Hamas Interior Minister. I'm pretty sure it's the Interior Ministry that's looking after Al-Jaffar. Mention me by name and make it clear that you are looking into the al-Jiffri story and want to interview Al-Jaffar. It might be a good idea to say that you've discussed this with Christopher Blakely. They trust the BBC, and of course Patrick Cavenagh and *News Report*."

"Do you think Cavenagh's been down there yet?"

"I don't think so. But he may have sent one of the younger British reporters hungry for a scoop as a glorified stringer. The unknown quantity is Husseini. I think he's there. I had the impression from the other day that he didn't take to you so readily, and Cavenagh may have poisoned the well there too. I've heard via the grapevine that Husseini's in with the *Ikhwan*."

"The Mohammed Brotherhood itself?" I translated the fuller Arabic phrase, *al-ikhwan al-muslimun*, the "brotherhood of Muslims," the name of the most influential yet secretive of all the Muslim radical groups; the Muslim Brotherhood, founded in Egypt by the school teacher Hassan al-Banna. "But I thought that Hamas was simply the Palestinian wing of the Muslim Brotherhood?"

"It was, and it is. But Husseini's connection with the Muslim Brotherhood started in Jordan, so his links are with the Brotherhood outside of the Hamas connection."

"What's the significance of that, and why, if Husseini really is in Gaza, has he gone there?" I didn't want to let Karim know that I'd heard of Husseini's Gaza visit from other sources – from Rayna.

"I think Husseini's a much bigger fish than he lets on. I wouldn't be surprised if Palestine-El Quds was a political front for Hamas here in East Jerusalem and on the West Bank."

"But Husseini doesn't *look* like an Islamist, and as far as I can tell, he doesn't act like one either. He's clean-shaven, wears rather expensive suits, even eats with the infidels at places where they serve liquor, like the Adelphia. How could someone like him be a big-shot with Hamas?"

"Don't under estimate the Islamists," Karim said, looking serious. "They may be pious Muslims, but they're also ruthless power-players. Husseini wouldn't be taken seriously on the West Bank and East Jerusalem if he were a conspicuous-looking Islamist. Indeed, he might even be physically attacked if he looked too much like a Hamas partisan. Fatah is still strong here, a lot stronger than Hamas for now. He can't afford to alienate people at this stage."

"So he's a cunning dissimulator," I said, half to myself.

"Dissimulator? What's that?" Karim asked, unfamiliar with the English term.

"Someone who pretends to be something or somebody he isn't."

There was an awkward silence between the two of us for a moment. I broke it.

"Karim," I resumed, "Who else do you suggest I see apart from Madani?"

"See whoever is willing to talk to you. I wouldn't venture off the beaten track of Hamas officialdom, if I were you. If they produce Al-Jaffar for you, that alone will have made the trip worthwhile." Then he looked at me with a strange expression on his face, a look that combined warmth and concern. Once again, I felt uncomfortable.

"Well, this isn't getting me any closer to Gaza," I said briskly, trying to cover my self-consciousness. "I'd better set off right now. Look, will you save me a lot of trouble by phoning Madani up and asking if he'll be willing to see me later this afternoon? Give me the number and I'll call to confirm my arrival as soon as I have passed through the Erez checkpoint. What was the name of that driver you organized for me in Gaza?"

"Butrus Rahman."

"Butrus? I've never heard that Arabic first name before."

"It's from the New Testament. It's the Arabic for Peter."

"You mean one of the disciples?"

"Exactly. Incidentally, he's not only a driver, he's a fixer too. He knows his way round Gaza and ought to be able to talk himself – and you – out of any awkward situations."

"Well, thanks, Karim. I'm not exactly on the lookout for awkward situations in Gaza."

I paid the bill and we walked back to the bureau. Margaret's eyebrows almost reached the ceiling when I walked in with Karim.

"So, you're really going to Gaza? My word." The polite English expression concealed a multitude of thoughts, ranging from amazement that I would do this to sympathy that I was going ahead with the plan. At this point, Benjamin Lifshutz came out of his office, loaded down as usual with camera equipment.

"There's been some kind of military confrontation between Israeli soldiers and Palestinian Authority police on the outskirts of Ramallah," he said, rushing out. "Apparently it's still going on."

"How do you know?" I asked. Nobody had called me on my cell phone – my original one – and Karim apparently didn't know anything about it.

"Oh, I have my sources," he said with a broad grin, great crow's-feet of good humor spreading out from his eyes in his tanned, wrinkled face. Karim watched him leave, amazed.

"Benjamin seems to find things out before they've even happened. No wonder he always gets such good pictures," he said after Lifshutz was out of earshot.

I shook hands with him, thanked him for all his help, and as casually as I could, said goodbye to Margaret. I wanted to make it appear as though the trip to Gaza would be no different from a trip to the IDF spokesman's office in Beit Agron.

But as I entered the underground garage to get my car, I felt anything but casual. There was a sort of heaviness, reminiscent of that terrible afternoon years ago in Grand Rapids when I'd come home from high school, seen an ambulance and police car in the driveway, and understood instantly what had happened. My brother, Calvin, after years of threats to end it all, after years of therapy, of treatment for depression, of medication, had finally done what he'd so often said he would do; he'd taken his own life. He'd been able to do it, moreover, because my own father, in a moment of supreme carelessness, had not locked up his shotgun after an afternoon's skeet-shooting with chums from work.

The gun had been left in the garage, in the back of the family sedan. It was in the trunk, not on the backseat. Someone who wanted to take it would have to know it was there. Calvin knew that his dad had gone skeet-shooting, sensed with the devil's knowledge that the gun had not been secured, and went into the garage immediately after coming home from one of his frequent walkabouts, one of the least damaging of the means to raise himself out the depths of despair. He'd entered the car by the driver's side, popped the trunk from the front seat, gotten out again, gone back, and taken the gun. There were even some shells carelessly lying on the carpet in the trunk near the gun. The adolescent, who had been plagued by black moods for much of his life, didn't even bother to go to his room and take his life in privacy. He'd shot himself standing up, between the car and the workbench at the end of the garage. It had taken forever to scrub the blood-stains off the car, the bench, and the floor. One slip-up by my dad; an end for all time of my brother.

Feeling this gloomy mood steal over me, I was momentarily drawn back to precise memories of the day of Calvin's death. I knew that, for the present, the heaviness had been induced by all the warnings to "be careful" in Gaza, by all the Job's comforters, all those well-meaning folk who seemed to take pleasure in reminding me what a dangerous place

Gaza was. Checking in the trunk for the overnight kit I always kept for unexpected overnight stays, the mere process of routine preparations helped partly to restore my normal cheerfulness. After all, if I got to Al-Jaffar and took down his story, it would not only be a scoop but one of the biggest scoops of the year in Israel. It pleased me particularly that if I managed to squeeze out of Al-Jaffar the information – which I suspected to be the case – that Al-Jaffar at most had seen some Israeli soldiers searching the hillside, never seen any Palestinian lying on the ground, and certainly never seen an actual execution taking place, it would be something I could stuff into Patrick Cavenagh's pipe for Patrick to smoke. I was no less offended by instances of Israeli heavy-handedness and sometimes thuggishness towards the Palestinians than Cavenaugh was; it's just that there was enough real evidence of that floating around not to need sheer fabrication.

I popped the trunk, momentarily remembering that this had been one of Calvin's last actions, confirmed that my carefully packed overnight bag was in the right place. I'd gotten into the habit of having one ready in my car trunk since arriving in Israel. You never knew when a story would force you to stay somewhere overnight, or even to take a sudden trip to some more remote part of Israel – though nothing was *that* remote in a country the size of New Jersey – for an ongoing story. There had even been times when I'd taken a brief trip to Cyprus or to Amman in Jordan following something up. I had never been a boy scout, but it was always useful to be prepared.

Once on a previous trip to Gaza I'd taken Benjamin Lifshutz with me. Benjamin was the perfect travel companion because he'd seen almost everything that had happened in Israel since independence in 1948 and was always calm and resourceful. He was also not only a supremely professional photographer but a man who could charm, if needed, an angry bear and persuade it to pose placidly in front of its cubs. Benjamin was especially helpful when deep in Palestinian areas. His ginning good humor and his genuine affection for children won him friends everywhere. A few times, his presence had smoothed ruffled Palestinian feathers in sensitive and potentially explosive situations. I would have loved to bring him on this trip, but I knew that having a photographer around might make Hamas officials especially nervous and certainly would completely spook Al-Jaffar. I'd brought my own digital camera in case an opportunity for photographs presented itself.

I drove out of Jerusalem the usual way to get to Gaza, initially on the freeway to Tel Aviv. I turned off the freeway to move south through Bet Shemesh, and then turned right again to approach the coast at Ashkelon. On the way, I soothed my nerves by listening to a cricket match on the BBC. If eleven grown men clad in white long pants could spend hours at a time crouched in general proximity to two others, similarly-clad, but holding funny-looking wooden bats, while two umpires in white coats looking like lab technicians from a pharmaceutical corporation stood at perpendicular or parallel positions to a field – the Brits and others who played it called it a "pitch" – in which two pairs of polished wooden sticks were stuck into the grass – the Brits called them "stumps" – for hours at a time; then, the human race was not completely lost to insanity. I loved the incomprehensible, but oddly soothing terminology of radio and TV cricket commentators, often delivered in a rich, English West Country accent or even an Australian drawl: "Pads it down to silly mid-off as though not quite sure of the bowler's pace," or, "That was a wild no-ball to Higgins that he barely flicked at with his bat before the umpire's call could be heard," or, "An elegant response to Howland's googly with a sweeping on-drive that was just low enough to keep from being caught out." *Epoch's* London bureau chief had once taken me to Lord's cricket field in London and tried to explain some of the esoteric peculiarities of the game. I remembered with a smile an AP colleague's anecdote of being told by the New York editors to "never mess with the cricket copy on the wire, because no one understands it anyway."

With the soothing cricket commentary in the background, the drive to the Gaza border went surprisingly quietly. I now saw that the Erez crossing point was just a few hundred yards ahead of me. I noticed how heavily fortified it was; countless numbers of suicide-bomb terrorists had been caught coming through there, and some had detonated their explosive vests before they could be searched by Israeli guards. The Israelis had thus developed a complicated array of walkways and inspection points that made entering or leaving Gaza similar to going in and out of a maximum security prison. No wonder the Palestinians living in Gaza often described themselves as living in a gigantic prison. But I had also met in Israel enough relatives of the victims of successful bombings to know that, cruel though the security measures seemed, whenever they failed to prevent a terrorist bombing, there was an appalling human cost to pay. Whose rights prevailed? Israel's to protect its citizenry, or the Palestinians' to live in genuine freedom? It was always a harsh choice to make.

The pedestrian traffic through the crossing was lighter than usual by the time I had parked my car in a designated lot and approached the first checkpoints. As usual, I produced both my US passport and my Israeli government press pass. The Israeli soldiers, looking bored, waved me through. My spirits now lifted a lot. If only the entire Gaza trip could be as similarly uneventful.

As I exited the checkpoint on the Palestinian side, Palestinian Authority officials – watched over by bearded Hamas security police – paid closer attention to my documentation than the Israelis had. I assumed the friendliest smile that I could in submitting to them my documents for examination. It seemed to work. The Palestinians grinned back; they knew, after all, that Western reporters entering Gaza were almost always more sympathetic to the Palestinian cause than to Israel.

Butrus Rahman was standing helpfully as close to the Palestinian checkpoint of entry into Gaza as it was permitted to come. He held a large white board with the letters on it, "I-R-E-L-A-N-D." I grinned as he approached and extended his hand. "It's close enough," I chuckled to myself.

THE DRIVER KARIM had arranged for me was short, middle-aged, and had a stubbly beard on his chin. His skin was unusually dark for a Palestinian, and I wondered if he had any Sudanese or Egyptian blood in his veins; many Gazans did, from the time Gaza had been under Egyptian control, from 1949 until the Six-Day War in 1967. He was wearing what seemed to me to be a tattered brown suit of rather heavy material, though the striped shirt beneath it had no tie. "Bleezed to meet you," said Butrus, also extending his hand for a warm shake and exposing a missing tooth in the front of his mouth.

"How is Garim? He's very nice man. I like Garim," said Butrus as we walked back to his dented, rather ancient-looking Renault with Butrus carrying my overnight case. "Last time he is in Gaza, Garim help my boy get into school. Garim is very nice man."

I was reassured by this initial exchange with Butrus. I agreed, of course, that Karim was a man of great kindness and integrity. I knew that it would be a waste of time trying to explain this to Butrus, whose English was okay for very simple tasks but quite lacked the depth to cope with any abstract terms such as "integrity."

In the car, as we negotiated Gaza's crowded streets – rickety belching trucks, donkey carts, noisy and polluting scooters, idle groups of men sitting around playing chequers – and despite the heat and the dust entering the car through the open windows, I felt myself relax even more. With people like Butrus working with me in Gaza, I thought I'd be pretty safe. From out of the partly open window I saw several groups of serious-looking people clad in black and wearing beards, either standing in knots on the sidewalk, AK-47 rifles hanging around their chests, or casting intimidating glances from the backs of trucks. They were, essentially, the thugs who had taken over Gaza since the summer of 2007, the "Executive Force" of Hamas, the enforcers of everything from political conformity to ever-tighter restrictions on permissible clothing for women and teenagers. I knew that they'd even disrupted at least one Palestinian wedding reception and beaten up the bridegroom because he had been playing music. Music is a serious sin for some strict Muslims.

Karim had arranged that my first call in Gaza would be on the Hamas official Hasan Madani who, Karim felt sure, probably knew where Al-Jaffar was and had the authority to put me in touch with him. In a mobile phone conversation I had driving down from Jerusalem, Karim had briefed me. "You probably have one shot at this," he said. "If you don't get through to Al-Jaffar after the meeting with Hasan Madani, I advise you not to try through any other official. Hamas bureaucrats can be quite unpleasant if they feel you are trying to make an end-run around them. On the other hand, they can sometimes be much more forthcoming than Fatah when it comes to contacts with journalists. Madani works for the Interior Minister Ahmed Sayyid and is probably in on most of the Interior Ministry decision-making.

"Don't underestimate Hamas," he continued. "They are not as worldly and as familiar with Western thinking as all those Fatah people you met a few months ago, but they are dedicated, ruthless, and rather clever. Good luck."

It would have been sound enough advice even if I didn't have one promising-sounding direct contact. I hoped to heaven that I wouldn't have to spend the night in the city and hang around for another morning, perhaps even an afternoon, too. I really disliked Gaza. It was not just because the city had become so dangerous to Western reporters – particularly to Americans and Brits – it was because the city itself was so squalid. "The armpit of the Middle East" was the phrase some grumpy

British journalist had used to describe Gaza. Unfortunately, in my view it was entirely accurate. On the way to the Interior Ministry building, I called the number for Madani that Karim had given me and spoke to a male assistant. Amazingly, or so it seemed to me, the man appeared to know that I would be coming. Karim had prepared the ground.

Butrus pulled up in front of a distinctly modern-looking office building on Al-Rasheed Street, parallel to the Mediterranean. There were the same knots of black-clad young men in beards standing in front of it on the sidewalk, and they acted as well-schooled doormen do when a celebrity limo arrives, rushing to the edge of the curb and opening the passenger door almost before the car had stopped. I got out and smiled as pleasantly as I could.

"Who have you come to see?" asked one of the young men in excellent English.

"I have an appointment with Interior Ministry official Mr. Hasan Madani."

"At what time?"

"He said to visit him as soon as I arrived in Gaza."

"Please enter the building and show identification at the reception desk," the man continued, never smiling. "They will inform Mr. Madani that you have arrived."

It seemed a cumbersomely redundant set of directions to me: obviously I'd have to identify myself on entering the building, and obviously they'd phone ahead from the lobby to Madani's office to let him know that I had arrived. Inside the lobby of the building, someone had given orders to make it clear that Hamas was now in charge, not Fatah, the secular Palestinian organization that had been the central group in the PLO but had been overthrown – with many of its officials murdered brutally – defeated in a violent coup by Hamas in June of 2007. Huge banners hung from the ceiling showing pictures of Sheikh Ahmed Yassin, the nearly blind paraplegic who'd been the founder of Hamas in 1987 and had been assassinated in a strike by an Israeli helicopter gunship in 2004.

As I stood gazing at them, a helpful man behind the main reception desk told me that the slogans all said, "Remember the Sheikh."

I politely thanked the man for his help and identified myself with my passport. The man picked up the phone and spoke in Arabic to someone at the other end.

"Please go up to Mr. Madani's office on the fourth floor," he said to me on putting the phone down. "The elevator is behind you."

"Thank you." I turned around and walked towards two elevators side-by-side, just as the doors opened. I was the only person to get on and quickly arrived at the fourth floor. Madani's office turned out to be at the end of a longish corridor leading away from the elevators. There was an air of brisk activity along the corridor, with people coming and going out of offices that led off from it. The official who'd answered the phone while I was still in Butrus' car was standing at the entrance of the office waiting for me.

He extended his arm and I noticed it had a limp and clammy feel to it as we shook hands. "Madani," he said simply, and I responded, "Richard Ireton." Although there was air-conditioning in the building the man, a surprisingly corpulent fellow probably in his forties, was perspiring heavily. He wore a white shirt, buttoned at the collar but without tie, like an Iranian diplomat, and I was surprised at how clean the shirt was and how well pressed. His shoes also looked a lot more expensive than most people's shoes in Gaza. I wondered what connections he had in order to dress himself so fastidiously.

Madani led me past another reception desk to an inner office that looked out over the city. In the distance you could clearly see through the window the Mediterranean sparkling in the late afternoon sun.

I was invited to sit down and was almost immediately offered a small cup of thick Arabic coffee, which I took gratefully. Most Americans, I had found, couldn't stomach the concentrated taste of the thick Arabic coffee, which was almost always served heavily sweetened and flavored with a touch of cardomon. I loved it and was always grateful when it was offered to me. This time, the scent of cardomon was apparent.

"Mr. Nasr phoned me and said that you wanted to see me," Madani began after inviting me to sit down on the one chair in the room that faced his desk and the chair behind it in which he was sitting. His rather heavily overweight body was surmounted by a round, smooth face. There was the beginning of what would probably eventually be a full beard on his chin. Around his eyes there were big, dark circles that made him look almost raccoon-like. He appeared to have been sleep-deprived for some time previously. Perhaps he had been. His English was good enough to suggest that he'd been around fluent English speakers quite a lot. I didn't think he'd spent any time living in an English-speaking country. There was just a hint of hesitation in his speech patterns, as though he were carefully putting together his syntax.

"How can I help you?" he began. I was a little perplexed by one of his eyes that seemed to wander without co-ordination with the other. I was confused at which eye to look at when speaking to him.

"I thought you might be able to help me in my investigation of the al-Jiffri incident," I began, delicately. I hoped earnestly that Madani knew nothing more about me than that I was *Epoch*'s bureau chief in Jerusalem, but I secretly doubted that was all he knew.

"You know, of course," he quickly replied, "that the Israeli soldiers shot three Palestinians in cold blood after they had already given up and surrendered? We are waiting for the UN team to come and investigate it fully."

"I saw most of the TV reports and read most of the newspaper stories," I said levelly. "I've also talked to Mr. Blakely of the BBC about it, and I know Mr. Patrick Cavenagh quite well. I think you may have a very strong case to bring before the world." This was a lie; I doubted whether they had a case at all. I felt a small twinge of conscience as I made the comment. "I know that my editors would like to see the whole truth fully exposed." *This much was true.* I paused, wondering if I should jump in with the request for an Al-Jaffar interview immediately or allow the conversation to lead around to the school teacher in a more serpentine way. I decided to proceed slowly. A modest amount of personal candor, I thought, might soften up this bureaucrat. I volunteered that I had been in the region only for six months, was still learning the ins and outs of the situation, and was eager to be corrected in any of my judgments. This wasn't really a lie. I was genuinely open to having my views changed on any matter involving Israel and the Palestinians. It was just that I was willing to allow Madani to believe that I might be "corrected" by him, which wasn't the case at all. As I quietly told him just a little of my various reporting experiences in Israel and the Palestinian territories, Madani's left eye seemed to make a tour of the whole room before, ever so briefly, returning to focus on my face.

"I've heard many stories of the difficulties faced by Palestinians with the Israelis" – this was true – I went on, wondering how long I needed to continue buttering him up, "and certainly this story puts most of those in the shade. My magazine is eager to take the lead in reporting this story."

Madani looked at me piercingly with his right eye, a deep brown, strangely hooded instrument of vision amid the dark circle that surrounded it. The left eye continued to wander off in all directions.

"Please excuse me just a moment," he said. He got up and went into another small office adjoining his main one. The door closed behind him, and soon afterwards I heard a phone conversation in Arabic. It wasn't loud enough for me to grasp, with my very limited Arabic, what was being said. Besides, I really only understood people who spoke classical Arabic slowly. I couldn't for the life of me follow an ordinary conversation taking place in front of me. Behind the closed door, I heard Madani raise his voice slightly once or twice before the phone conversation ended.

When he returned to his chair behind the desk, he was smiling slightly. The left eye, mysteriously, fell into co-ordinated movement with the right one.

"I am authorized to tell you," he said rather stiffly after rather fussily making himself comfortable in his chair, "that the school teacher who witnessed the al-Jiffri atrocity is in Gaza now. Also, the Interior Ministry has decided that you will be permitted to interview him, if you wish."

Jackpot. I couldn't believe my luck. I almost leaped from my seat. I wanted to pump Madani's hand in gratitude, but I was also as alert as a buck in hunting season that dangers were all around me.

"When might it be possible to meet with Mr. Al-Jaffar?" I asked unctuously. *Let it be today, please let it be today!*

"It will not be possible until tomorrow morning. Also, it will be necessary for you to share the interview with a foreign diplomat who has also asked to visit Mr. Al-Jaffar. I think you will understand that many people want to hear Mr. Al-Jaffar's story and we cannot accommodate everyone, certainly not individually. Also, we have decided not to have a press conference with Mr. Al-Jaffar yet. Our most immediate concern is for his security, and we do not think conditions are ripe yet for such a public presentation. But do not worry," Madani continued, as if about to announce a major concession in the arrangements, "You will be the first journalist to meet with Mr. Al-Jaffar in Gaza, and the diplomat who will also be at the interview is not a journalist. I know that beating the competition is very important to you Western reporters." He thought this uproariously funny and as he said these words the left eye was darting all over the room. "You will not have to compete with the diplomat." He smiled smugly, as though he'd conferred a great favor on me. "Please be ready to be here at 10.00 a.m. tomorrow. Now is there anything else I can do for you?"

I said no, there wasn't. As quickly and as politely as I could thank him, I got up from the chair and left the office. I found Butrus in the lobby of the building chatting cheerfully with two of the Executive Force guards who had been standing on the sidewalk when the Renault drove up. Obviously, he'd found a safe place to park the car. Butrus gave me a gap-toothed grin as I approached. "Where you want to go now?" he asked.

"I have another meeting here tomorrow morning," I said, "so I would like to find a hotel in Gaza to stay overnight." I tried hard to conceal my deep disappointment that staying overnight in Gaza would even

173

be necessary. "Let's try the Grand Palace Hotel, please, Butrus. Do you think there will be room there?"

"No broblem. Gaza has not many visitors now. There are many hotel rooms, but not so many visitors."

Over Butrus' shoulder I glanced at the glass entrance door to the building. What I saw suddenly made my blood freeze. It was Abdul Husseini walking into the building.

I had nothing in my hand to cover my face, but I turned my back on the glass door so abruptly that Butrus, whom I was facing, was startled. *What to do now? Think quickly.* I bent down, my back low and rendering me not quite as noticeable, pretending to have a sudden problem with my right shoelace. I thought that if I kept my head down for a few seconds, Husseini might pass by without even seeing me. But Butrus had started his conversation near the reception desk, and it was clear that Husseini would have to approach the desk to announce himself to whomever he was going to visit in the building. I hoped desperately that it would not be Madani.

As I continued to fiddle with the lace for longer than would have seemed reasonable to most people, Husseini came up to the desk less than ten feet from me. I heard him introduce himself in Arabic, produce an ID, and explain whom he wanted to see. There was no "Hasan Madani" in the dialogue. I was still frozen in my fumbling, bent, shoelace-fiddling position when I came to the conclusion that Husseini might have moved away from the desk in the reception area. But I couldn't escape the most chilling sensation that Husseini was now looking at me. *Should I rise to his feet as nonchalantly as possible, appear to notice Husseini for the first time, and then greet him as though there was nothing unusual for me to be in Gaza at this moment?* The problem with this idea was that Husseini would know for certain the European-looking man inside the Interior Ministry was me. My game with Al-Jaffar would be up. Either Husseini would do his best to block the interview, or he'd ask the Interior Ministry to let Cavenagh have the first access. Out of the corner of my eye, I saw

Husseini heading towards the elevator bank. But as he walked, he cast a glance again in my direction. A cold fear went through me. I had the clear impression that I had been noticed by him. I wasn't sure whether I was more frightened by the fact of his having seen me, or by the fact that he had done nothing to greet me.

With the sinking feeling that a sixth-grader has when told by the teacher that the principal wants to see him, I lingered in the bent position long enough to estimate that Husseini had entered the elevator and the doors had closed. I rose slowly to my feet and looked to my left at the elevator. But the door was still open and Husseini was standing in the elevator looking straight at me. The look in his eyes would have frozen a grizzly bear in its tracks.

Butrus noticed that I was subdued, even nervous, as we walked out of the building to the side street where the Renault was parked. "Is everything okay?" he asked helpfully.

"Yes, fine, thank you, Butrus. I think I am just a little tired."

"Okay, no broblem. Grand Palace Hotel has very comfortable beds. You sleep rest of day."

I said nothing. The hotel was barely three blocks down the street from the Interior Ministry. There were bullet marks on some of the buildings on the way, probably the result of the gunfights between Hamas and Fatah supporters in the summer of 2007, if not of the Israeli incursion into Gaza in December, 2008.

On arrival at the hotel, I asked Butrus to be back the next day at 9.30 a.m. Even though it was only a five-minute drive to the Ministry from the Grand Palace Hotel, I didn't want to take any chances on being punctual. Karim's "one shot" comment had hit home. There wouldn't be another shot at Al-Jaffar.

The hotel air-conditioning was working and I was assigned a larger-than-usual room overlooking the beach and the ocean. I stayed in the room only long enough to wash up and open my overnight case. I'd smelled the most pleasant of smells on entering the lobby, the odor of large prawns being cooked on an open grill. There was a restaurant just off the lobby, and that's where the cooking was probably going on. After all the tension of the day, I was famished, and the grilled prawns smelled awfully tempting. It was not yet six o'clock, but I couldn't see any reason not to eat right away. I gave Margaret a call on my mobile phone, omitting all the details of the day but making it clear that I would be overnighting in Gaza.

"Did you get to Al-Jaffar?" she asked.

"I can't tell you about this trip on the phone," I replied in as laconic a voice as I could muster, "but the fact that I am staying the night should give you some idea of what is going on." I hoped that this would be sufficiently vague not to raise interest in my activities on the part of any electronic eavesdroppers.

"Okay, I understand. Well, good-luck. When do you expect to be back?"

"I plan to leave Gaza by noon tomorrow. If I don't call you soon after that time, you can call out the fire department."

Margaret laughed. "Well, I hope there's nothing *that* inflammatory about your visit. Oh, and would you mind buying a Gaza tee-shirt for my nephew? He's eight and collects tee-shirts from all over the world."

"Sure thing. Oh, please call Karim and say that Mr. Madani was very helpful."

I imagined that, at the other end of the line, Margaret's eyebrows were rising. But if she realized what was going on, she was too discreet to comment.

"I will. Goodbye, then."

I had been standing in the center of the lobby idly watching the other guests. There were two European men talking quietly on one of the couches. In one of the leather arm chairs there was an Arab man apparently reading an Arabic newspaper intently.

I made straight for the small lobby shop and asked to see tee-shirts that would fit an eight-year-old. I paid thirty shekels to the woman behind the counter for two shirts with different, colorful illustrations of life in Gaza. She was wearing a *hijab* and a long-sleeved blouse that indicated she was a religiously conservative Muslim.

In the restaurant, I ordered the very prawns that had smelled so inviting when I had first entered the hotel. They were excellent. There was no alcohol being served on the premises, so I couldn't even order a cold beer. But the apple juice was at least chilled and was excellent.

I had time over dinner to think about the afternoon's disturbing encounter in the foreign ministry. Husseini was not only in Gaza, but had almost certainly seen that I was there too. I hadn't really understood why Husseini had seemed to take an instant dislike to me. I wasn't especially intuitive, and I was uncomfortable using the words "good" and "evil" of any person I was reporting about. But for some reason, Husseini had struck me as having a deeply malevolent disposition, and, for some unknown reason, had decided to direct part of that malevolence at me. It was disturbing. As a reporter, I tried to avoid definitive moral judgments at all costs. Who gave anyone the right to say, after all, what else or who else was definitively wrong?

By the end of my dinner, I had recovered something of my good humor. Dusk had now descended upon Gaza. The traffic was not quite so relentless and noisy as it had been. I returned to my room and looked out at the ocean. In the distance, the lights of an Israeli navy patrol launch on patrol against possible arms smugglers to Gaza blinked as the boat's searchlight swept the shore and the ocean. *Will this place ever be normal? Will these patrols, which the Palestinians hate so much, ever end? Will there ever be peace?*

On TV, one of the channels was showing the old Hitchcock movie, *Rear Window*. Murder is all right on TV under Hamas, I thought, but not sex. I caught the BBC TV news, but there were no new reports from the Middle East. In a way, I was relieved; the last thing I wanted while I was in Gaza was an escalation of violence between Israelis or Palestinians. I watched a little more of *Rear Window*, and then allowed sleep to take me away from it all. But I slept fitfully, getting up at least twice.

In the morning when I awoke, the morning cacophony of Gaza was already at high pitch. I ordered room service breakfast and caught up again on the news on my hotel TV. This time, there was speculation about the upcoming visit of the American Secretary of State to both Egypt and Jerusalem. I thought if I heard any more TV reporters referring to "the Middle East peace process," I'd really throw up. The term was not only an oxymoron, it was a lazy oxymoron. There hadn't been any "process," let alone peace, for years.

On the spur of the moment, before I had to be up and about for real, I decided to call Trish on my mobile. Her tour group was still in Galilee, and I badly wanted to hear her lovely Filipina accent. I also anticipated that hearing her burbling happily on about her touring of Galilee so far would sooth my nerves a little. She was thrilled to hear from me, and obviously relieved as well. Soon, she was rattling away about a visit to the Mount of Beatitudes and a trip on the Sea of Galilee aboard a boat rather loosely modeled on a fishing vessel of the time of Christ. I caught myself cynically imagining asking Trish and Clarissa if they had ice cold coke available on the Sea of Galilee at the time of Jesus. But I didn't want to foul the mood and so kept silent.

"Where are you today?" Trish asked.

"In Gaza. I've got an important interview in less than an hour. Look, I'll really be grateful for your running heavenly interference, if you can, on this one." I wasn't yet too comfortable in admitting that I was asking for "prayer," especially on a phone that was probably being bugged two or three times over. Trish drew in her breath audibly at this. But she, too, knew how carefully she must speak on the phone.

"When will you be leaving Gaza?" she asked.

"Well, I've told the bureau that I anticipate clearing the checkpoint around noon."

"Will you call me then?"

"Of course, princess."

Then she said something that I hadn't anticipated: "Remember, though you don't think of yourself as something special, I want you to know that you are. And I think my boss agrees."

"Your boss?" said I, momentarily flummoxed.

"Yes, my ultimate boss." I understood now. She was trying to convey some theological concept to me, something about God. I wasn't sure what it was and I wasn't sure why she was telling me this.

"Okay, princess, enjoy the rest of Galilee. See you in Jerusalem in a couple of days. I'll call this afternoon."

"You'd better," she said with a laugh. We both hung up.

Butrus was waiting for me in the lobby when I came down to check out of the hotel, his usual gap-toothed grin on his face. I felt good, not only because I had gone to bed quite early and had just come off the phone with Trish, but because I thought I was now on the final lap of the al-Jiffri story. I was curious to know which "diplomat" was going to be at the Al-Jaffar interview with me. Someone from the UN? I knew the delegation dispatched by the UN Security Council hadn't arrived yet. Had the Americans sent somebody? I seriously doubted that. For one thing, Hamas would almost certainly not allow them to be first up at bat on this incident. More likely some EU diplomat.

At the Interior Ministry building a few blocks from the hotel, the black-clad youths were posted outside, as on the previous day. This time, they recognized me and smiled at me. *A good omen*, I thought.

I went over to the reception desk to identify myself and was reminded immediately of Husseini's arrival in the building the previous afternoon. Feigning extreme casualness, I glanced all around the lobby to ensure that Hussein wasn't there. There was no sign of him.

On arrival at Madani's fourth-floor office, I saw that two extra chairs had been brought into the rather cramped space. Karim's "one-shot" remark came back to me again. What if I had the interview with the school teacher and couldn't get to the bottom of the atrocity story? I would certainly disappoint my boss Burton Lasch back in New York and I'd be something of a laughing stock to my fellow hacks in Jerusalem. I hoped to heaven that the diplomat, whoever he was, would let me do my job journalistically.

I sat down in one of the visitor chairs in front of Madani's desk and waited. But when the door opened behind me again no more than two minutes later I almost fell off my chair. Being ushered into the room by Madani was none other than Yao Fanmei. How had he gotten here? For that matter, did the Palestinians realize that he was not a diplomat, not even in the official sense of the word? He wasn't accredited to the Chinese embassy in Tel Aviv, and he was not even working officially for the Chinese foreign ministry. He was a "researcher" at a Beijing think tank, but in reality, working for Chinese intelligence. Had they grasped this?

I didn't think so. But taking it all in with great haste, I also understood that it would be vital – for the particular purposes of each – for Yao and me not to let on that we knew each other. As soon as I looked straight at Yao after being introduced by Madani, I realized with relief that Yao was going to play the same game; as far as Madani and Al-Jaffar were concerned, the two of us had never met before.

"Mr. Ireton, this is Mr. Yao from the Chinese Foreign Ministry. He's on a short-term visit to the region and the Chinese Embassy in Tel Aviv made a special request that he meet with Mr. Al-Jaffar."

"Pleased to meet you, Mr. Yao," I said, extending my hand for all the world acting as if I were being introduced to an insurance salesman. Yao also played his part well, expressionless, even bored-looking.

After the two of us had sat down and were busying ourselves setting up digital tape recorders, Madani curtly asked his assistant in English to invite Al-Jaffar to come in. I couldn't wait to see what he looked like, and nor, I think, could Yao.

When the Palestinian school teacher entered the office through the door behind me, I was surprised by his appearance. He was taller than the average Palestinian, was wearing a gray suit without a tie, and had a weary, almost furtive look on his face. He had the scraggly beginnings of a beard, or maybe it was just that he might deliberately not have shaved for about four days. I cast a sly glance at Yao as Al-Jaffar was being introduced. No one else would have noticed, but I thought that there was just the hint of wry humor showing on the face of the Chinese intelligence officer.

When all of us were seated, Madani turned to me as formally as if he were announcing my engagement, and said, "Mr. Ireton, since you are the journalist here, you may begin asking questions of Mr. Al-Jaffar."

"Thank you," I said, clicking on the digital recorder. I slowly turned to face Al-Jaffar.

"Well, I've read the report in the British newspaper of your experience and it's certainly very interesting. Can you tell me what you actually saw with your own eyes?" I asked.

"I was walking in the late afternoon outside the al-Jiffri village where I teach. Suddenly, I heard shooting, 'bang, bang.' Then silence, then more bangs. It was coming from the hillside, or below. I walked towards the edge of the slope to look. At first I couldn't see anything. Then quietness for a while. I crouched down. I think, perhaps if I stand up, someone will shoot at me. Then I see some Israeli soldiers climbing up the hillside from the road below."

"How many?" I interrupted. I noticed Yao looking sharply at me, as though annoyed at the interruption.

Al-Jaffar appeared to consider this question for a while, then answered slowly, "maybe twenty. I don't know because I didn't count them."

"Go on."

"There was a Palestinian man, much blood coming out. He was lying on the ground. Two other Palestinians were pulling him along. I think he was wounded very badly, maybe already dead. He was not moving. I was very scared. I moved back so that the Israelis could definitely not see me. Then I hear more shots, and now there are three Palestinians on the ground. The Israelis, they must have killed them after the Palestinians surrendered. That is murder. That is atrocity."

Now it was Yao who broke in. "Did you let anyone know what you had seen immediately after it happened?"

"Yes, I run back to my house and call Mr. Abdul Husseini. He is a very wise man with much experience. I know that he will tell me what to do."

"And what did he say?" Yao asked. I was surprised. Yao was asking questions like a journalist, focusing on the precise details of the story.

"He told me to stay in my home and said he would drive to meet me there. Then we would talk about what to do."

"Did you see the Israelis actually pointing their guns at the Palestinians after they came up the hill?" This time, it was I asking the question.

"Yes, I see the Israelis tell the Palestinians to lie on the ground and then an officer, he comes and points his pistol at them. Then he shoots."

I followed up with another question. "But didn't you just say that you moved away from the Israelis so that they wouldn't see you? It was then that you heard more shots?"

"Yes, that's right. After I moved away, then they shot the Palestinians."

Yao now followed up. "But if you moved away to a place where you were sure the Israelis couldn't see you, how were you able to see what they were doing?" There was a flash of panic in Al-Jaffar's eyes. Madani shifted uncomfortably in his chair and his face twitched slightly. The left eye went wandering around the room again.

"You know, when the Israelis catch you, they usually make you sit down or lie down on the ground first before they arrest you."

"How do you know? Were you ever taken into detention by the Israeli soldiers?" This was now Yao.

"No, I never have trouble with the Israelis." Now I knew that Al-Jaffar was lying. I remembered from the information at the Terrorism Center that Al-Jaffar had had two run-ins for minor transgressions like stone-throwing.

Yao went on like a terrier who's just been thrown a bone. "Well, perhaps the Israeli soldiers made the Palestinians lie down," he said. "But did you actually see them pointing their guns at the Palestinians?"

"Oh, they always point their guns at you when they arrest you," he said, attempting with bravado to evade the thrust of the question.

"But did you see it yourself?" insisted Yao. I was amazed. Yao was beginning to sound like a district attorney in an American TV court drama. There was another flash of panic in Al-Jaffar's eyes. Madani butted in. "You know," he said, "Mr. Al-Jaffar has already explained what he saw to other journalists. Perhaps you want to ask him other questions."

Yao looked at me, but still without the slightest indication that the two of us knew each other.

I smiled broadly at Madani, trying to assume a demeanor of innocent, reportorial charm. I said, "Mr. Madani, you must forgive me. I don't know about Mr. Yao, but when I was in journalism school they taught us never to take as established fact the words that a source had told another journalist previously. I certainly want to get to the bottom of this horrible story of what Mr. Al-Jaffar says he witnessed. I'm sure it must sound like boring repetition to you, but it's essential to make sure that I have gone over all the ground carefully." Madani said nothing, but his wandering left eye took off around to circle the room once more.

Madani then grunted at this and Al-Jaffar rubbed at the stubble on his chin. I thought the stubble was probably long enough to itch rather badly. Yao stared fixedly at a small, neat notebook he had taken out of the inner pocket of his suit jacket.

I resumed the questioning, taking a slightly different tack. "When you got back to your house and called Mr. Husseini, what did you tell him?"

Al-Jaffar looked annoyed. "I already tell you, I already tell the other journalists," he said with some exasperation. "I call Mr. Husseini on the telephone and say that Israeli soldiers are shooting, are coming up the hillside and are pointing their guns at Palestinians."

"And what did he say to you?" I replied.

"He say go back and try to see what the Israelis are doing now. Don't let them see you."

"But wasn't the first advice of Mr. Husseini to you to stay in your home and wait for him to come to you?" I asked, trying to sound as solicitous as possible.

"Yes, but I want to see what is happening on the hill. So I go back and I see that the Israeli soldiers are going back down the hill."

"Were the Palestinians still there, lying on the ground?"

"No, there was just much blood on the ground where they shot them."

"So what happened to the bodies?"

"I don't know. Maybe the Israelis take them away with their guns."

"So after you called Mr. Husseini and returned to where you had first seen the soldiers, they were already going back down the hillside and you think they were taking the bodies of the Palestinians with them?"

"Mr. Husseini tells me he thinks that is what happened afterwards."

I at this point really felt like a trial lawyer turning to the judge and then the opposing counsel and saying with quiet, but elegant finality, "Nothing further, your honor. Your witness." I wanted Yao to come back into the conversation. I ostentatiously closed my own notebook and pretended to be thinking deeply. Yao took the hint.

"But the bodies? Doesn't the Israeli army release bodies of killed Palestinians back to their families?"

"Usually yes," Al-Jaffar said, apparently feeling on safer ground now. "But maybe because they murder these men they don't want to leave… how do you say…?"

"Evidence?" I prompted helpfully.

"Yes, evidence. Maybe the Israeli army bury the bodies with no one knowing."

"I suppose that could happen," I said. "Did you see the Israeli soldiers taking the bodies away?"

There was a pause. Al-Jaffar looked at Madani who seemed to be trying to bring his errant eye back into its line of duty.

"No. I tell you, I was on the telephone with Mr. Husseini."

"Of course," I said smoothly, "you couldn't possibly have seen them do that because you had gone away to phone."

Al-Jaffar looked annoyed now and turned once again to Madani with a look that seemed to appeal for guidance. Madani shook his head slowly.

Yao now resumed the questioning. "I am very surprised," he said, "that An-Najah would say that three of its students were killed when no one could produce any bodies. Why didn't the university demand that the Israelis hand over the bodies?" I was astonished to hear Yao say this. How much digging into the al-Jiffri story had he done?

Al-Jaffar shrugged. "How do I know? They do many horrible things, the Israelis."

Yao continued. "My embassy made inquiries by phone of the An-Najah University yesterday. They asked for the names of the students and their home addresses. My embassy wanted to send a letter of sympathy to each of the families."

Madani seemed relieved that China was apparently on the right side of the atrocity investigation. He smiled and said, "Thank you. The Chinese people have always been good friends of the Palestinians."

"Unfortunately," Yao went on, as though he hadn't heard what Madani had just said, "the university could give us the names, but no addresses. They said that the students had not been living with their parents and had moved to other private homes. Also, unfortunately, they didn't seem to have the addresses of the parents."

There was a long, awkward silence. I tried to restore a sense that Al-Jaffar's story was still plausible by following up.

"Your friend, Mr. Husseini," I said, "How long was it before he came round to your home?"

"It was about forty minutes later," said Al-Jaffar, more subdued than he had been at the beginning of the interview.

"And by then, all the evidence had gone?"

"I'm sorry?" said Al-Jaffar, having forgotten what the word "evidence" meant.

"There were no soldiers, no Palestinian bodies by that time?"

"Just the blood on the ground," said Al-Jaffar.

"Of course, the blood." I said. I had a brief flash-back to my conversation with Yossi and Rayna and a reference to a blood-stained keffiyeh on the ground.

"And what did Mr. Husseini say you should do after he came?" I continued.

"He said that it is very important that the foreign reporters hear about this as soon as possible, before the Israelis have a chance to change the story."

"Of course," I said smoothly. "And who were the first reporters you spoke to about this?"

"Mr Cava…I don't know his name, and a man from the BBC."

"Mr. Cavenagh of *News Report*, and Mr. Blakely," I said unctuously.

I continued, "Why didn't you hold a press conference right away, so that other reporters could talk to you?"

"Mr. Husseini think that is a bad idea. There would be confusing questions." *Yes, there would*, I thought.

"Well, I expect that now you have been kind enough to allow Mr. Yao and me to interview Mr. Al-Jaffar," I said, still trying to seem just a simple-minded reporter, "Hamas will organize a press conference?"

I had put this question to Madani, whose errant left eye came instantly under control when he was concentrating, as he was now.

"There will be a press conference after the U.N. delegation has arrived," he said curtly. "Now if that is all, Mr. Ireton, I think Mr. Yao has some other matters he wants to discuss with me."

"Of course. Yes, I think I have enough material for the time being. I hope it is not too long before the press conference takes place. Mr. Yao, a pleasure to meet you. Thank you so much for your help, Mr. Madani."

Madani looked angry now, his left eye hunting the walls like a bat looking for moths. He said something in Arabic to his assistant who came in to escort me to the elevator. I thought I caught the word "Husseini" in his words, but I couldn't be sure.

The assistant, who still seemed to be perspiring as he had yesterday, led me not immediately back to the elevator, but to another room in the corridor. I was surprised and momentarily confused. "Mr. Madani said he wanted me to show you the materials we have in English about Hamas. He says he thinks many American reporters have wrong ideas about our movement."

I said nothing, but followed the assistant into a room larger than the office where the interview had taken place. There were tables neatly piled with booklets and pamphlets in English. Realizing I was expected to show interest, I flipped through some of the titles: *Sheikh Ahmed Yassin – in the footsteps of the righteous*, and *Palestine and Islam – the partnership of nation and faith*. "Please take as many of the books as you want," the assistant said. I wondered why his invitation to gather up Hamas propaganda literature was happening now, when I would have had more time to peruse the literature the previous afternoon. But apparently I was expected to show more than cursory interest in the leaflets and pamphlets on display. I lingered long enough to display politeness, took several leaflets and pamphlets, and then told the assistant that I had to leave to return to Jerusalem.

"Yes, you say 'Jerusalem,'" the assistant responded aggressively. "We say *Al Quds*, because that is the Arabic name of the city, the name of the ancient city that is the third holiest in Islam, after Mecca and Medina. Two great mosques of Islam are there, the Dome of the Rock and the El Aqsa Mosque, both built thirteen hundred years ago or more. Do you know what El Aqsa means?"

I was embarrassed. I didn't. I simply stared at the man who didn't wait for me to answer. "El Aqsa means 'the far distant place of worship.'" He went on, "In Arabic, *Al-Masdjid Al-Aqsa*. That is where our prophet Mohammed, peace be upon him, departed to heaven on his night-journey." He stared back at me. Then he said slowly, "One day you will know, one day when Islam takes its place as the true faith for the whole world." He seemed about to launch into a diatribe against the West, but apparently thought better of it. "Goodbye, Mr. Ireton." He extended the same clammy and limp hand that I had shaken the day before.

I was less cheerful than I had anticipated being on descending to the lobby in the elevator. I think I had clear evidence, on tape, that Al-Jaffar's allegations about an Israeli atrocity didn't hold up at all, and that in fact they had essentially been invented by Abdul Husseini. I had Al-Jaffar's voice saying it on my digital recorder, and I had a witness, Yao Fanmei. But the atmosphere of the interview had been unpleasant. Madani had become angry when it was obvious Al-Jaffar's story didn't hold up on close examination. Then I'd gotten the Hamas propaganda immersion treatment from Madani's assistant. I always hated it when, for the sake of journalistic access, I had to undergo these sessions of being hosed down by propaganda as if from a fire truck.

Butrus was in the lobby, but of the black-clad youths there was no sign. They had vanished. It didn't seem to bother Butrus, however, who was deep in conversation with a workman repairing floor tiles. He grinned his invariable grin, and I cheered up slightly. "Where have the blackbeards gone?" I asked. Butrus laughed loudly. At least someone in this theocracy-in-the-making still had a sense of humor. Then Butrus tried his own hand at subversive humor. He leaned in toward me and whispered conspiratorially, "I think they are all making the *haji*." He was referring to one of Islam's "five pillars" of correct living, a pilgrimage at least once in a lifetime to Mecca.

Butrus told me to wait on the sidewalk until he brought the car round because he hadn't been able to park it this morning in its usual spot close to the Ministry. I glanced up and down El-Rasheed Street and was surprised at how sparse both traffic and pedestrians were. Then I remembered: of course, it was Saturday, the day after the Muslim day off which many Muslims treat as a Sunday in the West.

Butrus drove up and opened the passenger door from the inside. Then he looked in the mirror to ensure that traffic was clear before pulling away from the curb. As he drove off, however, Butrus looked in the rearview mirror again and frowned. I turned around to see what the problem was and noticed a large delivery truck moving slowly down the street behind us. The van slowed to let Butrus pull away from the

Interior Ministry in the Renault, then fell in behind the Renault. My heart began to beat a little faster. The last thing I needed before leaving Gaza was to be involved in a major traffic incident.

Butrus went one block further along Al-Rasheed Street and then turned right to join up with the main road to the Erez crossing. In front of us now was yet another truck, this one apparently collecting garbage. It slowed to a crawl, and the garbage men jumped out and started picking up cans along the side of the street. Butrus had to slow to a crawl too. Suddenly, from down a side-alley off this Gaza cross-street, a dark green minivan roared up, screeching to a halt just in front of the Renault. Butrus understood instantly what was happening; we were both about to be seized by very nasty thugs.

X

BUTRUS RESPONDED WITHOUT a second's hesitation. He clutched at the steering wheel with both hands and, in a continuous sweeping movement, turned it until he'd completed the first part of a three-point turn, turning so fast that the Renault seemed for an instant about to turn over. As he rammed home the shift in place to go forward, however, the moving van behind him came to a halt diagonally across the entire road. From out of its cab leaped four men with ski masks on. Butrus almost choked and then started wimpering. I felt a sudden upward surge of fear into my whole system. Panic rose up, almost choking me; I knew more certainly than anything else that I was about to die. For a moment I simply couldn't breathe. My lungs continued to function, but in sort of jerky, desperate breaths. But just as suddenly, and to my great surprise, a sort of journalistic "training moment" came into play. I remembered the many times when I had seen soldiers on TV, having survived a fierce gun battle or ambush, explaining how their training simply "kicked in."

Well, my journalistic training "kicked in." I was terrified, but I was also almost unnaturally alert. I realized instantly what was happening – I was being kidnapped – and that the kidnapping could go badly wrong and I might be killed in the first few moments of it. But I found myself just as instantly paying attention to the precise details of what was happening around me. I saw, I heard, I felt, I even smelled with an intensity that I never had before.

The first thing that struck me visually was that, as I looked out of the passenger-side window of Butrus' Renault, I caught the impassive gaze of an old man on a donkey cart staring back at me. He was no more emotionally shocked by what he saw happening than if he had been overtaken by a passing bus. I was, for a split second, mesmerized by his impassive face. What life traumas had reduced him to this state of impassivity? But just then Butrus also instantly grasped what was happening and his face went white with fear.

The men in ski masks sprinted toward the driver's door and the passenger door of the Renault and began yanking violently at the handles of both of them. Neither Butrus nor I had thought to lock the car when we were driving around from hotel to Interior Ministry and back, and so the doors shot open. On the driver's side, two of the ski masks reached in to grab Butrus by both his arms, while the other two did exactly the same to me. The movement seemed to have been well-rehearsed, for there was no fumbling. Butrus continued to wimper, between shouting in English – I wondered later why he had not been speaking Arabic to them – "driver, driver, taxi, taxi." It made no difference. They simply flung him onto the road, as they did me. The sheer violence of the act of dragging me out of the car caused me to hit the ground hard. Immediately, I felt a searing pain in my right cheek and my right knee.

Blood was trickling down the side of my face. I lay on the ground for less than ten seconds, however, because the two men who had first pulled me out of the car hauled me roughly to my feet and frog-marched me towards the green van. One of them held an automatic pistol to my head, probably a nine-millimeter. The doors were open at the back of the van and two more men in ski masks were inside. I was half carried, half thrown into the back of the van. The two men who had grabbed me from the Renault jumped into the back behind me, and landed painfully on top of me. There was no sign of the other two men in ski masks or of Butrus. The van then roared off in the same direction that the Renault had been traveling before the road seizure. As the van rocketed into gear and weaved this way and that, I began to feel fierce pain. My face, with its bleeding cheek, was pressed down on the floor of the minivan. My legs were in agony too, because I had landed in the van in an unnatural position and my legs were being held down by the weight of my two captors.

I now felt my arms being pulled harshly back behind me and bound together with rope. Soon afterwards, a coarse cloth blindfold was pressed against my eyes and tied in a tight bow at the back of my head. It smelled utterly rank, as though it had been worn against someone else's sweating body and then never washed.

The whole action – from the screech of tires of the minivan coming out of the alley to the roaring off down the street – had taken less than half a minute. The kidnappers, whoever they were, had clearly practiced hard for this snatch. Perhaps they had done it in real life a few times before.

The van weaved for several minutes dangerously between oncoming traffic. At least, it seemed dangerous to me since I couldn't see anything because of the blindfold. I soon became quite disorientated and could not possibly have guessed in which direction the van was headed. It certainly seemed to have turned several times. The smell of the blindfold almost made me gag.

The pain in my legs from the weight of the men kneeling upon me was becoming so intense that I cried out, "My legs, my legs." At least this much seemed understandable to them and they shifted positions, still keeping me pinned to the floor by their body weight, but no longer putting all their weight on me through their knees.

I lost track of time. I had no idea what had happened to Butrus. I desperately hoped that no harm had come to the dear man. For what I guessed to be some ten minutes – I couldn't see my watch both because I was blindfolded and because my arms were pinioned – I felt the van continuing to travel at high speed through the teeming streets of Gaza. Then, without explanation, it slowed to a more normal traffic pace and seemed to be in a part of the city which was less busy and noisy. Finally, it stopped in what I guessed to be a driveway. There was the sound of an automatic garage door opening, then closing after the van had crept forward into the garage.

There was loud shouting in Arabic now and the sound of a door to the garage opening and slamming closed. I was beginning to feel sick, the combination of the foul smell of the blindfold and the swaying of the van, not to mention the stinging pain in my right knee and right cheek and the just recently relieved pain of two men's knees pressing onto my legs.

I heard the van doors being opened from the outside and more shouting. I guessed that there were two men in the garage and they had opened the door to the van. The men who had been sitting on me now stood up halfway in the van and helped me to my feet. It was difficult to keep balance because my arms were bound behind me and the blindfold deprived me of visual references. "Okay, sit down, sit down," one of the men in the van shouted to me in English, and I was grateful that I didn't have to risk toppling forward or sideways.

I was pushed along the floor of the van until my feet reached the edge of it at the door and dangled over. Then, the two men in the garage took me by both arms and led me, more gently now, through the garage and a door that opened out from it. I was taken to a staircase and ordered to climb the stairs. It seemed to me that I went up three flights, to a second floor, and then was taken into a room with a wooden floor. From the crack in my blindfold below my eyes I could see that there was a source of illumination in the room. By leaning my head back I saw that it was a single light-bulb hanging from the ceiling. I was still in considerable pain from my face hitting the pavement when I was first pulled from the Renault, but the bleeding seemed to have stopped. The skin on the entire right-hand side of my face felt raw and tingly.

The hands that had been holding my arms as I was led up the stairs now forced me to my knees. "Here you stay!" one of the garage men said brusquely. "You keep blindfold on until we say okay to take it off. Now we untie the ropes on your arms."

The rope had been tied so tight around my wrists that it was a relief to have it removed. Before I could enjoy the momentary freedom, however, I was told to place my arms together in front of myself. Someone then placed them in metal handcuffs. But no one objected when I rocked back on my knees and leaned against the wall, my legs in front of me.

Two men in the room with me were speaking Arabic to each other. I again thought I heard the word "Husseini" in the conversation, but I couldn't be sure. One of the men then started speaking to me in English.

"You know why we take you?"

"No. I have no idea, and I can tell you right up front that my company isn't going to pay any cash for me. I'm a reporter."

"Yes, we know that. And we know you are trying to stop the al-Jiffri story. We want United Nations to investigate and to condemn Israel. You are a bad reporter. You want to defend the Israelis."

I felt myself on safer ground now. However illogical the accusation, at least it was something I could respond to rationally.

"No, that's not true. I want to defend the truth. As a matter of fact, I want to defend the truth more than the Israelis. This is what I was trained to do as a reporter and this is what I have tried to do wherever I've worked."

"But we know you. You like the Jews. You think Palestinians and Hamas are bad people."

The criticism was so silly that, ordinarily, I would not have bothered responding to it. But I realized that the slim gangplank of discourse with my kidnappers was the only opening I had to get out of this situation.

"I will answer that in a moment. But first, what have you done to my driver, Butrus?"

The men both laughed. "Your driver? Oh, we let him go as soon as we are sure we have you. He is not important to us." I hoped that Butrus would have the sense either to leave Gaza, or if he couldn't do this, to lie very low for a few days, perhaps not even living in his home. I certainly hoped that he'd phone Karim as soon as he could.

"Good. He is completely innocent. He has no connection with me as a reporter other than to drive the car I am in."

"We know that. It is you we want."

"What on earth for? Don't you have any idea that by kidnapping reporters you are making the world think of Gaza as a mad house? How do you think you are going to get any support in the outside world if you keep kidnapping foreigners?"

Suddenly, I felt a stinging slap to my face, made more painful because I couldn't see it coming and I could do nothing to lessen the sting.

"You infidel American! You pig! You know we can kill you in ten seconds?" The shout was so close to my ear that it almost hurt.

"*Khalas, khalas, Khaffis 'anno* (stop, go easy on him)," the other man shouted in Arabic, evidently alarmed that I was being slapped around. "*Khalas, khalas.*" A loud argument developed, with the man who had slapped me evidently arguing that it was okay to do this, and the other one arguing that they shouldn't. Finally a third Arab came into the room, apparently drawn by all the noise. He started shouting too, but it was unclear at first whose side he was on.

"Okay, okay," said the man who had been alarmed by the slap to my face. "Ire-town. Your name is too difficult for say, so we call you reporter, okay?"

I wanted to give a smart-alecky reply, but didn't want to get another slap, so I held my tongue. "Suit yourself," was all I could manage.

"What's that?"

"You have the guns and the power, and I have nothing. You can call me Mickey Mouse if you want."

All three men thought this was hilarious and roared with laughter.

"Yes, that's right. We will call you Mickey Mouse! Ha, ha, ha!" They laughed again.

It was sickening. From their voices, none of my kidnappers seemed to be older than his early twenties. What I worried about most was that they all seemed to have the mental attitude of juveniles, which could be dangerous and forced you to pay constant attention to their moods. They seemed to have a sense of humor – at least about some things – but one of them at least had a mean, violent streak. I wasn't in a hurry to discover when that would next be displayed.

"Hey, you know why we take you?" the second of the two men resumed. I made a mental note of thinking of him as "Omar." I wanted to call the man who had slapped me "Tony," as in Tony Soprano in the TV series about the Mafia.

I decided to try to draw them out in conversation. "You say you took me because I like the Jews," I said, "and you say I don't like the Palestinians or Hamas. But if you think I don't like Hamas, why do you think I bother to come to Gaza to interview a Palestinian school teacher who has a story about the Israelis doing bad things? Does that show that I like the Jews?"

"Listen, Mickey Mouse," said Omar, "a brother told us that you ask to interview Al-Jaffar because you try to show that he tells lies."

So it was either Madani or Husseini who had engineered this. But Omar had apparently given away too much by even mentioning my interview with Al-Jaffar. Tony began to shout at him, "*Khalas, khalas.*" There was another heated exchange between the two men. Once again, a third Arab entered the room and began speaking very loudly, presumably berating both men again for arguing so loudly. Just as quickly as he had entered, he left. The two men guarding me continued to speak, but much more quietly.

I guessed, in fact, that it was probably Husseini, not Madani, who had ordered up the kidnapping. The warning about him by Rayna and by the Terrorism Center had indicated he was not a man to be trifled with. But who were these men, and what did they want from the kidnapping? Recent kidnappings of journalists and other Westerners in Gaza had been resolved either by an exchange of a sizable amount of money – allegedly two million dollars in the case of two American TV reporters kidnapped – or by a three-way negotiation involving the Israelis, or even by the ploy of a conversion to Islam at gunpoint.

Omar and Tony were muttering to each other in subdued voices.

Neither of them addressed my question.

I decided to risk asking them who they were.

"If I am Mickey Mouse," I said, hoping to get them to calm down by entertaining them, "who are you?"

This time, Omar and Tony responded almost in unison. "We are the Followers of the Caliph," they said. "Our job," Omar added, "is to make sure the world knows the truth about the Palestinian nation and the situation in Gaza."

"And you think you will succeed in doing this by kidnapping reporters?" I asked.

"Infidel pig!" Tony shouted, and I flinched as though I was going to be slapped again. But the blow didn't come. I heard the sound of flesh obstructing flesh. Omar had probably grabbed Tony's hand just before he could hit me.

Tony, still angry, went on. "You Western reporters, especially you Americans, you think you can come into our Arab nation and tell the world what is justice and what is not justice."

"No, we don't claim to know what justice is in the Arab nation. But we try to find out what the truth is." I surprised myself by this sort of forthright assertion of Western reporting principles.

"You do?" Tony responded. "Isn't it the truth that the entire Palestinian nation is in prison, especially here in Gaza? Why don't you report that?"

"We do. Hundreds of foreign reporters have come to Gaza and have accurately reported what they have been told by the people here and what they have seen. But since they started being kidnapped, they have not found it so nice to be here."

"Be quiet, pig!" Tony shouted, and I again anticipated another slap. I don't think Omar was physically restraining Tony, but the blow never came anyway.

My two guards continued to argue, though not as loudly as before, for several minutes. Then Omar abruptly left the room for no apparent reason. *Great*, I thought sarcastically, *now I'm alone with this brute Tony.*

There was the sound of a plastic bottle being opened and chugged. Tony was evidently not going to die of thirst. Suddenly, I felt the mouth of the bottle being lifted to my lips. I swallowed the water greedily, trying to suppress the thought of whose lips had been at the liquid before *mine*.

"All right, I tell you now who we are and what we want. Just remember, Mickey Mouse, don't argue with me. No smart replies."

"Okay," I answered warily. "Go ahead." I bit my tongue rather than add what I dearly wanted to say, "You have a captive audience."

"We are followers of the Caliph." Pause. I was unsure whether to respond to Tony as though repeating a catechism. *What does the man want from me? For that matter, what do his kidnappers want from anyone: from* Epoch *Magazine, from the American government, from the Israelis?*

"Please tell me who 'Followers of the Caliph' are. Please tell me what you want."

"Good. That is better. Now you are listening. We support Hamas. We think Hamas should be the rulers of Gaza and the West Bank. We despise the cowardly Fatah who blindly take orders from America. We think Hamas is better than Fatah, but we think they don't go far enough. Have you read the Hamas Charter?"

"Yes," I replied, even more warily now because the Charter was one of the most paranoid, idiotic documents I had ever read. It was wild rant as much as a serious political document. It accepted as true the notorious anti-Semitic forgery, the *Protocols of the Elders of Zion*, and rambled on about the Jews as the great enemy of mankind and the force behind the French Revolution, World War I and World War II, the League of Nations, Freemasonry, and the most idiotic accusation of all, the secretive cabal that had formed the Rotary Club and the Lions Club. It was a challenge to my imagination to accept that any normal person would take in such lunatic paranoia. But Tony obviously did.

"The Hamas Charter," he resumed, "says what we think about Palestine. It is the view of all good Muslims who are not slaves to Crusader culture. But we think in Gaza there should be the beginning of the rule of the caliphate over all Islam. The Followers of the Caliph say that not only should there be no Jews in Palestine – the sacred Muslim *Waqf* since the Caliph Omar captured Jerusalem – there should be no Crusader presence either. We want all Crusader and all foreign embassies to go out."

I thought I saw an opening here. "Forgive me," I said, trying to capture the tone of a fifth-grader asking to go to the bathroom, "but what do you mean by Crusader culture?"

"You Americans, the West, everything that is decadent, pornography, drunkenness, everything that is *jahiliyya*. You Crusaders brought this filth into the Muslim Umma, the Muslim community, and you seduced Muslim leaders into *jahiliyya*."

"What is *jahiliyaa*?"

"*Jahiliyya* is in the Koran. The Prophet, peace be upon him, said *jahiliyya* was the state of ignorance of the Arabs before Islam was revealed to the prophet by Allah. Jahiliyyah is the condition we Arabs were in before the Prophet, peace be upon him, brought us truth and purity. It also is the ignorance of Muslim rulers who are allied with Crusader countries. You know Sayyid Qutb?"

"The Egyptian Islamic thinker? Yes. I've read his book *Milestones*."

"You have? That is very good. Very few Crusaders have read *Milestones*, but you cannot understand why so many Muslims are ready to wage *jihad* in the world today without reading *Milestones*. In *Milestones* Qutb says, 'When a person embraced Islam during the time of the Prophet, he would immediately cut himself off from *jahiliyyah*. When he stepped into the circle of Islam, he would start a new life, separating himself completely from his past life under ignorance of the Divine Law.' Qutb is a pure Islamic philosopher of *jihad*, or revolution."

I was feeling a little easier. I had somehow pressed a button in Tony, and as long as I didn't contradict this angry and brutal man but appeared to listen to him, I felt that I wouldn't be hit across the face again. I would have liked to tackle Tony on the *Protocols of the Elders of Zion*, a plagiarism of a French 19th century pamphlet even before it was taken up by Adolf Hitler and the Nazis, extremist Arab nationalists, and, more recently, extremist Arab Islamists. I had come across an American Jewish researcher of the *Protocols* story while in my previous post, the Hong Kong bureau of *Epoch* and had learned more about the subject than most reporters.

Adolf Hitler, of course, in *Mein Kampf*, had referred to the *Protocols* as though they were genuine, and several modern Arab governments, including Syria, Saudi Arabia, and Egypt, continually referred to them as validating hatred of the Jews. Among the Palestinians, the Grand Mufti of Jerusalem – a successor to the odious Haji Amin al-Husseini, Abdul Husseini's ancestor – had even mentioned approvingly the *Protocols* on Saudi television quite recently. The *Protocols* purported to be the secret account of a gathering of Jewish leaders scheming to dominate the entire world by subverting insidiously entire societies and nations. This passionate hatred of the Jews baffled me and repelled me at the same time.

I wasn't Jewish myself and none of my relatives were. But my mother's life had been saved by a Jewish surgeon and one of my closest friends in graduate school at the University of Michigan had been Jewish. It seemed absurd that anyone wanted a world without such gifted people making contributions to it. But obviously some people did.

Omar, and Tony, and whoever the third man was, and the whole of the Hamas crowd in Gaza, and Hezbollah in Lebanon, and the mullahs running Iran; they not only *could* imagine a world without Jews, they wanted to bring it to pass.

Now Omar came back into the room. He started speaking.

"Mickey Mouse, we have instructions for you," he began. "We are going to take you to another place where it will be impossible for anyone to know where you are. Then you are going to make a video announcement for us in front of the cameras. The world will hear from your mouth who we are and what we want from it. So you get up now. We are going to move you."

I struggled to my feet from my sitting position, my blindfold still in place and my balance hard to keep. I felt Omar and Tony holding me by both arms and leading me back down the staircase. I felt myself being led back into the garage. I heard the doors of the van being opened and I was led once again to the back edge of the van. But I had the wit to sense that it was a different van, or at least it was parked now in a different part of the garage from where I had arrived in it. Perhaps it *was* a different van. Perhaps it was a different color, or even a different make, in order to confuse anyone who might have been able – unlikely though it was – to keep up with the green van's movement as it sped away from the street outside the Interior Ministry building.

With my handcuffs in front of me now, it wasn't so hard getting into the van. But when I had scooted forward, as instructed, to the space just behind the two front seats, I was told to lie down prone on the floor. It was painful folding my handcuffed arms above my head, but before I could complain, a heavy tarpaulin had been thrown on top of me. The van's engine was started and the garage doors ground opened up again. The van drew slowly out of the garage and drove at a stately pace along the roads in what felt like an upscale residential area of Gaza. For all the world, it felt as though I was being taken to a soccer game by a safety-conscious mum. I was more conscious of the time than I had been after the initial snatch, even though I could not see my watch. I reckoned the van cruised a long time, perhaps for thirty minutes. The street noises seemed to be much less here, and I presumed we were remaining within the more attractive residential areas of Gaza.

Just as suddenly as had happened on arrival at the first house, the van drove into what seemed to be another private compound. Though I was still on the floor under the tarpaulin, there was the distinct sound of a large iron gate being closed behind the vehicle. There seemed to be more men in this compound than in the earlier house for there was a lot of shouting as the van's rear doors were once again opened. I found myself once again being led up some stairs – perhaps an entrance stairway – into a room, then through that room to another room, and finally down a steep flight of additional steps that felt like the stairway into a cellar. I was guided into a room that had a concrete floor and, from the way the sound failed to echo in any way, was much smaller than the room of my first, temporary, detention. I was guided to a sitting position on a plastic, four-legged stool that had been placed at the far end of the room against the wall, and my blindfold was abruptly removed. Even though there was only one light bulb in the room – what was it about kidnappers that they seemed to enjoy the stereotype of having a single naked light bulb? – it was surprisingly bright. I blinked several times and tried to shade my eyes with my handcuffed hands. The walls had been painted a green color – green, of course, was the color associated with Islam – but somehow, they reflected the light bulb quite brightly. There was a low cot against one wall and a plain metal bucket in one corner. I figured out immediately what this was for; there wouldn't be any bathroom trips in this place of detention.

The room was no more than eight feet by six feet and when all three of us, Omar and Tony and I, were crowded into it, it certainly felt small. "You sit down on chair," said Tony brusquely, pointing to the stool. I did as I was told. Omar then uncuffed me, offering no explanation of this action. I wondered why they seemed to feel confident that I wouldn't pull any rough stuff and make an escape attempt. But as if reading my thoughts, Tony pushed open the door through which they had entered the cellar. Outside it, also sitting on a plastic stool just like the one in the cell, was a large, bearded man with an AK-47 cradled in his lap. He looked unpleasantly serious.

A new man now entered the cell, someone whom I had never seen before. He was carrying a video camera on a tripod, and he placed it directly opposite the stool on which I was sitting. He started adjusting the focus of the video camera. Tony and Omar, without a word, then exited the room briefly, and returned each with an AK-47 also. They donned ski masks as they entered the room and then took up position on either side of me. I began to feel fear rising again within me. It horribly resembled the situation of Westerners being executed brutally in front of cameras that I'd seen from several countries. But part of me wanted, illogically though it was, also to guffaw with laughter; the whole thing was such a cliché. Here were two bearded men in black ski masks standing with Kalashnikovs on either side of a kidnap victim. Couldn't these Islamist fanatics ever come up with an original way to pose a kidnap victim? Lounging poolside with a Tom Collins, for example, or seated in front of a bowl of popcorn taking in a Sunday night football game? I smirked as I thought of this ridiculous image, prompting Tony to elbow me in the ribs painfully. "Hey, Mickey Mouse," he said, "this is not funny. You want a bullet through the head? If you go on laughing you will get a bullet in the head. Yes, infidel, in the head."

Again, I held myself in. Being a smart aleck was not the way to prolong my life in this setting. Just then a third man came into the room. He was bearded but without a ski mask, and he looked quite a bit older than Tony and Omar who were still in their early twenties. This man was in his mid-forties, and he had graying hair on both temples. He had an intelligent-looking expression on his face. I thought immediately that he must be one of the intellectuals behind the Followers of the Caliph. I was tempted to ask whether he knew Abdul Husseini, but I thought if I asked the question, I'd probably get slapped around again by Tony, and I'd come to dislike that experience intensely.

The man took a folded piece of paper out of his pocket and handed it to me. "You read through this paper, and then you read it aloud in front of the camera when I tell you, okay?" He had a gravelly voice rather like a fifteen-season American college football coach. I simply nodded. I unfolded the paper and read it carefully twice. The first time, I was simply trying to take in what my kidnappers were demanding from me or anyone outside of Gaza. The second time, I was hunting for any word or phrase in English that I could mispronounce without the kidnappers knowing. This way, I'd send a signal to any watchers of the video in Israel or elsewhere that I was being totally controlled by my captors.

I looked at the paper hard for a couple of minutes, then nodded at the third man, who now stood behind the videographer in the tiny room. "Go ahead, Mr. Ireton. You can read our statement now." No "Mickey Mouse" from this man who was all business.

I decided to read the statement very slowly, so that my exaggeratedly slow delivery would be another clear sign that I was being coerced. The statement began, "To all my friends, to the editors of *Epoch* Magazine, and to the rulers of the Zionist entity." Well, at least the kidnappers weren't using the standard Arabic insult to Jews of "sons of pigs and monkeys."

"I am in the hands of the Followers of the Caliph," I continued, still reading as slowly as I dared in front of the camera. "They have treated me well and I have not been harmed." As I recalled the slaps from Tony, I angrily shrank from the words. I pronounced "well" as close to a Germanic-sounding "vell" as I dared to do without attracting the attention of either the videographer or this new, older man. I decided in my mind to refer to him as "Goodfellah," because he reminded me of one of that character in the 1990 movie about the Mafia. I paused, collecting my breath. "Continue without interruption," Goodfellah ordered.

"I am being held in a safe place in Gaza, far away from any place where foolish people might think they could rescue me. I ask you not to attempt any such thing. At the slightest sign of someone trying to interfere with the cause of the Followers of the Caliph, I shall be executed." I almost grimaced as I read this, but I kept reading, conscious of the gimlet eye of Goodfellah on me.

"I will only be released when the following conditions of the Followers of the Caliph have been met. First, all Crusader embassies in the Zionist entity must indicate within one week their decision to end diplomatic relations with the Zionist entity before the end of this month. Second, to show sincerity in this action, they must reduce their staff by half within two weeks." I pronounced "Zionist" as *Zeye-onist*, much as an Arab who spoke poor English would. Goodfellah didn't seem to pick it up. "Third, all Crusader countries must within seventy-two hours agree to recognize the Hamas-led Palestinian Authority in Gaza as the sole legitimate government of the Palestinian people. Fourth, the countries recognizing the Palestinian Authority must have at least one diplomatic representative in place in Gaza within one week of this video being released. Fifth, the Zionist" – again, I read *Zeyeonist* – "entity rulers must release from prison within one week one hundred members of Hamas currently being held. They will be named at the end of this video." As I read this, I felt my hands becoming clammy. If there was one thing I knew for certain, it was that the Israelis would almost certainly not release from prison terrorists who had been known to murder Israelis. They had done so once or twice, and they were harshly criticized by families of Israeli victims of terrorism. I was sure that at least some of the Hamas prisoners in the one hundred to be named at the end of the video would have committed murders of Israelis.

"These are the conditions of my release. The only way to guarantee my safe return to my family will be the completion, without exception, of all the conditions."

As I read the words "return to my family," I knew that these words alone would send a signal to *Epoch* and US government viewers that I was being held by a group that really didn't know very much about me. I didn't have any immediate family except my mother and sister back in Grand Rapids. The kidnappers didn't seem to have investigated whether or not I was married. Perhaps the kidnappers had made other mistakes as well.

"The Followers of the Caliph want it be known," I continued reading, "that, failing indications of a positive response to their demands within twenty-four hours, diplomats belonging to Crusader nations accredited to the Zionist entity will be liquidated at a time and place of the choosing of the Followers of the Caliph. If, after seven more days, there is no response, then I will be executed also."

I felt my pulse rate soar to almost panic levels as I uttered these words. Still holding the paper, I noticed that my hands were trembling. I looked up at Goodfellah. The man merely nodded to me to continue reading.

I had come almost to the end of the printed piece of paper. I read the last lines, "Now here is the list of names of the Hamas prisoners who must be released from Zionist prisons." There followed the whole tedious prisoner list of one hundred Arabic names. I concluded, "The motto of the Followers of the Caliph is as follows: 'Allah is our objective. The Prophet is our leader. Qur'an is our law. Jihad our way. Dying in the way of Allah is our highest hope."

So that was it. The Followers of the Caliph were a specific branch of the Muslim Brotherhood, the secret organization of radical Islamists founded in Egypt by Hasan al-Banna in 1928. The final words of the statement I had read were the actual motto of the Muslim Brotherhood. Hamas had proclaimed itself within its own charter to be the Palestine branch of the Muslim Brotherhood, but the Followers of the Caliph seemed to be trying to out-radicalize Hamas. Ostensibly, the Muslim Brotherhood was not a violent organization, but its influence was virtually ubiquitous in the Arab world; and many of its offshoots, including El Qaeda, had become extremely violent after ingesting the Brotherhood's ideology. Abdul Husseini's origins seemed to have been the Jordanian chapter of the movement.

After I had finished reading, I saw the red light on the video camera go off and the operator look up from the screen. I gazed at the unnerving eye of Goodfellah. He was still sitting on the stool, and Omar and Tony were edging out of the room with their Kalashnikovs.

"Mr. Ireton," Goodfellah said slowly, incongruously formal in his address, "You seem to be an intelligent man. I hope the editors of *Epoch* and the Zionist rulers are as intelligent as you. Your life depends on it. Incidentally, you could end the suspense over your life by accepting Islam with us. All you have to do is repeat the words *La ilaha illa allah, Mohammadur rasul allah*, which in English means, 'There is no Allah but Allah, and Mohammed is his prophet,' and we shall release you eventually. If you become a Muslim we shall not need to execute you."

This was an agonizing dilemma. I knew, of course, that I would not be blamed by *Epoch* or my colleagues if I converted to Islam at the point of a Kalashnikov, or more likely at the point of a kitchen carving knife that could also be used to behead me if I refused. But I didn't believe in Islam, and I didn't really believe in Christianity, though I would have termed myself an agnostic rather than an atheist. I thought of Trish and Clarissa, and I teared up almost instantly. Boy, I hoped they were doing some praying.

"Now we will leave you," said Goodfellah quietly. Under the cot is a blanket if you need it to cover you when you sleep. You know what the bucket is for. In an hour someone will come to you with some food. We will speak again in the morning."

With that, he followed the videographer man out of the room. The door was closed behind them and there was the sound of a key turning in the lock and of bolts being fastened outside the door at the top and the bottom.

I sat on the stool for a long time deep in thought. I wondered how *Epoch*, how the US government, how the Israeli government would respond. It looked pretty bleak. If I'd been a correspondent in Israel viewing the video, as all of my colleagues would be before long, I'd come to the conclusion that I didn't have a chance. The Israelis would never release any convicted Hamas murderers, and no Western embassy would dream of cutting off diplomatic relations with Israel because its diplomats were being murdered. The thought that this might happen, regardless of what *Epoch* or anyone else decided, slowly began to seep into my thoughts. Then, without any warning, a sort of catharsis happened. I just started sobbing uncontrollably, the heaving moans echoing off the green cellar walls.

XI

WHENEVER RAYNA WAS nervous, she tended to drum her fingers on the nearest available flat service. That is, she drummed her fingers when she wasn't clicking her ballpoint pen open and closed in a manner guaranteed to drive quite mad anyone who shared an office or a living space with her. She was nervous now, and her fingers were drumming so furiously on her desk that it was just as well the woman she shared an office with, an Israeli air force colonel, was away on a temporary assignment in the north of Israel.

"Come on, come on, come on, pick up, pick up." She was listening to the infuriating sound of the phone ringing at an office somewhere in Jerusalem and not being answered. "For God's sake," she said to no one in particular as she held the phone to her ear, "doesn't anyone work at this place?"

She decided to put the phone down and think through again what she would have to say to the man she was trying to reach. If she didn't play it just right, there was a good chance he'd tell her to go and get lost. It happened often enough that the IDF spokesman's office had been entirely uncooperative with the Israeli media. In response, some sections of the media responded in kind; whenever the IDF needed something that only the media could provide they stubbornly wouldn't co-operate. It wasn't confidential information that the IDF needed, simply a backgrounder on what had been said at a Palestinian press conference that was on the record, or how the Palestinian authorities were doling out – or not doling out – accreditation to Israeli or foreign reporters. Rayna hoped to heaven that the office she was now phoning in Jerusalem hadn't been snubbed by a sulky clerk at the IDF spokesman's office on a Friday morning, for example, just before the sabbath.

Had the Jerusalem office she was calling been able to identify her office on its caller ID? She had no way of knowing, and wouldn't have been able to do anything about it anyway. Or were they simply in a no-phone-answering mood? Rayna frequently came across businesses and organizations that, for no discernible reason at all, simply didn't bother to answer their phones for hours at a time. No one ever seemed to know what triggered this maddening decision simply to drop out of life for a while; but it did happen.

She got gloomier as she started speculating why no one answered; all sorts of discouraging ideas came to mind and she momentarily wondered if she was even in the right profession. But now all the discipline of her training and indeed her upbringing in a military family kicked in. She picked up the phone one more time and punched in the number.

It rang twice and then was picked up. In her surprise she almost forgot what she had been calling about.

"Er, is that Gideon Video Services?" she half-stammered into the receiver.

"Yes, Gideon Video Services here. Who is calling us?" The voice was pleasant and normal. It didn't seem to be that of a person who had spent the previous several minutes refusing to answer the phone.

Rayna bit her lip in uncertainty how to respond. Should she say she was with the IDF or not? Should she indicate which department of the IDF it was? How would this apparently unflustered, uncomplicated person at the other end of the phone deal with her request?

She decided to try the front-door approach. "I would like to speak with Jean-Louis David," she said.

There was the briefest pause at the other end of the phone.

"Well, he is not here. He is out on a story."

"Do you know when he will be back?"

"Before I tell you that," the man replied, suddenly rather suspicious, "Why don't you tell me who wants to speak with him?"

"This is the Israeli Defense Ministry," Rayna said, suddenly intuiting what she needed to say to get through to Jean-Louis. "I'm afraid I cannot discuss with you what the topic is, but I do need to speak with him."

"The Defense Ministry, is it? Is he in trouble with the censors this time?"

That was a stroke of luck. If Gideon Video Service was worried about having violated censorship regulations, the people there might be quite polite to her.

"No, he's not in trouble with the censors this time." Rayna, who'd never met Jean-Louis, took a chance that Jean-Louis might have run into difficulties before. "But he might be in the future if he's not prepared to meet with us."

"And who is 'us'?"

"I am Captain Rayna Shanach of the IDF."

"And how is Jean-Louis supposed to get in touch with you when he returns?"

"I will give you my office number. If Jean-Louis David is reachable by mobile phone, please call him right away and ask him to call me immediately. It is extremely important."

"So it's not about censorship, then, is it?"

Rayna was annoyed. The man was complicating things by being inquisitive. She started clicking her ballpoint furiously. She decided to take a chance with the man who had picked up the phone.

"Look, I'm sure Jean-Louis will explain everything when this is all over. Meanwhile, please have him call us. It's very, very important." She then gave her office number in the Hakirya in Tel Aviv.

She was drumming her fingers on the desk when her phone rang less than two minutes later. It was Jean-Louis. She was surprised at how rapidly he had returned her call until she remembered that he, like many recent immigrants, was rather overawed by the ID. It wouldn't be long before he'd be called up for his own compulsory military service of three years. He didn't want to do anything to earn black marks on his record before that happened.

"Jean-Louis David speaking." Poor Jean-Louis had discovered in his first weeks in Israel that, if he didn't speak Hebrew and didn't know Russian, he'd better pick up as much English as he could. Almost everyone in Israel who had finished normal schooling spoke some English.

"How soon can you get down to Tel Aviv?" Rayna asked.

"As it happens, I am in Tel Aviv right now. I'm in the Tel Aviv Hilton Hotel covering a press conference."

"Excellent. Can you come around to an office in Hakirya right away?"

"You mean the Defense Ministry complex on Kaplan Street?"

"Yes."

"Which entrance do I take?"

"The main one on Kaplan Street. Show your press ID at the main gate and give them my name, rank, and this phone number."

"I'll be there in about fifteen minutes."

As good as his word, Jean-Louis was taking the elevator to Captain Shanach's office on the third floor of the Defense Ministry building in Tel Aviv less than fifteen minutes later. He knocked on the door of room 415 and waited for an answer. A female corporal passing by in the same corridor looked at him quizzically; there weren't many offices in the building that required a knock at the door.

"Come in, come in," said Rayna impatiently.

It was a large office, surprisingly tastefully furnished. Handsome Palestinian rugs covered the floor, the walls were covered in finely painted water color landscapes of Israeli coastal views, and – most surprisingly – there was a vase with freshly-cut roses on a table in the center of the room. There were two desks in the room, one of them manned by a male lieutenant staring intently at a computer screen, the other – larger and set diagonally in one of the corners of the room – quite clean of any paper except a large brown notebook. Rayna was sitting behind it. Jean-Louis was taken aback at first by how extraordinarily pretty she was, and by how superbly her uniform seemed to be tailored to her shape. But she had a frown on her face and he didn't make any attempt at opening small-talk.

"Are you aware of the kidnapping that took place in Gaza a few hours ago?" she asked Jean-Louis after standing up and offering the briefest handshake. "Please sit down." Jean-Louis sat down in the comfortable, tastefully upholstered chair opposite Rayna's desk.

"No. What kidnapping?"

"An American reporter, the bureau chief for *Epoch* Magazine, has been kidnapped in Gaza. His kidnappers are a group called 'Followers of the Caliph.' We've never heard of them, but an Israeli news agency – I won't tell you which one – received a videotape to be broadcast publicly. Quite correctly, they let us know before they released it. It will be broadcast nationally and internationally in two hours' time. The American reporter's name is Richard Ireton."

"Ireton?" said Jean-Louis, startled. "Is he a tall American with hair that flops down over his forehead?"

Rayna smiled at the idea.

"Yes, that's him. Do you know him?"

"Well, I met him a few weeks ago at a new *olim* reception in Jerusalem. He introduced me to another new immigrant who in turn helped me find work. She's now my girlfriend."

"I'm very happy for you," she said. "I'm particularly happy you know Richard Ireton. We want him rescued as soon as possible, and we think you can help us do it."

Jean-Louis turned pale. "Me rescue someone?" he asked. "You've got the wrong man. I've not yet done my military service. I don't know one end of a rifle from the other."

Rayna grew impatient. "We are not expecting – and we are not asking – you to take part in a rescue operation. We are only asking you to go to

Gaza as a reporter with your video camera. You have the press credentials and you will have no problem getting in there."

"Maybe I will have no problem getting in, but what about getting out? Gaza is dangerous. Listen, you're just telling me that an American reporter has been kidnapped."

Rayna suppressed a sigh of impatience. The ballpoint in her hand started clicking. Jean-Louis might turn out to be a problem. She opened a drawer in her desk and pulled out a thick manila folder. She plopped it noisily on the flat and empty surface of her desk and began leafing through it. "Have you heard from Anne-Sophie recently?" she asked, without looking up from the dossier. "And how is Georges doing? And Daniel? I expect he's finding out how he can keep out of the way of Abdullah Farouqi and his boys."

Jean-Louis turned even paler. How much did the IDF know about him? He was silent as Rayna flipped through the documents on her desk.

"Ah yes," Rayna went on, "and I wonder if Chantal is still in Paris? Your teacher, Henri Brevard, has quite an eye for these African women. Did he tell about his earlier girlfriend, Marianna, from Nigeria? He didn't? Oh he's a rich one. By the way, have they fixed the elevator at 36 Place des Vosges?"

Rayna looked up now and stared straight at Jean-Louis.

"You've really done your homework on me," he said, twisting his fingers nervously in front of his lap.

"Of course," Rayna replied tersely. "We wouldn't have brought you here unless we knew a lot about you. Now, tell me about what happened in Paris."

Jean-Louis frowned. He'd told a few people about what had propelled him to make a decision to emigrate from France to Israel, to make aliya, but he didn't like doing it. The memories were still traumatic.

"I was returning from the Sorbonne to my home on the Avenue Beaumarchais with my friend Daniel. He'd just left me to take the metro in another direction. As I approached Bastille, I noticed a crowd of demonstrators approaching, shouting something or other. I didn't think it was a big deal at first. Demonstrators are always marching to Bastille down the Avenue Beaumarchais. It's a dull day in Paris if they are not.

"But there was something different about this group. Even from two hundred meters away it was clear that they were very angry. Then I started catching their shouts on the breeze. 'Death to the Jews!' and – incredibly – 'Back to the ovens!' It made my blood curdle to hear them. I thought I'd be able to avoid them by walking to the other side of Bastille, but a group of them ran across the road and seemed to make a bee-line towards me. I turned around and started to walk in the other direction, but they caught up with me, surrounded me and started kicking and beating me. I think they must have been immigrants from the *banlieus* north of Paris.

"I fell to the ground and tried to protect my head by curling up into a ball, but they were pummeling me with their boots. It was the most terrifying thing I've ever experienced in my life. Have you any idea what it is to be the target of hatred by people who don't even know you, who just hate you because you appear to belong to a group they hate? Finally, I heard the siren of an approaching police car, the whistle of the flics as they got out, and then everything went dark."

"You were in the hospital a few days, I see," said Rayna, flicking through the dossier. "Then what happened?" She appeared to be continuing to read, and didn't look at Jean-Louis.

"I realized that Paris just wouldn't be safe for me anymore. I decided to make *aliya*."

"Did your parents agree with that decision?"

"My mother thought it was okay. My dad, who is a dentist and thinks he's more French than General de Gaulle, totally disapproved."

"Tell me about the Place des Vosges," Rayna continued prodding.

"Well, since you seem to know everything about my earlier life, what do you need to know from me?"

"There's a reason why I'm asking you this. Go on."

Jean-Louis shrugged. "That was where I took the course in basic introduction to videography," he went on.

"Your teacher was Henri Brevard?"

"Yes," Jean-Louis replied slowly and carefully. "Is he going to be involved in this?

Rayna laughed. "Of course not. But we know who he is." She paused, looking carefully through the pages in front of her. Then she looked up and for the first time."Was there any incident in your three-week course that you hadn't expected?"

"Yes. We were at the Forum des Halles one afternoon just randomly shooting shoppers when a thief grabbed a woman's purse just meters from where we were and started running off with it. He hadn't gone very—"

"What did you do?" snapped Rayna, interrupting him brusquely.

"I and my buddy Georges, also a student at the school, grabbed our cameras and began chasing him. He must have been real dumb, because the place was crawling with plain-clothes flics, a couple of whom grabbed him. I shot the whole thing and it ran that night on France 24, the TV news channel."

Rayna smiled, leaned back in her chair, and clicked the ballpoint slowly three times. "That's what I wanted to hear," she said. "And that is why we chose you. You still have your French passport?"

"Of course."

"Do you have it on you?"

"Yes."

"Good. Now let's take a look at the video with Ireton."

At this comment, the lieutenant at the other desk rose from where he was sitting and pushed a DVD into a video player atop a table on the opposite wall. The image of Ireton came on the screen immediately, as did the words he'd been forced to read. "To all my friends, to the editors of *Epoch* Magazine, and to the rulers of the Zionist entity," the video began. Jean-Louis watched it through in silence. As it concluded with the chilling words, "failing indications of a positive response to their requirements within twenty-four hours, diplomats belonging to Crusader nations accredited to the Zionist entity will be liquidated at a time and place of the choosing of the Followers of the Caliph. If, after seven more days, there is no response, then I will be executed also," Jean-Louis began to breath rapidly. He started to perspire. Rayna watched him closely.

"By the way," she said as if absent-mindedly, "do you know who we think is behind the Followers of the Caliph? We think a Jerusalem-based Palestinian man called Abdul Husseini is connected with them. I thought you'd be interested in knowing that he and Abdullah Farouqi both joined the Muslim Brotherhood in Jordan at about the same time. You know who Abdullah Farouqi is, I suppose?"

"He was the man behind the anti-Jewish demonstrations in Paris. I've heard of Husseini. He's from the Palestine-El Quds center and he's supposed to be related to Haji Amin al-Husseini."

"He is related. By the way, have all your scars and bruises healed from that incident?"

"Yes," Jean-Louis answered grimly. "The ones on the outside are all healed. It's the ones on the inside that will never be healed." Jean-Louis tapped his head as he said this.

"I'm sure you are right," said Rayna impatiently. "I think the opportunity you have to work for the security of Israel will help that process. You realize that if we do not get Ireton out soon they will start murdering foreign diplomats in Israel within a matter of hours? The Americans will be fairly well protected, as will the British, the French, and the Germans. But do you think we can provide twenty-four hour protection for every assistant cook at the Costa Rican Embassy?" She shrugged cynically. Then she leaned back in her chair. "You know," she said, as much to the walls as to the two people in the room with her, "my father always used to say that if the Palestinians really wanted to make life difficult for us, they'd start murdering foreign diplomats on Israeli soil." She paused and went back to looking at Jean-Louis' dossier. She kept her head down and said slowly and quietly, "Perhaps that's exactly what they want to start doing now."

"What do you want me to do?" he said quietly.

Rayna replied, "Get into Gaza, go to the neighborhood where he is being held, and give us a really good video footage of the area."

"But how do you know where he is being held?"

"I can't tell you how we know, but we know."

Jean-Louis was baffled. "You've only just received this video," he said, "which was made probably a matter of hours ago. Nobody had officially reported Ireton as missing before that. And now you say that you know where he is? If that's the case, why don't you just go in and rescue him?"

"It's not as simple as that," Rayna said quickly. "We know the location, but we don't know much about the neighborhood."

Rayna watched Jean-Louis closely. He seemed to be thinking something over in his mind.

"All right," he said, "suppose I get down to Gaza. Will you tell me before I get there where I have to go to shoot the video footage you need?"

"Of course not. We cannot take the risk that you will tell someone in Israel where Ireton is being held, nor can we risk that once in Gaza, you will bumble your way into the wrong neighborhood and be followed all the way in. When you arrive in Gaza, you will be approached at different times by two different people. The second person will take you to the location of the kidnappers."

"Who? How will I recognize this person? How will I be sure that he is not a spy? Anybody might approach me in Gaza and say that he knows where the kidnapped American reporter is."

"When you reach Gaza and go through the Erez checkpoint, someone will come up to you and say something to you in French."

"You mean, 'It's a fine afternoon here in this armpit of the Arab world?'"

Rayna laughed out loud in spite of her attempt to be nothing but serious. "No," she said. "It will be a quotation from a famous French philosopher: 'tout va bien dans le meilleur de mondes possibles (Everything goes well in the best of all possible worlds)."

"Oh, Voltaire's *Candide*," said Jean-Louis relaxing. "I can play that game."

"Good. You will say 'Voltaire' after he says that phrase to you. The next person you meet who speaks French to you will take you to the location of Ireton's kidnappers. He will identify himself simply by saying 'Sartre.' You will reply with a phrase from one of Sartre's plays."

"Of course, you obviously want me to repeat that phrase from the Sartre play *Huit Clos* (No Exit)," said Jean-Louis, getting into the spirit of the thing, 'L'enfer, c'est les autres' (Hell is other people)."

"Very good, Mr. David, very good," said Rayna. "I should have known that someone educated in the Fifth Arrondissement of Paris would know his French literature."

"I may be educated in French literature," Jean-Louis said, "but I'll need more than a literary education to wander with my video camera into kidnap neighborhoods of Gaza without attracting the attention of every member of the Hamas Executive Force within five hundred metres."

"We will provide you with an escort of armed men who will be dressed like Hamas Executive Force gunmen," said Rayna. "Your sole job will be to use your video camera effectively once you are in the location and point your camera in the direction they tell you. As soon as the location shooting is completed, they will escort you back to the Erez crossing point. The Israeli soldiers on our side of the crossing will be expecting you and you will have no trouble getting back into Israel. The IDF officer in this room will meet you and take the video tape from you."

At this point, the lieutenant rose from his desk again and came towards Jean-Louis with his hand outstretched.

"Monsieur David, meet Lieutenant Shavit," Rayna said.

Jean-Louis rose from his chair and extended his arm to the young officer. *He looks barely twenty-two*, he thought. "Enchante (delighted)," he said in French without thinking.

Rayna then told Jean-Louis to call Gideon Video Services and explain that he'd been asked to discuss with the IDF one of his recent stories. It was a half-hearted attempt to keep up the pretence that censorship matters were what had prompted his summons to the Defense Ministry. All journalists in Israel, foreign and domestic, were required to submit to Israel censors in advance of transmission overseas any print or electronic material that the military considered might compromise national security.

"You understand that we are asking you to do something that might involve risks. We cannot order you to do this because you are a civilian. Is that clear?"

"A lot of things have become clearer to me in the months since it became obvious that I would have to come to Israel to live. Is Ireton Jewish?"

"No, but he is an honest reporter and he likes and respects the Jewish people. He doesn't like it when malicious people make up stories about us. And" – Rayna hesitated here – "I've met Mr. Ireton and I like him personally. I don't want him to come to any harm."

Jean-Louis was asked to sign papers absolving the IDF for any responsibility if harm came to him on this mission. He had to ask Rayna to translate it into English for him because he still read Hebrew only with difficulty. "Goodbye," said Rayna to him, shaking his hand with a surprisingly strong grip. "And good luck." The lieutenant asked him to follow him down the corridor to another room where he was introduced to a young sergeant charged with driving him to the Erez crossing point.

"What about my car outside Hakirya? It's parked on a meter."

"If you give me the keys and tell me where you have parked it, I'll park it in a safe place for you. The sergeant who brings you back from the Erez crossing will bring you back to me and you'll get your car back safe and sound." The lieutenant then returned to Rayna's office.

Rayna had already gone over to his computer screen after he'd gone and begun typing in several collections of coded passwords. A grid-map of Gaza streets suddenly flashed onto the screen. Just as the lieutenant re-entered the room, on the top right-hand corner of the screen a cursor was blinking.

"It seems to be close to the intersection of Salah al-Din Street and Gamel Abdul Nasser Boulevard," Rayna said, examining the on-screen map closely as the lieutenant came back to his position in front of the screen. "Isn't that a rather upscale neighborhood?"

"Yes," said the lieutenant. "It's out of Gaza City and much less built-up than other parts of the strip. It would be the logical place to take someone who'd been kidnapped. Now that we know *where* he is, we need to know what it looks like on the ground."

"Yes, we do," said Rayna. "Now, can we get him out before they start killing diplomats in Herzliya?"

* * *

Margaret Rosewood felt as if she had aged ten years overnight. She'd gotten a call from Rayna ten minutes before the hourly news bulletin on *Kol Israel*, the Voice of Israel, had broadcast the news of Ireton's kidnapping and the chilling recording of a portion of his coerced video. That had been around ten o'clock the previous evening. Since then, she'd been on the phone to Burton Lasch in New York, to Rick's mother in Grand Rapids, Michigan, to everyone in the bureau, to everyone she knew in the IDF, to Esther, Rick's landlady, and to Trish and Clarissa. The previous evening they'd still been in Galilee, but early in the morning they'd arrived in Jerusalem. Now they were both in the bureau, trying to take comfort from the fact that Margaret was as good a point person during the crisis as anyone could be. She was calm, orderly, and decisive. But she was under great strain.

"Can the IDF not do anything?" Clarissa asked as Margaret brewed a second pot of coffee for Trish.

"The IDF doesn't control Gaza anymore. It has had no presence in the city except during incursions in recent months to try to shut down the missiles that keep falling onto the Israeli border town of Sderot."

"Well, don't they have commandoes or something?" Trish asked, looking over her shoulder as Margaret walked by.

Margaret sighed. "Believe me," she said, "the IDF is treating this kidnapping as a much higher priority than some previous kidnappings. After all, the entire state of Israel will be affected if they start murdering foreign diplomats here."

At this point, Benjamin Lifshutz came into the bureau, his camera-bag over his shoulder and his lined, wrinkled face more careworn than usual. He introduced himself to Clarissa and Trish before Margaret could. He was clearly dazzled by Trish, whose dark skin was set off against an elegant pair of tight cream pants and a blue silk blouse. "So you're the secret Richard's been keeping from us," he said beaming at her, the crow's feet spreading out around his eyes as he smiled. "Well, I suppose Richard had to do something dramatic to make sure he got your attention just as you arrived in Jerusalem." And he laughed with such good humor that Trish and Clarissa laughed too. Even Margaret momentarily lost her frown.

"Well, I've always known Rick has a flair for the dramatic," Trish said, "but I think this is taking it a bit far." There was a hint of bitterness in her laugh. "Last year he was taking on half the Chinese army in Guangzhou. Now he seems to have gotten the attention of a gang of kidnappers in Gaza."

"I think he annoyed them," said Lifshutz, "because he rumbled them in an attempt to pin an atrocity on the IDF. You know, unfortunately the IDF has not always behaved perfectly towards the Palestinians. But in this case, I think he was about to demonstrate that they'd done nothing wrong. Margaret," he said, turning towards her, "at what time did you first hear from the IDF about the kidnapping?"

"About ten minutes before 10.00 p.m."

"And did they say how they had heard about the kidnapping?"

"They said they'd received news of the video, which had been sent to several news organizations and would be broadcast shortly."

"That's strange. It's not usually the IDF that breaks the news of a kidnapping. I think they must have known about it independently of the video's being delivered."

"How would they know that?" Margaret asked.

"Who called you from the IDF about the video?" he asked.

"A Captain Rayna Shanach."

"Rayna, eh?" A mysterious smile came over his face. "That's interesting. Then they certainly knew about it before the video was delivered."

"How do you know that?" Margaret asked, amazed at Benjamin's apparently private knowledge of the workings of the IDF.

"Oh, let's just say that I know the department of the IDF that she works for." Without saying another word, he went on into his office.

Clarissa made a face of theatrical astonishment. "Well, I've got work to do," she said, without explaining. "Trish, you know where to find me if you need me. I'm going back to the hotel room. Please call me if there are any further developments." She walked with great determination out of the bureau.

"Work?" said Margaret after she had gone. "I thought you two were here on vacation."

Trish looked a little awkward. "Well, not work in the sense of going to an office," she said hesitantly. "Clarissa's a missionary, and missionaries do a lot of praying. They sometimes call this 'work.'"

"Oh, I see," said Margaret, looking no less perplexed than before she heard this. "What's the time now?" she asked, suddenly looking worried again.

"It's just before noon," said Trish.

"Then it's almost twenty-four hours," she said.

"From what?" asked Trish.

"From the kidnapping, or at least from the video. The Followers of the Caliph said they would start killing diplomats in Israel if they hadn't heard from the Israeli government within twenty-four hours. Let's see what's on the news."

There was a large, rather old-fashioned-looking radio in the bureau reception area. Margaret turned it on and sat down in the chair behind her desk. As if on cue, Benjamin came out of his office and looked towards the radio. Just as unheralded, Ari came out of his office, and Ira as well. There was a tense silence as they all waited for the news to come on.

"The time is 12.00 o'clock," said the announcer. "Here is the news from the Voice of Israel. A Belgian diplomat was slightly wounded in Tel Aviv this morning when a gunman on a motorbike shot at his car as he was on his way to work. The gunman escaped from the scene on his motorbike. The government of Israel has issued a statement strongly condemning this attempted murder. Following the kidnapping in Gaza of American reporter Richard Ireton of *Epoch* Magazine, Foreign Minister Yitzhak Halutz said the situation in Gaza was now completely out of control. He called on the Hamas authorities in Gaza to ensure the swift and safe return of the American reporter and the suppression of all criminal acts against innocent civilians. The foreign ministry says it does not know whether the attack on the diplomat was related to the threat of future terrorism made in the Richard Ireton video. In other news…"

"Phew!" said Margaret. "So far no murders. Let's hope they keep on missing their target."

"I wouldn't count on that," said Benjamin Lifshutz quietly. "I think these people will learn very quickly from their mistakes." He frowned deeply.

"You mean next time they'll shoot straight?"

"Precisely."

Margaret turned away and dialed the number for Rayna. When the phone was picked up at the other end, a man's voice answered and apologized that Captain Shanach would not be available for phone calls for the next several minutes. She turned towards Benjamin, who had watched her making the call, and repeated what she had heard.

"Well, that is perhaps the first good news of the day. They're on to it."

"Who's onto it?" said Ira, barging into the conversation.

"The people in this country who know what they are doing," Benjamin said with mock solemnity.

"I hope someone knows what they are doing," said Margaret with sigh.

* * *

Jean-Louis spent the forty-five minutes from Tel Aviv to the Erez crossing point into Gaza talking to the sergeant who was driving him about video cameras. They spoke an inaccurate, but workable English with each other. Apparently, the sergeant was an amateur videographer and he was fascinated by the details of the profession. He looked serious when Jean-Louis told him about the circumstances that had prompted him to make *aliya* and to take a crash course in videography in Paris.

The transit through the border was surprisingly smooth. The sergeant with Jean-Louis leaned over and whispered in the ear of one of the two Israeli border guards on the Israeli side, and Jean-Louis was swiftly waved through. After watching carefully to make sure he was through to the Palestinian side of the border, the sergeant walked back towards his car on the Israeli side and waited.

Jean-Louis was nervous as he came up to the Palestinian immigration officers on their side of the border crossing, but he received a stamp in his French passport without any problem. As he cautiously walked into Gaza proper, however, he was without escort and felt nervous. His heart-rate skipped a beat when he was quickly approached by two men with long black beards carrying Kalashnikovs and wearing black turtle-neck sweaters.

"Tout va bien dans le meilleur de mondes possibles," the first man said in quite presentable French, with no trace of an Arabic accent.

"Voltaire," Jean-Louis answered. "Suivez-moi (follow me)," said the man who had spoken to him. Jean-Louis was impressed. The Israelis seemed to have French-speaking agents on the ground already in Gaza.

The second of the bearded men with the Kalashnikov followed closely behind Jean-Louis. To the Frenchman, it seemed that passersby in the street could not avoid thinking that he was being escorted under arrest. He was anxious, however, lest a real Hamas Executive Force patrol might intercept them and call their bluff.

They walked about eight blocks, but changed direction frequently as they did so. The gunman in the lead seemed to be making sure that, if anyone noticed the small procession at all, it would be seen going down a variety of different streets. Finally, the three-man team turned into an alley where small boys were playing a noisy game of scratch soccer. There were two motorbikes parked in the alley and two more bearded men, clad in identical black clothes, also carrying Kalashnikovs, standing by them. Jean-Louis' escort leader took him up to one of the motocyclists who looked him straight in the eye and said, so quietly that had he not known what he was expecting to hear, Jean-Louis would not have understood what he was saying. "Sartre," he said, this time with a heavy accent that made his quiet voice even harder to hear.

"Huit clos," Jean-Louis answered, as instructed.

"Is your video equipment ready?" asked the man in English.

"Of course," he replied. "That's what I am here for."

"Can you use your camera with one hand from the backseat of a motorbike?" the man asked.

"It's not ideal, but if it's necessary, I can film from there."

"Please get on the bike behind me, hold onto the strap on the seat with either your left or right hand and when we give you the signal, begin shooting with the other hand. We need video of the fronts of all the houses on the street we are going to be passing through. We will pass down the street only twice, once in one direction so you can photograph all the houses on that side, and once on the other so you can do the same there. Be very careful not to point your camera at anyone carrying a gun. They may be trigger-happy and get the wrong impression." Jean-Louis gulped. *Rayna didn't say anything about this*, he thought.

He mounted a bike behind the man who had spoken the name "Sartre" to him. Immediately, it set off out of the alley, the second bike following. They rode quite slowly for several blocks, apparently taking care to change direction every few blocks so that a casual observer would not know for sure in which direction they were headed. The streets of Gaza were the usual afternoon chaos of trucks, donkey carts, Mercedes sedans edging through traffic with dark-tinted windows, delivery vans, and constantly unpredictable pedestrians darting in and out between oncoming traffic in a sort of guerrilla war for priority on the road. Jean-Louis, his visual attentiveness sharpened by the tension and fear that this motorbike tour of Gaza had sparked in him, found himself noticing armed men long before the motorbike came close to them. He tried to feign a bored expression, as though it were a completely routine thing to be sitting pillion-style on a motorbike, holding a video-camera behind a bearded man with a Kalashnikov, while driving up and down the streets of Gaza. Whenever the motorbike approached groups of armed men, he tried to hide the video-camera behind his back. He just hoped that no gunman, idly gazing after a disappearing motorbike, would notice the video-camera, then observe it as it passed the same street location, this time in the opposite direction, a second time.

As the two bikes began to move deeper into Gaza city, the neighborhoods changed. Now Jean-Louis realized that they were entering what seemed like a more upscale residential area. The homes had high outside walls and were two or three storied high, inevitably with a satellite TV dish attached to the roof. Without warning, the bike Jean-Louis was riding slowed almost to walking pace, causing him to clutch desperately the strap atop the pillion-seat to steady himself. With his right hand, the motorcyclist slowly made an up-and-down motion and then swept his hand up and down the street. They had arrived at the street where serious footage was needed.

Jean-Louis raised his camera to eye-level and looked through the viewfinder rather than at the small video-screen that was the feature of most digital videocams. He thought this would look more amateurish and might attract less attention from people casually observing the motorbike procession. They moved slowly down the street with Jean-Louis trying to film every house on the right-hand side of the street before turning around at the end of the street and riding back to film the other side. There was one house in the middle of the block during the first pass down the street that had a heavy metal gate and in which, surprisingly, there were European-style shutters on all the windows. The shutters were closed. There seemed to be no sign of life in the house. Jean-Louis had an uneasy feeling as they rode by; on the flat roof of the house stood a bearded man with a Kalashnikov – what was it about Gaza and bearded men with Kalashnikovs? – who, miraculously, seemed to be looking in the other direction and didn't notice the small motorbike convoy. As they turned around and went up the other side of the street, the video camera was not so noticeable. Jean-Louis hoped against hope that the man on the roof was still looking in the other direction and still hadn't spotted the two bikes. But he couldn't be sure, and didn't dare look back. If the man on the roof had been facing them at that moment, he would have found Jean-Louis' movement suspicious.

The motorbike convoy rode on for two more blocks and then stopped in another alley. "Okay, that is all we need. Now we take you back to the Erez crossing."

Jean-Louis heaved a sigh of relief and carefully placed all the video equipment back in the camera case he had brought with him. Then the two-bike team, Jean-Louis still holding on to the strap on the pillion of the first bike, rode straight back to the border with Israel without any further zig-zags.

Jean-Louis was almost overcome with relief. He'd completed a difficult, potentially dangerous video assignment, but hadn't been stopped or questioned, much less shot at. Now all he had to do was cross over to the Israeli side of the Erez border point and hand over the tape to the IDF sergeant who had escorted him there originally. He was about to walk back to the formidable fortifications of the crossing point when his motor bicycle crewman told him to wait. A cell phone being carried in a jacked pocket by the motorcyclist broke into jarring life with a salsa dance ringing tone. *Right*, thought Jean-Louis, *we've got salsa dancing when half the Palestinian morals police are within earshot*. But after answering the call, his bearded motorcyclist spoke Hebrew to the person at the other end of the line.

There was a long conversation, during which the motorcyclist did little of the speaking and most of the listening. From time to time he glanced at Jean-Louis as he spoke. The Frenchman realized that they must be discussing plans for him. His heart sank. He now knew for sure it wouldn't be a simple matter of returning to Tel Aviv and Jerusalem right way.

"Please get back on the bike," said the man, and Jean-Louis did as he was told. The two bikes then roared off in convoy at great speed to another part of Gaza and approached a private residence whose front gate opened automatically as the bikes approached it. Then the iron gate closed automatically behind them. The two men got off their bikes and signaled to Jean-Louis to follow them into the house. Again, the door opened and closed automatically behind them.

Jean-Louis walked into a neon-lit room with a long, central table around which were a dozen chairs. No fewer than six of these were already occupied by dark, bearded types who seemed to be the spitting image of Jean-Louis' own motorcyclist and his comrade. But a seventh man at the table was a much smaller, almost completely bald man in his forties, the sparse hair on the backs and sides of his head of a salt-and-pepper color. He was smoking a cigarette with intense, deep puffs, and at first glance three of the other six men were smoking too. Jean-Louis' motorcyclist and his comrade remained standing, and did not smoke. But the air in the room was thick with cigarette smoke, and Jean-Louis started coughing. On seeing this, the small, bald man who was wearing a black turtleneck shirt and a dark brown jacket, stubbed his cigarette out and asked the others to do the same. With some shrugging of shoulders, they did so.

Jean-Louis was shown to a seat at one end of the table, opposite the small man, whom he instantly assumed was the leader of the team.

"You are Jean-Louis David and you agreed to a video assignment in Gaza requested by one of the IDF departments. Thank you for performing this. Unfortunately, our orders have changed and we cannot let you go back to Israel just yet. We need you here for something else. But first, can you please give us the video you took on the ride you just took?" Jean-Louis reached into his camera case, retrieved the tape, and handed it over.

"Thank you. You may call me Shimon," the older man said. "Please don't ask me to tell you anything else. What I can tell you is that twenty minutes ago a Dutch diplomat was murdered quite close to his embassy in Tel Aviv. The people who are holding Richard Ireton are extremely dangerous and may continue murdering diplomats even after Ireton is rescued. The government of Israel, however, must take immediate measures against this terrorism, and we may have to force Hamas to suppress the Followers of the Caliph, whoever they really are, immediately and harshly. If this were an Israeli journalist who had been kidnapped, we would have accepted that his life might have to be forfeited for larger concerns of national security. But for various reasons, our government has decided that we must try to rescue Ireton. Because the killings of diplomats in Israel has started, however, we must get him out of Gaza as soon as is humanly possible in order to be in a position to force Hamas to act against his kidnapers. Do you follow me?"

"Yes," said Jean-Louis, "but I told Captain Sha – "

"You do not need to mention any names of the Israeli officials you spoke with," interrupted Shimon impatiently.

"— the captain in Tel Aviv," Jean-Louis corrected himself, "that I am not a soldier, and certainly not a commando. I have never even held a rifle."

There were loud guffaws around the table among the bearded young men when he said this. Jean-Louis felt awkward and embarrassed.

Shimon looked at him steadily. "Don't worry," he said, trying to be reassuring. "We are not expecting you to do anything that a soldier might do. But we do think we need your help. We have to get the American out within a matter of two hours at the most. It's not only his life that is at risk, it is that of unknown diplomats who have entrusted their safety in Israel to Israeli security services. I think you can understand what the consequences would be for Israel if all of a sudden it became impossible for foreign diplomats to live here."

Jean-Louis was silent. Shimon looked at him carefully to see if he were paying attention and agreeing with him, then went on.

"We know where Ireton is being held. We now know exactly what the place looks like, and we have your videos to provide even greater detail. What we have to do is design a plan very soon – in no more than an hour – that we can execute swiftly and effectively. There's some coffee in the next room. Why don't you help yourself, or lie down for a few minutes if you like, while we work out how we are going to do this."

The six men were all staring intently at Jean-Louis. He realized that they wanted him out of the way while they made their plans. He realized also that they were probably speculating, each one separately, whether Jean-Louis could perform whatever it was that he was needed to do in order for the operation to be successful. He got up from his chair and went to the door that had been pointed to by Shimon, opened it, and found himself in a surprisingly pleasant and relaxing room. There were at least three comfortable sofas, each one long enough to accommodate a grown man stretched out, a small refrigerator, and a coffee machine that seemed to have percolated only recently, because the smell of coffee was fresh and the machine was still hissing and gurgling. On a low coffee table there were popular magazines lying about – in Hebrew.

So this must be one of Israel's undercover safe houses in Gaza, Jean-Louis thought. Since he had now seen so much more than any ordinary Israeli citizen should see, much less a brand-new *oleh*, of Israeli special forces in action, would they consider him a security liability after the event? That could certainly present problems.

He had made himself a cup of coffee in a Styrofoam cup, grabbed two cookies that were on a plastic tray, helped himself to milk from the fridge and was about to lie down on one of the sofas when the door opened from the room where the meeting had been taking place. It was Shimon. Without ceremony he sat down on a sofa opposite where Jean-Louis was sitting.

"Look," he said. "I realize you didn't volunteer for a dangerous job in Gaza, and what you were told in Tel Aviv involved only a relatively straightforward video shoot. But I need to tell you that you have an opportunity to be present at what may be a turning point in the survival of the State of Israel. This particular kidnapping could go two ways. Either we can rescue the American, eliminate his kidnappers and put enormous pressure on Hamas to suppress the kidnap organization and its supporters, or we lose possibly everything: the life of the American, the lives of several more foreign diplomats in Israel, and Israel's safety link through diplomacy with the outside world.

"I know you're a recent *oleh*. I heard briefly that you had an unpleasant experience in Paris. Would you tell me about that?"

Taken by surprise by Shimon's suddenly personal approach, Jean-Louis had to gather his thoughts for a moment and focus on the events of several weeks previous. But under Shimon's quiet, intense gaze, the horrifying experience near the Place Bastille quickly came back into his memory.

"I was coming home from the Sorbonne," he began. "My parents have an apartment on Boulevard Beaumarchais not far from Bastille. There was a crowd of Muslims shouting horrible things like 'Death to the Jews!' and other stuff. They had apparently come to hear a well-known imam give a rabble-rousing speech. For some reason, on their way back up Boulevard Beaumarchais, perhaps to Place de la Nation, they decided that I was Jewish and they could take out their rage on a representative of the ethnic community they hate. So they began beating me up. I fell to the ground and was being kicked and pummeled by them. I probably would have died if the flics – the police – hadn't come by very quickly. My physical wounds have healed, but as I told the captain in Tel Aviv, the inner wounds will never heal. Why do you want to know this?"

Shimon, who had relit a cigarette, took a deep draw on it.

"I wish one in ten Israelis today could sit here and listen to your story. As a nation we have become so successful that I think most of our citizens don't know what we are up against. We are not just Israelis. We are Jews, and just as Adolf Hitler tried to eliminate all the Jews of Europe six and a half decades ago, so there are many Hitlers within the world of Islam. Some of them are here in Gaza, and some of them want to have their own Wansee Conference right now."

"What is the Wansee Conference?"

"In January 1942, fifteen top Nazi officials gathered in a conference center in a suburb of Berlin to discuss 'the final solution to the Jewish question.' The man who took the minutes of the meeting was Adolf Eichmann. At his trial in Jerusalem in 1962, he made clear that he actually cleaned up the language of the meeting to cover the tracks of the people who attended. Words like 'extermination' and 'liquidation' were not mentioned in the official report. But they were freely banded about over the cognac that was served."

Shimon paused. Jean-Louis thought he detected the beginning of a tear in his right eye.

"You do understand what this is all about, don't you, Jean-Louis?"

"Yes," replied Jean-Louis quietly.

"And will you go through with whatever we decide you can best do for us?"

"Yes."

I WAS LOSING track of time. I'd spent more than twenty-four hours in captivity. A few hours after the video had been shot Tony had come with a plate of falafel. I was famished and scarfed it down greedily. I was also given a plastic bottle of water. I had no idea what had happened to the video. I assumed news of my kidnapping would have reached not only the bureau and all the relevant governments, but also Trish and Clarissa as they jauntily made their way through the Holy Land. I thought of them still in Galilee; the recollection that they were supposed to be in Jerusalem today had escaped me.

It had been an uncomfortable night. The cot on which I was supposed to sleep had been lumpy and uneven. But more than anything else, I realized a stopwatch had started ticking, a stopwatch leading to the probable deaths of innocent civilians in Israel, a stopwatch to my own mortality. "Within a week," the ultimatum by Goodfellah which I had been forced to read had said. Within a week I'd be dead if no concession were made by the government of Israel or the Western nations referred to as "Crusader countries," which had diplomatic relations with Israel. I was particularly horrified by the thought of a beheading. I wondered how many seconds of agony and screaming it would be until my windpipe was sliced through by a kitchen knife wielded by a bearded thug standing in front of a video camera.

I'd toyed with the idea of buying myself some time by making a formal conversion to Islam. If I got out of this captivity in Gaza, I'd tell everyone that I'd gone through the act under threat of execution. I knew that it wouldn't be held against me, at least not by *Epoch*, nor by my colleagues in Jerusalem, nor even by the Israeli or US governments. But I did wonder about Trish and Clarissa. They'd know as well, of course, that I'd performed a conversion ritual to buy time from my captors. But the thought nagged me: wouldn't they be just a little disappointed? Clarissa, I was quite sure, would allow herself to be shot rather than be forced to convert to Islam at gunpoint. I wasn't quite sure about Trish, but I thought that she would take the same option too. And I, Richard Ireton, direct descendant of Oliver Cromwell's son-in-law, had I just caved in to save my skin?

For the first time I started to wonder what my life was really worth. I was a successful reporter for the major American newsmagazine *Epoch*. I had already gained some fame – even a sort of fan club – in the US from my adventures the previous year in China. I had a mother who doted on me and would be inconsolable if anything happened to me. I had Trish, whose affection for me had apparently deepened – at least as far as one could tell by email and mail – in recent weeks. I had warm and supportive colleagues in the *Epoch* bureau in Jerusalem. They would surely be extremely upset if anything tragic happened to me. I had developed an unusual and potentially close friendship with the electrifying Rayna. She would probably be very saddened by my death. And, of course, there was Burton Lasch, my boss, the man who had hired me, my mentor – and perhaps something more; not quite a father figure, but pretty close to it. I was quite sure Lasch would not blame me if I converted to Islam at gunpoint. On the other hand, if I were to be killed anyway, wouldn't Lasch be rather proud of the fact that, though agnostic, I had not caved in?

But what about the remainder of the press corps in Jerusalem? If I were killed, would Patrick Cavenagh grieve for me? Probably not, though he would most likely come to the memorial service. It would be unBritish not to do that. And then there was Cavenagh's malevolent contact, Abdul Husseini of Palestine- El Quds. Out of perversity, I thought I'd rather like to disappoint Husseini by not converting to Islam under duress. Husseini's smirk might turn into a permanent scowl.

All this burrowed into my spirit with a sharpness that nothing else in my life ever had, not even my divorce from Marcia.

Down in the cellar, there was no way of telling night from day. They had taken away my watch, along with everything else except my shirt, pants, shoes and belt. "Please wear the belt for me," Rayna had written on the card that had been delivered with the belt. Why? Was this open flirtation? Then something began to dawn on me. I was about to take off the belt and look at it more closely when the sound of footsteps outside the cellar door caused me to stop. I quickly threw myself back down on the cot and feigned sleep. Since they had – thoughtfully, I felt – turned off that awful single glaring light bulb a few hours after my evening meal, it was virtually pitch black in the cellar. When the door opened and Tony came in with a plate with two pieces of bread on it, light streamed into the cellar from the stairs and hallway behind. I noticed that the man with the Kalashnikov on the stool was no longer there. Perhaps he was at the top of the stairs or on the stairway itself.

"Hello, Mickey Mouse. Here is some breakfast for you. I'm sorry there's no smoked salmon like the Jews like to eat at breakfast." He thought this was hilarious and laughed uproariously at his own humor. I noticed that he had a book under his arm, and was curious about it.

"This is a Koran in English," Tony said, putting it on the edge of the cot with great reverence. "You should read the Koran. When you become a Muslim you will read it a lot."

"When." *So they assume that I am going to cave in and convert within a matter of time?* When I heard this, I almost wanted to vomit. There was something so abusive about forcing a human being to change his religion at gunpoint. At the same time, an anger began to build inside me that would have prompted me to try to throttle Tony with my bare hands if the man had stayed a few more minutes in the cell. I was almost seething with the outrage of it all. It was personal now. I was not just a pawn in the mad fantasies of an extreme Islamist group in Gaza; I was being targeted for the allegiance of my own soul. Somehow this made it different.

The anger I felt surprised me. It was so different from the passivity and fear I had experienced when the kidnapping started. Now the kidnapping had turned into a personal assault on my being. The change in my disposition sharpened my mind. I decided that as long as there was breath in me, I was going to defy these people. What could I do to learn more about them?

I had lost track of the passage of time, but not of reality. Once I was alone again I decided to resume my examination of the belt. It was much thicker all around than most leather belts are. It also seemed to be a tad heavier. Clearly, there was quite a lot of metal in it. What for? Then it suddenly dawned on me. Rayna's gentle insistence that I wear it had nothing to do with any sentiment she may have felt for me. Almost certainly, the belt contained an electronic bug or a satellite tracking device that would tell the Israelis precisely where I was whenever I had the belt on. The realization that *people out there* knew my precise whereabouts was like a draught of a precious elixir. It made my spirit soar.

When Omar came in again after what seemed to be a passage of two to three hours, I was ready.

"That Koran which your friend" – I nearly blurted out "Tony" – "left a few hours ago, could we discuss it?"

Omar looked momentarily confused. He hadn't expected this.

"Let me ask Brother Ahmed," he said, and left the cell, closing the door behind him. *Who is "Brother Ahmed?" Is that Tony? Or is it Goodfellah? Or is it somebody completely different?*

A few minutes later he returned with Goodfellah. *So "Brother Ahmed" is the name that Goodfellah goes by in this group.*

Goodfellah was smiling, and had a demeanor which, in other circumstances, might have been termed congenial.

"Mr. Ireton, our brother tells me that you are interested in Islam?" He began.

No, you fool, I'm not interested in your religion the way you think I am. I'm interested in who you are and where you got the demented ideas about kidnapping and murder to further your cause.

"I have some questions about it," I said levelly. "But to make it a fair discussion, do you think you could unlock the handcuffs for just a few minutes. I am sure you will agree that a religious discussion with someone whose hands are bound is not really fair." I had no ulterior motive for saying this. I simply wanted to have freedom of movement for my arms.

He looked at me carefully for a few seconds, as if sizing me up. Then he reached into a back pocket and pulled out the handcuff key and uncuffed me. I felt an immediate physical relief.

"Thank you," I said, my sentiment being genuine.

"In our language," Goodfellah continued, "the book that you now have with you is called 'the Holy Koran.' It is what Allah revealed to the Prophet. It is Allah's exact words."

I, of course, had read the Koran through at least a couple of times. How could you be a serious reporter in the Middle East without doing so?

"Are you familiar with Surah 2:256?" I asked. "'There shall be no compulsion in religion'?"

"Of course."

"Then how do you propose to bring about the rule of Islam in the whole world through the sword?"

Goodfellah turned red with anger.

"You infidel pig! You try to use Allah's words against us? The word 'compulsion' here refers only to the Muslims, not to the infidels. Once you have submitted to Allah, there is no compulsion. But if you are not submitted, you are in a state of *jahiliyya*, a state of ignorance and rebellion against Allah's pathway. Look up Sura 9:29. What does it say?"

I picked up the Koran and opened it at the sura indicated by Goodfellah. I read slowly and clearly, "'Fight against such of those to whom the scriptures were given as believe in neither Allah nor the last day, who do not forbid what Allah and his apostle have forbidden, and do not embrace the true faith, until they pay tribute out of hand and are utterly subdued.'"

"That is our authority," Goodfellah said, "for conquering the whole world in the name of Islam, for bringing the true faith to all the people of the world. We are actually liberators of the world. We are saving the world from *jahiliyya*, from ignorance. We are going to re-introduce the caliphate, the rule of the world by the ruler of the Muslim *ummah*. I can tell you for sure, the people of the world will be grateful to us for showing them the way to paradise, and the way to avoid ending in the fires of hell. That is what we believe, and that is why we are sure that *jihad* is the only way."

"So you don't believe in freedom of conscience in religion? Everyone has to accept your truth, whether they agree with it or not?"

Goodfellah reddened again. "It is not our truth. It is Allah's truth. You crusaders think all religions are equal, or even worse, that your Crusader religion, Christianity, which always supports the Jews, is above the Koran."

In spite of myself, I started laughing. "Always supports the Jews?" I repeated. "I think the Jews would have a different view of how Christianity has treated them throughout history."

"The Jews were given Palestine by the Crusader British because Hitler treated them badly and the British had also been fighting Hitler. But the Jews started World War II and they even conspired with the Nazis to create the myth of the Holocaust so that the world would feel sorry for them. Even the so-called President of the Palestinian Authority, Mahmoud Abbas, who tried to stop Hamas from coming to power in Gaza and who was punished for it, said so. He wrote a PhD dissertation on the secret connection between the Zionist leaders and the Nazis."

My mind went into computer mode. I knew about the Mahmoud Abbas PhD thesis, and I also knew that, to his credit, Abbas had said in an interview with the Israeli newspaper *Ha'aretz* that the Holocaust was a hideous crime and should never be denied by anyone. What Goodfellah had just said was lunacy on a par with *The Protocols of the Elders of Zion*, or the *Hamas Charter*. But I desperately wanted to keep Goodfellah engaged in conversation. Without help from outside, I knew that there would be virtually no chance at all to escape from this dungeon, indeed this madhouse. But I needed to keep probing with the only instrument that I could deploy; namely, my mind.

"Why do you hate the Jews so much?" I asked.

"The descendants of pigs and monkeys opposed Allah's apostle," Goodfellah replied, "and Allah decreed punishment for them for this crime. When the day of judgments comes, according to the hadith, the rocks and trees will tell the Muslims that a Jew is hiding behind them."

"Yes, I'm aware of that *hadith*," I said, trying hard to disguise my disgust. I needed to draw Goodfellah out. "Do you anticipate the coming of the Mahdi?"

"The Mahdi will come and restore perfection to the world, along with Jesus. But we do not believe this is the same person as the Twelth Imam, as the Shia Muslims do. Why are you so interested in this?"

"Well, as a journalist I regard it as my job to investigate all kinds of beliefs that people have. I haven't been to Iran yet, but I expect—"

Suddenly, there was the sound of shouting, followed by automatic rifle gunfire somewhere in the house, followed by the sound of footsteps leaping down the stairway towards the cellar. The shouting and shots from automatic rifles continued, punctuated by shrieks and moans as people, somewhere, were struck by bullets. If the attackers had come from outside, then the kidnappers seemed to have been taken completely by surprise. I had been so intent on drawing Goodfellah out that it took several seconds for me to figure out what was happening. *Holy Moses, I was being rescued. But who by?* A school playground instinct suddenly sprang up in my mind. Acting on it without thinking, I found myself hurling my body through the air at Goodfellah, my fists, no longer handcuffed, screwed up into a weapon that was aimed directly for the man's face. I hadn't planned anything of the sort. I just acted. Goodfellah had not been carrying a Kalashnikov when he entered the cell, an obvious oversight based on a mistaken assumption that his captive had suddenly become compliant. But as he toppled to the floor under my weight, my fists thrusting as far as I could into his cheeks, I suddenly realized in mid-flight, so to speak, that Goodfellah probably had a pistol tucked into his belt. Even if my fists found their target of his face, as soon as he recovered from his surprise, Goodfellah would quickly be reaching for it. With all the intensity of the anger that had been building in me having found my fists' target of Goodfellah's face, I swept my arms down around his body as though embracing him, but in fact in order to squeeze him in a gorilla grip. I squeezed so hard that Goodfellah cried out with pain. This made me only keep on squeezing. I felt him struggling to escape but at six foot one and a half inches and one hundred seventy-five pounds to his less than five feet six inches, it was an unequal match.

Meanwhile, the sound of automatic weapons was continuing, and I heard rounds thudding into the closed cellar door. Whoever the attackers were, they had very quickly taken over the whole house. Somehow, I felt that I had to keep the cellar door closed. I had no idea where Tony and Omar were; they might well have been killed in the initial assault. But I was haunted by the fear that, as close as I might be to rescue, they might be under orders to shoot me dead as soon as any rescue were attempted.

In fact, the cellar door had been designed to open inwardly, something I'd noticed when the video camera operator had entered the small room the previous afternoon. I was still clutching Goodfellah with all the strength in my body, but we had fallen to the floor and we were flailing, he struggling to get free, I intent upon squeezing the life out of him, close to the door. As we both lay there panting, I still on top of him, there were more shots fired very close now directly into the door from close range. Then they stopped and I heard the incredible sound of shouted commands in Hebrew. There were Israelis in the house! Silence now ensued for a moment, and then a voice called out in English, "Richard Ireton, Richard Ireton, are you there? Are you safe?"

Not for a second relaxing my tight hold of Goodfellah, I shouted back, causing Goodfellah to grimace with discomfort, "Yes, I am here, behind the door. Come quickly."

Realizing Goodfellah and I, in our very unromantic position, were blocking the door from being opened, I rolled a few feet away from it, still cluthing him. He groaned now at each bruising turn of his body on the hard floor. The door was pushed violently open and for a moment I wondered if my last minute had arrived. Standing in the doorway were two panting, bearded men with dark beards wearing black ski masks. The Kalashnikovs in their hands were pointed at Goodfellah and me."

"Don't worry, we are Israeli special forces," said one of the two men, who seemed to be lightly bleeding from a wound on his forearm. "You are Richard Ireton, yes? Who is the man with you?"

I rolled away from Goodfellah now, confident that he wouldn't try to get at his pistol. I was panting as much from fear as the intense physical effort to keep Goodfellah's arms pinned. As the first Israeli soldier – commando, undercover agent, or whatever he was – kept Goodfellah and me covered with his Kalashnikov, the other man bent down and in one quick move secured Goodfellah's hands behind his back with plastic ties.

"He is Ahmed or something, one of the leaders of this group," I replied. I was still on the floor of my cramped cell, but reached out to be pulled up by the hand of the first Israeli, the one who was slightly bleeding.

"Are you all right? You were not wounded by the shooting?"

"No, I'm fine. I just want to get out of here. Have you taken care of the other kidnappers? I don't know how many were in the house."

"There was one on the roof. Our sniper got him at the moment we came in. There are two bodies on the staircase and we killed three more getting into the house. How many do you think were here?"

"I don't know, but when I was brought here there seemed to be as many as ten."

"Well, there were only six when we began our raid. Now, please come with me quickly. We have to move out of here very fast."

Dragging the partially bound Goodfellah with them, the two Israelis ascended the stairs as quickly as they could with a prisoner to handle, side-stepping the bodies half-way down, one of which was bleeding profusely from a bullet hole in the center of his forehead, and the guardian of the cellar who had died on his stool outside the door. His Kalashnikov was still in his hands and he lay face down over it, stretched out towards the door, blood oozing out of a wound in his chest.

As I stumbled up the stairs behind my two rescuers, I noticed other figures with beards and ski masks. When we passed through the main hallway of the house, however, I was astonished to see an unbearded young man sitting on a leather dining-room chair. For the first time, I took in the décor of the house. It was sumptuous in a truly tasteless way, with *faux* Louis XVI chairs, thick rugs and kitschy landscapes on every wall. Then I remembered that I had seen the unbearded young man before, but couldn't remember where. As our eyes locked, he spoke: "*Je suis Jean-Louis David. Vous me rappelez? Il y a quelque jours, a Jerusalem* (I am Jean-Louis David. Do you remember me? Some days ago, in Jerusalem)?"

I didn't have time to say more than "*oui*," before being hustled out of the front door of the house with the rest of the raiding party and Goodfellah as the sole surviving prisoner. I saw that Jean-Louis was being hustled out too.

"Quickly now. You must get into this pickup truck and lie face down. We will cover you with a rug. We have no time to lose." It was the bearded Israeli who had first greeted me who was speaking.

In the street outside the house a small group of bystanders had gathered, not at all sure what was happening. One of the ski-masked raiders then shouted something in Arabic, pointed his Kalashnikov ominously in the air and fired two shots, and the crowd rapidly dispersed. Remembering my painful abduction barely a day past, I wasn't comfortable with the prospect of lying face down again on the floor of any vehicle. But I did as I was told. With some satisfaction, I noticed that Goodfellah was now in the same uncomfortable position that I had been in the previous day, pressed face down in the back of the pickup truck with his hands tied behind his back. The truck roared off, the masked gunmen standing upright in the cargo area, their Kalashnikovs all pointed upwards. Suddenly I realized what was happening; the very chaos that had led to the takeover of Gaza by Hamas was now making it possible for an Israeli undercover group to raid a Gazan kidnapping safe house in the early evening and to attract no more attention than bearded, ski-masked men had been attracting ever since the first day of the Hamas takeover by force back in 2007.

My emotions were soaring and tumbling at the same time after I realized I had been rescued. I was ecstatic to be free, but I realized that the hardest part was still to come: how to get out of Gaza itself and back to Israel. The Palestinian territory was completely sealed off from Israel by barbed wire fences and in places cement walls. The sealing off – which the inhabitants of Gaza all considered made them essentially prisoners in a gigantic city-sized maximum security prison – was designed by Israel to keep terrorists out of Israeli territory. But it also made an exodus from Gaza by any route except the Erez checkpoint and a couple of other locations almost impossible.

The pickup truck drove fast and erratically in an apparently random way through Gaza before suddenly turning into the compound of a house whose gate closed automatically behind it. Jean-Louis, who had also been lying underneath a blue plastic sheet in the pickup truck, raised his head slightly. He seemed to recognize it.

The Israelis jumped out of the truck as quickly as they had boarded it and ran into the house. I learned later from Jean-Louis that it had been this house that he had been taken to when his return to Israel had been postponed after his video shoot. Three of the Israeli commandoes were joking with each other now, amazed at how quick the operation had been. But after everyone had entered a large recreation room in this new venue, a small, gray-haired, older Israeli came in and motioned everyone to be quiet. Goodfellah, blindfolded as well as handcuffed now, had been placed temporarily in a storage room adjoining the recreation room.

"You may call me Shimon," said the Israeli in charge. "Welcome back to freedom. Now my task is to get you and everyone here out of Gaza as quickly as possible. Forgive me if I speak Hebrew to the boys. But I will tell you and Mr. David first that we have to wait here totally unnoticed, if possible, until it gets completely dark and later in the evening. We don't know yet if anyone observed where we drove to after our raid. The neighbors here might have informed Hamas of suspicious things happening. It is going to be very tense. Everyone must stay out of sight of any window. Once it is night, we are going to proceed by truck to one of Gaza's beaches. We have an inflatable Zodiac boat with us. We will inflate it there and deploy it as soon as we arrive in the beach area we have selected. There will be some dangerous moments when we are still on the beach with the boat, and we will still be at risk of discovery even when we have put the Zodiac into the water. Hamas has a few patrol boats, but we just hope the place we are going to launch the Zodiac is far enough away from them to enable us to get into the water with a chance of making it offshore to an Israeli patrol boat. Do you have any questions?"

I looked at Jean-Louis and saw him going pale. I didn't know until later that he'd not volunteered for the original raid, and he'd not volunteered for this hazardous attempt to escape from Gaza either.

"No, sir," I said, as cheerfully as I could simulate.

"Very well. You two can make yourself some coffee and chat in that corner. I am going to brief our boys."

With that, Shimon began a rapid-delivery briefing of the commando team. I was surprised at the informality of it all. These bearded young men argued with each other and with Shimon, who didn't seem to mind at all. Interestingly, when Shimon seemed to be summing up a point – I merely guessed this was what he was doing, because I didn't understand Hebrew well enough – the tough-looking young men seemed to acquiesce in his leadership readily enough.

I tried a desultory conversation with Jean-Louis who was so nervous waiting for the departure that it was with difficulty that I was able to glean what his own role in the rescue had been. It turned out that he had been tasked with drawing the attention of as many people on the street as possible to his own activities with the video camera, but at the other end of the street from the house where the kidnappers were holding me. He'd been given a clown's disguise of bulbous red nose, great flapping shoes, and an outlandish wig. As the neighborhood children gathered around him, he made a great show of posing them for his video camera on a tripod. Just in case anyone came to ask questions, he'd been assigned one of the commandoes who spoke Arabic, with beard but without ski mask, to protect him. Jean-Louis said that a sniper among the commandoes had managed to climb unnoticed onto the roof of a house almost opposite the kidnap villa. His rifle, however, was fitted with a silencer, as had been the pistols of all of the men in the commando team. The initial break-in to the house where I was being held was therefore relatively quiet. The loud shooting occurred only when the raiders were already in the house and were being shot at by the kidnappers with Kalashnikovs. In fact, Jean-Louis said almost ruefully, he'd been so intent on his videoing of the children in the street that it took a cell phone call to his commando guard to let him know that he could now come into the house they had just raided.

The briefing of the commandoes concluded, and the boys passed the time playing cards and smoking uninterruptedly in a way that irritated me and made Jean-Louis' eyes weep. There didn't seem to be a minute when smoke wasn't being blown into the air or allowed to drift aimlessly into the upper reaches of the room from an untended cigarette. But Jean-Louis and I agreed that it was a small price to pay for having some very brave young men risk their lives to get us out of Gaza.

Finally, the Mediterranean night was upon us, sweeping in decisively after that lustrous moment before nightfall when all seems suffused with a dark golden aura. The relentless noise on the street quietened down.

At one point, we all had quite a scare when police sirens could be heard approaching the neighborhood and even whining down the street. But their apparent destination was not in our immediate neighborhood.

Shimon had decided we'd leave Gaza at the earliest possible moment of nightfall, though tonight it wouldn't be fully dark at all because the moon was almost full. The longer we remained in town, the greater the risk of discovery, particularly when word got out that an attack had been made on the Followers of the Caliph's headquarters. It might have been possible that Hamas itself didn't know that the kidnapping would be going down when it did, but Hamas would have been as infuriated as anyone that Israeli special forces had penetrated Gaza successfully and gone into action. They might be ordering up a block-by block search of the city at any time. If they discovered the Israeli safe house, it would be all over. The Israelis might be able to call in helicopter gunships and hold off their attackers for a while, but they would be heavily outnumbered and would have to fight to the end or surrender. I didn't fancy either of those outcomes.

Thus at eight o'clock, when the last stragglers from work had gone home and Gaza was settling into the evening TV programs, the signal was given for all of us to board the pickup truck.

The Israelis carried the Zodiac in a package they had extracted from a cupboard in the house. The package was not much bigger than a large suitcase, and two of the men brought out an outboard motor and two cans of gasoline from the garage. Then we all boarded the pickup. Goodfellah, blindfolded, his hands still bound by the plastic ties and a duct tape gag over his mouth, was lifted up gently onto the truck by two commandoes. I and everyone else was told to lie down in the back of the pickup under a blue tarp. When the truck set off over the poorly maintained roads of Gaza, I seemed to feel its every jolt.

As I had now noticed what seemed to be a standard evasive tactic, the truck meandered in several directions through the streets spreading out from the safe house until it had traveled quite a distance away. Then we turned towards the Mediterranean beaches some ways north of Gaza City, almost at the border with Israel. After coming on to the coastal road that ran north and south, the driver slowed down and appeared to be scanning the beach. There weren't many really deserted areas. Few areas of Gaza were ever more than "relatively deserted." With 1.3 million people living in a territory only twice the size of Washington DC, Gaza had one of the highest population densities of any urban area in the world. Shimon had decided that a stretch of beach quite close to the border with Israel in the north of Gaza would be the only stretch where it might be possible to launch the Zodiac without being spotted or intercepted by Palestinian patrols. The particular spot was less frequented than most because there had been incidents of stray shells landing there as a result of Palestinian artillery duels with Israel. After one such duel in 2006 several members of a Palestinian family were killed in an explosion on the beach which the Palestinian Authority claimed was from a hitherto unexploded Israeli artillery round. Many Gazans feared that there might be more artillery rounds inadvertently buried in the beach sands in Gaza.

That was a risk that Shimon had been prepared to take in his choice of the site. But one other advantage of the selected location was that it lay in an area of desolate sand dunes with almost no houses close by. If the truck could negotiate the sand and get to the beach itself, we might get away with it. That is, we might make it to a suitable location on the beach. Whether we could reach it without being spotted by the Hamas Executive Force or other watchers was another question.

Though the truck had four-wheel drive, the closer we got to the shore before the actual beach, the looser and more treacherous became the sand. Several times the truck had to stop, back up, and take a different route to gain traction for forward movement. It made an enormous amount of noise each time it did so and I couldn't imagine that no Hamas patrol had heard the noise and would not come sooner or later to investigate.

At first, we thought lady luck had been with us all the way. When we

249

arrived after a drive of some forty minutes, we quickly clambered out of the truck and began helping the commandoes inflate the Zodiac and then carry it from the sand dunes to the water's edge. We'd not gone more than a dozen yards, however, before we heard a loud shout from a ridgeline about one hundred yards away. I was startled, and I notice Jean-Louis instinctively duck down, as though that might make us all less conspicuous. Just seconds later, there was a burst of gunfire from the same location. Instantly, one of the Israeli commandoes cried out that he had been hit. Everyone immediately fell prone on the sand, using the Zodiac as a barrier. Of course, the inflatable rubber wouldn't stop any bullet, but it would make people harder targets to pick out.

The shooting at us intensified, and I heard the sound of bullets whizzing overhead or making a "thwack" sound as they hit the sand or even a curious jarring noise as they ripped into the rubber surface of the Zodiac. After several seconds, it appeared that we were pinned down and couldn't move in any direction. I thought the noise of the gunfire alone must have alerted every Hamas patrol within half a mile. Though we were being fired at from only one position right now, we might soon be completely surrounded and subjected to a hail of bullets from all directions.

Shimon, whose voice had immediately rung out with orders after the shooting first started, apparently had foreseen something like this happening. He shouted an order, and two of the Israeli troops began crawling away from the Zodiac for several yards, and then jumping up and bolting off sideways. There was a good chance that they would not be spotted in the darkness. But Shimon had told us that we would need the light of the moon to launch the Zodiac. The one we had been carrying, and then sheltering behind, however, was now useless for carrying us on the water. Several of the bullets were hitting the rubber skin of the Zodiac and penetrating it with a wishing sound. I figured that the boat wouldn't float by itself, let alone carry several commandos, a prisoner, and two civilians out to sea. We had to suppress the immediate gunfire and launch the back-up Zodiac that was still on the truck.

To add to our woes, the moon would be coming up very soon now, and we might be sitting ducks when that happened. We still had about one hundred yards before the dunes and the edge of the Mediterranean.

A new sound now came from the ridgeline, that of an exploding grenade, and the shooting from that direction stopped. The Israeli flanking movement had evidently paid off.

What to do now? Shimon started barking orders again, and a special forces soldier near me translated that we would have to return to the truck and unload the second folded Zodiac, a spare one that had been brought along in case of something like just what had happened. I now heard an ominous sound in the distance, that of one of more heavy trucks heading in our direction. Shimon started shouting more urgently, and then to Jean-Louis and me in English, "Quick! We are going to have to run as fast as we can to the beach with the second Zodiac. We are in a race against time – against approaching Hamas trucks! We are going to need both of you to help carry either the Zodiac, or the wounded soldier, or the prisoner."

Jean-Louis and I looked at each other quickly. The moon was beginning to rise over the Mediterranean and Jean-Louis' facial features were beginning to become clear. "Let's take the wounded man," he said quickly. "I think they'll have a stretcher in the pickup truck!"

We scrambled as fast as we could through the sand, shouting to Shimon as we passed him that we would take the wounded Israeli, and reached the truck just as the driver was passing down a folding canvas stretcher. Then, as the troops ran panting past us with the new Zodiac, we made our way back to the old one and found a medic treating a deep bullet wound in the left shoulder of the wounded man. We laid down the stretcher, and the medic told us how to pick the man up carefully and place him on it. He then quickly tied Velcro straps around the man's chest and thighs to prevent him falling off.

He was an Israeli of average height and quite trim, so we were grateful not to have to carry a giant. But he was still heavy and very soon we were falling behind the soldiers running ahead with the Zodiac. At an order from Shimon, two of them then fell away from the Zodiac group and came to help us. Now with four men carrying the stretcher we were able to half walk, half run, almost as fast as the Zodiac crew.

With the moon now climbing higher and higher in the sky, we knew we would be targets if the truck burst through the last of the sand dunes and hit the beach. Pausing for the briefest of stops to catch our breath as stretcher-bearers, I glanced quickly over to the Mediterranean. It was now twinkling in the moonlight. If we hadn't been in a race for our lives, I would have said it was almost romantic.

I had presumed that everyone in the pickup – commandoes, Shimon, Jean-Louis and myself and the driver, would board the Zodiac for the return trip to Israel. But to my surprise the driver of the pickup, presumably also Israeli, had started back across the dunes as soon as we had unloaded the second Zodiac. He had heard the approaching truck and had ground in four-wheel drive as quickly as he could at an angle perpendicular to the direction the trucks seemed to be taking. *Brave man,* I thought. *I wonder if he'll make it.*

There were some nervous moments when the new Zodiac, now fully inflated, first hit the water and everyone boarded it. The outboard motor at first wouldn't start. While one commando frantically yanked at the starter cord, I was handed a paddle and told to begin moving the Zodiac out to sea as quickly as human power could get it there. The sound of the truck engine was getting closer. In fact, two of the commandoes had apparently suggested to Shimon that they establish a perimeter on the beach and hit the truck and the people in it before they could fully dismount. That way, they wouldn't have a chance to establish a firing position on the shore against us when we were in the water. But Shimon had vetoed that idea, gambling that we could start the engine and get out of useful automatic rifle range before the patrol was in a position to aim at us properly. It was a gamble whose success depended on our firing up the outboard motor literally within seconds of being in the water. I had a flash of insight about Clarissa and Trish in their prayer mode. "Let it start, let it start," I found myself muttering, causing Jean-Louis to give me an odd look.

Whether Providence heard that prayer or sheer luck happened, the engine roared to life after a few very strong pulls of the starter cord by one of the commandos. Immediately, we surged at high speed out to sea. At the stern of the boat, however, the same commando who had started the engine was now steering the boat, and he sent it into a sharp turn to the right, changing direction so fast that I was all but thrown overboard and only prevented from hitting the water by a commando's hand grabbing the back of my belt.

I realized why he had made the sharp turn after I heard bullets hitting the water close to where the boat had just been. Until we got out of AK-47 range, we would have to zigzag back and forth to make us as elusive a target as possible.

Another sharp turn, and another cascade of rounds hitting the water where we had been. I wondered if the commandos when training to handle the Zodiacs had been taught at what intervals to make zigzag turns most effectively in order to render a retreating boat to be as elusive a target as possible. But the shots seemed to be falling short now and by the time we all noticed that, we headed on a straight course. I'd been sitting in the boat in a position that enabled me to watch the receding shore, but as we got farther away from the beach, I craned my neck to look at where the Zodiac was headed.

Its destination now became apparent: the looming dark outline of an Israeli patrol boat lying – it seemed to me – perilously close to the Gazan coast. If the troops in the truck had mortars or even large-caliber machine guns, the patrol boat would be a target.

We were approaching the boat fast, and I saw that, far from being anchored, it was moving at a few knots through the water. The Zodiac approached fast from a shallow angle, and I noticed a ladder with narrow wooden steps slung over the patrol boat's deck. The Zodiac then slowed quickly, one of the commandoes grabbed the ladder, and another caught a line thrown from the patrol boat by a sailor.

The first task was to get the wounded Israeli aboard. I was surprised by how quickly a winch was lowered from the deck of the patrol boat to the Zodiac and attached to the four wooden polls of the stretcher, and then the stretcher was lifted onto the deck by a powerful motor. After that the rest of us, one by one, with two of the commandos carrying Goodfellah rather perilously trussed up like a sack of potatoes, clambered up on board. Lastly, the Zodiac itself was winched up onto the deck of the patrol boat which was already accelerating fast in a northern direction towards Israeli waters. On shore, the truck evidently did have some mortar tubes, and a couple of rounds were fired at us, but both fell harmlessly several yards behind the patrol boat. The naval vessel was now also increasing its distance from the shore rapidly as it headed towards its base in Ashdod, the nearest Israeli naval base. The patrol boat accelerated to its maximum speed, and the lights of Gaza receded into the distance.

XIII

THE NEXT NINETY minutes passed in a daze for me. I was still trying to come to terms with what had happened: both the kidnapping and the just-completed rescue. I realized that I had brought out of the kidnappers' house none of my own personal possessions. I had with me neither my mobile phone nor my overnight bag with toiletries, nor my passport, nor anything that established who I was. In an odd but different way, I felt almost as vulnerable as I had felt in the cellar. I had had nothing but the shirt on my back, my pants, and my shoes. But I *did* have the belt. It obviously must have had some GPS device embedded in the leather. Was that why Rayna had been so insistent on my wearing it? It had to be the only reason.

I was about to take the belt off and examine it closely when I realized that this would look rather strange in full view of the commandos in the wardroom of a patrol boat. I kept it on, and turned to Jean-Louis.

"How is Svetlana?" I said, remembering with a rush the Russian Jewish immigrant to whom I'd introduced Jean-Louis at that Absorption Center reception.

Jean-Louis grinned almost stupidly. "She will certainly be very happy now," he replied.

"Good," I said distantly. I was thinking of my own return now.

Within less than an hour the patrol boat was easing into its berth in Ashdod. Prepared for everything, the IDF had ordered two ambulances to the dockside in case there were any medical emergencies from the rescue. This turned out to be a blessing, because the wounded Israeli commando had passed into unconsciousness on the patrol boat and needed serious medical attention quickly. Once again, we waited until the stretcher had been unloaded from the boat and the wounded man moved onto a regular, wheeled stretcher to be loaded into the ambulance. The whole area was surrounded by soldiers. There was not a camera crew in sight, a point that at first perplexed me. But I remembered with a "duh" moment that the operation had been entirely secret and this base itself wasn't open to the media. I certainly didn't want any media contact myself at this point.

Jean-Louis and I disembarked from the patrol boat after the bearded commandoes had all gone ashore with their still bound and gagged captive, Goodfellah. "What will happen to him now?" I asked Shimon as he lingered on the quayside.

"I expect he'll be faced with a very inquisitive and very attentive audience of new friends," Shimon replied with a laugh.

As we walked away from the quay towards an administrative building into which the commandos, Shimon, and the captive Goodfellah had already moved, an Israeli sergeant approached me and Jean-Louis. "Could you two please come with me? A rather senior person wants to meet you both."

He led us both away from the quay to a two-story building set back behind the first administration-looking building. This new structure was built so solidly that I at first thought it was some kind of bunker. Perhaps it was. We entered an empty lobby area which, to my surprise, had a flooring of marble. It was well lit and for a moment I didn't know if we were supposed to wait there or go through one of the doors that led off the reception. Then a door opened from a well-lit room and a female figure almost rushed out to me. Rayna. She was in uniform.

Without thinking, I opened wide my arms and she rushed to embrace me. We held each other for a few seconds, and then I noticed an older man standing a few feet behind Rayna looking a little embarrassed. I gave him a second glance and realized instantly who it was. He introduced himself right away.

"I am Yoram Messinger," the man said quietly, "We have met via telephone. I see that you have already become quite well acquainted with my senior analyst, Rayna. Welcome back to Israel. I am delighted. Now, after all your adventures, how are you feeling?"

"Well, sir," I said, "incredibly better now than I did three or four hours ago. Thank you a thousand times for what you pulled off there in Gaza. My life would have been snuffed out within days if you hadn't come."

"Actually, within hours. The cabinet had authorized a retaliatory raid on Hamas in order to force them to suppress the Followers of the Caliph. By the way, after the death of the Dutchman, we lost another diplomat a few hours ago, a Japanese. We couldn't go on taking these terrorist deaths among diplomats accredited to Israel. Because of Rayna, however, I knew where you were in Gaza. Because of another operation that we had been planning there, we also had a commando team already in the territory. It all came together very, very quickly. I have to say, you are a very lucky man to get out."

"I know, sir, and I will be indebted to you and your boys for the rest of my life. But can I ask a question? How did you know where I was?"

Rayna now burst out laughing. "Don't you know, Rick? It's obvious. Your belt. Our technicians had recently developed a way to conceal a GPS satellite transmitter inside a belt. We had never tried it out, even in a peaceful situation. But when I realized that you were definitely going to go into Gaza after Al-Jaffar, I knew that the chances of your being taken hostage were extremely high. The only way we could then get you out for sure would be to know exactly where you were located. That's why I made special efforts to get the belt back to you overnight after it had been inscribed with your name."

Messinger chimed in. "Sometimes a gift from a lady can save your life," he said with a broad smile.

I reddened in embarrassment. I tried to change the subject.

"And what about the al-Jiffri incident and Al-Jaffar?"

"After your interview with him in Gaza," Messinger said, "his handler,

Husseini, knew that the game was up. He knew that you had essentially punctured Al-Jaffar's version of the story. In fact, it was the realization that you would now completely destroy the atrocity story that tipped Husseini's hand and unleashed the Followers of the Caliph kidnapping.

"How did you know I was interviewing Al-Jaffar?" I interrupted.

Rayna answered. "You don't think with as serious an allegation as this, with a UN investigative team about to bear down on us, with the US Secretary of State due in a few days, we would leave anything to chance, do you? It was obvious you were going to try to meet Al-Jaffar once you knew for sure that he was in Gaza." she said. "So we had you tracked. What we didn't expect was that you would be kidnapped almost immediately after your interview. That took us by surprise. And it was your belt that made this clear to us. We knew that, in the normal course of things, you would have either returned to the hotel in Gaza or gone straight to the Erez crossing point for the return to Israel. When the GPS showed you rambling around Gaza, we knew you were in trouble. It was Mr. Yao, your Chinese friend, who informed us of the details of your interview with Al-Jaffar."

"What'll happen to Husseini now that his cover is blown?"

"He'll have to stay in Gaza. He's useless now in Jerusalem because – though nothing can be proved until we debrief him – everyone will assume he masterminded the kidnapping."

"Excuse me now," it was Yoram interrupting, "I have a phone call to make to the Prime Minister. Rick, I look forward to seeing you before too long in more relaxed circumstances in Tel Aviv."

"Thank you, sir."

"We think, however," Rayna continued having acknowledged the departure of Messinger, "that Husseini's finger prints are all over the kidnapping. We intercepted a call a few days ago between Husseini and a man we couldn't identify referring to a 'hostage situation.' That had to be about you. We also know" – here Rayna hesitated momentarily before continuing – that Cavenagh was trying without success to reach

Husseini by phone just before the kidnappning."

"You're not suggesting that Patrick Cavenagh – "

"No, I'm not for a moment suggesting that Mr. Cavenagh had the remotest idea about the kidnapping. I'm only saying that Husseini would have answered the phone at his office if he had been in Jerusalem. We thought he might be in Gaza, but we didn't know for sure. We only realized that later."

I was about to ask a follow-up question about Cavenagh, but I realized in the nick of time that this would be unprofessional.

Messinger had now returned and wanted to be part of the conversation again.

"The Prime Minister is very pleased," he said, "and wants to congratulate you for not doing anything foolish or embarrassing."

"Like what?" I asked.

"Oh, offering some craven plea for mercy, converting to Islam – you know, some of the things that frightened hostages do."

I frowned and was about to admit that I might very well have done either of those things given more time alone in that cellar. But I changed the subject.

"What will happen to the Followers of the Caliph now?" I asked.

"We don't know how big a group it is. It may be very small. But you can be sure that their members will surface again, perhaps under another name."

"Well," I responded, "there won't be any Omar, Tony, or the bearded man who guarded my cell."

"Tony? Omar?" Rayna asked in fascination. "Who are they?"

"Oh, Tony was one of my guards who slapped me around a bit, and Omar was another of the guards. They were both killed in the rescue."

Now the Defense Minister interrupted us.

"We can never be sure to have suppressed permanently any terrorist organization," he said. "What's more important is that Hamas will be forced to suppress any reappearance of this group inside Gaza. Now that we have Ahmed, they don't have any leader."

"You mean the man I called Goodfellah, who was brought back to Israel?"

"Goodfellah? What is that?"

I laughed. "Oh, just a name I gave the man who was talking to me in that house about Islam. I took it from a movie about the Mafia called *Goodfellahs*."

"Well, Goodfellah will be out of the Mafia for quite a long time," Messinger said. He laughed.

"Seriously, though," he went on, "if we hadn't managed to get you out quickly, we'd have had to act against Hamas immediately, and this terror gang would probably have quickly murdered you."

"But even if I were dead," I asked, strangely fascinated by the cold reality of it all, "wouldn't the Followers of the Caliph be able to continue their murderous rampage against diplomats in Israel?"

"Yes, of course," Messinger replied. "But not even Hamas is suicidal. They know the limits of what can be done against us from Gaza."

"Well," Rayna now said, "I'm sure you don't want to spend the whole evening speculating about Gaza terrorism with us. You certainly want to get back to Jerusalem as soon as possible. Oh, and don't worry about Clarissa and Trish. We've told them that our rescue effort was successful."

Now I was doubly embarrassed. I had talked about Clarissa the first night I had met Rayna in Jerusalem, when Clarissa had called my cell phone. But I'd been been duplicitous about Trish, not indicating to Rayna at all the extent of our closeness, and giving the impression that I might be available for a new romantic connection. Rayna had at first responded positively to that impression. But by now, no doubt with phone calls to Margaret, and perhaps to Clarissa and Trish already made, she could be in no doubt that I was certainly not available for a fling with her. I probably looked crestfallen, like a third grader caught cheating. Deep down, I was humiliated because I'd misled Rayna into thinking I *was* available, and I'd betrayed Trish by flirting with Rayna.

Messinger now came to my rescue. "Well," he said, "we've arranged separate transportation for you and Jean-Louis to Jerusalem. I expect you don't want to spend a second longer in Ashdod."

"No, sir. Thank you, sir, for everything." Messinger quickly walked out of the room. I turned to Rayna. "Rayna, my life saver, what can I honestly say to you? You saved my life and yet I have to confess I flirted with you shamelessly when I was not in a position to do that honestly. Will you forgive me?

"There's nothing to forgive, Rick. I enjoyed every part of our friendship. Besides, I wasn't born yesterday."

I felt myself turning crimson. Then she quickly added, "Come on. You've got a sensational girlfriend who's eager to see you. You and I remain good friends and I don't hold anything against you. But priorities, Rick, priorities. It's okay, Rick. Really, it's okay."

The trip back to Jerusalem was a breeze. After all the adrenaline rushes of the past two days, I slept soundly in the back of the Ministry of Defense car that delivered me to my home in the German Colony. As I alighted, though, it suddenly occurred to me that my own car was still somewhere in an Israeli parking lot near the Erez crossing point to Gaza and I had no keys or anything. I was about to explain to the diver that I didn't know how to enter my apartment when a light went on at the main entrance. It was Esther, waiting up for me like a fussy aunt of an errant teenager.

"The Ministry of Defense called me earlier, Rick," she said with a smile. "I realized you wouldn't be able to get into your apartment and that I'd have to be here to greet you. Oh, and by the way – Congratulations. I think you will be happy to see that your two friends have waited up for you. I'm so glad nothing bad happened to you." Behind Esther, coming out of the shadows of the house's front entrance were Trish and Clarissa. Trish almost sprinted towards me and kissed me fully on the lips.

* * *

She and Clarissa chatted only for a few minutes. It was obvious to them both that I was sinking into a sleep from which nothing would quickly wake me. They helped me up to the apartment, helped me off with my shoes, helped my lie down fully clothed on the bed, and then placed a blanket atop me to keep away the cold of the Judean nights.

The next day, even before I had a chance to be reunited with Trish and Clarissa, the first person I saw was Burton Lasch. "This is becoming a habit, Rick," he said with a broad grin as he got out of a car that had pulled up outside the house at 8.00 a.m. Fortunately, he'd phoned me on my home phone before arriving, and I scrambled to shower and dress in time to meet him. "Every time I send you on a new assignment the news around you goes into overdrive and I have to get on a plane to see you safely delivered from some life-threatening international news emergency. Rick, how about, for your next assignment, a couple of years in Detroit? I hear the auto industry is making a slow comeback. I think you'd be good at covering that. Hey, anyway, you don't want to spend all morning with me. Seems I'm to escort you yet again to your girlfriend and her chaperone. They're waiting for you at the Renaissance Hotel."

Trish, as expected, was looking radiantly beautiful when I pulled up to the hotel. Clarissa was standing beside her, but after I had given her a hug, tactfully withdrew. I needed to spend several minutes just enjoying the proximity to Trish, and we wandered into the coffee shop where we sat side by side in a booth.

Lasch stayed three days and used the time well, having serious talks with everyone in the bureau and managing to arrange a meeting with the Israeli foreign minister. Karim drove him up to Ramallah and he listened with his usual seriousness both to senior members of the Palestinian authority and to a small group of Palestinian professionals Karim had rounded up. Lasch had always had a special liking for the Palestinians and was much more patient at untangling their legitimate grievances from the usual anti-Israeli hyperbole than were many experienced reporters. As always, he left Israel sobered by what he heard on both sides, and looking serious.

For me, however, the week that followed my rescue was a giddy round of celebrations. At Christopher Blakely's even Patrick Cavenagh appeared to be relieved that I had escaped with my life. Diplomatically, I did not bring up in conversation with him either Al-Jaffar or Husseini. Blakely was in his usual wine-bibbing mode and was spouting off about a new Argentine Merlot he claimed to have "discovered."

One of the first people to call on the *Epoch* bureau the day after the rescue was Yao. Having shared the Al-Jaffar interview with me in Gaza, he seemed to feel partly guilty for my kidnapping. Of course, as I kept insisting, there was no connection at all between our meeting together with Al-Jaffar and my seizure by the Followers of the Caliph. I had not been in the bureau when Yao came by, and it was not until that evening that we could meet over dinner. Trish and Clarissa were also there, and I had also invited Jean-Louis and Svetlana. We decided to dine in the King David Hotel.

"So, Fanmei," I asked over a glass of Israeli wine, "What impressions are you taking away from the region after all this excitement? Do you think there is any hope for a peaceful settlement between Israelis and Palestinians?"

Yao assumed his most serious expression. "I see no prospect of a permanent settlement in the near future," he said. "But I do think that both sides can work towards that ultimate goal by co-operating on practical matters that are of mutual concern; ending the sexual trafficking of foreign women through the Sinai from Egypt, for example. Surely even Hamas must be against that?"

"I don't doubt that they are," I said, "but the cost of cracking down on such a social evil is co-operation with a political entity they don't recognize as really existing: the Jewish state itself. Nothing will persuade them to agree to that."

Svetlana chimed in now. "You know, everybody, I am new to Israel, to this region. I know only what I have read, or heard, or what Jean-Louis has told me. Of course, I have been here longer than him, so I have more personal experiences. But not that much. Please, someone, answer this question: why are so many people against the Jews? What have we done that offends so many people? Can you tell me?"

"What did the people say to you who didn't like you – the Jews – in Russia?" Clarissa asked.

"They said we should go back to Israel."

"How ironic," said Trish. "In Russia they want you to go back to your original homeland, but as soon as you get here – your original homeland – your neighbors say they don't want you *here*. There's no way you can win."

Clarissa said, "That's true. There is no way in human terms that anyone can solve the Arab-Israeli issue. That's why I don't believe in human terms."

Svetlana looked puzzled. "What do you mean?" she asked.

"Clarissa is a very serious Christian," Trish said. "She believes in prayer and she believes in the Bible."

"She means," said Clarissa, "that there are so many things that we can never explain, and never predict using our limited, normal understanding. I think the answer to Israel's dilemma is in the Bible."

"Well, what is it?" Svetlana said, bouncing the ball back. "Does the Bible explain why Jews are hated in so many places? Does it explain when the hating will stop and the Jews will be safe?"

"Yes, actually," said Clarissa. "But it will be at the end of the story."

"You mean when the Messiah comes?"

There was a momentary, awkward pause around the table. Then Yao, who hadn't said much all evening, chimed in.

"The Christians believe he has already come," he said. "They think the end of time will be when he returns."

Clarissa and Trish turned towards him almost together.

Trish said, "That's very well said, Mr. Yao. How do you know that?"

"Oh," he said so quietly we all had to strain to catch his words. "You now that I've been in a research institute for the past several months. Well, I've been researching many things."

I noticed that Clarissa was about to leap into the conversation, but

Trish quietly put her hand on the African-America's arm and silenced her. Then Yao looked straight at me. "Well," he said with great seriousness, "I think it's time that Rick spent some time researching things."

Both Trish and Clarissa burst into laughter. "Mr. Yao," Trish then said, "do you mind if I say a word you might not have heard before?"

"Of course not. What is it?"

"Maranatha."

I must have looked blank. I had never heard this word before. But apparently Yao had. "Yes," he replied. "Maranatha."

I looked in confusion at Trish and Clarissa. "Pardon me, but what does that mean?"

"I think you'll have to ask Mr. Yao."

I turned to the Chinese. He was shaking with mirth.

About The Author

David Aikman is an award-winning print and broadcast journalist, a best-selling author, and a foreign affairs commentator based in the Washington, D.C.-area. His wide-ranging professional achievements include a 23-year career at *TIME Magazine* with reporting spanning the globe of nearly all the major historical events of the time. Since leaving *TIME*, he has authored ten books, including *The Mirage of Peace: Understanding the Never-Ending Conflict in the Middle East* (Regal 20009).

The list of previously published books is as follows:

- Hope: the Heart's Great Quest
- When the Almond Tree Blossoms (a novel)
- Great Souls: Six Who Changed a Century
- Jesus in Beijing: How Christianity is Transforming China and Changing the Global Balance of Power
- A Man of Faith: the Spiritual Journey of George W. Bush
- Qi (hardcover) or Awaken the Dragon (soft cover: a novel)
- Billy Graham: His Life and Influence
- The Delusion of Disbelief: How the New Atheism is a Threat to Your Life, Liberty, and Pursuit of Happiness
- The Mirage of Peace: Understanding the Never-Ending Conflict in the Middle East

- **(forthcoming)** One Nation Without God? The Battle for Christianity in an Age of Unbelief.

Current and Forthcoming Titles from Strategic Media Books

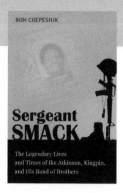

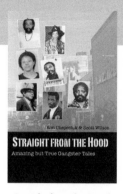

The Trafficantes
Godfathers from Tampa, Florida:
The Mafia, The CIA and The JFK
Assassination
978-0-9842333-0-4

Sergeant Smack
The Legendary Lives and Times
of Ike Atkinson, Kingpin, and
His Band of Brothers
978-0-9842333-1-1

Straight from the Hood
Amazing but True
Gangster Tales
978-0-9842333-3-5

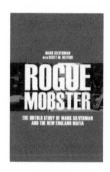

Chili Pimping in
Atlantic City
The Memoir of a
Small-Time Pimp
978-0-9842333-
4-2

Queenpins
Notorious Women
Gangsters of the
Modern Era
978-0-9842333-
5-9

Scapegoat
The Chino Hills
Murders and The
Framing of Kevin
Cooper
978-0-9842333-
8-0

Rogue Mobster
978-0-9842333-
8-0

COMING IN 2012

Gorilla Convict
The Prison Writing of Seth Ferranti

THE BEST OF AMSTERDAM IN 6 WALKS

WALK **1** > CENTER p. 18

The Center has more to offer than just the Kalverstraat and Red Light District. Discover unusual eateries and medieval sites, and explore the peaceful canals.

WALK **2** > JORDAAN & NEGEN STRAATJES p. 38

The Jordaan is Amsterdam's most pleasant neighborhood. Wander through streets with historic buildings and shop in the Negen Straatjes.

WALK **3** > OUD-WEST & VONDELPARK p. 58

You'll find the chicest part of town around the Vondelpark. Less well-known is creative Oud-West.

WALK **4** > WEST & WESTERPARK p. 78

West and Westerpark have undergone a transformation since 2010 or so. The raw vibe remains, but today you'll also find vintage clothing and pop-up stores.

WALK **5** > OOST & DE PIJP p. 98

Oost and De Pijp are Amsterdam's most lively multicultural neighborhoods. Here good restaurants, markets, and shops blend together seamlessly.

WALK **6** > EILANDEN & NOORD p. 118

The Eilanden (islands) are fascinating, thanks to many architectural highlights, while the industrial character of Amsterdam-Noord has led to it becoming the city's number-one hotspot.

MOON AMSTERDAM WALKS

Step off the plane and head to the newest, hippest café in town. Find out where to get the best fish in the city or where there is locally brewed beer on tap. In *Moon Amsterdam Walks*, you'll find inside information on numerous hidden gems. Skip the busy shopping streets and stroll through the city at your own pace, taking in a local attraction on your way to the latest and greatest concept stores. Savor every second and make your trip a truly great experience.

AMSTERDAM-BOUND!

Amsterdam is a compact city and a multicultural melting pot with open-minded inhabitants. There's a reason people say anything goes in Amsterdam. What makes Amsterdam so special are its numerous, splendid museums and the incredibly diverse range of shops—from vintage and design to trendy pop-up stores—all to be found in central neighborhoods, together with the most varied restaurants, new eateries, and pubs. The suburbs also provide a raw industrial feel with numerous festivals, underground parties, and secondhand markets. We'll take you to Amsterdam's most fascinating places.

ABOUT THIS BOOK

In this book, you'll discover the genuine highlights of the city we love. Discover the city by foot and at your own pace, so you can relax and experience the local lifestyle without having to prepare a lot beforehand. That means more time for you. These walks take you past our favorite restaurants, cafés, museums, galleries, shops, and other notable attractions—places locals like to go to. So who knows, you might even run into us.

None of the places mentioned here has paid to appear in either the text or the photos, and all text has been written by an independent editorial staff.

CITY
AMSTERDAM

WORK & ACTIVITIES
**PHOTOGRAPHER
AND BLOGGER**

LOCAL
FEMKE DAM

Femke knows the city better than many of its natives and likes nothing more than sharing her love of Amsterdam. She especially enjoys discovering new cafés, picnicking in Westerpark, and relaxing on Sunday evenings when Amsterdam has that village feel. A personal favorite of hers: taking the ferry to Amsterdam-Noord—it's almost like going on vacation.

PRACTICAL INFORMATION

The six walks in this book allow you to discover the best neighborhoods in the city by foot at your own pace. The walks will lead you to museums and notable attractions; more importantly they'll show you where to go for good food, drinks, shopping, entertainment, and an overall good time. Check out the map at the front of this book to see the areas of the city where the walks will take you.

Each route is clearly indicated on a detailed map at the beginning of the relevant chapter. The map also specifies where each place is located. The color of the number tells you what type of venue it is (see legend the at the bottom of this page). A description of each place is given later in the chapter.

Without taking into consideration extended stops at various locations, each walk should take a maximum of three hours. The approximate distance is indicated at the top of the page before the directions.

PRICES
For each listing, a suggested price indicates how much you can expect to spend. The price appears next to the address and contact details. Unless otherwise stated, the amount given in restaurant listings is the average price of a main course. For sights and attractions, we indicate the cost of a regular full-price ticket.

FESTIVALS & EVENTS
Amsterdam hosts many festivals, which are held throughout the city, especially during the summer.

LEGEND

● >> SIGHTS & ATTRACTIONS   ● >> SHOPPING
● >> FOOD & DRINK   ● >> MORE TO EXPLORE
☼ >> WALK HIGHLIGHT

Rollende Keukens—May and June (www.rollendekeukens.nl)
During this festival, the Westergasterrein and Westerpark turn into one giant
outdoor restaurant with food trucks, live music, and lots of finger food.

Amsterdam Roots—June (www.amsterdamroots.nl)
This world music and culture festival features around 60 concerts each year at
different locations throughout the city, plus the Roots Open Air festival in
Oosterpark.

ITs Festival Amsterdam—June and July (www.itsfestivalamsterdam.com)
A new generation of national and international performing artists presents their
graduation show performances at the International Theater School Festival.

Amsterdamse Bostheater—June, July, and August (www.bostheater.nl)
Outdoor performances, including theater (Shakespeare and other classics),
concerts, and children's shows are held in the Amsterdamse Bos (Amsterdam's
largest wooded park).

Summer in the Tolhuistuin—June, July, and August (www.tolhuistuin.nl)
This cultural festival in North Amsterdam, in Tolhuistuin Park, features an
outdoor stage, music, a wooden dance floor, and good food.

Keti Koti Festival—July 1 (www.ketikotiamsterdam.nl)
This festival is a celebration and remembrance of the abolition of slavery in the
former Dutch colonies, with an exuberant music party in Oosterpark.

Over het IJ Festival—July (www.overhetij.nl)
This is a pop-up theater festival in Amsterdam-Noord that features
performances at various locations, including the NDSM Wharf area.

Julidans—July (www.julidans.nl)
Performances take place throughout the city, from West to Zuidoost, during this
renowned festival of international contemporary dance.

Appelsap—last Sunday of July (www.appelsap.net)
This is a music festival in Oosterpark with hip-hop, urban, soul, and contemporary jazz.

Kwaku Summer Festival—July and August (www.kwakufestival.nl)
This multicultural festival takes place over four consecutive weekends in Bijlmerpark.

Grachtenfestival—August (www.grachtenfestival.nl)
Classical concerts are held at special locations on and near the canals in the city, the IJ waterfront, and in Noord.

Amsterdam Gay Pride—early August (www.amsterdampride.nl)
The largest gay event in the Netherlands, this festival features cultural and sporting activities, parties, and the flamboyant canal parade.

Parade—first half of August (www.deparade.nl)
This traveling outdoor theater festival in Martin Luther King Park showcases unique (and surprising) theater, music, and dance.

Magneet Festival—August (www.magneetfestival.nl)
Two weekends revolve around all things creative with crazy themes and a mix of music, theater, and art at the tip of the Zeeburgereiland.

Uitmarkt—last weekend of August (www.uitmarkt.nl)
A sneak preview of Amsterdam's upcoming cultural season, featuring performances, festivities, and market stalls at locations such as Museumplein and Leidseplein.

IDFA—November (www.idfa.nl)
The International Documentary Film Festival Amsterdam screens the best documentaries.

PUBLIC HOLIDAYS

In addition to Easter, Ascension Day, and Pentecost (whose dates vary each year), the Dutch celebrate the following official national holidays:

January 1 > New Year's Day
April 27 > King's Day
May 5 > Liberation Day
December 25 & 26 > Christmas

HAVE ANY TIPS?

Shops and restaurants in Amsterdam come and go fairly regularly. We do our best to keep the walks and contact details as up to date as possible. We also do our best to update the print edition often. However, if there is a place you can't find or if you have any other comments or tips, please let us know via email at info@momedia.nl.

TRANSPORTATION

Amsterdam is most easily reached from other European destinations by **train.** Exiting Amsterdam Centraal Station takes you directly into the city center. If you come by **car,** it's best to use a parking lot if you want to **park** in the Center. Parking rates on the street vary, depending on the district—from €1.40-€5 per hour. The closer to the Center you are, the higher the rates. Day tickets are also available. If you want to keep costs down, head for **P+R (Park & Ride)** from Amsterdam Arena, Sloterdijk train station, VU Medisch Centrum, Bos en Lommer, Olympisch Stadion, and Zeeburg. The rate is €8 per 24 hours (with a maximum stay of 96 hours).

The Amsterdam transport authority (GVB) will provide you with a P+R chip card for travel to the city center by tram, bus, or metro. From Sloterdijk and Arena, you will be given a train ticket to travel into the city center. Check the website www.iamsterdam.com/en/visiting/plan-your-trip/getting-around/parking for details.

You will need an **OV chipkaart** (smart card for public transport) with credit when traveling around Amsterdam. You can buy one at the machines in the train and subway stations, or you can buy an hour or day ticket on the tram, although this is generally more expensive. See www.ov-chipkaart.nl.

In the city center, the **tram** is your best option. Amsterdam has 15 tram lines, most of which depart from Centraal Station to the city's various districts. The **bus** is a good option if you're heading further out. There are special bus services from Centraal Station at night. Check www.gvb.nl for details.

Metro lines 53 and 54 connect Amsterdam Centraal Station with the Zuidoost area. Line 51 runs from Centraal Station via Buitenveldert to Amstelveen, and line 50 takes you from Amsterdam Sloterdijk station via Station Zuid to Gein. **Taxis** can be hailed on the street, and you'll find various taxi stands in the city center. You can always catch a taxi from Centraal Station. The best-known taxi company is TCA (tel. 020-7777777). The initial rate is €2.89 plus €2.12 per kilometer and €0.35 per minute. Make sure the driver observes the rules. You'll see bright yellow electric taxis, too, which are clean, silent, and resemble London cabs. In the Center, try a **bicycle taxi** for €1 per person per 3 minutes.

Real tourists take the **"hop-on, hop-off" boat** (with four lines and 20 stops). The boats navigate the canals and stop near the most important museums, shopping areas, and places of interest. A day ticket (€22) allows you to hop on and off all lines for the entire day. Evening tours are an option as well (reserve at www.canal.nl). Or take a trip with one of the **canal boats** departing from the Rokin. You'll also have nice views from the **"hop-on, hop-off" bus** (12 stops). A one-day ticket is €18 (www.citysightseeingamsterdam.nl).

BIKING

If you really want to experience Amsterdam and get around fast, hop on a bike. There are lovely cycling paths throughout the city, and it's a great way to explore the suburbs. You can also take your bike on the ferry and cycle around Amsterdam-Noord. The signs for cyclists are everywhere—look for the white signs with red letters. You can also buy maps of various cycling routes at the VVV tourist office at the Centraal train station.

Amsterdam is, of course, a cyclist's city, so most drivers are aware of the many cyclists on the road. But do be careful—it can get really hectic and busy, especially in the Center around Dam Square. As a cyclist, remember to watch out for pedestrians, other cyclists (visitors from abroad are not used to cycling here), buses, trams, and cars. Follow the rules of the road, even if most Amsterdammers don't, and, most importantly, steer clear of the tram tracks. A bell is highly recommended.

Bicycles can be rented from many places around Amsterdam, but first check if your hotel has them for free. If not, you can try **Macbike** (www.macbike.nl) or **Yellowbike** (www.yellowbike.nl). Both offer particularly nice guided tours in and around Amsterdam. If you really want to make a special afternoon of it, hop on a vintage **Velox bike** (www.veloxbikes.nl) and cycle around Amsterdam-Noord to picturesque Waterland, where a farmer will welcome you to Zunderdorp and invite you to milk the cows with him. Enjoy a fresh glass of milk afterward, which is a typically Dutch thing to do. The farmer's tour takes two and half hours and costs €29.50.

Do you live in the Netherlands? If so, you can arrange an **OV-fiets** season ticket (www.ns.nl/en/door-to-door/ov-fiets) before you visit Amsterdam. This free ticket is linked to your OV chipkaart and allows you to rent a bike at nearly every train station (including Amsterdam Centraal) for €3.85 a day. You can take two bikes at a time per ticket.

1 Experience amazing **CT Coffee & Coconuts** > p. 111

2 Food and a phenomenal view at **REM Eiland** > p. 93

3 Try a little of everything at **De Hallen**'s food court > p. 76

4 Everything at **Café Modern** is wonderful > p.130

5 For delicious pizzas and Bloody Marys head to **Bar Spek** > p. 85

6 **Gartine** serves a fantastic high tea > p. 32

7 Savor high-quality Dutch cuisine at **Wilde Zwijnen** > p. 106

8 Head to **Scheepskameel** for an elaborate dining experience > p. 126

9 Enjoy a sustainable meal at creative hangout **Pllek** > p. 130

10 Visit **Buffet van Odette** for great classics > Prinsengracht 598

TOP 10 | **MUSEUMS**

1 Enjoy unusual films and exhibitions at **EYE** > p. 125

2 The renovated **Rijksmuseum** is a must-visit > p. 62

3 Explore worlds and cultures at **Tropenmuseum** > p. 102

4 **Tassenmuseum Hendrikje:** handbag history > Herengracht 573

5 View amazing images at **Foam** photography museum > p. 25

6 There's plenty to do at action museum **NEMO** > p. 136

7 Travel back in time at the **Scheepvaartmuseum** > p. 122

8 Visit the **Hermitage** for treasures from around the world > p. 22

9 Admire the Amsterdam School architectural style at **Museum Het Schip** > p. 85

10 Learn about resistance during WWII at the **Verzetsmuseum** > p. 102

1 Get a good start at **The Breakfast Club** > p. 69

2 Have a peaceful wander around scenic **Prinseneiland** > p. 42

3 Sit back and relax on the waterfront at **Hangar** > p. 129

4 A Sunday morning concert at The **Concertgebouw** > p. 77

5 Visit the beautiful greenhouses at **Hortus Botanicus** > p. 117

6 Grab an afternoon drink on lively theater street **Nes** > p. 37

7 Browse the lovely little boutiques on **Utrechtsestraat** > p. 21

8 Take a bike ride through the **Amsterdamse Bos** > p. 138

9 Sample beers outdoors under the windmill at **Brouwerij 't IJ** > p. 126

10 Catch a film at **The Movies,** Amsterdam's oldest cinema > p. 57

NIGHTLIFE

1 **Paradiso** is Amsterdam's pop temple > Weteringschans 6-8

2 **Pacific Parc** has live music and DJs > p. 90

3 **Club AIR** knows how to throw a good party > Amstelstraat 24

4 For live jazz head to **Bourbon Street** > Leidsekruisstraat 6-8

5 Visit **Brouwerij De Prael** for beer tasting in the Red Light District > p. 37

6 **Canvas** offers dancing with a view > Wibautstraat 150

7 Watch films in style at **Tuschinski** > Reguliersbreestraat 26-34

8 **Melkweg** hosts great parties and concerts > Lijnbaansgracht 234A

9 **Tolhuistuin** always has a diverse program > p. 137

10 **The Waterhole** is for rock lovers > Korte Leidsedwarsstraat 49

CENTER

ABOUT THE WALK

This is the most touristy walk in the book, featuring places for which Amsterdam is most famous, such as the Red Light District, multicultural Zeedijk, and the Canal District. Varied and with a rich history, this walk leads through both busy and quieter areas. It's quite long, so you can also split it in two by walking back down the Oudezijds Achterburgwal, after you've gone halfway, to return to the starting point.

THE NEIGHBORHOODS

If you arrive by train at Centraal Station, you'll step right out into Amsterdam's vibrant center. Many tourists get no further than Damrak, the Red Light District, and the Kalverstraat. But the Center has a lot more to offer. Amsterdam owes much of its fame to the **Canal District,** which was designated a UNESCO World Heritage Site in 2010. During the 17th century (the Netherlands' Golden Age), monumental buildings were built with large inner courtyards, transforming the Kalverstraat from a muddy livestock market into a chic shopping street. Although today it's full of many of the usual chains, it's still possible to find some beautiful spots around the Kalverstraat, such as the **Begijnhof, Beurs van Berlage,** the **Royal Palace** (Koninklijk Paleis) on Dam Square, and the **Amsterdam Museum.** Around the large shopping streets, you can also find many small streets with boutiques and specialty stores.

Wandering past the canals with their stately mansions, it's easy to forget that Amsterdam dates not from the Golden Age but from much earlier and was granted city rights in 1342. From modern maps, you can see how the medieval city was built around the port. There was once open sea where the Centraal train station now stands. Today, only the stretch of water next to Damrak remains.

The world's most famous red-light district, the **Wallen,** forms the oldest part of the city. Although you may regularly stumble across drunken bachelor parties, you shouldn't miss this part of the Center. The **Zeedijk** and **Nieuwmarkt** are full of countless cozy cafés, Asian shops, and eateries. In Amsterdam's Chinatown, you'll also find the Buddhist temple **Fo Guang Shan He Hue,** Europe's largest temple built in the traditional Chinese palace style. The city of Amsterdam is currently busy with large-scale Project 1012, the goal of which is to make the Red Light District and Damrak more attractive. There are already various fashion studios nestling in between the prostitutes.

SHORT ON TIME? HERE ARE THE HIGHLIGHTS:

13 WATERLOOPLEIN + 16 MAGERE BRUG + 18 FOAM + 26 BEGIJNHOF + 36 BROUWERIJ DE PRAEL

TIPS

// Must-see sights for first-time visitors
// You can split this walk into two parts
// Perfect route for a quiet Sunday evening stroll

CENTER

WALK 1 DESCRIPTION (approx. 4.4 mi/7.5 km)

Walk from Centraal Station to Prins Hendrikkade for some slow food ❶. Follow the street over the canal and admire the Schreierstoren ❷. Turn onto Oudezijds Kolk, then left on Zeedijk for a treat ❸. Dive into Chinatown ❹ ❺ ❻ ❼ ❽ or continue walking to café-restaurant In de Waag ❾. Cross the Nieuwmarkt and walk along Sint Antoniebreestraat for vintage clothing ❿ or a treat ⓫. Continue to the Rembrandthuis ⓬. Cross Waterlooplein ⓭ next to the town hall, then cross the bridge over the Amstel and head down Staalstraat to get some gifts ⓮. Turn left on Kloveniersburgwal and continue down Halvemaansteeg. Cross Rembrandtplein diagonally, enter Utrechtsestraat, and turn left on Herengracht. Walk to the Amstel for the Hermitage ⓯ and Magere Brug ⓰. From the bridge continue alongside the Amstel, turn right onto Prinsengracht and right again on Utrechtsestraat, where you'll find a nice concept store ⓱. Cross the water and turn left on Keizersgracht, past the photography museum ⓲. Turn right on Vijzelstraat and keep going past the Munttoren ⓳. Continue to Nieuwe Doelenstraat and turn left to walk through the Oudemanhuispoort ⓴ to Oudezijds Achterburgwal. After the bridge, turn left and immediately right to walk down theater street Nes ㉑. Turn back and visit De Laatste Kruimel for a nice slice of cake ㉒ or cross the street for high tea at Gartine ㉓. Walk back and turn right before the canal on Rokin. Turn right onto Olieslagersteeg and right again on Heiligeweg to reach restaurant Blue° ㉔. From the Kalvertoren continue to Voetboogstraat for the best Flemish fries ㉕. Keep walking down Voetboogstraat until you reach the gate leading to the Begijnhof ㉖. Turn left down Gedempte Begijnensloot and through the Amsterdam Museum ㉗ to Nieuwezijds Voorburgwal ㉘. Turn right through Mozes en Aäronstraat to reach the Dam, Koninklijk Paleis ㉙, and Nieuwe Kerk ㉚. Cross the Dam and turn left onto Warmoesstraat for experimental art ㉛ and chocolate heaven ㉜. Turn left on Paternostersteeg to admire the Beurs van Berlage ㉝. Walk back and head down Wijde Kerksteeg to the Oude Kerk ㉞. Follow the street, turn left and walk down Oudezijds Voorburgwal, turning left again on Lange Niezel and heading back to Warmoesstraat for some homemade pasta ㉟. Turn right on Oudezijds Armsteeg for special homebrewed beer ㊱ and right to see an unusual church ㊲. Walk back and finish at the oldest pub in Amsterdam ㊳ on the Zeedijk.

SIGHTS & ATTRACTIONS

❷ Dating from 1487, the **Schreierstoren** (Weepers' Tower) was once part of the city wall that ran along the harbor. Its name is said to come from the days of the Dutch East India Company, as it was here that the women of Amsterdam bade tearful farewells to their men. Although a great story, it's probably no more than urban legend. *Schreien* means weeping, but *schray* means sharp and most likely refers to the sharp corner of the old city wall. These days, you can stop for coffee and lunch on the terrace over the water or inside the tower's nicely decorated interior.

Prins Hendrikkade 94-95, www.schreierstoren.nl, tel. 020-4288291, café open daily from 10am-1am, Fri-Sat 10am-2:30am, Sun noon-1am, free, Tram 2, 4, 11, 12, 13, 14, 17, 24, 26 Centraal Station, Metro 51, 52, 53, 54 Centraal Station

❽ The **Fo Guang Shan He Hue Temple** is the largest Chinese Buddhist temple in Europe. It's in active use for Buddhist celebrations, and you can take Chinese or Buddhism classes there. Guided tours need to be booked in advance.

Zeedijk 106-118, www.ibps.nl, tel. 020-4202357, open Tue-Sat noon-5pm, Sun 10am-5pm, free, Tram 2, 4, 11, 12, 13, 14, 17, 24, 26 Centraal Station, Metro 51, 52, 53, 54 Centraal Station

❿ A visit to the **Rembrandthuis** (Rembrandt House) gives you a good impression of the famous painter's living and working quarters from 1639 to 1658. Some of his paintings, etchings, and drawings are exhibited on the walls.

Jodenbreestraat 4, www.rembrandthuis.nl, tel. 020-5200400, open daily 10am-6pm, entrance €12.50, Tram 14 Waterlooplein, Metro 51, 53, 54 Waterlooplein

⓯ The **Hermitage Amsterdam** is the only foreign branch of the world-famous museum in Saint Petersburg. Extending more than 43,000 square feet (4,000 square meters), the museum displays art treasures from around the world and also hosts regular workshops and film screenings so visitors can learn more about the rich history of Saint Petersburg and Russia.

Amstel 51, www.hermitage.nl, tel. 020-5308755, open daily 10am-5pm, entrance €15, Tram 14 Waterlooplein, Metro 51, 53, 54 Waterlooplein

🔴 The **Magere Brug** (Skinny Bridge) is one of the most attractive drawbridges in Amsterdam. It's beautifully lit at night. The Mager ladies were two wealthy sisters who lived on either side of the Amstel, and allegedly built the original bridge in 1670 in order to visit each other more easily. It's more likely that the bridge got its name simply because it's so narrow.

Amstel, between Keizersgracht and Prinsengracht (extension of Kerkstraat),
Tram 2, 4, 11, 12 Prinsengracht

🔴 Photography enthusiasts can indulge at **Foam,** Amsterdam's photography museum. Alongside works by big names such as Erwin Olaf and Jim Goldberg are displays by lesser-known talent. There are usually three or four exhibitions on at the same time.

Keizersgracht 609, www.foam.org, tel. 020-5516500, open Sat-Wed 10am-6pm,
Thur-Fri 10am-9pm, entrance €10, Tram 2, 4, 11, 12 Keizersgracht

🔴 **De Munt** (The Mint) is a remnant of the Regulierspoort, a city gate that was built in 1487 and was rebuilt after a fire in 1620. It was part of the medieval city wall. The tower got its name during the French occupation when it was no longer possible to transport silver and gold to the mints in Dordrecht and Enkhuizen.

Muntplein, not open to the public, Tram 24 Muntplein

🔴 The **Oudemanhuispoort** is a covered passageway running from Oudezijds Achterburgwal to Kloveniersburgwal. The gate used to lead to the Oude Mannen- en Vrouwe Gasthuis (Old Men's and Women's house). Nowadays it leads onto the Binnengasthuis Terrein, an enclosed area that is part of the University of Amsterdam. The passageway houses a used books market.

Oudemanhuispoort, open book market Mon-Sat 9am-5pm, free, Tram 24 Muntplein

🔴 In the middle ages, the **Begijnhof** was a place where single, religious women could live together, nurse the sick, and offer classes. Today it's an oasis of calm in Amsterdam's busy downtown district.

Begijnhof (use entrance gate at Spui), www.begijnhofamsterdam.nl, open daily 9am-5pm, free, Tram 2, 11, 12 Spui, Tram 4, 14, 24 Rokin, Metro 52 Rokin

㉗ Unsurprisingly, you can learn all about Amsterdam at the **Amsterdam Museum.** Seven centuries of history are recounted through stories of city life, old movies, photos, sound recordings, and paintings.
Nieuwezijds Voorburgwal 357 and Kalverstraat 92, www.amsterdammuseum.nl, tel. 020-5231822, open daily 10am-5pm, entrance €13.50, Tram 2, 11, 12 Spui, Tram 4, 14, 24 Rokin, Metro 52 Rokin

㉙ Originally serving as the city hall, this building assumed its current function as the **Koninklijk Paleis** (Royal Palace) in 1808. It's still used for ceremonial occasions—Queen Beatrix abdicated here in 2013. The interior is beautiful, thanks to the restored chandeliers, furniture, and artistic masterpieces.
Dam 1, www.paleisamsterdam.nl, tel. 020-6204060, open daily 11am-5pm (closed during official engagements), entrance €10, Tram 2, 4, 11, 12, 13, 14, 17, 24 Dam

㉚ The **Nieuwe Kerk** (New Church) was built in the 14th century because the Old Church could no longer accommodate the growing number of churchgoers. The official inaugurations of seven generations of the royal family of Orange-Nassau have taken place here. Crown Prince Willem-Alexander married Maxima in this church and was sworn in here as the king of the Netherlands on April 30, 2013. Great photo and art exhibitions are regularly held here.
Dam 12, www.nieuwekerk.nl, tel. 020-6386909, opening times vary, entrance fee varies, Tram 2, 4, 11, 12, 13, 14, 17, 24 Dam

㉝ Grain, securities, and commodities were originally traded at the **Beurs van Berlage.** The architect, Berlage, was inspired by Italian architecture. He longed for a more just society in which exchange trading was abolished. No longer a stock market, the building now hosts conferences, concerts, and exhibitions. On Saturdays, you can take a tour reviewing Berlage's career as an architect.
Damrak 243, www.beursvanberlage.nl, tel. 020-5304141, weekly tour on Sat 10:30am-noon, tour €14.50 including drinks, Tram 2, 4, 11, 12, 13, 14, 17, 24 Dam

34 The **Oude Kerk** (Old Church) is Amsterdam's oldest building. The church was probably originally a wooden chapel. The first stones were laid around 1306, and the church gradually assumed its current form over the subsequent centuries. Exhibitions and concerts are regularly held here.

Oudekerksplein 23, www.oudekerk.nl, tel. 020-6258284, open Mon-Sat 10am-5:30pm, Sun 1pm-5pm, entrance €7.50, Tram 2, 4, 11, 12, 13, 14, 17, 24 Dam

37 The attic of this canal house hides a Catholic church from the 16th century. At that time, the official religion was Calvinism, and non-Calvinists were allowed to hold services only in places that were unrecognizable as churches. And so the church of **Ons' Lieve Heer op Solder** (Our Dear Lord in the Attic) came to be and can now be visited as a museum.

Oudezijds Voorburgwal 40, www.opsolder.nl, tel. 020-6246604, open Mon-Sat 10am-5pm, Sun and holidays 1pm-5pm, entrance €8, Tram 2, 4, 11, 12, 13, 14, 17, 24, 26 Centraal Station, Metro 51, 52, 53, 54 Centraal Station

WIJS BIER

x Blonde Poes.

x Kopi Luwak.

FOOD & DRINK

① You wouldn't expect to find a place as cozy as **Dwaze Zaken** (Foolish Matters) opposite Centraal Station, but you'll soon feel completely at ease in this arty café. The menu offers drinks as well as vegetarian, organic, fair trade, and locally produced food options. On Monday nights, you can have a potluck for just €6.90. The café also often has live jazz performances and temporary exhibitions.

Prins Hendrikkade 50, www.dwazezaken.nl, tel. 020-6124175, open Mon-Thur 9am-11pm, Fri-Sat 9am-midnight, price €18, Tram 2, 4, 11, 12, 13, 14, 17, 24, 26 Centraal Station

③ Home-roasted coffee beans are in, though that's nothing new, as **Hofje van Wijs** can testify—the business has been importing coffee and tea for more than 200 years. In the peaceful courtyard, the bustle of the Zeedijk seems far away, and you can sample what used to be luxury beverages, which are now consumed daily.

Zeedijk 43, www.hofjevanwijs.nl, tel. 020-6240436, open Tue-Sun noon-11pm, coffee from €2.10, tea from €3, Tram 2, 4, 11, 12, 13, 14, 17, 24, 26 Centraal Station, Metro 51, 52, 53, 54 Centraal Station

④ Somewhat hidden between the many Asian restaurants and shops on Zeedijk you'll find **Sugar & Spice Bakery.** As the name suggests, this cozy coffeehouse offers a variety of many different treats, both sweet and savory. It's a welcome change in this old Amsterdam neighborhood. Their flavorful sweet-and-savory brunch platters come highly recommended, wand they also have vegan options.

Zeedijk 75, www.sugarspicebakery-amsterdam.nl, tel. 065-5701765, open Sun-Mon & Sat 10am-6pm, Tue-Fri 9am-6pm, brunch platter €17, Tram 2, 4, 11, 12, 13, 14, 17, 24, 26 Centraal Station, Metro 51, 53, 54 Nieuwmarkt

⑤ **Thai Bird** is a known fixture on Zeedijk. Don't come here expecting an elaborate dining experience that will last all evening. But if a fast and tasty meal is what you're after, then this is the place. This popular restaurant is so tiny, it can feel rather crowded. But what it lacks in space, it certainly makes up for in charm. You will probably need to wait awhile for a table, but the fresh and delicious Thai dishes served here are well worth it.

Zeedijk 77, www.thaibird.nl, tel. 020-4206289, open Sun & Thur-Sat 1pm-10:30pm, Mon-Wed 1pm-10pm, mains from €13, Tram 2, 4, 11, 12, 13, 14, 17, 24, 26 Centraal Station, Metro 51, 53, 54 Nieuwmarkt

9 De Waag originally formed part of the medieval city walls. The building, which dates to before 1425, used to be called Saint Anthony's Gate. In the 17th century, it was converted into a weighing house. Since then, it has housed a guild, museum, fire station, and the anatomical theater that formed the setting for Rembrandt's painting *The Anatomy Lesson of Dr. Nicolaes Tulp.* Today, you can lunch, snack, or dine at the restaurant **In de Waag.** There's a lovely view from the outdoor seating area of the imposing Weigh House.

Nieuwmarkt 4, www.indewaag.nl, tel. 020-4227772, open daily 9am-4pm, 5pm-10:30pm, from €23, Tram 2, 4, 11, 12, 13, 14, 17, 24, 26 Centraal Station, Metro 51, 53, 54 Nieuwmarkt

11 Pizza for breakfast? Then head to **Betty Blue.** Alongside standards such as pancakes and fried eggs, the menu also features breakfast pizzas. This little gem on the corner of Snoekjessteeg is a great place for breakfast, brunch, or lunch. And with an extensive selection of pies and cakes, you are spoilt for choice. Their outside terrace is the perfect place to relax and watch city life pass you by—a quiet and peaceful spot in the middle of a buzzing neighborhood.

Snoekjessteeg 1, www.bettyblueamsterdam.nl, tel. 020-8100924, open Sun 9:30am-6pm, Mon-Sat 8:30am-6pm, from €8, Tram 14 Waterlooplein, Metro 51, 53, 54 Waterlooplein

22 Just try walking past the window of **De Laatste Kruimel** (The Last Crumb) without your mouth watering. Tantalizing cheesecakes, moist brownies, and scrumptious cakes are all there to tempt you—and they are all the more delicious when you know that everything is made with natural ingredients. If you're lucky, there might be a seat along the water, though it's also a pleasure to sit inside with a view of the kitchen.

Langebrugsteeg 4, www.delaatstekruimel.nl, tel. 020-4230499, open Mon-Sat 8am-8pm, Sun 9am-8pm, slice of cake €3.50, Tram 2, 4, 11, 12, 13, 14, 17, 24 Dam

㉓ Hidden away in Taksteeg—an alleyway in the middle of the busy city center, between Kalverstraat and Rokin—you'll find **Gartine:** a hole in the wall that is one of Amsterdam's best-kept secrets. Many of their fruits and vegetables are freshly picked from their own garden—and you can taste the difference. Try the nettle cheese on sourdough bread with homemade chutney or the ginger and pear pie. This is also the perfect place for high tea. Remember to make reservations if you come here for lunch because they're always packed.

Taksteeg 7, www.gartine.nl, tel. 020-3204132, open Wed-Sat 10am-6pm, lunch €10, high tea starting €18.95, Tram 4, 14, 24 Rokin, Metro 52

㉔ De Kalvertoren shopping center is a cut above the rest, which is reflected in restaurant **Blue°.** Making the most of the location, there's a beautiful view through the glass facade from virtually every table. Take the glass elevator to the top for a sandwich or a glass of wine, and take a walk around the restaurant to view the city on all sides.

Singel 457, www.blue-amsterdam.nl, tel. 020-4273901, open Mon 11am-6:30pm, Tue-Wed & Fri-Sat 10am-6:30pm, Thur 10am-9pm, Sun noon-6:30pm, sandwich €7.50, Tram 2, 11, 12 Koningsplein, Tram 24 Muntplein

25 For the very best fries in town, head to **Vlaams Friethuis** (Flemish fries shop), where 55 years of experience have certainly paid off. Choose from 25 sauces—from mayonnaise to samurai sauce, and from ketchup to yellow curry.
Voetboogstraat 33, www.vleminckxdesausmeester.nl, tel. 020-6246075, open Sun-Mon noon-7pm, Tue-Wed & Fri-Sat 11am-7pm, Thur 11am-9pm, fries and sauce €2.80, Tram 24 Muntplein, Tram 2, 11, 12 Koningsplein

28 At **Stadspaleis** you are spoiled for healthy choices like wraps, salads, and soups—all made with pure ingredients and fair-trade products. Try the organic Flemish fries with homemade tartar sauce, a delicious accompaniment to the organic burger. It's healthy yet scrumptious eating in this teeny-tiny lunchroom.
Nieuwezijds Voorburgwal 289, www.stadspaleis.com, tel. 020-6256542, open daily 11am-7pm, sandwich €6.50, Tram 2, 11, 12 Spui, Tram 4, 14, 24 Rokin, Metro 52 Rokin

32 The chocolate served at **Metropolitan Deli** is reminiscent of the romantic film *Chocolat*. It's a dangerous place—here they do anything and everything with chocolate. Try the homemade Italian ice cream, too. The deli sometimes organizes tastings.
Warmoesstraat 135, www.metropolitandeli.nl, tel. 020-3301955, open daily 9am-1am, chocolate tasting €7.95 (minimum of four people), Tram 2, 4, 11, 12, 13, 14, 17, 24 Dam

35 Italian restaurants abound in the center of Amsterdam, though the quality of the pasta often leaves much to be desired. At **Pasta Pasta,** they understand that making pasta is an art in its own right. The pasta is purchased fresh from the market every morning. The result: handmade pasta topped with fresh ingredients.
Warmoesstraat 49, www.pasta-pasta.nl, tel. 020-3311199, open Sun-Thur 11am-midnight, Fri-Sat 11am-2am, from €5, Tram 2, 4, 11, 12, 13, 14, 17, 24 Dam

38 Taste the atmosphere of old Amsterdam at café **Int Aepjen** (Old Dutch meaning "at the monkey"). The Dutch saying *in de aap gelogeerd* (literally, "stayed at the monkey," meaning to be in a bad situation) apparently originated here. The story goes that during the 15th century, if guests couldn't pay their bill, the owner would accept payment in kind—in the form of monkeys that sailors often brought with them. Apparently, the monkeys often had fleas, so if

someone was spotted walking along the seafront scratching vigorously, it was said, "He must have stayed at the monkey!"

Zeedijk 1, tel. 020-6268401, open Sun-Thur noon-1am, Fri-Sat noon-3am, drink €3, Tram 2, 4, 11, 12, 13, 14, 17, 24, 26 Centraal Station, Metro 51, 52, 53, 54 Centraal Station

SHOPPING

❻ Toko Dun Yong is by far the largest Asian shop in the city and one of the oldest, dating back 60 years. You'll find more than just food and drink in the building's six stories—this is the place for all things Chinese, from cookware to books, music, and porcelain. Check out the restaurant on the second floor for some good noodle soup.

Stormsteeg 9, www.dunyong.com, tel. 020-6221763, open Mon-Fri 9am-7pm, Sat 9am-6pm, Sun noon-6pm, Tram 2, 4, 11, 12, 13, 14, 17, 24, 26 Centraal Station, Metro 51, 52, 53, 54 Centraal Station

❼ Asia is not only a source of ancient culinary traditions but also various new trends. **Asia Station** collects all the novelties the continent has to offer—from bubble tea to beautiful Asian-style dresses and from gadgets you've never seen before to cosmetics by special Asian brands.

Zeedijk 100, www.asiastation.nl, tel. 020-3032628, open daily 11:30am-9pm, Tram 2, 4, 11, 12, 13, 14, 17, 24, 26 Centraal Station, Metro 51, 52, 53, 54 Centraal Station

❿ Bis! is a must for all lovers of vintage clothing, with a whopping three shops filled to the brim with clothes, shoes, hats, and accessories. They sell unique fashion items—whether you're looking for a special 1950s evening gown or a funky pantsuit from the '70s. One of the three shops is dedicated to army and navy apparel. They also have a good selection of menswear.

Sint Antoniesbreestraat 25a, www.bis-vintage.nl, tel. 020-6203467, open Sun noon-5pm, Mon noon-6pm, Tue-Sat 11am-6pm, Tram 14 Waterlooplein, Metro 51, 53, 54 Waterlooplein

13 Located behind the Town Hall and Music Theater, the market on **Waterlooplein** has 300 stalls selling mostly secondhand wares. "If it's not for sale here, then it doesn't exist," as the saying goes. The market's not cheap, but it's still fun to visit.

Waterlooplein, waterlooplein.amsterdam, open Mon-Sat 9am-6pm, Tram 14 Waterlooplein, Metro 51, 53, 54 Waterlooplein

14 Handmade buffalo leather bags, Japanese crockery, or sketchbooks from handmade paper. If you're on the hunt for an original present for yourself or a friend, **Biec** is the place to be. Time flies in this curiosity shop because there is so much to see and choose from. They focus on sustainable products from all over the world, and there is something to be had for everyone.

Staalstraat 28, https://biec.nl, tel. 020-2620316, open Sun-Mon noon-6:30pm, Tue-Sat 11am-6:30pm, Tram 24 Muntplein

⓱ MaisonNL is a fun concept store that constantly changes its stock. You can find anything here from Scandinavian clothing to home accessories made of natural materials and lingerie from Amsterdam Love Stories clothing.
Utrechtsestraat 118, www.maisonnl.com, tel. 020-4285183, open Mon 1pm-6pm, Tue-Sat 10:30am-6pm, Sun 1pm-5pm, Tram 2, 4, 11, 12 Prinsengracht di-za 10.30-18.00, zo 13.00-17.00, tram 4 prinsengracht

MORE TO EXPLORE

㉑ At first sight, **Nes** might look a bit drab, but don't be fooled—in the evenings and on Sundays, this street comes to life with animated theater-goers heading for Frascati (the oldest theater on the street), the Comedy Theater, Brakke Grond, or the Torpedo Theater. While here, take a look down Gebed zonder End (Prayer without End), an alley that refers to one of the many monasteries located in the city during the Middle Ages.
Nes, Tram 2, 4, 11, 12, 13, 14, 17, 24 Dam

㉛ W139 is an internationally renowned exhibition space and haven for fine art. It's a place where artists can experiment. Festivals, concerts, dance performances, and other activities are regularly held here. Drop in and be surprised by the variety of contemporary art projects in this industrial-style gallery.
Warmoesstraat 139, www.w139.nl, tel. 020-6229434, open daily noon-6pm, free, Tram 2, 4, 11, 12, 13, 14, 17, 24 Dam

㊱ You can now find **Brouwerij De Prael** on a street formerly known as de Bierkade (beer quay). Take a tour through the brewery and then hang out at the bar with beers named after heroes from the Dutch tears-in-your-beer-type ballads. The tasting room also doubles as a learning center for people with a history of mental illness who find it hard to find work.
Oudezijds Armsteeg 26 (Proeflokaal), www.deprael.nl, tel. 020-4084469, open tasting room Mon-Wed noon-midnight, Thur-Sat noon-1am, Sun noon-11pm, tours every hour Mon-Fri 1pm-6pm, Sat 1pm-5pm, Sun 2pm-5pm, tour €8.50, tasting room €10, tour and tasting €17.50, Tram 2, 4, 11, 12, 13, 14, 17, 24, 26 Centraal Station

JORDAAN & NEGEN STRAATJES

ABOUT THE WALK

This walk leads you past historical canal houses and shops. You'll stroll down the charming Haarlemmerstraat to the lovely, quiet Prinseneiland and on to the lively Jordaan with its many cafés. The Negen Straatjes (Nine Little Streets) are an absolute must for any shopaholic. The walk is worth it, even you don't like shopping—this neighborhood is in the most beautiful part of town, with scenic views of many bridges and canals.

THE NEIGHBORHOODS

The **Jordaan** is considered Amsterdam's most pleasant neighborhood. Previously a blue-collar quarter, it has been increasingly gentrified over the years, now that anyone with money is willing to fork it over for a property. The quaint streets and scenic canals are now dominated by yuppies on designer cargo bikes and affluent expats.

It's easy to forget that this neighborhood used to be far removed from the riches of the canal belt. The Jordaan was constructed in 1612 for workers and immigrants. It became increasingly impoverished from the 19th century onward, until the 1970s when the municipality began extensive rejuvenation. Since then, the Jordaan has been transformed from a working-class neighborhood into an expensive area, home to the well-educated.

It might seem as though the special atmosphere of yesteryear—of folk songs, pubs, and tacky jokes told in the broad Amsterdam dialect—are a thing of the past. Trendy shops and living spaces now occupy the buildings that once housed traditional businesses. But the good old days is far from forgotten. On **Johnny Jordaanplein,** for example, the Dutch *levenslied* (tear-jerking beer ballad) is honored. Like the Jordaan, the **Negen Straatjes** have also become a must-see for any Amsterdam visitor. And for good reason—the area is lined with unique boutiques, delicatessens, home decor stores, and lovely cafés. The nine streets run parallel to one another between the canals and are considered Amsterdam's finest shopping district.

SHORT ON TIME? HERE ARE THE HIGHLIGHTS:

8 PRINSENEILAND + 13 APPLE PIE AT WINKEL 43 + 17 HET OUD-HOLLANDSCH SNOEPWINKELTJE + 24 CHOCOLATERIE POMPADOUR + 34 ANNE FRANK HUIS

TIPS
// A must for shopaholics
// Nice on Mondays when there's a market
// Lots of cozy, traditional Dutch pubs

casa de **anne frank**
Um museu com uma história

JORDAAN & NEGEN STRAATJES

WALK 2 DESCRIPTION (approx. 5.5 mi/9 km)

Start on Haarlemmerstraat ❶ ❷. Bear left for the West-Indisch Huis ❸ and keep going ❹ ❺ ❻ ❼. Turn right onto Buiten Oranjestraat. Walk under the railway and on Hendrik Jonkerplein head for Bickersgracht. Take the first bridge left and walk left over Prinseneiland ❽. Turn right at the end of the street, then right again onto Galgenstraat, and then left over the water. Turn left again, under the railway and cross the road until you get to Haarlemmerdijk. Turn left ❾, right, and right again onto Vinkenstraat ❿. Turn left at the end, then left again onto Brouwersgracht. Cross the first bridge, turn left, and walk alongside the water to Café Thijssen ⓫. Turn right onto Lindengracht and left via the Noorderkerkstraat to the Noordermarkt ⓬ ⓭. Turn right onto Westerstraat and take the first right. When you arrive at Boomstraat, take a left. Cross Tweede Boomdwarsstraat diagonally to Karthuizerstraat ⓮. Walk left onto Tichelstraat and past ⓯ ⓰ ⓱. Cross Egelantiersgracht and go left until you reach Prinsengracht. Turn right and take the first right to check out some special T-shirts ⓲. Walk down Nieuwe Leliestraat, take the second street left and then take the first right onto Bloemgracht. Follow the street to the next bridge, cross over, turn right onto Bloemstraat, then take the first left. Continue walking to Elandsgracht, then turn left for Palladio ⓳ and to reach Holland's famous folk singers ⓴. Turn right onto Prinsengracht, right again onto Oude Looiersstraat, then the first left. Cross the canal, turn right to reach Lijnbaansgracht, then turn left. Head over the canal, turn left, then right for the Turnzaal ㉑. Turn around and go via Raamplein to Passeerdersgracht ㉒ until you reach Prinsengracht. Turn left and take the first bridge on the right for Negen Straatjes ㉓ ㉔ ㉕. Cross to the other side of Herengracht and turn left for a liqueur ㉖. Cross Herengracht again. Walk down Prinsengracht along the right side of the canal. Take the first right for good food ㉗ ㉘ ㉙ and great shopping ㉚ ㉛. Walk down Singel on the left, and turn left again. Walk through the shopping arcade and cross the road at Westermarkt for some noteworthy sights ㉜ ㉝ ㉞. Continue over Prinsengracht and turn right onto Leliegracht. Finish the walk with dinner ㉟ ㊱ ㊲.

SIGHTS & ATTRACTIONS

West-Indisch Huis, the former head office of the Dutch West India Company, which participated in the Atlantic slave trade, is the place where its directors decided to build a fort on the island of Manhattan that was to later become New York.

Herenmarkt 99, not open to the public, Tram 2, 4, 11, 12, 13, 14, 17, 24, 26 Centraal Station, Metro 51, 52, 53, 54 Centraal Station

This often-overlooked part of Amsterdam is quite beautiful. The Dutch West India Company used the neighborhood's shipyards and warehouses to store herring, grain, tobacco, wine, salt, anchovies, cat skins, pitch, and tar. In the first half of the 20th century, **Prinseneiland** fell out of favor and was almost deserted until after World War II when it was rediscovered by artists. The oldest 17th century houses are at numbers 269 and 517.

Prinseneiland, Tram 3 Zoutkeetsgracht

The real Jordaan still survives in places such as the **Jordaanmuseum,** where you'll also find an exhibition about life in the Jordaan. In this nursing home, you can learn more about the district's many upheavals, street life, theaters, and artists. If your Dutch is up to par, try and have a chat with one of the residents, and if you're lucky, you'll hear all about "the good old days." The people behind this initiative would like to purchase the property to house their collection, so feel free to give a donation.

Vinkenstraat 185, www.jordaanmuseum.nl, tel. 020-6244695, open daily 10am-5pm, free, Tram 3 Haarlemmerplein

The icons of the Jordaan's popular folk songs can be found on **Johnny Jordaanplein,** which is actually part of Elandsgracht. The feelings Johnny Jordaan captures in his hit song "Geef mij maar Amsterdam" ("I prefer Amsterdam over any other city") are almost tangible around his statue and those of fellow Jordaan singers. The rumor is that a sculpture of Johnny Jordaan's nephew, Willy Alberti, will soon join his uncle on the square.

Elandsgracht, Tram 5, 7, 19 Elandsgracht

㉑ The Neo-Renaissance **Turnzaal** (Gymnasium) was built in 1887 after gymnastics became compulsory in Amsterdam's primary schools in 1862. In addition to a large gymnasium and an outbuilding, there is also a caretaker's house and bartender's lodgings (there was a beer cellar in the basement). Since 1978 the building has been home to an educational youth theater, Jeugdtheater de Krakeling that also rents out the foyer, theater hall, and basement.
Nieuwe Passeerdersstraat 1, not open to the public, Tram 5, 7, 19 Elandsgracht

㉒ In the days before recruitment agencies and job centers, you had to come here if you were looking for work or workers. Founded in 1887, the **Arbeidsbeurs** (Labor Exchange) moved to this specially constructed building, designed in the Amsterdam School style, in 1918. Men entered on the left, women on the right. Eighty employees shared various jobs, with a clear division of labor not only between the genders but also between professional groups.
Passeerdersgracht 30, not open to the public, Tram 5, 7, 19 Elandsgracht

㉜ The 270-foot-high (85-meter-high) tower of the **Westerkerk** is the symbol of the Jordaan. Princess Beatrix of the Netherlands and Prince Claus were married in this 17th-century church on March 10, 1966. Weekly services are still held here.

Prinsengracht 281, www.westerkerk.nl, open Mon-Fri 10am-3pm, Sat 11am-3pm, free, Tram 13, 17 Westermarkt

㉝ It's estimated that 10,000 homosexuals were killed in concentration camps during World War II. The pink triangle they were forced to wear later became the symbol of the gay movement. The **Homomonument**'s three pink triangles symbolize the past (the triangle at street level, pointing to the Anne Frank House), present (the triangle in the water, pointing to the National Monument on the Dam), and future (the triangle above street level, pointing to the headquarters of gay rights group COC).

Westermarkt, www.homomonument.nl, Tram 13, 17 Westermarkt

㉞ At the world-famous **Anne Frank Huis,** you can visit the hiding place of the Frank family via the stairs behind the bookcase and view Anne's original diary. Arrive as early as possible—the lines are often very long.

Prinsengracht 263-237, www.annefrank.org, tel. 020-5567100, open Nov-Mar, Sun-Fri 9am-7pm, Sat 9am-9pm, Apr-Oct daily 9am-10pm, entrance €9, Tram 13, 17 Westermarkt

FOOD & DRINK

❷ You're welcome in the early morning hours throughout the week at this slick café with Danish designer chairs and Dutch designer lamps. The chefs at **Vinnies Deli** work as much as possible with organic, fair trade, and eco-friendly products—by simply cooking with seasonal vegetables. All the ingredients, such as home-cooked granola and organic quinoa, are also for sale.

Haarlemmerstraat 46, vinnieshomepage.com, tel. 020-7713086 open Mon-Fri 7:30am-6pm, Sat 9am-6pm, Sun 9:30am-6pm, sandwich €8, Tram 2, 4, 11, 12, 13, 14, 17, 24, 26 Centraal Station, Metro 51, 52, 53, 54 Centraal Station

❹ The tiny cakes at **Petit Gâteau** look like works of art—almost too beautiful to eat. Almost, because they taste divine! The atmosphere is akin to a proper French patisserie in Paris. Everything is made on the premises, so you can watch every mouthwatering morsel as it's created. Beware though: before you know it, you'll be ordering seconds—just watching will be enough to make you hungry for more!

Haarlemmerstraat 80, petitgateau.nl, tel. 020-7371585, open daily 10am-6pm, from €4, Tram 2, 4, 11, 12, 13, 14, 17, 24, 26 Centraal Station, Metro 51, 52, 53, 54 Centraal Station

⓫ Where typical "Jordanees" (people born and raised in the Jordaan neighborhood) meets preppy—this is probably the best way to describe **Café Thijssen.** You'll feel right at home in this cozy bar where young and old from all walks of life mingle seamlessly. If you like a bit of buzz, come here in the evening, or on Saturdays when the weekly market is held. During the week, this is a great place to sit and read the paper or have a chat at the bar. The sandwich with Amsterdam *osseworst*—raw beef sausage—is not to be missed! In the summertime they offer some of the best outdoor seating in the Jordaan.

Brouwersgracht 107, www.cafethijssen.nl, tel. 020-6238994, open Sun 8am-midnight, Mon-Thur 8am-1am, Fri 8am-3am, Sat 7:30am-3am, Tram 13, 17 Westermarkt

✺ **Winkel 43** (Shop 43) is a favorite hangout in the heart of the Jordaan for a drink or a bite to eat. The apple pie is particularly delicious here—many consider it to be the best in Amsterdam, but of course you can decide for yourself! In summer, the long, wooden tables outside are always busy. It's the ideal place to relax after a visit to the Noordermarkt on a Saturday or Monday.

Noordermarkt 43, www.winkel43.nl, tel. 020-6230223 open Mon 7am-1am, Tue-Thur 8am-1am, Fri 8am-3pm, Sat 7am-3pm, Sun 10am-1pm, apple pie with cream and coffee €5.80, Tram 3 Nieuwe Willemsstraat

⓯ This is one of those bars that most tourists will walk past. And that isn't such a bad thing because here you can enjoy the company of genuine locals. **Café de Tuin** is a no-nonsense place with the typical interior decor of an authentic "Jordanees" bar. The walls are filled with prints, the shelves are lined with

ornaments, and the vibe is great. If you manage to secure a place out front on a nice day, expect to be here for a while. This buzzing little street has lots to see.
Tweede Tuindwarsstraat 13, www.cafedetuin.nl, tel. 020-6244559, open Sun 11am-1am, Mon-Thur 10am-1am, Fri-Sat 10am-3am, from €8, Tram 3, 5 Marnixplein, Tram 13, 17 Westermarkt

16 If you've ever been to Northern Spain, you probably know what *pintxos* are: small slices of bread with a variety of toppings. This and much more can be found on the menu of **La Oliva**. Together with some great Spanish wines and incredibly friendly staff, this is the perfect place for a Spanish evening in the heart of the Jordaan. Expect unique flavor combinations—and if you love Spanish ham, this is the place to be.
Egelantiersstraat 122-124, www.laoliva.nl, tel. 020-3204316, open Sun-Wed noon-10pm, Thur-Sat noon-11pm, from €15, Tram 3, 5 Marnixplein, Tram 13, 17 Westermarkt

19 You won't find bottles hanging from the ceiling or rustic murals on the wall at restaurant **Palladio**. Instead, there are plenty of light, fresh flowers, chandeliers, and lovely outdoor seating. The menu may also be a little different from what you'd expect at an Italian restaurant—there are no pizzas, but homemade pasta and fresh vegetables, fish, and meat instead. Try the seafood special: a catch of the day from the Dutch Wadden Sea.

Elandsgracht 64, www.restaurantpalladio.nl, tel. 020-6277442, open Tue-Sun 6pm-10:30pm, pasta €14.50, Tram 5, 7, 19 Elandsgracht

27 **Pluk** offers healthy juices, salads, and sandwiches, as well as delicious cakes and pastries, all available to take away. On the upper floor of this lovely, light space you can enjoy an extensive lunch. In addition to food and drink, Pluk is a great place to shop if you're looking for an original gift. Cookbooks, vases, cups, and dish towels are just a few of the lovely goods.

Reestraat 19, www.pluk9straatjes.nl, open Mon-Sat 9am-6pm, Sun 10am-6pm, from €10, Tram 2, 4, 11, 12, 13, 14, 17, 24 Dam

28 With the advent of venues such as **Ree7,** pubs with good-quality menus— "gastropubs"—have arrived in Amsterdam. You'll find tasty, no-frills sandwiches at lunch, and spareribs, chicken satay, or burgers for dinner. Try to find a spot by the door or at the window—it's a great place to do some people watching.

Reestraat 7, www.ree7.nl, tel. 020-3307639, open daily 9am-6pm, from €17, Tram 2, 4, 11, 12, 13, 14, 17, 24 Dam

29 At **Screaming Beans,** they know their coffee—and it shows. Here coffee is brewed with the utmost precision and they use their own selection of beans, procured from small farmers and roasted in-house. They're always on the hunt for new flavors, and tasting is all part of the experience. Drip coffee is brewed at your table, and if you're not a big fan of the black gold there is a special selection of teas.

Hartenstraat 12, tel. 020-6260966, open Mon-Tue and Thur-Fri 8am-5pm, Wed 8am-6pm, Sat 9am-5pm, from €3.50, Tram 13, 17 Westermarkt

35 Vegan food is certainly not boring at **Vegabond,** thanks to owner Babet. The business is colorful and sells surprising vegan produce and meals, such as (mostly gluten-free) cupcakes, pizza, or sandwiches. Choose a spot overlooking the canal or browse through the products. Be sure to try the beer from Amsterdam microbrewery Oedipus!

Leliegracht 16, www.vegabond.nl, tel. 020-8468927, open Tue-Sat 11am-7pm, Sun noon-7pm, sandwich €5, Tram 13, 17 Westermarkt

36 The name of this restaurant, **De Luwte** (The Shelter) is no accident. It's wonderful to relax in this sheltered nook, situated on one of the Jordaan's idyllic canals. The menu is international with a nod to Mediterranean cuisine. If that doesn't whet your appetite, it's also nice to sit inside by the fireplace with a glass of red wine or sip a cocktail overlooking the canal.

Leliegracht 26, www.restaurantdeluwte.nl, tel. 020-6258548, open daily 6pm-10pm, from €20, Tram 13, 17 Westermarkt

37 The romantic Art Deco/Art Nouveau decor alone is reason enough to visit restaurant **De Belhamel,** but the unique menu is a temptation as well. It includes, for example, French toast with *foie gras* and apple, and baked gnocchi with diced eggplant, tomatoes, and spring onions. The terrace, located at the intersection of the Herengracht and Brouwersgracht, is one of the most beautiful spots in Amsterdam.

Brouwersgracht 60, www.belhamel.nl, tel. 020-6221095, open for lunch daily noon-6pm, dinner Sun-Thur 6pm-10pm, Fri-Sat 6pm-10:30pm, from €24.50, Tram 2, 4, 11, 12, 13, 14, 17, 24, 26 Centraal Station, Metro 51, 52, 53, 54 Centraal Station

SHOPPING

1 **The Gift Lab** is a store full of must-haves for anyone who loves to shop. Whether you're looking for home accessories, a beautiful item of clothing, or jewelry, you can choose from a large selection of sustainable and fair-trade brands. This bright and beautiful shop on Haarlemmerstraat also has perfect presents for baby showers. What about a baby coat made from old blankets? Come here to shop for some original gifts.

Haarlemmerstraat 38, www.giftlab.nl, tel. 020-3627737, open Sun noon-6pm, Mon 11am-6pm, Tue-Sat 10am-6pm, Tram 2, 4, 11, 12, 13, 14, 17, 24, 26 Centraal Station, Metro 51, 52, 53, 54 Centraal Station

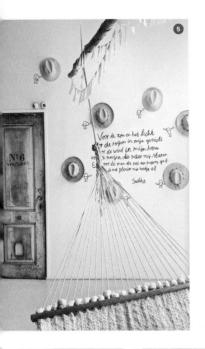

❺ Sukha means "joy" in Sanskrit, and that's exactly what the owners of this eco-friendly store want to create. Handwritten poems and doodles to make you smile hang from the walls. The common thread here is love and attention, from the special home accessories to sustainable clothing and books. Sukha also has its own label with artisan products from India, Nepal, Peru, and Indonesia.
Haarlemmerstraat 110, www.sukha-amsterdam.nl, open Mon 11am-6.30pm, Tue-Sat 10am-6.30pm, Sun noon-5pm, Tram 2, 4, 11, 12, 13, 14, 17, 24, 26 Centraal Station, Metro 51, 52, 53, 54 Centraal Station

❻ If you're in search of something special for your home, **Store Without a Home** is a must. The owner is always on the lookout for furniture, lighting, and home accessories that are otherwise virtually impossible to find in the Netherlands. The collection consists of international interior design from both established and new designers, such as cupboards by Seletti, porcelain by Lenneke Wispelwey, and lamps by Fraumaier.
Haarlemmerdijk 26, www.storewithoutahome.nl, open Mon 1pm-6pm, Tue-Sat 10am-6pm, Tram 3 Haarlemmerplein

❼ In this shop, less is more and "simple" is key to everything they sell. **Restored** has a stunning assortment of minimalist bags, jewelry, clothing, and ceramics, mostly from young designers and niche brands. Some of the items are even one of a kind. The shop itself is a sight to see, with attention paid to the smallest detail. Make sure to check out the beautiful Art Deco details on the storefront before you leave.
Haarlemmerdijk 39, www.restored.nl, tel. 020-3376473, open Sun 1pm-5pm, Mon 1pm-6pm, Tue-Sat 11am-6pm, Tram 3 Haarlemmerplein

※ At **Het Oud-Hollandsch Snoepwinkeltje** (The Old Dutch Sweet Shop) you can purchase sweets your grandmother might have bought, individually and wrapped in a paper bag. Among the traditional Dutch sweets are ones with enchanting names such as *toverballen* (magic balls) or *duimdrop* (salty licorice).
2e Egelantierdwarsstraat 2, www.snoepwinkeltje.com, tel. 020-4207390, open Tue-Sat 11am-6:30pm, Tram 3, 10 Marnixplein, Tram 13, 17 Westermarkt

⓲ Universe on a T-shirt prints its own designs on its T-shirts and tops. The T-shirts are not only humorous, they are above all original. Plus they feel good because everything is made from organic cotton and guaranteed to be sweatshop-free. Feeling inspired? Then why not buy your own DIY T-shirt box to liven up your old T-shirts. If you can't get enough, there's also a shop on the Bloemstraat.

Nieuwe Leliestraat 6, www.universeonatshirt.com, open daily 11am-6pm, Tram 13, 17 Westermarkt

㉓ You'll find no mild cheese geared at tourists at **De Kaaskamer van Amsterdam**—here you can buy cheeses soaked in *calvados* (a French apple brandy), wrapped in grape leaves, or a simpler mature cheese. This strong-smelling shop not only sells an incredible selection of local produce, but also stocks cheeses from out-of-the-way French mountain areas and small Italian islands. There are also nuts and tasty sausages to complete your picnic basket.

Runstraat 7, www.kaaskamer.nl, tel. 020-6233483, open Mon noon-6pm, Tue-Fri 9am-6pm, Sat 9am-5pm, Sun noon-5:30pm, Tram 2, 11, 12 Spui

㉔ The fragrance and atmosphere of the beautiful **Chocolaterie Pompadour** are enough to make your mouth water as you enter. But perhaps the proprietors also want to teach visitors a thing or two about style—here, craftsmanship is king and the ingredients are as pure as possible. Take note of the paneling, which was created in 1795 for the town hall of Mortsel (Belgium) and has now been given a second life at Pompadour.

Huidenstraat 12, www.pompadour-amsterdam.nl, tel. 020-6239554, open Mon-Fri 10am-6pm, Sat 9am-6pm, Sun noon-6pm, pastry €3.80, eat in €5.25, Tram 2, 11, 12 Spui

㉕ We Are Labels sells things by small, exclusive brands. The team travels all over Europe in search of suppliers. You'll find a selection of 30 exciting brands such as Eleven Paris, Nümph, and Mina UK and accessories by Club Manhattan. We Are Labels has another shop in Huidenstraat and two in Utrechtsestraat.

Hoek Huidenstraat/Herengracht 356, www.welikefashion.com, open Mon noon-6:30pm, Tue-Fri 10:3am0-6:30pm, Sat 10am-6pm, Sun noon-6pm, Tram 2, 11, 12 Spui

30 meCHICas, run by owner Debbie, conjures up images of Mexico, color, and passion. The jewelry is handmade from natural materials such as shells, fruit stones, and gems. Alongside its own collection, meCHICas also sells silver jewelry by Mexican designers, hand-painted Mexican pottery, and bags.

Gasthuismolensteeg 11, www.mechicas.com, tel. 020-4203092, open Mon-Wed and Fri 11am-6pm, Thur 11am-7:30pm, Sat 11am-6:30pm, Sun 1pm-6pm, Tram 2, 4, 11, 12, 13, 14, 17, 24 Dam

31 This well-stocked record shop is regularly frequented by many internationally renowned DJs. The owners of **Waxwell Records** have collected some 60,000 records with some real gems among them. While the shop specializes in soul and funk, it also sells old-school rap and other genres. If you're looking for something specific, the staff is happy to help.

Gasthuismolensteeg 8, www.waxwell.com, open Mon-Sat noon-7pm, Sun noon-6pm, Tram 2, 4, 11, 12, 13, 14, 17, 24 Dam

MORE TO EXPLORE

9 The oldest cinema in Amsterdam is not, as you might expect, the Tuschinski, but rather **The Movies.** This stylish cinema, dating from 1912, not only has a beautiful Art Deco interior, but the chairs are also comfortable. It generally shows more unusual art house films.

Haarlemmerdijk 161-163, www.themovies.nl, restaurant open daily from 5:30pm, last film showing usually around 7:45pm, entrance €11, Tram 3 Haarlemmerplein

12 Visit one of the Jordaan's markets for a real taste of this neighborhood's atmosphere. Every Monday, the **Noordermarkt**'s flea market attracts vintage hunters from miles around. You can find some real gems going for a song between the mountains of clothes and shoes. There are also more than enough knickknacks for everyone. On Saturdays, there's an organic farmers' market.

Noordermarkt, www.noordermarkt-amsterdam.nl, open Mon flea market 9am-2pm, Sat farmers' market 9am-4pm, Tram 3 Nieuwe Willemsstraat

14 The Jordaan is known for its many courtyards. You need only know where to find them, as they are often hidden behind a nondescript door or gate. The **Karthuizerhofje** (1650) was originally built for poor widows, but today the houses are rented out to individuals by a housing association. Take a look behind one of those doors and step into another world—a green oasis of tranquility.

Karthuizersstraat 89-171, tram 13, 17 Westermarkt

26 Entering **Proeflokaal de Admiraal** (Admiral's Tasting Room), located in a former coaching inn, is like stepping back into the Netherlands' Golden Age. Sample from among 60 types of liqueur and 16 gins, all artisanally produced according to original recipes. Take a good look around if you visit the restroom—it's constructed in a 10,000-liter oak barrel.

Herengracht 319, www.proeflokaaldeadmiraal.nl, tel. 020-6254334, open Mon-Fri 4:30pm-midnight, Sat 5pm-midnight, Tram 2, 11, 12 Spui

OUD-WEST & VONDELPARK

ABOUT THE WALK

This walk is for culture lovers who enjoy visiting museums. Museumplein is, of course, not to be missed. You'll also see a lot of interesting architecture, both modern and historical. And the walk also caters to those who like to eat well—there are numerous cafés and restaurants on the Overtoom and in the new Hallen. It's a long walk that can also easily be done by bike.

THE NEIGHBORHOODS

If Amsterdam's elite are to be found anywhere, it's here. And you can't blame them—this is considered one of the best areas of the city, with Amsterdam's most exclusive shopping street **(P. C. Hooftstraat)** and a variety of townhouses, stately mansions, and fine cafés all just around the corner, and the **Vondelpark** as its backyard.

Bordering the Vondelpark, the museum district also offers a significant selection of Amsterdam's most important cultural attractions, such as the **Concertgebouw** (Concert Hall) and the city's three largest museums: the **Rijksmuseum,** the **Stedelijk Museum,** and the **Van Gogh Museum,** which have all been significantly renovated in recent years. The Rijksmuseum reopened its doors in 2013 after a 10-year renovation and is now more impressive than ever. It opens almost directly onto **Museumplein,** and you can once again cycle underneath its grand arch.

Oud-West is characterized by its innumerable, lovely neighborhood cafés and shops. As a result, it has become really popular among young people in their 20s and 30s. On the Overtoom, you'll come across many students and young people who have pulled up a chair for a quick, reasonably priced snack.

An important new hotspot in Oud-West lies in the **Kinkerbuurt** (Kinkerstraat neighborhood). There is new life where Amsterdam's first electrical trams were serviced. The tram depot was built in the early 20th century and since 2014 has been open to the public as **de Hallen**—a center for media, culture, catering, and crafts. It's a great place to eat, drink, or go to the cinema, and interesting events are organized there monthly.

SHORT ON TIME? HERE ARE THE HIGHLIGHTS:

1 RIJKSMUSEUM + 4 VONDELPARK + 16 DE HALLEN + 23 BELLAMYSTRAAT + 36 STEDELIJK MUSEUM

TIPS

// Perfect for culture lovers
// Great during the week if you plan to visit a museum
// You can also follow this route by bike

OUD-WEST & VONDELPARK

LEGEND

>> SIGHTS & ATTRACTIONS

>> FOOD & DRINK

>> SHOPPING

>> MORE TO EXPLORE

>> WALK HIGHLIGHT

WALK 3 DESCRIPTION (approx. 7 mi/11.5 km)

Start with the Dutch Masters ❶. Walk to Stadhouderskade, cross the bridge and turn left onto Lijnbaansgracht. Keep right and continue on Korte Leidsedwarsstraat to Leidseplein ❷. Walk past the Stadsschouwburg theater, cross two streets and turn onto Vondelstraat. Take the first left and the next right past the Zevenlandenhuizen ❸. Continue to Vondelpark ❹ ❺ ❻ ❼. Exit the park via Vondelstraat and turn right at the church ❽ in the direction of Overtoom ❾. Cross the street and walk down Tweede Constantijn Huygensstraat. Take the first right, then the first left for coffee ❿ ⓫ and a nice shop ⓬. Continue walking for Asian street food ⓭. Go back and turn left onto Kinkerstraat for more coffee ⓮. Turn right at Bilderdijkkade, then the first left for Hannie Dankbaarpassage ⓯ ⓰. Turn right onto Tollensstraat toward Bellamyplein ⓱. Take a left on Ten Katestraat, turn right twice, take Jan Hanzenstraat and continue to Da Costakade. Turn left for two historical buildings ⓲ and continue to De Clercqstraat. Cross the street and turn left on Bilderdijkstraat, then left again into Bilderdijkpark ⓳. Continue to Bilderdijkkade, turn left, then take a right onto De Clercqstraat ⓴ ㉑ ㉒. Take a left on Tweede Kostverlorenkade. Cross the park to Korte Schimmelstraat and continue right onto Jan Hanzenstraat. Turn left and then right at Bellamystraat ㉓ ㉔. Turn right onto Van Effenstraat, turn right at the end and then left on Jan Pieter Heijestraat ㉕ ㉖ ㉗. Cross the bridge and turn left, then right on Nicolaas Beetsstraat. Take a left on Arie Biemondstraat to view art installations ㉘ on the grounds of an old hospital. Zigzag to Ite Boeremastraat, turn right, then take a left onto Kanaalstraat. At Jan Pieter Heijestraat turn left ㉙ ㉚. Turn right on Eerste Helmersstraat and continue until you reach Rhijnvis Feithstraat for a pizza with the locals ㉛. Take a left and right onto Overtoom. Cross the street and follow Frederiksstraat to enter Vondelpark. Exit the park at Van Eeghenstraat, turn left on Cornelis Schuytstraat ㉜ and left again on Valeriusstraat. Turn left at the end on Van Breestraat ㉝. At the end of the street, turn left. Continue until you reach Van Eeghenstraat, turn right, then take a left onto Van Baerlestraat. Cross the street and take the second street to the right: P. C. Hooftstraat ㉞. Turn right onto Van de Veldestraat, which ends in front of two of the city's most famous museums ㉟ ㊱ and the Concertgebouw ㊲.

SIGHTS & ATTRACTIONS

1 After a thorough renovation, the **Rijksmuseum** reopened in 2013. On display are 8,000 objects in 80 magnificent rooms, spanning 800 years of Dutch art and history. Highlights include Rembrandt's *The Night Watch* and Vermeer's *The Milk Maid*. Make a detour on your way out through the museum's beautiful garden.
Museumstraat 1, www.rijksmuseum.nl, open daily 9am-5pm, entrance €17.50, Tram 2, 5, 12 Rijksmuseum

2 The **Stadsschouwburg** offers the chance to see quality theater and dance daily. It's home to the Netherlands' largest repertory theater company, Toneelgroep Amsterdam (TA), which performs on Thursdays. Now catering to an international audience, the Stadsschouwburg also features international theater productions, in particular from Germany and the UK, and provides subtitles in English and other languages as appropriate.
Leidseplein 26, www.ssba.nl, opening hours dependent on performances, see website for programming and prices, Tram 1, 2, 7, 11, 12, 19 Leidseplein

3 Travel through Europe down one street, thanks to Sam van Eeghen who decided (120 years ago) to build the **Zevenlandenhuizen**: seven houses, each in the style of a different European country. You'll recognize Germany (romantic style), France (in the style of a Loire Valley castle), Spain (inspired by Moorish architecture), Italy (reminiscent of a palazzo), Russia (onion dome), the Netherlands (northern Renaissance), and England (Tudor cottage).
Roemer Visscherstraat 20-30, not open to the public, Tram 1, 11 1e Constantijn Huygensstraat, Tram 3 Overtoom

7 Pierre Cuypers, one of Amsterdam's most famous architects, built his dream home in 1877 alongside Vondelpark: **Villa Pierre Cuypers.** It's directly opposite the much-loved Vondelkerk (also one of his designs) and has both neo-Gothic and neo-Renaissance features. There's a very unique tile panel that shows three men and the old-Dutch text: *Jan bedenckt et, Piet volbrengt et, Claesgen laeckt et. Och wat maeckt et* (Jan invents it, Piet accomplishes it, Claes reproaches it, but who cares). Jan is the architect, Piet the builder, and Claes symbolizes the city that opposed Cuypers's plans.
Vondelstraat 75, not open to the public, Tram 1, 11 1e Constantijn Huygensstraat, Tram 3 Overtoom

⑨ The **Vondelkerk** is an attractive neo-Gothic listed building near the Vondelpark. The church was built in 1872 to a design by Pierre Cuypers, who also designed Centraal Station and the Rijksmuseum. On weekends, the church's main hall can be rented for parties and other gatherings.
Vondelstraat 120d, not open to the public, Tram 1, 11 1e Constantijn Huygensstraat, Tram 3 Overtoom

⑩ Once, there was a brewery on almost every street corner in Amsterdam. The building at number 102 with its red-brick façade recalls those times. It also once served as a wine warehouse. It was designed in 1903 in an eclectic style, with influences from both Neo-Renaissance and Art Nouveau. The tasting rooms were located in the attic. Today it is home to **De Nieuwe Liefde,** a cultural center for public debates, spiritual reflection, and poetry events.
Da Costakade 102-106, www.denieuweliefde.com, opening hours dependent on events, see website for programming and prices, Tram 3 de Clerqstraat 13, 19 Bilderdijkstraat

㉟ There is nowhere else in the world where you can see so many works by artist Vincent Van Gogh in one place. More than 200 paintings are on display at the **Van Gogh Museum,** including *The Potato Eaters*, 500 drawings, 700 letters, and a collection of Japanese prints. Besides works by Van Gogh, there is also a collection of 19th century Post-Impressionist art.
Paulus Potterstraat 7, www.vangoghmuseum.nl, open daily from 9am, see the website for current closing times, entrance €18, Tram 2, 3, 5, 12 Van Baerlestraat

㊱ The **Stedelijk Museum** has undergone years of renovation. Now completed, perhaps the most striking feature is the new wing that, thanks to its shape, is now popularly referred to as the bathtub. In the old building you can view highlights from the museum's large contemporary art collection, while the new section houses temporary exhibitions.
Museumplein 10, www.stedelijk.nl, open Fri-Wed 10am-6pm Thur 10am-10pm, entrance €15, Tram 2, 3, 5, 12 Van Baerlestraat, Tram 24 Museumplein

FOOD & DRINK

5 This unique round building that dates back to 1937 is located smack in the middle of Vondelpark. **'t Blauwe Theehuis** is a relaxed place to have a drink or something to eat. It has an enormous outside terrace where you can always find a spot to relax on a sunny day. On warm summer evenings there are movie nights or free yoga classes, and occasionally there's a party.

Vondelpark 5, www.blauwetheehuis.nl, tel. 020-6620254, open Mon-Fri 9am-6pm, Sat-Sun 9am-7pm, coffee and cake €6.50, Tram 2, 3, 5, 12, Van Baerlestraat

6 After a thorough renovation, the Vondelpark's former pavilion now houses restaurant **Vondelpark/3** and a number of cultural foundations. The restaurant offers Mediterranean-style lunch and dinner with a modern twist. You can also breakfast in style in the stately dining room or have a coffee outside on one of the two large terraces.

Vondelpark 3, www.vondelpark3.nl, tel. 020-6392589, open Sun 10am-8pm, Mon-Tue 10am-6pm, Wed-Sat 10am-midnight, from €14, Tram 1, 11 1e Constantijn Huygensstraat, Tram 3 Overtoom

10 **De Koffie Salon** is worth a visit not only for the coffee (a few years ago nominated the best in the Netherlands) but also for its location in a beautiful Art Deco building from 1933. Admire the colorful stained-glass windows and geometric designs or enjoy the pleasant terrace outside.

Eerste Constantijn Huygenstraat 82, www.dekoffiesalon.nl, tel. 020-6124079, open daily 7am-7pm, coffee from €2.40, Tram 3 Overtoom

11 Leonie does what many can only dream of—in 2013, she succeeded in making a living baking cakes. At **Baksels** (Bakes), the cakes are simple but tasty. Take a piece of cake to go, or tuck in on a cozy window seat. Leonie's favorite is the raspberry cheesecake brownie.

Bilderdijkstraat 201, www.baksels.nl, tel. 020-3892001, open Tue-Fri 10am-6pm, Sat 11am-5pm, piece of cake €3.50, Tram 3, Kinkerstraat, Tram 7, 17 Bilderdijkstraat

⑬ At **Happyhappyjoyjoy** you'll feel like you've been transported to an Asian street food market with sizzling pans, tantalizing scents, mesmerizing prints, and vibrant colors. It's hard not to feel happy when you're here! The menu features an array of small Asian dishes, all meant for sharing. Choose from a variety of dim sum, noodles, and curries. Pair your meal with a cup of tea or an Asian beer.

Bilderdijkstraat 158, www.happyhappyjoyjoy.asia/en, tel. 020-3446433, open Sun-Thur noon-1am, Fri-Sat noon-2am, dim sum starting at €6.25, tram 3 kinkerstraat, tram 7, 17 bilderdijkstraat

⑭ Step inside **Lot Sixty One Coffee Roasters** for a coffee to go. Speed, however, is not a priority here—the barista likes to create a moment of tranquility around every cup and enjoys involving you in the process. Drop by on a Monday or Tuesday if you can, because that's when the coffee roaster's working—a delight to the senses!

Kinkerstraat 112, www.lotsixtyonecoffee.com, open Mon-Fri 8am-5pm, Sat 9am-5pm, Sun 10am-5pm, coffee from €2, Tram 3 Kinkerstraat, Tram 7, 17 Bilderdijkstraat

17 What better way to start the day than with a delicious Parisian- or New York-style breakfast? **The Breakfast Club** is located on the corner just across from the massively popular Hallen. Come here to indulge in a stack of pancakes with fresh fruit, overnight oats, or eggs made however you like them, with salmon, avocado, or bacon. Wash it all down with a good cup of coffee or a fresh smoothie and you'll be ready to take on the world.

Bellamystraat 2-h, https://thebreakfastclub.nl, tel. 020-2234933, open Mon-Fri 8am-4pm, Sat-Sun 8am-5pm, breakfast starting at €7.50, Tram 7, 17 Ten Katestraat

19 Mexico meets California in Amsterdam! At **Flora,** hidden inside the small and charming Bilderdijkpark, are the best tacos. The small wraps come with a variety of surprising fillings. Try the vegan tacos with black beans and cashew crema or roasted cauliflower with sliced radish, pomegranate seeds, and zesty lime sauce. The cocktails are delightful as well, and on a summer's night this is a great place to relax and enjoy an entire evening.

Bilderdijkpark 1a, open Sat-Sun noon-11pm, Wed-Fri 6pm-11pm, three courses €25, Tram 3 De Clercqstraat, 13, 19 Bilderdijkstraat

20 There's nothing clichéd about Greek restaurant **To Ouzeri,** from its blue awning to its bright decor, surprising menu, and fresh food. Try the *mezedes*, Greek tapas that can easily match the more famous Spanish variation. What about *tiri saganaki*—mature, melted cheese flambéed with Greek brandy? The *kolokithokeftedes* is also worth a try, provided, of course, you can pronounce it!

De Clercqstraat 106, www.toouzeri.nl, tel. 020-6181412, open Wed-Sun 5pm–11pm, from €7, Tram 3 De Clercqstraat, Tram 13, 19 Bilderdijkstraat

22 If you enter this authentic pub, it's hard to believe it opened only about ten years ago. **Café Thuys** is a bit like the Kinkerbuurt's local, where everyone joins in the pub quiz, watches soccer, and orders an affordable dish of the day (ranging from schnitzels to casserole). The terrace opens as soon as the sun shines. The view from the pub is never boring, with all the activity on the water and the passing traffic.

De Clercqstraat 129, www.cafe-thuys.nl, tel. 020-6120898, open Sun-Thur 11am-1pm, Fri-Sat 11am-2pm, from €15, Tram 13, 19 Willem De Zwijgerlaan

27 Deegrollers (Dough Rollers) is a pizzeria with a traditional Dutch name but real Italian pizza made by an Italian chef. You can taste it too—in the thin crust, fresh ingredients, and the truly Italian combinations, such as truffle with pecorino, and pancetta with mushrooms. Traditional pizzas like Margherita and *cinque formaggi* have not, however, been omitted from the menu. For an original Italian atmosphere eat inside at long, wooden tables or in good weather sit outside overlooking the canal.

Jan Pieter Heijestraat 110, tel. 020-2212098, open daily 5pm-10pm, pizza €13, Tram 1, 7, 11, 17 J. P. Heijestraat

29 Soup with meatballs—it sounds Dutch, but **Voldaan** proves this combination can be created in any cuisine. There's a delicious Arabic version of lentil soup with spicy lamb meatballs. There's always a vegetarian and a gluten-free option on the menu, too, and the delicious dips, chutneys, and compotes are for sale in storage jars, so you can reminisce at home.

Jan Pieter Heijestraat 121, open Tue-Sun noon-8:30pm, from €7.95, Tram 1, 7, 11, 17 J. P. Heijestraat

31 Forno's pizzas are among the most popular in Oud-West, keeping this trendy restaurant's *pizzaiolos* constantly busy. The idea is simple: straightforward decor, a large terrace, and pizzas straight from the wood oven. And that's not all, Forno's has good antipasti (oysters and roasted beetroot, for example), unusual toppings (what about pizza calzone with venison?), and high-quality wines and proseccos.

Rhijnvis Feithstraat 43, tel. 020-6187415, open daily 11am-1pm, pizza €13, Tram 1, 11 Rhijnvis Feithstraat

32 The Bertram family opened its first bakery in 1890 in the Amsterdam neighborhood Jordaan. Nowadays **Bakker Bertram** is located on the corner of the lively Cornelis Schuytstraat. Enjoy your freshly made sandwich and coffee out front or find a table inside this cozy neighborhood store. Everything you see is baked on the premises. And for early birds the doors open at 7:30 am. It's a great place to pop by on a morning walk through Vondelpark.

Cornelis Schuytstraat 34, www.bakkerbertram-amsterdam.nl, tel. 020-3319042, open Sun 8:30am-4pm, Mon-Fri 7:30am-5pm, Sat 8am-5pm, coffee starting at €2, Tram 2 Cornelis Schuytstraat

SHOPPING

9 Amsterdammers who love to travel know that **Pied à Terre** is the largest travel bookstore in Amsterdam. The shop has a huge collection of travel guides, globes, hiking maps, and much more for anyone with any interest in travel.
Overtoom 135-137, www.piedaterre.nl, tel. 020-6274455, open Mon 1pm-6pm, Tue-Wed & Fri 10am-6pm, Thur 10am-9pm, Sat 10am-5pm, Tram 1, 11 1e Constantijn Huygensstraat

12 Sisters **Jutka & Riska** sell vintage clothing—their own designs and creations by young designers—here and at three other locations in Amsterdam, Antwerp, and Haarlem. Conveniently sorted by color and constantly changing, the store's unique garments are also a great value. The collection includes a wide range of bags, jewelry, sunglasses, and shoes.
Bilderdijkstraat 194, www.jutkaenriska.nl, tel. 020-6188021, open Fri-Wed 10:30am-7pm, Thur 10:30am-9pm, Tram 3 Kinkerstraat, Tram 7, 17 Bilderdijkstraat

15 Stop in **The Gathershop** for handmade jewelry and other beautiful fair-trade items—all with a story to tell and many by boutique designer studios. Magazines, succulents, skincare supplies, and stationery—each item is as beautiful as the next. The white space has a minimalist décor, and it's the perfect place to pick up a present for someone or for you. The shop is located in the "Kleine Hallen," a passage with a number of different stores.

Hannie Dankbaarpassage 19, www.gathershop.nl, open Sun & Tue-Sat noon-6pm, Tram 7, 17 Ten Katestraat

21 If office supplies conjure images of boring paper clips, staplers, and binders, then you've never been to **Misc Store.** The online store was a huge success, with its stationery to make you smile. Now the wonderful (traveler's) notebooks, calendars, and pens can be admired in a showroom. Your desk will never look the same again!

De Clerqstraat 130, www.misc-store.com, tel. 020-7009855, open Tue-Fri 11am-6.30pm, Sat 10am-6pm, Tram 13, 19 Willem De Zwijgerlaan

24 The founders of the **Creative Garage** refer to their initiative as a "drop-off shop." It's a platform for twenty artists who make unique products but can't afford to open their own store. There's a special selection of handmade bags, jewelry, clothes, and home accessories—ideal gifts for a great price. Both adults and children are welcome for workshops and other activities, and also just for a drink.

Bellamystraat 91, decreatievegarage.wordpress.com, tel. 061-9979967, open Tue-Sat 11am-5pm, Tram 7, 17 Ten Katestraat

25 **Bullitt**'s amicable owners are incredibly enthusiastic about design, art, styling, and fashion, something they have managed to transmit through their store. They don't limit themselves to a particular style but rather stock what they find attractive themselves, whether clothing or accessories, homemade jewelry, or vintage hi-fi, lighting, or glassware.

Jan Pieter Heijestraat 91-93, www.bullittamsterdam.nl, tel. 020-6180007, open Tue-Fri 11am-6.30pm, Sat 11am-6pm, Tram 7, 17 J. P. Heijestraat

26 At **Frankie's Corner,** *kwarkbollen* (quark balls, similar to scones) are made with farm-produced quark and cranberries, organic corn bread with pumpkin, or whole wheat bread with walnuts. Every week, baker Frank introduces new creations that are healthy, organic, and preservative-free. And as befits any real corner store owner, he knows exactly what's happening in the neighborhood and is always up for a chat.
Jan Pieter Heijestraat 95, tel. 020-6121776, open Mon-Sat 7am-6pm, Tram 1, 11 J. P. Heijestraat

30 This slick store that sells athletic shoes, demonstrates that sneakers can be as desirable as high heels. The impressive collection has been inspired by London's love of the athletic shoe. Brands such as Supra, Creative Recreation, Goliath Shabbies, and Radical are stylish, different, and striking—precisely the vibe that **Label 1401** aims to create.
Jan Pieter Heijestraat 153, https://label1401.com, tel. 020-6161734, open Tue-Wed & Fri 10am-6pm, Thur 10am-8pm, Sat 10am-5pm, Tram 1, 11 J.P. Heijestraat

33 **&klevering** sells original home accessories and gifts by its own label &K amsterdam, together with other leading brands such as HAY, littala, and firm LIVING. From cabinets to cushions and from lamps to toys, all items are equally fun. There is also a secondhand store in the Jordaan on Haarlemmerstraat.
Jacob Obrechtstraat 19a, www.klevering.nl, tel. 020-6703623, open Mon noon-6:30, Tue-Fri 10:30am-6:30pm, Sat 10am-6pm, Sun 11:30am-6pm, Tram 2 Cornelis Schuytstraat

MORE TO EXPLORE

4 For many Amsterdammers, the **Vondelpark** is their garden. It's the ideal place for romantic picnics or family celebrations with a party tent and a barbecue. In summer, the Openluchttheater (open-air theater) also offers free dance, drama, and musical performances, from Wednesday to Sunday.
Constantijn Huygenstraat, www.hetvondelpark.net, open daily, Tram 2, 3, 5, 12, Van Baerlestraat

🔟 In the late 19th century, **De Hallen** was the largest tram depot in the city. The large complex has recently been developed into a location for creative enterprises, with several TV studios, a cinema with an Art Deco room, a library with a literary café, restaurants, and an industrial hotel. In addition, there's the monthly Local Goods Weekend Market with products from Amsterdam.
Hannie Dankbaar Passage 33, www.dehallen-amsterdam.nl, tel. 020-7058164, open Sun-Thur 7am-1am, Fri-Sat 7am-3am, Tram 7, 17 Ten Katestraat

🔟 Entering this charming street is like taking a step back in time. The **Bellamystraat** is still at the old, lower polder level of all the villages around Amsterdam before the city's expansion in 1865. Now the street stands out among the "new" buildings from the second half of the 19th century.
Bellamystraat, Tram 7, 17 Ten Katestraat

28 Lab111 is hidden away in a former anatomical pathology lab in the Wilhelmina Gasthuis complex. Enjoy excellent food, watch movies you won't see anywhere else, check out various art projects, and enjoy experimental music.

Arie Biemondstraat 101-111, www.lab111.nl, tel. 020-6169994, open Mon-Thur noon-1am, Fri noon-3pm, Sat 2pm-3am, Sun 2pm-1am, movie tickets €9, mains from €15, dinner and movie €20, Tram 7, 17 Ten Katestraat

34 Celebrities, expensive cars, and tourists jostle on **P. C. Hooftstraat** where it's all about seeing and being seen. The street boasts some of the chicest brands. If "the PC" is somewhat beyond your budget, then it's the perfect place to just sit and people watch.

P. C. Hooftstraat, www.pchooftstraat.nl, Tram 2, 3, 5, 12 Van Baerlestraat

37 The **Concertgebouw** is one of the most popular classical concert halls in the world, renowned for its perfect acoustics. If you'd like to attend a concert, it's best to book well in advance. Or go to one of the free performances held every Wednesday 12:30-1pm (arrive early)!

Concertgebouwplein 10, www.concertgebouw.nl, tel. 090-06718345, see website for program and prices, Tram 3, 5, 12, 24 Museumplein

WEST & WESTERPARK

ABOUT THE WALK

If you're interested in going for a stroll through a colorful neighborhood with many creative initiatives, then this walk is for you. Discover interesting shops and small cafés on Jan Evertsenstraat and enjoy the greenery as you walk through Erasmuspark and Westerpark. If you want to know more about the interesting Amsterdam School architectural style, don't miss a guided tour of Museum Het Schip. From Centraal Station, take tram 13 to Admiraal de Ruijterweg, where the walk starts.

THE NEIGHBORHOODS

De Baarsjes and **Bos en Lommer:** until a few years ago, these were neighborhoods Amsterdammers avoided. Their dubious reputation means they're hardly mentioned in any city guide. It's a shame because these are some of the most exciting, up-and-coming areas of Amsterdam. Local businesses and residents took it upon themselves to make improvements to their neighborhoods. Initiatives such as "Geef om de Jan Eef" (Care about **Jan Evertsenstraat** shopping street) and BoLo Boost (Boost Bos en Lommer) have brought new life into impoverished streets and neighborhoods. Now they're bubbling with pop-up stores and weekend markets, making the area great for shopping. You may not find any big chain stores here, but there is more space for small entrepreneurs with unique ideas.

West Amsterdam is still very much alive and kicking and is characterized by multicultural diversity and many creative enterprises. **Westergasterrein** in the **Westerpark** is an important hub for this creative scene. Many years have passed since its factories supplied the city with gas. Today the buildings that used to house transformers and machines are home to cafés, a cinema, and creative businesses. During the summer, the Westerpark is a venue for weekend festivals, and once a month there's the Sunday Market.

It's nothing new that Amsterdam West is a focal point for creative energy. Around 100 years ago, architects from the Amsterdam School gave free rein to their imagination. The result is the **Spaarndammerbuurt,** where you'll find an incredible concentration of buildings in this style.

SHORT ON TIME? HERE ARE THE HIGHLIGHTS:

8 BAR BAARSCH + 17 PIZZAS AT BUURMAN & BUURMAN + 25 WESTERPARK + 27 WESTERGASTERREIN + 34 MUSEUM HET SCHIP

TIPS
// An interesting walk off the beaten path
// Ideal for weekends because of the activities in the park
// You can follow this route by bike

WEST & WESTERPARK

WALK 4 DESCRIPTION (approx. 7.5 mi/12 km)

Start on Admiraal de Ruijterweg ❶ ❷ ❸, which turns into Jan Evertsenstraat, the beating heart of trendy Amsterdam West ❹ ❺ ❻ ❼ ❽ ❾ ❿ ⓫. Take a tour of the special architecture on Mercatorplein ⓬, walk under the arch to Mercatorstraat, turn right onto Jan Maijenstraat and continue to the Jeruzalemkerk ⓭. Turn right onto James Cookstraat, then turn left twice to reach the green Vespuccistraat ⓮. Continue to Erasmuspark ⓯. Take the first left ⓰. Cross the water on the right and walk down Mercatorstraat ⓱. Continue for a while alongside the water until you reach Hoofdweg. Turn right over the bridge and walk to the left to Wilde Westen ⓲, or immediately turn right alongside the water. Turn left onto Griseldestraat and continue until you reach Tijl Uilenspiegelstraat. Turn left. Via the little street on the right and the stairs you'll reach Bos en Lommerweg. Cross the road and turn onto Gulden Winckelplantsoen: now you're in Bosleeuw Midden ⓳. Turn right onto Leeuwendalersweg and check out the so-called piggelmee-houses, then turn right onto Hofwijckstraat to return to Bos en Lommerweg, where you turn left ⓴ ㉑ ㉒. Follow the street until you reach Willem de Zwijgerlaan. Turn right and left onto Adolf van Nassaustraat for some tasty pickles ㉓. Continue on to Nieuwpoortstraat and turn right. Head left on Nieuwpoortkade, walk past the windmill ㉔, and turn right onto Haarlemmerweg. Continue until you can turn left over the water to head to the Westerpark ㉕. Turn right and pass by Mossel & Gin ㉖ onto the Westergasterrein ㉗ ㉘ ㉙. Head left in the direction of the railway and turn right, following the railway until the second tunnel. Go through the tunnel to reach the Spaarndammerstraat ㉚. Turn left for a short diversion to Hammam ㉛, or continue to two special restaurants ㉜ ㉝. Turn left onto Knollendamstraat and walk clockwise around the Spaarndammerplantsoen to view one of the highlights of the Amsterdam School architectural style ㉞. Walk via Oostzaanstraat to Hembrugstraat, turn right and walk to the water. Continue to Houthavens ㉟ to ㊱ ㊲ or take a right onto Stettineiland that becomes Memeleiland. Walk until you can't go any farther. Take a right and the first left toward Tasmanstraat, follow this street, cross the water and through Van Diemenstraat to end at Bak Restaurant ㊳.

SIGHTS & ATTRACTIONS

⑫ Designed by the famous Dutch architect H. P. Berlage, **Mercatorplein** was destined to become the focal point of Amsterdam West in the mid-1920s. But its cafés, theater, cinema, and department store never materialized, and the square took on a purely residential and business function. It wasn't cheap to live here, so at first it attracted mainly affluent newcomers. By the 1980s, however, the area had fallen into disrepair and had earned a bad reputation. It has since gone through two renovations—in 1998 and again in 2008—that have breathed new life into the square and its surroundings.

Mercatorplein, Tram 7, 13 Mercatorplein

⑬ Amsterdam West is a magnet for lovers of the Amsterdam School, an architectural style that developed in the Netherlands between 1910 and 1930. The **Jeruzalemkerk** (Jerusalem Church) is without doubt one of the finest buildings constructed in that style (1928-1929). The architect deliberately designed the church so it would be attached to housing, to express God's desire to live among the people. The symmetry of the façade and the fact that the church is oriented north-south, rather than the usual east-west, is striking. The seven stained-glass windows symbolize the seven days of creation.

Jan Maijenstraat 14, www.jeruzalem-kerk.nl, Tram 7, 13 Mercatorplein

⑭ The **Vespuccistraat** is a good example of how the neighborhood has taken matters into its own hands. Nearly one hundred years ago, the street was designed as a green avenue leading to the Erasmus Park, with front gardens, rare trees, and houses in Amsterdam School style. Over recent years, half of the gardens were lovingly maintained by the residents, with the other half left in the uninspired hands of the municipality. Then, residents decided the gardens should be restored to their 1920s appeal. Fortunately, 40 Japanese ginkgo trees have stood the test of time—they are some of the few that can be found in the Netherlands.

Vespuccistraat, Tram 13, 18 Marco Polostraat

⑮ **Bosleeuw Midden** now seems to be a typical residential area, but in 1935 it was a revolutionary idea in the context of the "Bosch en Lommer expansion plan." Architect Cornelis van Eesteren worked with open housing blocks, open courtyards, and lush greenery. It was an example of "new construction" in which home, work, and recreation were separated and accommodation was affordable. Behind, on the Leeuwendalersweg,

you'll find the *piggelmeewoningen* ("gnome homes"—Piggelmee is a gnome in an Old Dutch book for children). They're probably the most intimate single-story family homes in the city at 366 square feet (34 square meters)—though not for long, as they're due to be demolished.

Tussen de a10, Admiraal de Ruijterweg, Wiltzanghlaan En Leeuwendalersweg, Tram 7 Bos en Lommerplein

㉔ Molen de Bloem (Flower Mill) might look as though it's been here for centuries, but that's not the case. From 1786 to 1878 it stood in the center of Amsterdam, on the Bloemgracht (Flower Canal), from where it got its name. When the Marnixstraat was laid in the 1870s, the mill had to move. It was rebuilt in 1921 and has since been modernized several times. Flour was still ground here until 1960, but now the mill runs only occasionally.

Haarlemmerweg 465, not open to the public, Tram 19 Bos en Lommerweg

㉗ When the Westergasfabriek was built in 1883, it was the biggest coal and gas plant in the Netherlands. The factory still produced gas until the 1960s. Nowadays, the **Westergasterrein** is a green cultural complex. Spaces are rented to creative, cultural, and innovative entrepreneurs, from restaurants to clubs and galleries to studios. For partygoers there's Pacific Parc, plus a host of fun festivals taking place throughout the year.

Polonceaukade, www.westergasfabriek.nl, tel. 020-5860710, open daily, Tram 5 Van Hallstraat

Museum Het Schip was built in 1921 as a combination of post office and residences in Amsterdam School style. For several years, it has served as a museum for the Amsterdam School. The property should be seen from the inside—only then does it become clear how the architects intended to reconcile the interior and exterior. The museum house still has an authentic 1920s interior.

Spaarndammerplantsoen 140, www.hetschip.nl, tel. 020-6868595, open Tue-Sun 11am-5pm, entrance €7.50, Tram 3 Haarlemmerplein

35 The **Houthavens** were dug in 1876 for transshipping and storing wood. It was the first harbor in Amsterdam that was man-made. Nowadays the area is being redeveloped and is set to become a brand-new city district. A 269-foot-high (82-meter-high) building known as Pontsteigergebouw, designed by Arons en Gelauff Architecten, was erected on the former ferry dock at Tasmanstraat. It made headlines at the start of 2016 because the penthouse apartment—which was yet to be built—sold to Amsterdam hospitality entrepreneur Won Yip for 16 million euros.

Houthavenkade, Tram 3 Zoutkeetsgracht, Bus 48, 248 Koivistokade

FOOD & DRINK

1 Cozy corners, beautiful industrial lamps, and a large sofa—start your day at **Bar Spek** (Bacon Bar) with a latte, tasty tea, or an unusual smoothie, like the green monster or Bloody Mary. Or choose from oysters, tasty pizzas, and other Italian delicacies such as *melanzane alla parmigiana*, and an extensive selection of mouth-watering desserts.

Admiraal de Ruijterweg 1, www.barspek.nl, tel. 020-6188102, open Mon-Thur 8am-1am, Fri-Sat 9am-2am, Sun 9am-1am, pizza €12.50, Tram 12, 13, 14 Willem de Zwijgerlaan

3 Falafel and beer—that's what **Bar Kauffmann** is all about. And the falafel is unlike any you've tasted before. It's served in pita bread or as a salad, homemade and flavorful. This is the perfect spot for vegetarians and beer lovers alike, with some 30 kinds of craft beer in all. For those in the know, this place is located just off-route on a side street. It also has a small outdoor seating area in the sun, making it a popular summertime hangout.

Reinier Claeszenstraat 4b, barkauffmann.nl, tel. 020-8461606, open Sun-Thur 5pm-11pm, Fri-Sat 5pm-1am, falafel starting at €10.50, Tram 13, 19 Willem de Zwijgerlaan

❺ Radijs (Radish) is proud of its location in the newly spruced-up West district of Amsterdam and features menu items inspired by the neighborhood, including Oude Baarsjes, a sandwich with mini pickles and mustard. You can't get more Amsterdamese! Try a special beer from a local brewery or sample honey from the city beekeeper while enjoying the industrial interior with an extensive use of wood. Or sit outside on the terrace overlooking the water.

Jan Evertsenstraat 41, www.radijs-amsterdam.nl, tel. 020-7513232, open Mon-Fri 8:30am-2am, Sat 10am-2am, Sun 10am-1am, from €16.50, Tram 13, 18 Marco Polostraat

❻ At **Deli-caat** you'll find homemade French bread and quiches, fruit, vegetables, and organic food. Sit down for a cup of coffee by White Label or a sandwich. The owners describe their business as a mix between delicatessen, lunchroom, and coffee bar. They like to talk through your choice with you. Their priority? Everything should be really tasty.

Admiralengracht 223, www.deli-caat.nl, tel. 063-8103649, open Mon, Sat & Sun 4pm-9pm, Tue-Fri 11am–9pm, from €12, Tram 13, 18 Marco Polostraat

✿ With a relentless stream of clientele in this busy location, it would be no exaggeration to call **Bar Baarsch** the focal point of the Baarsjes. Business lunches, Friday afternoon drinks, spontaneous dinners, lively parties, and hearty breakfasts—everything goes here. It's a local pub but with a more contemporary feel, good food, an extensive beer list (many American specialty beers), 30 varieties of whisky, and fresh ginger tea.

Jan Evertsenstraat 91, tel. 020-6181970, open Mon-Thur 10am-1am, Fri 10am-3am, Sat 11am-3am, Sun 11am-1am, from €16.50, Tram 13, 18 Marco Polostraat

❾ Burgers and beer—that's what **Bar Frits** serves. The large outdoor seating area on Mercatorplein is a great place to hang out. This is a friendly neighborhood bar with great character, and the staff is equally cheerful. It's the type of place where you can enjoy a tasty burger (vegetarian options available) and find yourself staying easily until the wee hours of the morning. The beer menu is so extensive, you can try something new from a different part of the world every time you visit.

Jan Evertsenstraat 91, frits-amsterdam.nl, tel. 020-2339796, open Sun-Thur 4pm-1am, Fri & Sat 4pm-3am, burgers start at €9.75, Tram 13, 18 Marco Polostraat

⑪ **White Label Coffee** aims to evoke the raw atmosphere of Brooklyn with its slick, rugged business. The coffee here is freshly roasted and takes center stage, preferably without milk and unaccompanied by plates of cakes. The tea comes from Amsterdam Monkey Chief Tea and chocolate from Chocolatl Amsterdam. Coffee is also sold separately, including all the things you need to prepare that perfect cup of coffee.
Jan Evertsenstraat 136, www.whitelabelcoffee.nl, tel. 020-7371359, open Mon-Fri 8am-6pm, Sat-Sun 9am-6pm, Tram 7, 13 Mercatorplein

⑯ At **Terrasmus,** situated in Erasmus Park, you'll find juices, smoothies, and ice creams, perfect for the summer months, when nothing could be better than sitting on the terrace or taking your snack and drink to sit on the grass. During summer, you can also enjoy all kinds of musical activities that are organized in or around the café. In bad weather, take refuge inside with a hot soup or drink, wraps, or a luxury sandwich. Note that the café is closed November-February.
Erasmuspark, www.terrasmus.nl, tel. 020-3343468, open Mar-Oct daily 10am-6pm (sometimes later), toasty €3.75, Tram 7 Jan Van Galenstraat

⑰ The friendly neighbors who run **Eetwinkel Buurman & Buurman** wanted to breathe new life into this dark corner building. And with the help of friends they succeeded to magically turn it into a local place to cook and eat. The wood-fired oven at its heart is guaranteed to produce the best pizzas. Ingredients for all dishes are sourced locally. You can also buy Amsterdam limoncello, Himalayan salt, and Turkish olive oil.
Mercatorstraat 171, www.eetwinkelbuurmanenbuurman.nl, tel. 020-2628262, open daily 5pm-midnight, from €12, Tram 7 Erasmusgracht

⑱ **Wilde Westen** is located in the basement of the old GAK-building (a now defunct government agency) in the Bos & Lommer neighborhood. The interior is industrial, but it has succeeded in creating a living room atmosphere with a hipster vibe where you'll feel right at home. During the day, young creatives come here to work and to eat lunch. In the evening great pizzas are served from a wood-fired oven. On "Cheap Mondays," every pizza on the menu costs €9. Try their pizza Arabica!
Bos en Lommerplantsoen 1 , www.wilde-westen.nl, tel. 020-7608290, open Sun 10am-1am, Mon-Thur 9am-1am, Fri 9am-3am, Sat 10am-3am, mains from €13, Tram 7 Erasmusgracht

22 It's not trendy, and there's no excessive decoration. It's simply an Indonesian restaurant, as was intended. **Betawi** started here more than thirty years ago now. The *nasi rames* is famous, and the vegetarian dishes are also delicious; the aubergine dish is a must.

Admiraal de Ruijterweg 337, www.betawi.nl, tel. 020-6821885, open Tue-Sun 4-10pm, from €10, Tram 19 Bos en Lommerweg

26 **Mossel & Gin** specializes in—you guessed it—mussels and gin and tonics. This fun food bar in the middle of Westerpark knows how to surprise with both taste and presentation. This is not a rustic place where you'll find the classic black pans filled to the brim with mussels. Try the Thai mussels with coconut curry and lime or the Surinamese mussels with peanut sauce and long beans. The homemade signature gin mayo, found on every table, can be purchased by the tube and makes for a great souvenir.

Gosschalklaan 12, www.mosselengin.nl, tel. 020-4865869, open Sat & Sun 1pm-midnight, Tue-Thur 4pm-midnight, Fri 2pm-1am, mussels €16.50, Tram 5 Van Hallstraat

28 Quirky is perhaps the description that best fits rock 'n' roll **Pacific Parc** restaurant. The interior of this large industrial space is nicely messy, while the benches lining the wall are a good place from which to people watch. A cozy fire burns in the winter, and in the summer, you can sit in princely splendor on the terrace. From Thursday to Saturday evenings, the tables are pushed aside to make room for live music and DJs.

Polonceaukade 23, www.pacificparc.nl, tel. 020-4887778, open Mon-Wed 11am-1am, Fri-Sat 11am-3am, Sun 11am-11pm, from €17, Tram 5 Van Limburg Stirumplein

32 "You're crazy if you don't come to eat here," said former mayor Job Cohen at the opening of **Restaurant Freud.** You would be crazy to miss the delicious food as well as the restaurant's special and particularly dedicated staff. The 80 employees have all struggled with mental illness or addiction and are given a special opportunity here. Everything is homemade, right up to the cakes and chocolates. In addition, dishes contain only free-range meat, responsibly caught fish, and, wherever possible, organic vegetables. Your dinner couldn't be more socially responsible!

Spaarndammerstraat 424, www.restaurantfreud.nl, tel. 020-6885548, open Tue-Sun 11am-11pm, from €19.75, Tram 3 Haarlemmerplein

33 First the bad news—from five o'clock in the afternoon, it's only possible to get take-away. Now for the good news—Westerpark is around the corner, and **DopHert** goes all out to give a new dimension to all things vegan. Everything at this lunchroom is completely vegan from lattes made with almond milk, sandwiches with vegan cheese, and meatloaf made from lentils. It even sells vegan accessories, including cosmetics and condoms!

Spaarndammerstraat 49, www.dophertcatering.nl, tel. 020-7520581, open Wed-Fri noon-9pm, Sat 10am-9pm, Sun 11am-5pm, sandwiches €6.50, Tram 3 Haarlemmerplein

36 Father Ad and son Steven are the brains behind the brilliant concept that is **Wilde Kroketten.** Here you eat handmade *kroketten* (traditional Dutch croquettes) with bread and salad. They make the broth that serves as the base themselves, producing the best croquettes imaginable. Choose from some twenty varieties: besides the classic beef croquette, there is Asian duck, spicy Indonesian meat, and lentil and goat cheese croquettes. In the evening a four-course dinner is served, consisting of croquettes and other delicacies.

Danzigerkade 27, wildekroketten.nl, tel. 020-7372909, open Sun & Wed-Sat noon-10pm, Mon & Tue noon-4pm, mains from €16, Bus 48, 248 Koivistokade

㊲ Once upon a time **REM Eiland** was a platform located 6 miles off the coast of Noordwijk in the North Sea. From here Radio and TV Noordzee broadcast its rebellious pirate radio and television shows. Nowadays this unique building is located in the Houthavens and houses a restaurant with phenomenal views over the Amsterdam harbor. Order the chef's menu and indulge in the pure and fresh ingredients that are used.

Haparandadam 45-2, www.remeiland.com, tel. 020-6885501, open daily noon-10pm, mains from €25, Bus 48, 248 Koivistokade

㊳ If you love unique ingredients and original combinations, **Restaurant BAK** is the place to be. There are no *à la carte* dishes but instead a tasting menu that changes with the seasons and availability of the ingredients. Let the chef surprise you with fresh heirloom vegetables and other organic—mostly locally sourced—products. Many of the dishes are works of art on a plate, and the wine list boasts a beautiful selection. This is the perfect place for a truly exquisite dining experience.

Van Diemenstraat 408, www.bakrestaurant.nl, tel. 020-7372553, open Sat & Sun 12:30pm-1am, Wed-Fri 7pm-1am, chef's tasting menu €60, Tram 3 Zoutkeetsgracht, Bus 48 Houtmankade

SHOPPING

❷ With their knowledge and love of wine, the nice guys behind **The Wine Spot** demonstrate that purchasing wine is far from dull and could even be one of the world's most enjoyable pastimes. They'll happily advise you on the right wine to accompany that dinner dish. The wines are imported from seven European countries, including Romania. Chilled wine and specialty beers can also be purchased here.

Admiraal de Ruijterweg 43, www.thewinespot.nl, tel. 020-7372212, open Mon 2-7pm, Tue-Fri 11am-7pm, Sat 10am-7pm, Sun noon-6pm, Tram 13, 19 Willem de Zwijgerlaan

❿ Reap the rewards of Sanne and Petra's choosy collector mania at **Things I Like Things I Love.** Their carefully selected mix of vintage and new clothing, created by prominent designers, also includes knitwear from neighbor Willie. Sanne and Petra also furnish houses, offices, and hotels on request, such as Hotel Dwars.

Jan Evertsenstraat 106, www.thingsilikethingsilove.com, tel. 020-2239254, open Mon-Tue 1-5:30pm, Wed-Sat 11-5:30pm, Sun 1-5pm, Tram 13, 18 Marco Polostraat

20 It was risky to open this bookshop in Bos en Lommer (BoLo), a gritty neighborhood undergoing urban renewal. However, **De Nieuwe Boekhandel** has become a lively meeting point. It's the place to buy BoLo goodies. As befits a bookshop, lectures, book reviews, and workshops are also organized here. Don't forget to check out the Wall of Fame! Owner Monique has her own claim to fame, as book panel member on *De Wereld Draait Door*, a popular Dutch talk show broadcast live from Amsterdam.

Bos en Lommerweg 227, www.libris.nl/denieuweboekhandel, tel. 020-4867722, open Mon 1-6pm, Thur-Fri 10am-6pm, Sat 10am-5pm, Tram 19 Bos en Lommerweg

23 If you're a fan of onions, pickles, and Dutch mustard, chances are those came from **Kesbeke Zoet & Zuur,** supermarket brands included. Today, the 70-year-old business is the sole supplier of Amsterdam pickles. Apart from pickles, it's also the place for special oils and vinegars—indeed, everything you need to pickle fruit and vegetables yourself. Before you know it, you'll have left laden with dragon oil, porcini, and preserving jars.

Adolf Van Nassaustraat 3, www.zoetenzuur.nl, tel. 020-3032650, open Wed-Fri 11am-5pm, Sat 10am-5pm, Tram 19 Bos en Lommerweg

30 **Kweek Stadstuinwinkel** has everything anyone with green fingers but not much space could ever wish for—organic herbs, organic vegetables that can be grown in pots or in a roof garden, small tools, hanging gardens, and mini gardens in boxes. The store sells only organic products, from soil to fertilizers and plant protection.

Spaarndammerstraat 54, www.spaarndammerstraat.nl/winkel/kweek-stadstuinwinkel, tel. 020-3705181, open Tue-Fri 10am-6pm, Sat 10am-5pm, Tram 3 Haarlemmerplein

MORE TO EXPLORE

4 **TOON Amsterdam** is a podium shop that offers creative entrepreneurs, artists, and designers a place to show their work. At TOON you'll find small gifts and exclusive pieces of art. There are cultural events on a regular basis, such as "living room performances," album launches, and book presentations. A visit to this dynamic place is always surprising.

Jan Evertsenstraat 4-6-8, www.toon.amsterdam, tel. 064-2011831, open Tue-Sat 10am-6pm, Sun noon-6pm, Tram 13, 19 Admiraal de Ruijterweg

WELCOME TO OUR
A PLACE WHERE NEW I
E MIXED WITH VINTAG
E SECOND HAND
WHERE
THING
NGS
VE

7 Following a successful crowdfunding campaign **Kattencafé Kopjes** opened its doors in 2015, with no less than 600 cat lovers lined up on the waitlist. The café is home to eight different cats that want for nothing. Here you can enjoy a *catuccino* with a slice of cake or something from the lunch menu. They can accommodate only 20 people at a time, so be sure to make reservations. Patrons pay an additional "cat tax" of 3 euros, used to help keep the cats happy and healthy. Marco Polostraat 211, kattencafekopjes.nl, tel. 020-7370999, open Wed-Sun 10am-7pm, entrance €3, Tram 13, 18 Marco Polostraat

15 **Erasmus Park** is not just a park—it was laid out where only a hundred years ago there was nothing but polder, complete with meadows and ditches. As a Mondrian painting seeks harmony in surface, color, and line, so the park seeks to create harmony between paths, trees, and grass. There's a rose garden in the middle of the park, and on the side of Jan van Galenstraat you'll find various statues. Erasmuspark, Tram 7, 19 Jan Van Galenstraat

㉑ The former Pniëlkerk has grown to become the cultural heart of the Bos en Lommer district. **Podium Mozaïek**'s repertoire includes dance, theater, world music, and cabaret. It's also home to a number of studios and workshops. Works by new artists are displayed in the exhibition space, and on weekends between 10am and 3pm you can enjoy a traditional Turkish breakfast in the theater café.
Bos en Lommerweg 191, www.podiummozaiek.nl, tel. 020-5800380, open theater café Sun-Thur 9:30am-midnight, Fri-Sat 9:30am-1am, see website for performance timings, sandwich €5.75, Tram 19 Bos en Lommerweg

㉕ Mention the **Westerpark**, and Amsterdammers think first of the Westergasterrein, but the park is also worth a visit. It's spacious, with plenty of water, undulating lawns, and a children's zoo. The construction of the park began in 1890, a number of years after the earlier Willemspoort Station was closed and from where for 35 years trains departed for Haarlem on the first Dutch railway. After the former gasworks closed in 1967, the site was so polluted that the upper layer of soil had to be removed before it could be transformed into the park you'll find today, which is now ideal for a stroll or some grassy relaxation.
Westerpark, Tram 10 Van Limburg Stirumstraat

㉙ **Het Ketelhuis** (The Boiler House) is also known as "the canteen of Dutch film and TV," but the cinema also shows quality European films. If you're tired of no longer being able to find popcorn at many cinemas, here you can have dinner—the menu changes daily.
Pazzanistraat 4, www.ketelhuis.nl, tel. 020-6840090, see website for film showings, movie €10, Tram 5 Van Limburg Stirumstraat

㉛ This bathhouse was built in 1916 for workers from the Spaarndammerbuurt. Now the **Hammam,** with its several pools, is open to everyone.
Zaanstraat 88, www.hammamamsterdam.nl, tel. 020-6814818, open Mon 6-10pm (men), Tue-Fri noon-10pm (women), Sat-Sun noon-10pm (women), entrance €17, Tram 3 Haarlemmerplein

OOST & DE PIJP

ABOUT THE WALK

On this walk, you'll encounter a cultural melting pot that's also rich in history, from typical Amsterdam markets to Jewish traditions. There are many trendy foreign restaurants that offer lunch or dinner. Artis, Amsterdam's zoo, is also on this walk—for children, combine a stop there with the fascinating and often-overlooked Tropenmuseum (Museum of the Tropics).

THE NEIGHBORHOODS

Oost (East) is perhaps Amsterdam's most varied neighborhood. Here you'll find the **Indische buurt,** where street names and the **Tropenmuseum** recall a colonial past. Hip and exotic blend perfectly here—on the Javastraat, there are a growing number of trendy coffeehouses, boutiques, and restaurants interspersed with multicultural shops. The locals actively encourage this melting pot and rightly so. What could be nicer than buying reasonably priced vegetables and then drinking a perfect cup of coffee nearby?

Next is the Dapperbuurt, with its genuine old Amsterdam character and the famous **Dappermarkt. Linnaeusstraat** has a nice bar on every corner. The **Dapperbuurt** borders on the green **Plantagebuurt,** where, in addition to **Artis** zoo, you'll find the former Jewish Quarter. Jewish traditions are respectfully preserved at the **Jewish Historical Museum** and the **synagogue.** At the **Verzetsmuseum** (Dutch Resistance Museum), you can learn all about Jewish history and World War II.

In the middle of all this lies the vibrant **Oosterpark,** where the cultures of East Amsterdam come together. The monuments in the park recall a turbulent history of slavery, as well as more recent events, such as the 2004 murder of Dutch film director Theo van Gogh. At the Tropenmuseum, which sits at the edge of the park, you can discover more about cultures and customs from around the world.

Oost can be combined with **De Pijp,** a melting pot of yuppies and market sellers. The De Pijp area has since become very trendy, as it was once a district for blue-collar workers. There's always something happening on the **Albert Cuypmarkt,** with its many shops, stalls, and cafés. In the middle of the market you'll find the **statue of André Hazes,** who was born and raised in the area. **Sarphatipark** is situated near the market and is one of the city's smaller but perhaps most beautiful parks.

SHORT ON TIME? HERE ARE THE HIGHLIGHTS:

13 BIERTUIN + 15 TROPENMUSEUM + 18 HORTUS BOTANICUS + 28 ALBERT CUYPMARKT + 35 SARPHATIPARK

TIPS
// A melting pot of cultures
// Walk this route on a market day
// The best walk for children

OOST & DE PIJP

Het IJ

SUMATRAKADE

OOSTELIJKE HANDELSKADE

C. VAN EESTERENLAAN

WITTENBURGERSTR.

LONRADSTR.

EERSTE LEEGHWATERSTR.

ZEEBURGERSTR.

Nieuwe Vaart

Lozingskanaal

INDISCHE BUURT

MOLUKKENSTR.

DAPPER-
BUURT

PONTANUSSTR.

BORNEOSTR.

SUMATRASTR.

JAVASTR.

De
Biertuin

WALK 5

EERSTE VAN SWINDENSTR.

REINWARDTSTR.

PONTANUSSTR.

LINNAEUSSTR.

START

INSULINDEWEG

LEGEND

- >> SIGHTS & ATTRACTIONS
- >> FOOD & DRINK
- >> SHOPPING
- >> MORE TO EXPLORE
- >> WALK HIGHLIGHT

0   400 yd

0   400

WALK 5 DESCRIPTION (approx. 7 mi/11 km with detour)

Start at Drover's Dog ❶. From here cross the square, turn left down Sumatrastraat, and turn right onto Javastraat ❷ ❸. On Javaplein check out a cozy bar/restaurant ❹ and behind it another interesting restaurant ❺ and a vintage shop ❻. Cross the street and turn down Borneostraat to Amsterdam East's hotspot ❼. Then cross the street diagonally and take the first left. Turn right onto Javastraat ❽ ❾. Walk under the railway to the Dappermarkt ❿. Follow the road ⓫ ⓬. Turn right on Linnaeusstraat ⓭ ⓮. Continue and cross the road at the roundabout for the Tropenmuseum ⓯. From here, decide whether to follow the optional detour or take the regular route.

Detour (approx. 2 mi/3 km): Turn onto Mauritskade, cross the first bridge and follow Plantage Middenlaan ⓰ ⓱ ⓲. Continue until you reach Meester Visserplein, bear left, then turn left after the synagogue ⓳ onto Jonas Daniël Meijerplein ⓴. Cross the bridge and turn left onto Hortusplantsoen. Bear right at the fork and cross over Plantage Muidergracht. Walk through the Plantagebuurt until you reach Plantage Middenlaan again. Head to the Tropenmuseum to continue the route.

Regular route: Follow Linnaeusstraat to the entrance of the Oosterpark ㉑. Walk through the park and exit at the monument to slavery. Walk to the intersection with Eerste Oosterparkstraat ㉒. Walk down Beukenweg to Beukenplein ㉓. Turn back and head left onto Tweede Oosterparkstraat. Take the first right and at the end of the street turn left onto Eerste Oosterparkstraat. Continue to Wibautstraat, cross the road, turn right and take the second left ㉔. Exit the street over Nieuwe Amstelbrug, continue on Ceintuurbaan ㉕ and take the second right to De Pijp. Continue until you reach Tweede Jan Steenstraat. Turn left and then right onto Eerste Sweelinckstraat ㉖. Turn right onto Govert Flinckstraat, then take the first left. Continue to the concept store ㉗, or turn earlier onto Albert Cuypstraat ㉘ ㉙ ㉚. Turn right onto Eerste van der Helststraat and walk to Gerard Doustraat ㉛ ㉜. Cross Ferdinand Bolstraat and continue on Saenredamstraat ㉝. Turn left onto Frans Halsstraat, then left again on Govert Flinckstraat. Take a right at Eerste van der Helststraat ㉞ and walk to Sarphatipark ㉟, entering through the first entrance on the right. Follow the path to reach the exit. Turn left and walk a short distance ㊱, then turn right onto Ceintuurbaan ㊲ ㊳. Turn left on Ferdinand Bolstraat and walk to Cornelis Troostplein ㊴.

SIGHTS & ATTRACTIONS

③ Architect Hendrik Petrus Berlage didn't design only Amsterdam's stock exchange—he also built the **Berlageblokken** (1911-1914) to accommodate workers. The complex was inspired by British social housing and today these are historically listed buildings. It was important to include sufficient greenery, so the accommodation includes small parks as well as inner courtyards with gardens. The apartments underwent a substantial renovation at the end of the 1960s.
Balistraat, Benkoelenstraat, Javaplein, Javastraat En Langkatstraat, not open to the public, Tram 14 Javaplein

⑮ The **Tropenmuseum** (Museum of the Tropics) is a unique museum housed in a beautiful building where you can wander through lifelike replicas of dwellings, rooms, and shops from countries around the world. It houses an enormous collection of objects from numerous cultures—a door from Marrakech, an altar from Mexico, African musical instruments. That's not all that this inspiring museum has to offer, though. There are films and wonderful interactive and temporary exhibitions with special activities for children.
Linnaeusstraat 2, www.tropenmuseum.nl, tel. 088-0042840, open Tue-Sun 10am-5pm, also open on Mon during school holidays , entrance €15, Tram 19 1e Van Swindenstraat

⑰ The **Verzetsmuseum** Amsterdam (Resistance Museum) is located in the Plancius building, opposite the entrance to Artis zoo. In this permanent exhibition a lifelike decor of city streets and a floor-to-ceiling visual display help create an atmosphere reminiscent of Amsterdam during WWII. Authentic historical objects, photos, documents, film, and audio tell the story of the people who lived here during wartime. There's also an interactive children's museum where the story is told through the eyes of children.
Plantage Kerklaan 61, www.verzetsmuseum.org, tel. 020-6202535, open Sat-Sun 11am-5pm, Mon-Fri 10am-5pm, entrance €11, Tram 14 Artis

⑲ This **Portuguese Synagogue** (also called Esnoga or Snoge) is situated in the heart of Amsterdam's former Jewish Quarter. The first Jews to settle in Amsterdam in the 16th century came from Spain and Portugal. The synagogue not only continues to fulfill its original function, but the interior has been preserved in its original state. In the 17th century, Snoge was the world's

largest synagogue and formed part of an extensive synagogue complex. Today, the other synagogues house the Jewish Historical Museum.

Mr. Visserplein 3, www.portugesesynagoge.nl, open Apr-Oct Sun-Thur 10am-5pm, Fri 10am-4pm, Nov-Mar Sun-Thur 10am-4pm, Fri 10am-2pm, entrance €12, Tram 14 Mr. Visserplein, Metro 51, 53, 54 Waterlooplein

20 At the **Joods Historisch Museum** (Jewish Historical Museum), you can learn about the culture, religion, and history of the Jewish people who lived in the Netherlands and its former colonies. The museum has a large collection of war documents. Many personal belongings such as letters, diaries, and photos are also on display, along with films.

Nieuwe Amstelstraat 1, www.jhm.nl, tel. 020-5310380, open daily 11am-5pm, entrance €15, includes all five locations of the Jewish Cultural Quarter, Tram 14 Mr. Visserplein, Metro 51, 53, 54 Waterlooplein

25 Take a good look at the **Huis met de Kabouters** (House with the Gnomes) because there's a lot more to it than meets the eye. The architect designed the three houses in 1884, giving free rein to his imagination. It has Swiss

chalet-style elements, with abundant wood carving, most striking of which are a pair of green gnomes playing with a ball. Almost as old as the house is the associated tale—that now and then the gnomes toss the ball—so that every so often you'll find the ball in the hands of the other gnome.

Ceintuurbaan 251-255, not open to the public, Tram 3 Van Woutstraat, Tram 4 Ceintuurbaan

㉙ Probably the most famous inhabitant of de Pijp was born on the third floor of No. 67 Gerard Doustraat. The beloved Dutch folk singer **André Hazes** spent his youth in and around the Albert Cuypmarkt. It was here he drank his first beer, and it was here he was discovered in 1959. His **statue** was unveiled in September 2005, the day his ashes were fired into the air with 10 flares. Fans still place a beer or some flowers next to his statue.

Albert Cuypstraat, Tram 4 Stadhouderskade

FOOD & DRINK

❶ Start the day with a taste of Australia. **Drover's Dog** has a super-friendly Aussie atmosphere. And Australians know how to breakfast—choose from sweet, savory, spicy, or crispy. "Bog in" to the Drover's own full-cooked *brekkie*—a *ripper* combination of fried eggs, sausages, tomatoes, spinach, and mushrooms. "Don't knock it till you've tried it!" That goes for the *roo*, too!

Eerste Atjehstraat 62, www.drovers-dog.com, tel. 020-3703784, open Tue-Thur 11am-11:30pm, Fri-Sun 10am-11:30pm, brunch €10, main course €18, Tram 1, 3 Muiderpoortstation

❹ **Badhuis Javaplein** was one of the last bathhouses to be built in Amsterdam (1942) and is now a trendy restaurant-café. The building also previously housed a Hindu temple and a secondhand shop. Today it has again become the meeting place for the neighborhood. Shower heads have made space for beer taps and an open fireplace. Only the tiled wall behind the bar recalls the place where women once washed.

Javaplein 21, badhuis-javaplein.com, tel. 020-6651226, open Mon-Thur 10-1am, Fri-Sun 10-3am, €15, Tram 14 Javaplein

5 One of the best places to sample high-quality Dutch food in atmospheric surroundings is at **Wilde Zwijnen** (Wild Boar). Seasonal dishes are made, as far as practicable, with local Dutch produce. In autumn the menu includes dishes with such wonderful names as *in Limburgs grottenbierbeslag gefrituurde mergelgrotchampignons* (fried Limburg Mergel cave mushrooms in beer batter) or venison stew. Reserve a place and look for your name chalked on the table.
Javaplein 23, www.wildezwijnen.com, tel. 020-4633043, open Mon-Thur 6-10:15pm, Fri-Sun 12-4pm & 6-10:15pm, three course menu €30.50, Tram 14 Javaplein

12 Anyone who has visited Suriname (a former Dutch colony) knows that **Roopram Roti**'s *roti* ("pancake" with a spicy filling) is among the best. It was a smart move on the owner's part to export the concept. And with the Oosterpark just around the corner, you can have a Surinamese picnic in the park.
Eerste Van Swindenstraat 4, www.roopramroti.nl, tel. 020-6932902, open Tue-Sun 2pm-9pm, from €5, Tram 19 1e Van Swindenstraat

13 You'll have to try really hard to think of a beer that's not on this beer garden's menu. On offer at **De Biertuin** are beers such as Brouwerij 't IJ, wheat beer (witbier) and specials with names such as Snake Dog and Lamme Goedzak (Drunken Softy). In the evening, the restaurant serves six main courses, including spit-roasted chicken.
Linnaeusstraat 29, www.debiertuin.nl, tel. 020-6650956, open Sun-Thur 11am-1am, Fri-Sat 11am-3am, beer from €2.20, Tram 19 1e Van Swindenstraat

14 On the corner across from the Tropenmuseum you'll find **Louie Louie,** an all-day café with a fantastic outdoor seating area where you can easily spend hours. The menu features dishes inspired by South American cuisine, including tacos, quesadillas and of course, a variety of meat dishes. They make a mean cocktail, or you can order their 1.5-quart pitcher of sangria. Perfect if you want to raise a glass with friends.
Linnaeusstraat 11, louielouie.nl, tel. 020-3702981, open Sun-Thur 9am-1am, Fri-Sat 9am-3am, mains from €12, sangria pitcher €21.50, Tram 1, 3 Alexanderplein, Tram 19 1e Van Swindenstraat

22 **Bar Bukowski** is a must for its roaring '20s interior and delicious breakfast. But these are not the only reasons it has become a social hotspot in East Amsterdam. Everything fits—from the rough-intellectual interior, inspired by writer and lover of alcohol Charles Bukowski, to Henry's cocktail bar and the fresh juices. As Bukowski himself wrote, "There's always a reason to drink!" Oosterpark 10, www.barbukowski.nl, tel. 020-3701685, open Mon-Thur 8am-1am, Fri 8am-3am, Sat 9am-3am, Sun 9am-1am, sandwich €6, Tram 1, 3 Beukenweg

23 To taste, to smell, and to see, is to know that the owners of **Coffee Bru** got their inspiration from South Africa's coffee bars. Plants grow between the characteristic furniture and the smell of coffee hangs in the air while homemade banana bread and cakes and pies—devil's food and key lime—line the counter. Visiting tea lovers drink Chinese leaf tea called Chief Monkey, a brand established by one of the owners. Beukenplein 14, www.coffeebru.nl, tel. 020-7519956, open Mon-Fri 8am-6pm, Sat-Sun 9am-6pm, coffee from €2.30, Tram 1, 3 Beukenweg

24 **De Ruyschkamer** is a Berlin-style café, with soft drinks and beers to match. Concoct your super healthy drink at the juice bar, lounge with your pizza on the couch, or sample macaroons with flavors beyond your wildest dreams, such as cinnamon with a ganache of cherries and soft caramel. Alternatively, you might like to try your hand at the legendary German bingo or contemplate buying one of the beautiful pieces of furniture. Or perhaps you'd rather just have a cup of coffee while perusing the newspaper at the reading table. Ruyschstraat 34, www.deruyschkamer.nl, tel. 020-6703622, open Wed & Thur 5pm-1am, Fri-Sat 5pm-2am, Sun 3pm-11pm, from €1.90, Tram 3 Wibautstraat

26 The trendy **Little Collins** is a tribute to its Melbourne namesake, which means an impressive brunch and dinner menu. You can brunch here all day long on cauliflower hashes, baked puddings, and Florentines. On Thursdays and Fridays, there is also dinner—choose from an international selection of small dishes. Bloody Marys make an excellent accompaniment to brunch, and for dinner choose from an extensive selection of wines. Eerste Sweelinckstraat 19, www.littlecollins.nl, tel. 020-6732293, open Mon-Tue 9am-4pm, Wed-Sun 9am-10pm, lunch €13, Tram 3 Van Woutstraat, Tram 4 Ceintuurbaan

㉚ "Come as you are, pay what you like," is the motto at **Café Trust,** a peaceful oasis in the heart of the busy Albert Cuypmarkt. You pay what you feel the food is worth.

Albert Cuypstraat 210, tel. 020-7371532, opening times vary, prices vary, Tram 4 Stadhouderskade

㉝ Casual yet luxurious with a menu full of great food and wines, **Maris Piper** feels very much like a Parisian bistro. However, it's in the middle of the Amsterdam neighborhood De Pijp. The menu has something for everyone and includes seafood platters, beef Wellington, and of course steak-frites. The kitchen, located in the back of the restaurant, features a "chef's table"—an exclusive table with a separate menu. Great for an exceptional dining experience!

Frans Halsstraat 76hs, maris-piper.com, tel. 020-7372479, open daily noon-10:30pm, chef's menu €115, Tram 24 Marie Heinekenplein, Metro 52 De Pijp

㉞ At **My Little Patisserie** you can choose from an assortment of mouthwatering pastries. Owner Audrey used to have a career in marketing, and when she needed a change of pace she enrolled at the prestigious Parisian bakers' school École de Boulangerie et de Patisserie. She eventually moved to Amsterdam for love, and her dream became a reality with the opening of her own French patisserie. Enjoy yours indoors in the petit café or outdoors in the Sarphatipark around the corner.

Eerste Van Der Helststraat 63, mylittlepatisserie.nl, tel. 020-4706949, open Mon-Fri 9:30am-5:30pm, Sat 9am-6pm, pastries from €4, Tram 3 2e Van Der Helststraat, Metro 52 De Pijp

㊱ Lots of wood, an open floor plan, the food and clothing, all conjure Scandinavia—clean and sustainable. Scandinavia has a vibrant, sophisticated coffee culture, which you can experience for yourself here at the **Scandinavian Embassy.** The coffee comes from small coffee producers in Stockholm, Helsingborg, and Oslo, among other places. On the menu are dishes such as spit-roasted lamb, fermented herring, and Danish cheese.

Sarphatipark 34, www.scandinavianembassy.nl, tel. 068-1600140, open Mon-Fri 8am-6pm, Sat-Sun 9am-6pm, from €13, Tram 3 2e Van Der Helststraat, Metro 52 De Pijp

37 SLA raises the average salad to delicious new heights. Some of the vegetables (as far as possible organic) are grown along the wall and in the business's own greenhouse. The accompanying meat, fish, grain, and dairy products are all organic. In the large industrial interior, healthy eating can be combined perfectly with a glass of wine or beer, though it's not easy to choose from the wide variety of salads on offer. SLA also has its own lab where you can take inspiring workshops.

Ceintuurbaan 149, www.ilovesla.com, tel. 020-7893080, open daily 11am-9pm, from €8, Tram 3 2e Van Der Helststraat, Metro 52 De Pijp

38 The former Ceintuurtheater dates back to the 1920s and was closed for a long time, but after a thorough renovation it now houses **CT Coffee & Coconuts.** Grab a bite at this city venue with three floors where trendy Amsterdam hangs out with good coffee and healthy food.

Ceintuurbaan 282, www.ctamsterdam.nl, tel. 020-3541104, open daily 8:30am-11pm, full breakfast €10.50, Tram 3, 12, 24 De Pijp, Metro 52 De Pijp

ALL
THE
LUCK
IN
THE
WORLD
.NL

SHOPPING

② Java Bookshop was once a bit out of place in this neighborhood, but the hidden gem of a bookshop has now come into its own. Take time to browse among a wide selection of Dutch and English literature, cookbooks, and children's books, all in a homey atmosphere. The enthusiastic staff is happy to let you make up your mind over a cup of coffee and something tasty.
Javastraat 145, www.javabookshop.nl, tel. 020-4634993, open Tue-Fri 10am-6pm, Sat 10am-5pm, Tram 14 Javaplein

⑥ Step into this shop that's hidden behind the baths, and you'll find you've stepped back into rooms from the 1950s and '60s. Everything at **Jansen Vintage** is for sale. All items have been carefully curated, from the lamps to the glassware, the tableware and the special bedside tables, and the rough stools and furniture from known and unknown brands.
Javaplein 31, www.jansenvintage.nl, tel. 061-0125018, open Wed-Sat 11am-6pm, Tram 14 Javaplein

⑧ Hartje Oost (Heart of East) is one of the latest additions to the Javastraat. It's a coffee boutique, which means good coffee, fashionable clothing, fresh sandwiches and cakes, and handmade jewelry. The boutique's owners aim to sell only products that tell a story—ecological, sustainable, fair trade, local, and original. They combine foods from businesses in and around Javastraat, such as Peking Duck from the Asian shop, with sourdough bread from De bakker van Oost.
Javastraat 23, www.hartjeoost.nl, tel. 020-2332137, open Mon-Fri 9am-6:30pm, Sat-Sun 9am-6pm, Tram 14 Javaplein

⑨ Tough guys can confidently stroll into **Div. Herenkabinet.** The selection is uncluttered and clean and is only from the most stylish, trendiest brands (including Pointer, Obey, and Carhartt). The owner can tell you something about everything, from the Japanese jeans to the Swiss knives, and from the Swedish backpacks to the Belgian sunglasses.
Javastraat 8, www.divamsterdam.com, tel. 020-6944084, open Mon-Fri 10am-6:30pm, Sat 10am-6pm, Sun 12-6pm, Tram 1, 3 Dapperstraat, Tram 14 Zeeburgerdijk

11 Now that secondhand has become "vintage," recycled clothing has largely become unaffordable. But things are done differently at **We Are Vintage** (note the ceiling!)—clothing can be purchased by the pound, and it's still good quality. Much of the collection is sorted by color and type. Lovers of suede and leather will feel right at home.

Eerste Van Swindenstraat 43, www.wearevintage.nl, tel. 020-7852777, open Mon-Wed & Fri-Sat 11am-7pm, Thu 11am-8pm, Sun noon-6pm, Tram 19 1e Van Swindenstraat

27 **Hutspot** (Stew) stocks only products by new, exciting brands, designers, artists, and entrepreneurs, including clothing, accessories, furniture, and household items. There is also an industrial-style bar on the second floor, where you can hang out with special beers and exclusive cocktails until the early hours of the weekend. Hotspot has a second branch on Rozengracht.

Van Woustraat 4, www.hutspot.com, tel. 020-2231331, open Mon-Sat 10am-7pm, Sun noon-6pm, Tram 4 Stadhouderskade

31 Fans of fashion from the 1940s through '60s can't help but pay a visit to **The Girl can't help it.** This pink boutique is filled to the brim with brand new retro designs that would've suited iconic figures such as Marilyn Monroe and Audrey Hepburn. It's all feminine, elegant, and sexy. The staff here loves to help find an outfit that will enhance your figure and leave you feeling fabulous. The owner has her own line of skirts and can customize clothing in her atelier for the perfect fit.

Gerard Doustraat 87, www.thegirlcanthelpit.nl, tel. 020-2333399, open Tue-Sat 11am-6pm, Tram 24 Marie Heinekenplein

32 **All the Luck in the World** is the perfect place to find unique gifts for someone—or for you. From beautiful new and vintage home accessories to postcards, posters, kitchen gadgets, and bags. The shop sells Danish design and unique pieces made by Dutch designers. Everything is displayed and combined beautifully, making you spoilt for choice. Their own jewelry line features delicate necklaces, bracelets, earrings, and rings made of silver, or gold plate.

Gerard Doustraat 86hs, www.alltheluckintheworld.nl, tel. 065-5022230, open Sun 1pm-6pm, Mon noon-6pm, Tue-Wed & Fri-Sat 11am-6pm, Thur 11am-8pm, Tram 24 Marie Heinekenplein, Metro 52 De Pijp

MORE TO EXPLORE

7 **Studio/K** is a space for film, theater, music, food, and drink—all brought together in an old trade school, with a colorful clientele. For a perfect night out, purchase the "film package," which consists of dinner (one main), and a movie ticket.
Timorplein 62, www.studio-k.nu, tel. 020-6920422, open Sun-Thur 11am-1am, Fri & Sat 11am-3am, movie €9.50, dinner & movie €17, Tram 14 Javaplein

10 The **Dappermarkt** has been named the best market in the Netherlands several times. You'll find endless stalls that sell wares from around the world. What you won't find are many tourists, as this market has a distinct neighborhood feel to it.
Dappermarkt, www.dappermarkt.nl, open Mon-Sat 10am-5pm, Tram 1, 3 Dapperstraat

16 With or without the kids, **Artis** is fun. The zoo first opened in 1838 to bring nature closer to the city, and it's still popular today. Right next door you'll find

café-restaurant Plantage. Its stunning 19th century conservatory looks out upon the freely accessible Artisplein (Artis Square).

Plantage Kerklaan 38-40, www.artis.nl, tel. 020-5233670, open daily Nov-Feb 9am-5pm, Mar-Oct 9am-6pm, Jun-Aug every Sat 9am until sunset, entrance €23, Tram 14 Artis

⑲ Dating from 1638, the **Hortus Botanicus** is one of the oldest botanical gardens in the world. It includes an exotic mixture of 6,000 plants spread over an enormous outdoor garden and several greenhouses.

Plantage Middenlaan 2a, www.dehortus.nl, tel. 020-6259021, open daily 10am-5pm, entrance €8.50, Tram 14 Artis

㉑ In the **Oosterpark** you'll find the national monument that recalls the history of slavery and *De Schreeuw* (*The Scream*) sculpture that was created in memory of film director Theo van Gogh, who was murdered nearby in 2004 by a Muslim extremist. There are also a number of festivals held here during summertime.

Oosterpark, Tram 1, 3 Linnaeusstraat, Tram 19 Wijttenbachstraat

㉘ Stroll down the **Albert Cuypmarkt,** which is alive with the cries of market stall holders. There is an array of snacks—everything from waffles, pancakes, to fresh stroopwafel. Also explore behind the stalls, where there are some interesting shops.

Albert Cuypstraat, www.albertcuypmarkt.nl, open Mon-Sat 9am-5pm, Tram 4 Stadhouderskade, Metro 52 De Pijp

㉟ In the mid-19th century, the original plan was to build Centraal Station at this location. Fortunately, Samuel Sarphati, a Jewish doctor and philanthropist who initiated many projects to improve the quality of life in Amsterdam, came up with a better idea to create this English landscape park, the **Sarphatipark.**

Sarphatipark, Tram 3 2e Van Der Helststraat, Metro 52 De Pijp

㊴ Beer doesn't come fresher than at **Brouwerij Troost.** It is brewed on-site by enthusiastic young beer lovers. They picked the perfect location—a former monastery with a beautiful courtyard. The beers go down easy, combining perfectly with meaty menu items such as burgers, steaks, and spare ribs.

Cornelis Troostplein 23, www.brouwerijtroost.nl, tel. 020-7371028, open Mon-Thur 4pm-1am, Fri 4pm-3am, Sat 2pm-3am, Sun 2pm-midnight, beer from €2.50, Tram 12 Cornelis Troostplein

EILANDEN & NOORD

ABOUT THE WALK

This walk takes you through what was once a lively port. On the eastern islands (Eilanden) you'll pass architectural highlights and interesting bridges. Once you've crossed the IJ (the river dividing the center of Amsterdam from Amsterdam Noord), you'll discover Amsterdam's trendiest neighborhood, with its raw industrial edge and countless culinary and art initiatives. Cycling this route is also ideal—you can take in a larger area of Noord.

THE NEIGHBORHOODS

"If you come from north of the IJ, you're not one of us," was long the view of many Amsterdammers. But times have changed. Today, the ferries are busy transporting trendy passengers to and from the north. It's the place to be for the **IJ-hallen,** which houses Europe's largest indoor flea market, the futuristic **EYE** film museum, and industrial cafés, restaurants, and vintage shops. **Noord** is Amsterdam's Brooklyn and is increasingly listed as one of the world's trendiest neighborhoods.

It still has space for creativity and relaxation. There's the recently constructed promenade along the IJ and the **Oeverpark,** from where you can view the city and clear your head. Cafés and restaurants are spacious, with entire gardens and urban beaches where you won't be bothered by screeching trams or hordes of visitors.

What was once a no-go area is now attracting more and more young families to the other side of the IJ. You're outside the city but can still reach it in no time. And today, there's always something going on. Creative entrepreneurs and businesses are springing up everywhere, attracted by the charm of Noord with its raw edge and great old shipyards with an industrial vibe.

Java-eiland and **KNSM-eiland,** prized as new architectural highlights, have also become popular, conjuring up today's Rotterdam with their trading and shipping history. Here you can chill out on the quays and check out the architecture. More and more, well-educated Amsterdammers are moving here with their kids.

SHORT ON TIME? HERE ARE THE HIGHLIGHTS:

🟋 **SCHEEPVAARTMUSEUM** + 🟋 **ROEST** + 🟋 **JAVA-EILAND** + 🟋 **EYE** + 🟋 **NOORDERLICHT CAFÉ**

TIPS
// Route through Amsterdam's trendiest neighborhood
// For architecture lovers
// Good biking route

EILANDEN & NOORD

LEGEND

- >> SIGHTS & ATTRACTIONS
- >> FOOD & DRINK
- >> SHOPPING
- >> MORE TO EXPLORE
- >> WALK HIGHLIGHT

© MOON.COM

WALK 6 DESCRIPTION (approx. 11 mi/18 km)

Start at Oosterdokskade ❶. From the library ❷, turn left and, at the intersection, walk to Hannekes Boom ❸ or continue to Scheepskameel ❹. Follow the route to the right for NEMO ❺. Walk around the museum and turn right at Oosterdok ❻. Follow the water to the Scheepvaartmuseum ❼. Continue to Kattenburgergracht and follow this street until you reach the flour mill ❽ and the brewery ❾. Walk back to the bridge, cross the canal and walk down Czaar Peterstraat ❿ ⓫ ⓬ ⓭. At the end of the street, before the railway, turn left to the former Werkspoor factory grounds, then go left again ⓮. Turn right, walk around the building to Roest ⓯ and continue to the overpass. Turn right under the railway until you reach Piet Heinkade. Cross the road and after the tram stop, turn left to cross the tram tracks. Now you're in Rietlandpark. Continue to Lloydplein via Lloyd Hotel ⓰ to Veemkade and turn right. Follow the road and turn left over the bridge to Java-eiland ⓱. Turn left and walk through Bogortuin to the Nine Bridges ⓲. Walk back through the gardens and continue to Levantkade on the KNSM-eiland ⓳ ⓴. Turn left onto Levantplein, then right and left again onto KNSM-laan ㉑. Walk to Azartplein and take the free ferry from here to Amsterdam Noord. Once there, you can sit on the waterfront ㉒ ㉓ ㉔. Follow the water, turn left onto Aambeeldstraat and at the intersection, turn left onto Gedempte Hamerkanaal. On the industrial site you'll find a fish restaurant ㉕. Walk back, turn left onto Gedempte Hamerkanaal until you reach the water, then turn right. Take the first left past the supermarket, then turn left. Take Motorwal to Noordwal, walking along the water to where the ferry docks. Turn right and take the first left to Sixhavenweg. Follow until you reach the water. Cross the sluices, turn left and walk along the water to Buiksloterweg. Take a right for some good restaurants ㉖ ㉗. Turn back and walk along the canal to Tolhuistuin ㉘. Follow the route in front of the building, cross the bridge and turn right for coffee ㉙. Walk toward IJ and turn right via IJ-promenade toward EYE ㉚. Walk along the waterfront and into the Oeverpark ㉛. Turn onto Bundlaan and bear right on Grasweg. Turn left onto Asterweg and then right on Chrysantenstraat ㉜. Continue until the end of the road, turning left onto Distelweg, and continue until you can turn right over the canal. After the bridge, take the first left ㉝ ㉞. Continue and finish on the NDSM-wharf ㉟ ㊱ ㊲ ㊳ ㊴.

SIGHTS & ATTRACTIONS

6 The **Museumhaven** gives you a good idea of what Amsterdam looked like during the 17th century—ships from the navy moored here, and it was also home to the Dutch East India Company's shipyard. The port was an important hub for inland navigation until well into the 20th century. Today it's the final resting place of ships aged 50-150 years old, including barges, clippers, luxurious motor boats, and tugs.

Oosterdok, between Nemo and Het Scheepvaartmuseum, www.museumhaven amsterdam.nl, always open, free, Tram 26 Muziekgebouw Bimhuis

7 There couldn't be a better location for **Het Scheepvaartmuseum** (The National Maritime Museum). From 1656 the building was used as a warehouse for Amsterdam's naval war fleet. Now you can view a selection of paintings, different types of ships, weapons, and old maps of the world. Outside you can climb on board a replica of a 1749 ship from the Dutch East India Company.

Kattenburgerplein 1, www.hetscheepvaartmuseum.nl, tel. 20-5232222, open daily 9am-5pm, entrance €15, Tram 26 Kattenburgerstraat, Bus 22, 246 Kadijksplein

8 Between the 17th and 19th centuries, the defensive walls of the Outer Singel canal were lined with windmills. The last mills were demolished around 1900, but Korenmolen **De Gooyer** managed to survive. Built in 1725, the mill played an important role until the end, grinding corn for the citizens of Amsterdam during World War II. Unfortunately, the mill is not open to visitors, but it's still a pretty sight in the middle of the city.

Funenkade 5, Tram 7 Hoogte Kadijk, Tram 14 Pontanusstraat

16 Drop into the Lloyd Hotel. This former jail is one of Europe's most unique hotels. The corridors of this building, listed on the historic register, are a delight to any design enthusiast. The hotel is also a cultural embassy—guests can gain a deeper insight into Dutch culture through art, workshops, lectures, and concerts.

Oostelijke Handelskade 34, www.lloydhotel.com, tel. 20-5613636, open daily, Tram 10, 26 Rietlandpark

17 Does the atmosphere on **Java-eiland** remind you of something? Yes, it's the center of Amsterdam with a modern twist. In the early 20th century, the Netherlands' Steamship Company, whose liners serviced the Dutch East Indies, was located on the artificial island in the IJ (the lake that is Amsterdam's waterfront). With decolonization, trade virtually stopped and the island fell into disuse. For a long time, it was occupied by squatters until everything was demolished in the 1990s. Now the island is covered with postmodern canal houses. Regular concerts and events take place at the head of the island.

Java-Eiland, Tram 7 Azartplein

18 The **Negen Bruggen** (Nine Bridges) over Java-eiland's four canals were designed with the aim of seamlessly fusing art, architecture, and construction. Belgian artists' duo Guy Rombouts and Monica Droste based the bridges on their own "Azart" alphabet. In this typeset, every letter is represented by a shaped line and a color. For example, "C" is for curve and citrus yellow. Together the lines form a word. Although the original intention was for the letters to be given different colors, the architects decided the result would be too toylike.
Java-Eiland, Tram 7 Azartplein

19 As with Java-eiland, **KNSM-eiland** was also an important location for trade and transport to the Dutch East Indies until the 1950s. The Royal Dutch Steamship Company (KNSM) was located here from 1903. Today, next to the modern, high-rise buildings you'll still find the doctor's house, the customs building, and the canteen of the Dutch Dock and Shipbuilding Company. The old statues and fountain of Amphitrite have also stood the test of time.
KNSM-Eiland, Tram 7 Azartplein

21 Around 1950, when competition from the airlines began in earnest, the Royal Dutch Steamship Company pulled out all the stops to win over travelers. The result was the **Kompaszaal** (Compass Hall), a luxurious arrivals and departure hall that breathes the grandeur of the ships from olden days, and where nowadays you can enjoy high tea or lunch. High tea is served Wednesdays through Sundays, with reservations only.
KNSM-Laan 311, www.kompaszaal.nl, tel. 020-4199596, open Sat & Sun 11am-1am, Wed 10am-5pm, Thur & Fri 10am-1am, high tea from €17.50, Tram 7 Azartplein

30 Watch a film or visit an exhibition at **EYE,** which now houses the Netherlands' largest film library with at least 46,000 films, 50,000 photos, and 41,500 posters. The futuristic building opened in 2012.
IJ Promenade 1, www.eyefilm.nl, tel. 020-5891400, open Sun-Thur 10am-10pm, Fri-Sat 10am-10pm, free entrance, film €10, Ferry 901, 907 Buiksloterweg, Ferry 902 Ijplein

31 Thanks to the **Oeverpark,** Amsterdam now finally has a promenade on the waterfront. The park includes an elm arboretum with 30 varieties of elm. There's a view across the IJ to the imposing Centraal Station, where the roof of the bus station has at least 4,500 sheets of glass.
Oeverpark, Ferry 901, 907 Buiksloterweg

FOOD & DRINK

❶ This is a piece of Manhattan on the Amsterdam waterfront. Enjoy a spectacular panoramic view of the city, the IJ, and North Amsterdam with coffee or cocktails in the **SkyLounge Amsterdam.**

Oosterdoksstraat 4, doubletree3.hilton.com, open Sun-Tue 11am-1am, Wed-Thur 11am-2am, Fri-Sat 11am-3am, sandwiches from €15, Tram 2, 4, 11, 12, 13, 14, 17, 24, 26 Centraal Station, Metro 51, 52, 53, 54 Centraal Station

❸ Amsterdam's trendiest know the way to this café-restaurant. **Hannekes Boom** has its own dock complete with a picnic terrace on the water. The food is organic, and on the weekend it's time to dance!

Dijksgracht 4, www.hannekesboom.nl, tel. 020-4199820, open Sun-Thur 10am-1am, Fri-Sat 10am-3am, from €16.50, Tram, 26 Muziekgebouw Bimhuis

❹ The folks at **Scheepskameel** pay close attention to high-quality food and to their patrons. The stark cuisine excels in pure, fresh, and familiar flavors. An extensive wine list features only German wine. The restaurant is a bright and open space in a beautiful building located in the naval yards (Marineterrein). The owners are known for their other restaurant Rijssel (Marcusstraat 52)— a popular fixture in the Amsterdam food scene.

Kattenburgerstraat 7, scheepskameel.nl, tel. 020-3379680, open Tue-Sat 6pm-1am, from €45, Tram 26 Muziekgebouw Bimhuis

❾ **Brouwerij 't IJ,** next to Korenmolen De Gooyer, brews the best beer in Amsterdam. Beer lovers come for beers with humorous names like *Natte* (wet) and *Zatte* (drunk), or seasonal beers called *Paas IJ* (Easter egg). On the weekend you can take a guided tour.

Funenkade 7, www.brouwerijhetij.nl, tel. 020-5286237, open daily 2pm-8pm, Fri-Sun guided tours in English 3:30pm, Dutch 4pm, beer €3, guided tour + 1 beer €4.50, Tram 7 Hoogte Kadijk, Tram 14 Pontanusstraat

❿ **Coffee and Friends** is the perfect place to start your day with a great cup of coffee. The people who run this place are super friendly and will make you feel right at home. This cozy café has a laid-back vibe and great outdoor seating

area, where you can watch people, bicycles, and trams rush by. Their smoothie bowls are highly recommended!

Czaar Peterstraat 135, www.coffeeandfriends.nl, tel. 062-7262621, open Sat & Sun 9:30am-5pm, Mon 11am-5pm, Tue-Fri 8:30am-5pm, lunch €8.95, Tram 7 1e Leeghwaterstraat

14 Rosa & Rita likes to keep it simple. Choose from a pizza or steak—both are prepared on-site. Eat while sitting comfortably in the former warehouse, next to a wood fire. Fun fact: contrary to what you might think, Rosa and Rita are not the owners of this small establishment. It was named after two tankers built in 1935 when the area was still a shipyard.

Conradstraat 471, www.rosaenrita.nl, tel. 061-1122373, open Wed-Sun from 3pm, pizza €9.50, steak €12.50, Tram 7, 26 Rietlandpark, Tram 7 1e Leeghwaterstraat

20 Kanis & Meiland 3.0 could be described as the islanders' local pub. Non-islanders are also welcome for a beer or a board game.

Levantkade 127, www.kanisenmeiland.nl, tel. 020-7370674, open Mon-Fri 8:30am-1am, Sat-Sun 10am-1am, drinks from €2.20, Tram 7 Azartplein

㉒ If you arrive on the ferry from Azartplein, you'll see the beautiful hangar made of green and gray corrugated sheet metal come closer and closer. The letters *P-e-r-o-n-i* glisten from the rooftop, as **Hangar**'s sunny terrace beckons you to spend long summer nights on the waterfront. Industrial and tropical go hand in hand at this place that was once part of a booming harbor. Now you can come here to enjoy Mediterranean dishes from Southern Europe and North Africa. The flavors are pure and pleasantly surprising, and the menu changes with the seasons.

Aambeeldstraat 36, hangar.amsterdam, tel. 020-3638657, open Sun-Thur 10am-1am, Fri-Sat 10am-3am, three-course menu €34.50, Ferry 915 Zamenhofstraat, Bus 38 Hamerstraat

㉓ This gigantic hangar houses one of the best restaurants in Amsterdam. At **Hotel de Goudfazant** you can order a seasonal meal for a great price in a fine, relaxed atmosphere indoors. In the summer you can dine at the picnic tables that beckon from the waterside.

Aambeeldstraat 10, www.hoteldegoudfazant.nl, tel. 020-6365170, open Tue-Sun 6-10pm, three course menu €30, Ferry 915 Zamenhofstraat, Bus 38 Hamerstraat

㉕ **Stork** is a seafood restaurant with high ideals. Working with Stichting Vis&Seizoen (Fish and Season Institute), Stork ensures that the fish appearing on the menu are fresh caught daily. Consideration is also given to the way in which the fish are farmed or caught. Add to this the restaurant's industrial character, the view of the IJ, and the huge terrace, and you'll understand why this is the perfect place to enjoy a fish soup or sea bass.

Gedempt Hamerkanaal 201, www.restaurantstork.nl, tel. 020-6344000, open daily 11am-10:30pm, from €20, Ferry 902 Ijplein, Ferry 915 Zamenhofstraat, Metro 52 Noorderpark

㉖ You can't miss this bright-orange building on the water—though 10 years ago, a river cruiser somehow did miss it and sailed up onto the patio! At **Il Pecorino,** you can have a panini during the day, and a crispy, traditional Neapolitan pizza straight from the oven at night. In the summer it's lovely to sit on the sunny deck and look out over the IJ.

Noordwal 1, www.ilpecorino.nl, tel. 020-7371511, open daily 5pm-11pm, pizza €12, Ferry 901, 907 Buiksloterweg, Metro 52 Noorderpark

27 This place is a must-visit for foodies. But beware, at **Café Modern** you don't get to choose anything yourself. Instead, the chef will present you with four courses that are guaranteed to tickle your taste buds. The menu changes each day, and the dishes are always flavorful and highly original. Be sure to mention any dietary restrictions—they will be happy to adjust things to your taste. This beautifully decorated space used to be a bank. Be sure to visit the restrooms, as they are located inside the old vault.

Meidoornweg 2, https://modernamsterdam.nl, tel. 020-4940684, open Mon-Thur noon-midnight, Fri & Sat noon-1am, four course menu €40, Ferry 901, 907 Buiksloterweg, Ferry 902 Ijplein, Metro 52 Noorderpark

29 As the name suggests, **The Coffee Virus** is all about the coffee. Here, beans are roasted locally, and the selection changes on a regular basis. The quality, however, is consistently high: they aim for the perfect brew, served up exactly as you like it. Pies and lunch dishes are equally recommendable. The café is located inside A.Lab, a creative space where a lot of freelancers work.

Overhoeksplein 2, thecoffeevirus.nl, tel. 020-2442341, open Mon-Fri 9am-4:30pm, filtered coffee €4.50, Ferry 901, 907 Buiksloterweg

36 From the outside, **Noorderlicht Café** (Northern Lights Café) resembles a greenhouse, thanks to its glass dome. Inside you'll discover it's beautifully decorated with materials from town and country alike. The interesting location, live music, and menu all ensure that Noorderlicht is one of the finest places in Amsterdam. It's located at the NDSM shipyard, where ships were once built and repaired. The transformation of the shipyard is currently in full swing, with trendy cafés springing up everywhere.

NDSM Plein 102, www.noorderlichtcafe.nl, tel. 020-4922770, open daily from 11am, kitchen closes at 10pm, from €9.50, Ferry 903, 905, 906 NDSM, Bus 35, 36 Atatürk

37 **Pllek** is more than just a café and restaurant. The venue is marketed as a "creative hangout," where you can take yoga classes on weekends, watch films with a social conscience, or down a detox cocktail. It also serves sandwiches or meals made with local, organic, and sustainable produce. Outside the building, which has been largely constructed from shipping containers, you can relax on the beachlike terrace.

TT Neveritaweg 59, www.pllek.nl, open daily from 9:30am (kitchen closes at 10pm), from €17.50, Ferry 903, 905, 906 NDSM, Bus 35, 36 Atatürk

39 Built by NDSM's shipbuilders, the industrial **IJ-kantine** once formed the shipyard's office building, assembly yard, and canteen. When the canteen went bankrupt in the 1980s, the Unemployed Shipbuilders Association took over the building for use as a community center, where members could play cards and billiards and have a drink. Now you can have something to eat or drink in the colorfully decorated café-restaurant overlooking the IJ.

Mt. Odinaweg 15-17, www.ijkantine.nl, tel. 020-6337162, open daily from 9am, half a lobster €23.50, Ferry 903, 905, 906 NDSM, Bus 35, 36 Atatürk

SHOPPING

10 At **de werkwinkel +meer** (literally: the workshop and more) you can purchase unique designer items and artworks from artists all over the world. Lian Aelmans, founder of the shop, selects everything with care and consideration—and it shows with wares such as beautiful ceramics, stunning graphic prints, and fine jewelry. This is the perfect place to hunt for that all-important one-of-a-kind gift. Combine your visit with a walk around the Oostelijke Eilanden!

Czaar Peterstraat 104, www.dewerk-winkel.nl, tel. 020-3636972, open Tue-Fri 10am-6pm, Sat 11am-6pm, Tram 7 1e Leeghwaterstraat

⓫ Czaar Peterstraat now has its own concept store in the form of **CP113.** Try a coffee from the roasting plant in Amsterdam-Noord, accompanied by a cake from the mobile Van Moss bakery, while taking a look at the clothing in this well laid-out shop. Hanging from the rails are a mix of vintage and new clothing originating from anywhere from Amsterdam to Scandinavia. The furniture is also for sale.

Czaar Peterstraat 113, cp-stores.com, tel. 020-2231976, open Tue-Sat 11am-6pm, Tram 7 Eerste Leeghwaterstraat

⓭ Debby's desire on setting up shop in this former launderette was to fill it with products that she herself would be delighted with. The result is **Olie & Zo** (Oils & So On), a specialty store selling high-quality products for the kitchen. There are at least eight kinds of oil in barrels, half of which are organic. The "& Zo" part of the shop is also worth a visit—its shelves display fresh bread, sausages, special cheeses, unusual mustards, and Himalayan salt.

Czaar Peterstraat 128, www.olieenzo.com, tel. 020-6223832, open Tue-Fri 10am-6pm, Sat 10am-5pm, Tram 7 Eerste Leeghwaterstraat

㉜ Brothers **Blom & Blom** share a passion for forgotten items: objects that had an industrial life but are destined to be scrapped. The brothers love to explore the former East Germany, scouring factories for forgotten gems. The furniture and lamps are given a second life in their workshops in Berlin or Amsterdam and are sold through the webshop and at this store. Every object comes with a document certifying the product's origin.

Chrysantenstraat 20a, www.blomandblom.com, tel. 020-7372691, open Wed-Fri 10am-5pm, every 1st and 3rd Sat of the month 11am-5pm, Ferry 900 Distelweg, Ferry 901, 907 Buiksloterweg, Ferry 902 Ijplein

㉝ You've never seen so many vintage, design, and industrial products as are in this warehouse. **Neef Louis** (Cousin Louis) is an expert in collecting fine furniture, lamps, and accessories: he's regularly invited to decorate shops, film

sets, and fairs (such as the famous Bread & Butter in Berlin). Louis's mission is to enable his customers to make something beautiful of their surroundings.
Papaverweg 46, www.neeflouis.nl, tel. 020-4869354, open Thur-Fri 10am-6pm, Sat 10am-5:30pm, Ferry 900 Distelweg, Bus 35, 36, 293 Floraweg, Bus 38 Klaprozenweg

34 The people behind **Van Dijk and Ko** like to visit Hungary and Romania because that's where they know they can find beautiful cabinets, chests of drawers, beds, and dressers that deserve a second life. Besides these showpieces, you'll also find imaginative, handmade lampshades and lamp stands from the Gezusters Stoop Lampenkappenatelier (Stoop Sisters Lampshade Studio) and a great book department. Everything here is unique, and the collection changes daily, so if something tickles your fancy, don't think about it too long!
Papaverweg 46, www.vandijkenko.nl, tel. 020-6841524, open Tue-Sat 10am-6pm, Sun noon-6pm, Ferry 900 Distelweg, Bus 35, 36, 293 Floraweg, Bus 38 Klaprozenweg

38 At this first furniture store in the NDSM shipyard, you'll find some vintage furniture plus numerous designs by Esther from **Woodies at Berlin.** Esther works with wood and steel and has three furniture lines—sleek, organic, and natural. The store displays her earlier work, or you can also get started on your own design with Esther's assistance. In addition to furniture and lighting, the store also sells fair-trade clothing.
Ms. Van Riemsdijkweg 51, www.woodiesatberlin.nl, tel. 064-3008100, open Sat noon-5pm, Ferry 903, 905, 906 NDSM, Bus 35, 36 Atatürk

MORE TO EXPLORE

2 The **Centrale** Openbare **Bibliotheek** Amsterdam (the Amsterdam public library) opened on the seventh day of the seventh month in 2007. It's the Netherlands' largest library. Although as a visitor it doesn't make sense to join the library, do drop in anyway. Admire the modern design, and above all check out the wonderful panoramic view of the city from the restaurant on the seventh floor.
Oosterdoksekade 143, www.oba.nl, tel. 020-5230900, open daily 10am-10pm, free, Tram 2, 4, 11, 12, 13, 14, 17, 24, 26 Centraal Station, Metro 51, 52, 53, 54 Centraal Station

⑤ NEMO is the largest science museum in the Netherlands. All manner of interactive scientific and technological installations are spread over five floors. Whizzkids, nerds, and adults alike—even those with little knowledge of science and technology—can happily spend a very entertaining afternoon here and learn something in the process. The roof terrace is open to all and is a great place for a drink.

Oosterdok 2, www.e-nemo.nl, tel. 020-5313233, open daily 10am-5:30pm, also on Mon during school holidays, roof terrace open until 7pm during summer, entrance €15, Tram 26 Muziekgebouw Bimhuis

⑮ Roest (Rust) opened a few years ago on the site where Dutch East India Company ships were once built. Today it's a combined café, theater, music venue, exhibition space, beach, and club. Buy snacks and drinks in a "camping shop" or double-decker bus, and head for the beach or restaurant.

Jacob Bontiusplaats, www.amsterdamroest.nl, open Sun-Thur 1am1-1am, Fri 4pm-3am, Sat 11am-3am, free, Tram 7, 26 Rietlandpark

㉔ Not a soccer team or football club, but a boutique cinema, complete with a petit-restaurant and wine bar—that's **FC Hyena.** You can watch the movie in one of two screening rooms while seated on homemade couches, and afterward it's discussion time. All this while enjoying some natural wine and tasty snacks from a wood-fired brick oven. You're even allowed to take food and drinks with you into the cinema. FC stands for "Film Club," but the interior is more reminiscent of a sports canteen, albeit it a very cool one!
Aambeeldstraat 24, fchyena.nl, tel. 020-3638502, open Sat-Sun noon-1am, Mon-Fri 4pm-1am, mains from €14, Ferry 915 Zamenhofstraat, Bus 38 Hamerstraat

㉘ For seventy years, this was the canteen for Shell employees. Today, the company restaurant and associated garden (laid 150 years ago as a city park) have become one of the cultural hotspots of North Amsterdam. Paradiso holds concerts at **Tolhuistuin,** and in the summer there's a program of live music, DJs, and theater in the garden every weekend. Even if there is no event going on, it's a fine location with the café-restaurant, a large roof terrace, and the mysterious atmosphere of the garden. The Tolhuistour is recommended, which is an audio tour obtained at the nearby EYE or via an app. Download the free Tales&Tours app and then select the Tolhuistour for €2.69.
Tolhuisweg 5, www.tolhuistuin.nl, tel. 020-7604820, garden open Thur-Sun noon-10pm, see website for program and other opening times, Ferry 901, 907 Buiksloterweg

㉟ Unfortunately it's open only one weekend a month, but that's partly what makes it so special and well worth a visit. With 750 stalls, the flea market in the **IJ-hallen** is one of the largest in Europe. Thanks to the market's growing popularity you'll need to search for the real bargains, but the atmosphere is always fantastic, and special items are up for grabs.
TT. Neveritaweg 15, www.ijhallen.nl, open one weekend a month Sat-Sun 9am-4:30pm, see website for calendar, entrance €5, Ferry 903, 905, 906 NDSM, Bus 35, 36 Atatürk

WITH MORE TIME

The walks in this book will take you to most of the city's main highlights. Of course, there are still a number of places worth visiting that are not included in the previous walks, and those are listed here. Note that not all of these places are easily accessible by foot from town, but all are accessible by using public transportation.

Ⓐ If you are tired of the crowded center, just hop on a bike or take the bus to the **Amsterdamse Bos.** This nature and leisure park between Amsterdam and Amstelveen is a lovely place to go for a walk or ride a bike. There are also two children's paddling pools, a goat farm, exciting climbing courses among the trees at Fun Forest Climbing Park, and canoe and paddleboat facilities on the Grote Vijver. There are a couple of famous Dutch hockey and soccer pitches at the edge of the forest. A rowing club has regular competitions, which are held on the Bosbaan. Every summer, theater performances are held outdoors at the Openluchttheater and attract large crowds—some people gather on the benches hours in advance with picnic baskets and bottles of wine, soaking up the pleasant, relaxed atmosphere.

Bosbaanweg 5, www.amsterdamsebos.nl, Visitors Center open Tue-Sun 12-5pm, free, Tram 26 Vu Medisch Centrum, Bus 62, 246 Vu Medisch Centrum

Ⓑ Apart from Blijburg, a pleasant hippie city beach, **IJburg** is virtually unknown to many Amsterdammers, which is a pity because there is lots to see and do here as far as the new area's architecture, restaurants, and cafés are concerned. IJburg consists of six islands, of which Steigereiland Zuid is the most interesting in terms of architecture—residents were allowed to design their own homes, which are clearly visible on, for example, J. O. Vaillantlaan. There are also floating homes on the Haringbuis Dijk. On Haveneiland Oost try a modern take on pancakes at Firma Koek, while Haveneiland West harbors the lovely Greek restaurant I-Grec.

Ijburglaan, Tram 26 Lumierestraat

Ⓒ Many researchers work and study in the **Science Park**'s modern buildings. These are the offices of the science faculty at the University of Amsterdam, the

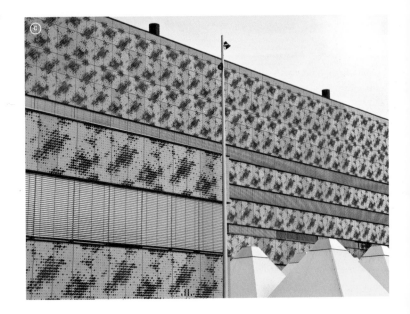

Amsterdam University College, dozens of research institutes in the area, and some 120 other companies. Even if you have little to do with information technology, life sciences, advanced technology, or sustainability, this campus is worth a visit. Several of the buildings were nominated for the Golden AAP (Amsterdam Architecture Prize), including Amsterdam University College. Also take a look at the installation, *Raw Paradise*, located in the tunnel under the train station, where artificial light from hundreds of LED lights merges with the natural light from outside.

Science Park, Bus 40, 240 Science Park, Train Science Park

ⓓ On the other side of the IJmeer is the **Muiderslot.** This imposing medieval castle with a moat was built around 1285 by Count Floris V. The castle is situated about 10 miles outside of Amsterdam in the picturesque village of Muiden. Paintings and artifacts reveal more about life at Muiderslot during the Netherlands' Golden Age. The famous Dutch writer C. Hooft lived in the castle 400 years ago. The period rooms still have 17th-century furnishings. You can also wander around the castle's beautiful gardens. A visit to Muiderslot makes a great family day out with the children, who can climb the towers or go on an exciting treasure hunt.

Herengracht 1, Muiden, www.muiderslot.nl, open Apr 1-Oct 31 Mon-Fri 10am-5pm, Sat-Sun noon-5pm Nov 1-Mar 31 Sat-Sun noon-5pm, entrance €13.50, Bus 327 From Amstel Station

(E) **Broek in Waterland** is a stone's throw from Amsterdam. This village of wooden Dutch houses is surrounded by meadows and dykes. For much of its history it was a thriving village, but during one harsh period the colorful houses were all painted shades of gray. This area has large pieces of land that are accessible only by water, so it's nice to rent a boat at the edge of Broek in Waterland and take yourself on a boat trip past the dykes and through the lakes. The *fluisterboten* ("whisper boats") have silent electric motors, so you can fully enjoy the natural environment—and if you're lucky, you might be able to spot some of the many birds native to this area.

Drs J. Van Disweg 4, Broek in Waterland, www.fluisterbootvaren.nl, 3-hour rental for 5 people €50, Bus 316 from Amsterdam Centraal or get there by bicycle

(F) For a long time, the polder region on the outskirts of Amsterdam between West and Halfweg was a run-down, undefined area. Then, a couple of creative, enterprising folks fell in love with this piece of nature, and now there is a lot to see and do in the **Tuinen van West.** It's a unique place where you can walk, pick fruit, ride a horse, or go for a bike ride. You'll also find **Het Rijk van de Keizer** here, hidden among the greenery. Plop down on soft cushions and enjoy an organic lunch. The venture began in the Jordaan where founder John Hannema organized evenings with theater and food. But the venue soon became too small, and John picked a perfect location in the heart of Amsterdam's pasturelands. Here you really feel that you can get away from it all, in a lovely, relaxed atmosphere.

Joris and Den Berghweg 101-111, www.hetrijkvandekeizer.nl & www.tuinenvanwest. info, open Wed-Sun 11am-7pm, Bus 21 from Amsterdam Central or get there by bike

(G) **Ruigoord** lies in the heart of Amsterdam's port and has a long history. At the beginning of the 1970s, the village had 200 inhabitants and was in danger of being swallowed by the port. The local priest and a couple of village inhabitants opposed the plans and were supported by a group of Amsterdam artists. At the end of July 1973, the priest handed the artists the keys to the church with the hope they would save the village. From that day on, Ruigoord was a cultural haven with a hippie feel, where many illicit substances were taken. It became known for its anything-goes atmosphere. Although initially Ruigoord was supposed to be demolished as part of the expansion plans for the port, in 2000 it was decided that part of the village could remain. No one lives there anymore, but there are numerous galleries and studios where alternative and cultural activities are organized, and every summer sees the annual festival Landjuweel.

Ruigoord 76, Amsterdam, www.ruigoord.nl, Bus 82 from Amsterdam Centraal or get there by bike

(H) If you take the ferry from behind Centraal Station to the other side of the IJ and keep walking straight ahead down Buiksloterweg, you will come to **Van der Pekstraat.** What was once a slum is now a bustling street with all sorts of interesting shops. The Pekmarkt happens on Wednesdays, Fridays, and Saturdays. Every Saturday, there's an open street podium where anyone who feels like it can perform in front of an audience. The result is often-surprising moments and lots of fun. You can buy lovely home textiles at Club Geluk, or head to Fashion & Tea for trendy clothing or a cup of tea in a cozy inner garden. You can also eat your heart out on Van der Pekstraat. Try Soepboer for the most delicious soup, Café Modern/Jaques Jour for culinary highlights, and Semifredo on weekends for an elaborate lunch.

Van Der Pekstraat, www.pekmarkt.nl, Ferry 901, 907 Buiksloterweg

(I) The Netherlands, as you've seen on the postcards, features picturesque little houses, windmills, and meadows. That's the **Zaanse Schans.** This area of the Zaan waterway was set up to protect historic heritage, dating from the 18th and 19th centuries. The wooden mills, barns, and houses in typical Zaans wooden architecture were transported here from 1961 onward. Traditional crafts are still practiced in the mills and barns. There's a clog maker, a cheese farmer, and a distillery where you can taste liqueur. The area

has an interesting history rich in crafts and craftsmanship, which you can learn more about at the Zaans museum and the Verkadepaviljoen. The Verkadefabriek has stood on the banks of the Zaan for more than a century. Originally a bread and biscuit factory, over the course of its long history, Verkade produced 48 varieties of cookies and many types of chocolate, sweets, biscuits, and even tea-light candles. The Verkade family always kept a careful record of the business's development, and the result is an extensive collection of 9,000 photos, 1,000 posters and advertisements, the packaging for 2,000 items, and working machines. The collection gained a permanent home in 2009 when the Verkadepaviljoen was opened. The area is an important attraction not only for tourists from overseas, but also for locals. Mondays and Tuesdays are quieter days to visit the Zaanse Schans, or head there in the afternoon.

Schansend 7, Zaandam, www.dezaanseschans.nl, Bus 391 from Amsterdam Centraal

NIGHTLIFE

There are all sorts of ways to enjoy Amsterdam's nightlife. The main nightlife attractions are situated around the Leidseplein, the Rembrandtplein, and the Red Light District, which is also where you'll find most of the tourists. But you can still find some more mainstream clubs such as **Paradiso** and **Melkweg**, which both have good concerts.

Perhaps you prefer something more underground? Alternative options are scattered across the city in Noord on the NDSM wharf, in West on Hugo de Grootplein, or in the Westerpark. If you're looking for a drink, head for the Jordaan's cozy pubs. For same-day theater performances, look for the Last Minute Ticket Shop on the Leidseplein, and there's a good chance you'll find a half-price ticket!

HOTELS

A good bed, a tasty breakfast, and a nice interior—these are all ingredients for a pleasant hotel stay. Even more important, however, might be location. A hotel is really only good if you can walk out of the lobby and straight into the bustling city. Staying the night in the center of Amsterdam is often very pricey. Fortunately, there are a few hostels in the Center for an affordable overnight stay. There are plenty of nice areas around the Center where you can stay for a reasonable price, such Bos en Lommer, Oud-West, or De Pijp. The Center is always accessible with public transportation, but renting a bicycle makes it even easier to get around. Going out for breakfast is also no problem—there are loads of nice breakfast and coffee places around the Center. If you'd prefer a quieter start to the day, try Noord or the Eilanden.

INDEX

INDEX

MOON
AMSTERDAM WALKS

SECOND EDITION

AVALON TRAVEL
Hachette Book Group
1700 Fourth Street
Berkeley, CA 94710, USA
www.moon.com

ISBN 978-1-64049-775-7
Concept & Original Publication
"time to momo Amsterdam"
© 2019 by mo'media.
All rights reserved.

time to momo

MO' MEDIA

Text and Walks
Femke Dam

Translation
Cindi Heller

Design
Studio 100% &
Oranje Vormgevers

Photography
David in den Bosch,
Evelien Vehof, Saskia van Rijn,
Tijn Kramer, Judith Zebeda,
Hans Zeegers

Project Editor
Sophie Kreuze

AVALON TRAVEL

Project Editor
Lori Hobkirk

Typesetting
Cynthia Young

Copy Editor
Beth Fraser

Proofreader
Sandy Chapman

Cover Design
Faceout Studio, Jeff Miller

Printed in China by
RR Donnelley
First US printing,
December 2019

Trips to Remember

TRIP OF A LIFETIME

ANGKOR WAT

BELIZE
TRIP OF A LIFETIME

TRIP OF A LIFETIME

GALÁPAGOS ISLANDS

COSTA RICA

FIJI

JAPAN
JONATHAN DEHART

TRIP OF A LIFETIME

MACHU PICCHU

MOROCCO

NEW ZEALAND

TRIP OF A LIFETIME

PATAGONIA
Including the Falkland Islands
WAYNE BERNHARDSON

VIETNAM
DANA FILEK-GIBSON

Grand Adventure

Drive & Hike
APPALACHIAN TRAIL

THE BEST TRAIL TOWNS, DAY HIKES,
AND ROAD TRIPS IN BETWEEN

TIMOTHY MALCOLM

PACIFIC COAST HIGHWAY

CALIFORNIA,
OREGON & WASHINGTON

IAN ANDERSON

MOON

USA NATIONAL PARKS

THE COMPLETE GUIDE TO ALL
59 PARKS

BECKY LOMAX